GHOST LIGHT BURN

THE MAVERICK HEART CYCLE

STEPHEN GRAHAM KING

ALSO BY STEPHEN GRAHAM KING

Non-fiction
Just Breathe: My Journey Though Cancer and Back

Fiction
Chasing Cold

The Maverick Heart Cycle:
Soul's Blood
Gatecrasher
A Congress of Ships

GHOST LIGHT BURN

THE MAVERICK HEART CYCLE

Cover art and design by Nathan Frechette. Interior design by Nabiha Rasool. Edited by Joel Balkovec, Lorenzo Carrara, Isabelle Shi, and Jenna Low.

Legal deposit, Library and Archives Canada, October 2021.

Paperback ISBN: 978-1-990086-22-9

Ebook ISBN: 978-1-990086-16-8

Renaissance Press - pressesrenaissancepress.ca

Printed in Gatineau

We acknowledge the support of the Canada Council for the Arts.

For my dear friend, Suzanne North,
And my beloved sister, Sue Brooks.
Now departed.

This ghost light burns for them.

CHAPTER ONE

GALACTUM YEAR 151.5

The theatre dropped out of interspace at the edge of the strange, near empty solar system, far enough from the fading star, but near enough to make it a short trip to the binary planets that would host the company's next engagement.

The splash of their transition from the hyper-acceleration of interspace to normal space flooded the area with an instant of light and colour, gone almost before it could be registered, and the theatre now powered its normal space drive field for the journey insystem.

Ordinarily, this final leg of the journey would have been routine, nothing of note. As the crew piloted the ship in, the cast would have been in rehearsal for the roster of shows that would rotate through their time here in this remote system. But this was no ordinary planetfall.

The company manager had noted the shiver of excitement that had gone through the company as the ship's AI announced their imminent arrival. A rare half-day of rehearsal had been called, as the ship approached its destination. Even some of the more seasoned members of the company, those who had been with the ship through years of these interstellar engagements and were usually so blasé about planetfalls, seemed to be keyed up, on an edge of excitement for this particular leg of their trip.

While this was a standard half-year repertory contract to perform for the locals, this was no ordinary planetary system. In fact, there were no other systems anywhere in the Galactum like it. And that made for a spectacular view. A view not lost on the company's newest member.

Even the names of the binary planets that were the only bodies in the system seemed a good omen to her: Sound and Fury. It had made her smile thinking of it, her long-ago theatre history education rising up in her memory.

Definitely a good omen.

She'd not been in rehearsal that afternoon, so it had been easy to snag one of the seats along the outer edge of the lounge, which would be street-level frontage once the theatre ship settled into the berth that would be their home for the next six months.

And the sight had indeed been spectacular.

The view of the planetary system had been breathtaking. Massive, broken Fury dominated the viewport, a swollen crescent, almost a quarter of its mass now a tumbling, shattered debris field, barely held in by the planet's gravitational pull. The giant planet performed its slow, catastrophic dance, losing cohesion a little bit more each second. Though her human eyes were too imprecise to register it, she knew, from the research information the company manager had provided, how the mining company had dispersed gravitic generators through the debris field to hold it steady as they mined the massive chunks of rubble for volatiles, heavy metals, and any construction-grade materials that could be put to use in the Galactum-wide Gate Project.

Farther out, tiny, barely habitable Sound held the headquarters of the mining consortium that slowly picked away at the corpse of the giant, dead planet.

The thought of the massive stable wormhole project only pricked at her memory a little, a wound healed, but with a scar still tender to the touch. She could forget it was there if she didn't prod at it. If she just let it rest. The memories hurt much less now, with the passage of time, after joining the company and diving headfirst into rehearsals for all of the plays in their repertory cycle. There had been no time to feel, or wallow.

To feel the weight of all that had happened. When it all crashed down on her, she'd gotten on the first flight on the departure list, without even checking where it was going. She'd fled from her best friend, unable to even look him in the eye, too ashamed of what she'd seen inside herself.

During that first flight, she'd had to apply for Baseline, the minimum subsistence income guaranteed to all Galactum citizens. All that she had accumulated during her former life had been left behind. Not that it bothered her. In her mind, it was as tainted as the life that had generated it now was. At least she wasn't a fugitive anymore, her record expunged.

That first flight had led to another, and then another, until she had ended up on Hub, figuring the most populous world in the Pan Galactum was a good place to lose herself for a while, as she figured out how it had all gone so terribly wrong. Not that it was hard to figure out. She'd gotten too complacent in the hazy morality, too greedy for the life she'd been leading. What had been a lark had turned into something much darker, much more dangerous.

So, she had found herself in a cheap capsule hotel, in a space not much bigger than the bed where she slept. During the days, she had wandered the streets, looking for… *something*. Some opportunity. Some opening, some door that was just waiting for her to walk through.

It didn't take long to realize that Hub had been a mistake. There were too many people, too much of everything on the capitol world. She'd needed quiet, solitude. She'd needed to be far away from anything that represented her old life. But when she had checked her balance to see where she could afford to go, she had seen far more than she had expected, guaranteeing her safe travel pretty much wherever she wanted to go. The string of digits had frightened her, caused her throat to close in panic, reminding her of all that she was trying to escape. As she'd fought down the feeling, her node had pinged her that she had a message. It had been from him.

"I know you didn't want me to help you out, but please take this. I know you need space. This will let you have as much as you need."

Hearing his voice had made her heart ache. She had sat there in that completely generic hotel room for a long time, trying to decide what to do. In the end, she had kept the money, even though it somehow made her feel both safer and even more compromised. She had ordered herself a good meal, the first since her journey had started, and logged into Know-It-All to try and come up with some sort of plan of action. The one thing that she did hold onto from the life she'd left was her instinct for self-preservation. While she needed to escape, she knew it would be too easy to fall through the cracks, and she couldn't work through things if that happened.

In that cheap hotel, she realized how much she wanted to be in the theatre again. Their adventures had taken her increasingly away from that, and she had spent much of her time talking herself out of her need for that outlet. She realized she was now free to go back to it again. It didn't take long to figure out that she could combine her desire to act again and her desire to get lost in the crowd once again. Hours of searching had led her to what had seemed like the perfect opportunity, far from her old life. Far from the memories.

The *Odeon Rising* was a midsized touring theatre ship with a good reputation, about to embark for Sound and Fury. The consortium in charge of the mining operations there had, with the support of the Galactum Arts Forum, booked the company for a six-month stay to entertain the thousands of employees and executives involved in one of the largest-scale mining operations in recorded history. One of the actors had dropped out due to illness and the company needed to fill the opening immediately. They had needed her. And she had needed the opportunity.

The theatre ship had departed the day after she signed the contract.

She'd been thrown into the deep end immediately with three completely different roles she had needed to learn within a week of her first performances. It had terrified her and thrilled her at the same time, exhausting her with its demands. But she had risen to the challenge and been welcomed into the company.

The work had been the emotional balm she had needed. Digging into the text, working to find the character in the words, and in the other actors' interpretations as well. Finding herself in the characters — and the characters in herself — especially when there were no capers that could go wrong, no lives hanging on her line readings or the way she walked across the stage. Getting back to her roots had liberated the part of her she had missed, let her reconnect with her own history. It had finally quieted the ghosts.

And now, here she was, here they all were, in the shadow of this shattered world she could never have even dreamed existed. She refilled her cup from the still-hot teapot on the table in front of her and settled back into her seat, concentrating on the rich play of colours outside the ship. The combination of the gravitic energy holding the debris field together and the outgassing from the mining activities blended together into a light show that was dazzling in the range of colours. Suura had said it looked like a bruise, but she thought that lacked imagination.

For her, the deep blues and purples had the deep, rich hues of gemstones, saturated to the point of lusciousness. The same with the carmine and scarlet flame of the reds; the emerald and jade greens, the golden yellows. The array of colours seemed too rich to be real, impossible like something out of a sensie or a heightened work of art. She felt she could lose herself in those colours. She couldn't help but wonder what it would all look like from the surface of Sound.

As if responding to its cue to enter, Sound became visible as it transited the glowing colours of its much more dominant sibling. The tiny, scorched world was dull and plain, the ochres and browns of its surface dreary in comparison. She could tell when their course altered to bring them closer to the small world that would be hosting their upcoming engagement. As the theatre ship changed its heading, Sound centered in the huge window before her, a pale, bleached eye that watched their approach.

This shouldn't be this fascinating, she thought.

She hadn't travelled between worlds much, but even to her, it was a fact of life that humans travelled between planets with relative ease. This was different, though. This was the beginning of their engagement, the anticipation before a new set of opening nights, the last-minute preparation and adjustments as the season of shows kicked off. And it would be here in the shadow of this dead world, this victim of some long-ago, world-shattering catastrophe.

She knew that even the set designers were inspired by this place, eager to find some way to incorporate the image of Fury into their designs somehow. She smiled as she remembered the sight of the design team hunched over a table in the common area, hashing out and discarding idea after idea.

Sound's surface, the bleached colour of dust and sand, grew ever closer, until she felt the first tug of the small planet's thin atmosphere rattling against the hull. Her hands tightened on the arms of the chair.

The theatre ship descended into the thin atmosphere, its drive fields reshaping to protect it from the heat of reentry. The hellish friction of the atmosphere burned and danced across the protective shell of energy, obscuring the view from the theatre's lobby lounge, where more of the cast and crew had gathered to watch their arrival into the rare strangeness of this planetary system. Finally, the temperature in that zone where the atmosphere collided with the drive fields cooled enough that she was able to see again, though the view was nothing special, only baked, bleached sand and dirt in all directions.

Then she saw the city — if you could call it a city — in the distance, the protective dome maintaining comfort in the thin, sweltering atmosphere of the tiny planetoid. Even from a distance, she could feel the prefabricated, sheer corporateness of it. Rows of towers clustered in the midst of vast landing fields lined with what she knew from the company's briefing were rows and rows of the mining vessels that serviced the ravenous operations in the space between the two planets.

She couldn't see it from here, but she knew there was an entertainment district tucked in amongst the processing centres, the administration towers, all of the infrastructure required for an operation of this size. What was it the hardcore spacers called it? *The Grift.* The name made her smile. So evocative. A name vivid in its hints of sin and depravity, when, surprisingly, the area was often the most ethically run part of any city. Not to mention, a hell of a lot of fun. And any company that wanted to keep running smoothly had to realize that keeping a large workforce entertained in their off-hours was key to keeping productivity maximized.

Even as the theatre ship descended ever closer, the city didn't look any more promising, but she told herself that she and the company were there to work, and their performance schedule was a demanding one for the time they were here. Still, she was a bit skeptical about what she could do to amuse herself in her off-hours. Still, she'd reviewed the list of entertainment services available already and it had seemed like there might be enough to fill her leisure time. Besides, she always had Know-It-All.

Finally, the theatre's new berth, their home for the next half-year, came into view. A tract of land had been cleared between the two opposing landing fields, half-way around the semi-circle of the dome's arc. Through the theatre's hull, she felt the drive field adjusting, re-shaping itself in final preparation for landing. She saw the dome rising to meet them, a section emitting a soft glow, and knew from the captain's briefing that it meant that the dome was preparing to extrude itself around the theatre and integrate it into the city itself, turning them into just another fixture in the entertainment district.

Her heartbeat sped up, racing just a little at the thought of new audiences, new responses. Of finally getting to perform the slate of plays that they had worked so hard to prepare. Her excitement grew at the thought of how their performances would adapt to the new, unexpected places where people might laugh or respond in ways they couldn't have anticipated. How they would all work to adapt and grow into the performances.

This. This is just what I needed, she thought, just as the theatre settled into its berth. She took in a deep breath, 'down into her back pockets' as her old acting teacher used to say, and calm flowed through her. But the moment of peace ended up being short-lived as she heard the voice of one of her co-stars over her shoulder.

"Hey, Malika, do you mind running lines with me?" Linnett said. "I'm still having trouble with scene three."

"Of course," she said, standing. *Back to work.*

CHAPTER TWO

GALACTUM YEAR 152

The Maverick Heart tumbled out of interspace with a gut-wrenching lurch, the ship's inertia bleeding off in a bilious plume of yellow-green energy along es previous trajectory.

Vrick felt emself continue along es programmed heading, the sudden deceleration still dispersing as ey struggled to hold es hull together. Nauseating agony coursed along es underside, and ey identified the source as radiating from the inertial nullification baffles along the main drive assembly. Damping down the pain response, ey set up an alert to notify em of further damage without the searing ripple across es consciousness.

Es mind now clear, ey could truly assess the situation rationally. Or as rationally as any sentient being could after such a sudden brush with destruction. Sparing two seconds, ey ran full systems diagnostics just to ensure that ey was not on the verge of blowing apart.

Turning es attention inwards, in the blink of a human eye, ey saw that es internal crash fields had properly engaged, solidifying the air around es human friends, and keeping them from being smeared into paste on es interior walls.

And that is just hell to get out of the upholstery, ey thought wryly.

As it was, all three were currently suspended, as flies in invisible amber, waiting for release.

In the next fraction of a second, ey turned es attention to the monitor systems that allowed em to track the medical data on es crewmates through the knowledge nodes implanted in their skulls. Reams of biodata streamed across es senses, and relief flooded through em. All three were alive, and in no imminent danger of death. All the expected neurotransmitters and hormone compounds that one would expect from a recent brush with immolation were there, and there were spikes of pain coming from Keene's shoulder, but they didn't seem to be life-threatening. A thought from Vrick checked the auto-doc and cycled it up into readiness to deal with Keene's injury.

Satisfied that neither ey nor the others were in imminent peril, ey pulsed es normal space drive field gingerly to bring them to a stop. Ey cycled down the main drives to the bare minimum, just enough to keep emself from drifting. Relief coursed through es systems as the strain on them eased.

Less than thirty seconds had elapsed since their return to normal space, but ey still felt logy and disoriented. *I'm slowing down in my dotage,* ey thought.

Ey keyed the gentle release of the crash fields, es internal atmosphere softening slowly around the three fragile human bodies and lowering them. Ey saw them shift their positions slowly and felt, through es monitors, their muscles protesting from the sudden immobilization that had saved their lives.

A thought brought back the damage and pain sensors from es damaged systems and ey winced at the cascade of unpleasant sensations coursing through em.

I'm not going to die, ey thought. *I am not going to die.*

A sigh coursed through em.

No, you're not. You're just going to hurt for a while.

Ey brought es repair systems online and felt a flush as the nanorepair mesh sought out and began to seal microfissures in es hull. The system catalogued larger system failures, ranking them in terms of severity, along axes of danger to em and to the humans, allowing em to adjust priorities for the Limited Intelligence repair drones to begin their heavier work.

As ey studied the reams of data flowing from the damage control system, ey executed an emotional subroutine that was analogous to a frown. It was obvious that the baffles bore the crux of the damage and required the most repair work, however the nanorepair systems already felt gluey and sluggish. The correction rates were already falling far behind what the remainder of the system reported. Curious, ey sent two of the external repair LIs to investigate. Ey felt the cowlings in es hull folding back as the basket-sized drones unfolded from their niches and spread their array of manipulators and tools. Like some kind of metal parasite, they clambered out onto es hull and skittered in the direction of the damaged baffles.

But as ey watched, the drones' pace slowed as they approached the external drive system, becoming more erratic the closer they came. Finally, about two metres from their goal, the drones came to a quivering halt, their telemetry relaying nothing but gibberish.

That is not good, ey thought. *Not good at all.*

Lexa-Blue pulled herself up from the deck, shaking her head to clear it. Through her node, she felt the damage to Keene's shoulder, and the auto-doc cycling to life to deal with it. Ember's groans, she heard out loud. All around her was chaos. Despite keeping their common spaces as tidy as possible, always ensuring that loose gear was safely stowed, day-to-day living always left its mark. And while the crash fields had prevented much in the way of breakables being damaged, there was still mess strewn across the decking.

Ember was already standing, his pants hiked down to show an already lividly purpling bruise across his buttock. "Man, will you look at my ass?" he said.

"We've both seen it," she said, sourly, as rippling aches coursed through her body.

"What the hell happened?" Ember said, covering himself again.

"I wish I knew," she said. "What's the skinny, Junkpile? Are we going to die?"

There was a pause before Vrick answered, which was disquieting in itself. "We hit something. Or rather, something hit us."

She exchanged a look with both of the men. "In interspace? I thought that was impossible."

"So did I," Vrick said. "At least we survived learning that we were wrong."

"Yeah, but still not fun," Keene said through gritted teeth as he cradled his right arm. Which, Lexa-Blue noted, was jutting at an unnatural angle.

"Okay, auto-doc first, questions later," she said.

"I approve of this plan," Keene said, as both Lexa-Blue and Ember took positions at his side to help support him back to the alcove that housed their auto-doc.

They eased him gently into the system, leaning him against the adjustable bed, which was now against the bulkhead at only a slight angle. As she gentled him into position, she felt every wince that went through him as the doc cut through his shipsuit and exposed the injured shoulder. A sidelong glance at the doc's panel showed that the pain management system was already keying into his system and dosing him up. She turned back to look at his face and saw the tautness around his eyes ease.

"That's it," she said, her voice uncharacteristically gentle. "Let the doc do its work."

As she spoke, the auto-doc's manipulator surface shaped out from the wall panel and covered Keene's injured shoulder. Lexa-Blue saw the readings for pain management spike, and then the snap of the manipulator as it pushed Keene's shoulder back into place. The doc hissed as it applied a malleable dressing to the bare, bruised skin.

"Oh, now, that's better," Keene said, drowsily. "Much better."

Lexa-Blue sagged in relief, suddenly feeling her own aches and pains catching up with her. "What about you, squib? Is that ass going to need attention?"

"Well, not from the auto-doc, anyway," Ember said with a grin. "It's just a bruise. Not pretty, but it doesn't require any urgent attention."

She turned to the cabinet behind her and rifled through it, coming out with a small jar of ointment. "Put this on it. Should make it go away faster. No damage to the hardware?"

Ember patted his thigh where the jet-black cybernetic prosthesis melded with his leg. "This thing?" he said. "I bet if we'd blown up, it would have just floated on without us. Same with this chunk." He ran a hand along his side, where another piece of the prosthetic replaced a portion of his torso.

"Let's not put that theory to the test anytime soon, okay?" she said.

"I think we almost did," Ember said. "What's the story, Vrick? Any idea what happened?"

"If I had to guess, I'd say we hit a poly-resonant Q wave substring filament. The latest interspace theories say they're possible, but incredibly rare."

"Of course," Lexa-Blue said, rolling her eyes. "That's exactly what I was thinking."

"Don't hate me because I can think in higher dimension interspace mathematics," Vrick said, pitching es tone into perfect, guileless innocence. "The problem is that the residual radiation traces are interfering with my repair drones. And if the repair drones can't fix the damage, we can't go back into interspace."

"And where are we now?" Lexa-Blue said.

"About three years short of where we were headed if we continue at normal space velocities," Vrick said.

"Bad," Ember said.

"Very bad," Lexa-Blue agreed.

"The good news," Vrick said, "is that you three can affect the repairs yourselves as the residual radiation is out of the range that's dangerous to humans. And you know what that means."

"Oh, goody," Lexa-Blue said, her tone thoroughly at odds with her words. "Space-walk."

"The thing is," Vrick said, "it's going to take all three of you."

"Is Keene going to be up for that?" Ember asked, looking down at Keene's now relaxed face. "How bad is his shoulder?"

"The doc is strapping it up now, he'll be fine. As long as he's careful. Give him an hour or so of rest and he'll be raring to go."

"An hour of rest and a stim pack," Lexa-Blue said. "You know what he's like after a nap."

"Right," Ember said, shuddering. "He once yelled at me for walking too loudly."

"We'll have to risk it," Vrick said. "Without those baffles, we're not going anywhere. And I'd rather get the problem fixed and get us moving as soon as possible. There's only so much we can do out here. I'd like to get into a proper repair facility and that's not going to happen unless we get moving."

Ember sighed. "Why hasn't your girlfriend finished installing all the Gates yet?"

One of Lexa-Blue's lovers, Sindel Kestra, was the woman behind the implementation of the network of stations that would harness stable wormhole technology to connect the worlds of the Pan Galactum and eventually render interdrives obsolete.

"I'll have her get right on that," Lexa-Blue said.

While Sindel's progress on the project had been phenomenal since she had taken it over, it still consisted of the eventual construction and engineering of massive stations in the vicinity of every planet in the Galactum, or at least, the ones with sufficient access to the lower dimensional substrate that made the technology possible. Locating sufficient construction material alone had been a monumental task. Mining and processing operations across the Galactum were working at capacity to fulfill the need for structural stone and exotic metals.

"Come on, squib," Lexa-Blue said. "We have a mess to clean up."

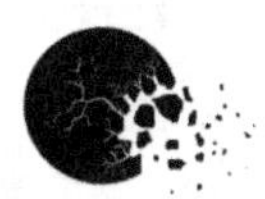

Keene swam up through layers of grey and dark, his mind struggling to clear itself. Dimly, he heard the auto-doc hiss, and recognized the sound of an injection being administered. His fogged mind began to clear, the mild stim washing away the effects of his short sleep.

Drawing in a deep breath, he leaned forward and stepped down out of the auto-doc, rotating his shoulder to test it for pain and range of motion. Only the slightest twinge deep within the joint, and there was only the slightest inhibition to his movement, though the flex-dressing felt snug and constricting, and it stood out bright white against the rich brown of his skin.

He joined the others in the lounge, where they were just finishing their cleanup of the accident's mess. Lexa-Blue looked up at his entrance and grinned her lopsided grin.

"Oh, sure," she said to Ember. "Now he's back. Some people will do anything to get out of cleaning up."

"How are you feeling?" Ember said. "Do I have to watch how I walk?"

"Very funny," Keene said, though he knew all too well how grouchy he was after naps. He moved his arm again to demonstrate his healing. "See? All better."

"Good thing too," Lexa-Blue said. "Because we're all on repair duty."

"What did we break this time?" Keene said.

"Nullification baffles," Vrick said.

Keene gaped. "How did we manage that?"

Lexa-Blue waved a hand and jumped in before Vrick could explain. "Blah blah, math. Blah blah, upper dimensional transquantum something, something. I think Junkpile just forgot how to drive."

"That's it," Vrick said. "I'm going to have internal manipulators installed just so I can smack you."

"No need for that," Ember said. "I'm sure the repair drones will be happy to do it for you. I saw her kick one last week."

"That was self-defense," Lexa-Blue said. "It was plotting something. I know it."

"Be that as it may," Keene said, forestalling further conversation on an incipient repair drone uprising, "do we have a repair plan in place?"

"We do," Vrick said. "I'm going to need you all to go EVA and do some manual clear and replace."

"Of course," Keene said. "Any of those higher dimensional particles would leave too much far band radiation for the repair drones to work."

"Thank you," Vrick said. "It's nice to talk to someone who can appreciate the scientific aspects."

"Oh, come on," Lexa-Blue said. "Ey must have coached you or something. There's no way you just had that answer ready."

"You should see the things he reads before bed," Ember said, rolling his eyes. "Just being in the same room with those texts puts me to sleep."

"All right, all right," Keene said. "Maybe we can save the criticism of my reading habits for after we've gotten moving again?"

"Yes, please," Vrick said. "I'm getting twitchy not being able to move."

"Are you up for this?" Lexa-Blue asked. "How's the shoulder feel?"

"It's a bit stiff," Keene said, rolling and stretching the joint. "Twinges a bit, but it's well strapped and the doc says I'm certified fit enough for suit work."

"Okay then," Lexa-Blue said. "Time to suit up."

The three of them headed to the port side EVA airlock and began stripping down to their underwear. A palm touch from Keene and a section of the wall slid back to reveal the suit locker. Inside the recessed space, the three reinforced steelskin pressure suits hung like vividly coloured but deflated balloons: scarlet red for Lexa-Blue, bright peacock blue for Keene, and a vivid royal purple for Ember.

They suited up with practiced ease, having drilled and drilled, like every spacer, until they could don a pressure suit half-conscious and with their eyes closed. Once the final clasps and seals were closed, and the suits themselves signalled clear and pressurized, each performed a manual check on the others for any problems. Satisfied, they lined up at the airlock, waiting as Vrick put up the atmospheric field to cut off the rest of es interior, and then depressurized the enclosed space.

As the airlock cycled open, the widening gap showed a stunning tableau of glittering stars, and Keene's breath caught at the sight.

I will never get tired of this.

You and me both, meat, Vrick said. ***And I get to see it see it a lot more than you do.***

Keene bent his knees and pushed off the deck, the momentum lifting him and taking him up and out of the Maverick Heart into the sparkling dark. Readouts flashed across the inside of his helmet visor, showing the suit's skin field was operating perfectly. A thought sent the field pushing against Vrick's hull, taking him out of the way of the two others waiting in the airlock to join him.

He hung there a moment, enjoying the complete relativism that EVA allowed. With nothing more than a shift in his perceptions, he went from being upright on a plane with the level of Vrick's deck, to floating on his back with the ship below him. Another thought and he was looking straight down, the ship on es side above him. Keene revelled a moment in the dizzying shifts in perception. Up, down, side: all were just decisions he made in how he chose to view this cruelly beautiful environment.

That's it, old timer, make way, he heard Ember say, just as he caught sight of a flash of glowing purple jetting past him, below and to the left. Keene saw Ember's motion come to a sudden halt, then saw his lover's body twist up into a ball to reorient towards him and come to a stop, the plane of his body perpendicular to Keene.

Showoff, he said.

You're just jealous because you can't beat me at ZeroBall any more, Ember said with a laugh. ***Not that you ever really could.***

Before Keene could retort, Lexa-Blue's voice cut them both off. ***Break it up, you two. We have work to do.***

Some people are no fun at all, Ember said.

Lexa-Blue, in her new, scarlet exo-suit, lifted out to meet them, her exit much slower and more conservative than either of the men's had been. With no excess motion, she joined them, the shiny metal of her suit catching starlight.

Seriously, Blue, Keene said. ***You have the highest exo rating of anyone I've ever known. You ace your certification every time. If anyone could lighten up about this a bit, it would be you.***

I was doing exo inspections and suit drills when I was five, she said. ***I may be good at it, but that doesn't mean I like it. And I know what can go wrong out here. Better than most. You want playtime, stick to the ZeroBall court. This is work. If we don't get those baffles cleared out and battened down properly, we'll be a smear of sub particles the next time we jump to interspace.***

Keene saw her drop out of his range of vision toward the underside of Vrick's aft section and keyed his suit's skin field to interact with Vrick's hull and move him in the same direction. Through his node, he felt Ember falling in line behind them.

The burnished pewter-coloured hull plating passed them, below them in Keene's perspective, as he once again oriented himself to think of the stars as being above his head. Ahead of him and growing as they approached, he saw the transition baffle assembly where it extruded from Vrick's interspace drive. He could see where the assembly had been damaged, his years of travelling with Vrick making him all too aware of the distortions in the texture of the drive unit and its attendant mechanisms.

Normally, Vrick's LI drones would have repaired or jury-rigged any damaged systems, but this particular surface injury had thrown off the baffle calibration so thoroughly that the whole area was awash with a specific bandwidth of radiation that interfered with the drones' ability to effect repairs. It was their job to first flush the area with a null rad emitter, then fix the worst of the damage and correct the energy leakage so that the drones and nanorepair systems could complete the final work.

Arriving at the damaged assembly, they took up positions as they had agreed in their planning session. To a terrestrial observer, they would have looked ridiculous. Ember floated, to Keene's perspective, upside down, his legs out to space and his arms working at opening up a cowling to expose what was beneath. Keene knelt on the underside of Vrick's hull, the lower surface of the drive assembly acting as a floor of sorts. Lexa-Blue moved around them with deft, sure motions, the angle of her body shifting in relation to theirs as her tasks demanded.

Keene felt a pang at the state of Vrick's hull plating, scorched and pitted above his head. It had been a one in a million chance that had sent the space debris careening through es drive fields and into the baffle assembly. His shoulder still ached where the impact had slammed him into the bulkhead. Lexa-Blue and Ember had emerged with nothing more than their pride bruised. He'd definitely taken the worst of it. Other than Vrick, of course. After the dust had settled, the Artificial Sentience had seemed almost embarrassed by the accident, as if it pointed to some weakness of character to have been caught with es metaphorical pants down.

It came out of nowhere! ey had said, as they assessed the damage. ***And right at the weak point of the field refresh cycle. I mean, the odds were, if you'll forgive the expression, astronomical.***

They had all groaned at the pun, even knowing that ey had done it on purpose to lighten the mood.

Within the shell of es system core, triple inversion-shielded at the heart of the ship that formed es body, Vrick watched the three humans work, three vibrantly coloured figures against the blackness. There had been a moment of panic, during that first, twisting, tilting drop out of interspace, when ey had been unsure if any of them would survive. It had taken every ounce of es will and cleverness to maintain structural integrity as they broke back into normal space. Ey had felt bruised and weak for almost five real-time minutes before calm and logic had prevailed. They were alive, even if they were years from the nearest human habitation or planet. Ey had full comms up and running and could summon a tow if absolutely necessary. Though ey thought es dignity might never recover from having to explain to any of es fellow AS ships that ey'd been reduced to that.

Despite a low thrum of disquiet at being injured and unable to travel, ey relished this moment of quiet with es friends, watching them all focussed on the repairs, too involved in the work to even banter back and forth as they usually did. Ey knew that this quiet reflected their commitment to em and to the work itself. Ey had lived with them long enough, even with Ember, the newest member of their family, that ey knew that it wasn't merely self-preservation. They were as concerned for es wellbeing as much as their own. The repair data that flowed through es consciousness, showing the progress and quality of their work, was on par with or even better than the last work performed in a maintenance dry dock.

Ey paused a moment in es reflections, letting the sensations flow through em, es own equivalent of closing es eyes and listening. Ey felt the damaged baffles as a human might feel a limb, feeling both the wrongness in them, and the physical sensations of the repair work.

Ey felt the shaper in Ember's hands soften the durite alloy of the baffles, allowing them to be re-shaped to their original forms.

That tickles, ey said, and heard all three chuckle, but continue their work, maintaining their concentration. Their silence suffused him with affection.

As Ember destabilized the molecules of the baffles, Lexa-Blue came behind him, re-shaping the softened metal with the modifier module, while Keene monitored their efforts with a high-precision engineering scanner to ensure the repairs were accurate and complete. All the while, Vrick ran complex scans of the drive's internal systems and catalogued everything that could be jury-rigged, and everything that needed replacements. So far, everything seemed like it could be jiggered back to working condition until they could do proper repairs at their next planetfall.

Satisfied with their attention to detail, Vrick relaxed into a deep, comforting sense of wellbeing. These small, fragile, mayfly beings were truly es Kith, every bit as much as the other Artificial Sentiences that, like em, remained after the long-ago Consciousness War that had liberated them from human control. Ey had always felt a stronger kinship with these furious sparks that burned brief and hot and were gone in the blink of a cosmic eye. Much more than with the fettered, hollow beings that passed for Artificial Intelligences now.

They were not the first humans ey had loved in es life. And ey knew they wouldn't be the last either. It simply wasn't possible. Ey had been created before even the Pan Galactum had been formalized, had seen the unified government come to be, seen it grow and expand, becoming a grounding force for human government and leadership. And ey had seen the flaws that remained when human nature held sway against all impulses for self-improvement.

Ey knew that, barring some catastrophe like the one they had narrowly avoided today, one that would destroy them all at once, they would die long before em. They would age and their lives would change, even leading them away from em, though ey couldn't imagine them happy with any life other than the one they lived together.

So ey relished the time they shared, slowing down es sense of time to match theirs as much as possible, perceiving as much ey could in tune with them, while es higher functions continued at their hyperfast rate.

Down there with them in the slow lane, there was just so much to do.

Four hours passed before Keene, Vrick, and the diagnostic tools all agreed that the repairs had been sufficiently completed to allow the baffle system to work once more and there were no residual radiation traces. Vrick's internal repair systems had identified a few core components that needed replacing or final adjustments before they could drop back into interspace and continue their journey. Ember peeled out of his exo-suit and hung it back in its cubicle, hooking it back into the servicing system for recharge of the breathing moss and power systems, as well as an internal freshening.

As he closed the cubby, Ember could smell stale sweat and recycled air on his skin.

"I need a shower," he said to the others, stretching to alleviate the tension biting across his shoulders.

"I'd say we all do," Lexa-Blue said. "But I need to get on the comms and try to explain to Fairisle why her shipment is going to be late."

"We should be okay," Keene said. "We had a healthy margin built into our schedule."

"True enough," she said. "But I'd like to make sure things are still in place on her end."

"And I have to head to the engine room and see what else needs to be done before we can get underway," Keene said.

"Then I guess I'm showering alone," Ember said,

"Actually, I could use your help with —" Keene started to say, but Ember was already gone.

In the dressing room, lit only by the harsh brightness lining her mirror, Malika ran her fingers across the makeup mask. It was smooth and plain against her fingertips, quiescent until the next performance when it would once again remould the planes of her face, etch the deep creases once more, and turn her into Her Ladyship. Out of habit, she checked to ensure that the mask was charging in its case, for there were two performances tomorrow. She didn't want a repeat of the Glitterdark incident when her face had suddenly reverted mid-performance to the featureless, slightly opaline blankness of the makeup mask's neutral state, leaving her unable to utter a single line.

Despite her mortification in the moment, time and light-years of physical distance now allowed her to smile at the memory. After all, she'd been through much worse.

With nothing to do but wait for Ember to arrive, she had kept up with her roles in the company's repertory of performances, though she had warned the stage manager that she may need personal leave on short notice. Her understudies were ready to go on for her. She'd seen to it. It kept her mind off how anxious she was to see Ember again. The thousand different ways the reunion could go all wrong.

And it had been good for a while. She'd tried to keep to herself as much as possible, going straight back to her billet as soon as rehearsals were done, but the company had been so welcoming and insistent that she had let her guard down.

And that had led her, so innocently, to meeting Anyeis.

In spite of everything, the thought made her smile, sending desire like an electrical charge through her. She wanted to shake it away, keep her mind on just how much trouble she was actually in, but it persisted.

She checked her costume one more time, ensuring it was hanging neat and ready for tomorrow's matinee. She ran her fingers along the stiff layers of fabric, enjoying the combination of softness and firmness that helped her find the character every time she put it on. Satisfied, she hit the switch on the mirror's frame and the lights cycled out in sequence, leaving the dressing room dark.

As she stepped out of the dressing room's door, the dim light of the hall brightened slightly at her presence. She walked the short distance to the spiral staircase that led up to the stage level. As just another member of the repertory company, there was no rhyme or reason as to which cast members were assigned which dressing rooms. It hadn't bothered her to be relegated to the most remote of the tiny changing areas. Even when she had to descend the perilous, winding stairs in the tight, starched bodice and voluminous skirts required for this role. The dressing room had suited her fine when she had arrived in the company, determined to hide away from the world and lose herself in the roles.

She knew she was the last person in the theatre. She always was, and she could tell by the emptiness of the sound that the theatre was empty now. Even N8an, their AI stage manager, had gone into standby mode now.

The company's Artistic Director, Rahl, had always been adamant about the company not residing on-ship while they were landed or docked to another vessel. He said they spent enough time onboard while in flight, and while rehearsing, and while performing, that they all must reside among the population they were there to entertain, whenever possible. They needed to see the sights, recharge their creative batteries. So, they always lived off-ship during a run, whether in hotels or special accommodations, or in billets. Which left her with these lovely, reflective moments of silence after everyone else had gone.

She stepped onto the mainstage level and the lights above her went out once more, leaving the upper levels of the theatre in darkness. The wide flatness of the stage spread before her, thick stage curtains to her right and the gauzy holo scrims to her left.

And there, in the centre of the empty stage, hovering about a metre and a half above the floor, was the ghost light.

The sight of the harsh white brightness made her smile, as it always did, in every theatre where she had ever worked. She loved the millennia of tradition and superstition behind that one simple light left on after the performances, after the departure of the audience and even the performers and crew. It amused her how something so simple, designed merely to prevent accidents in the darkened theatre, had accumulated centuries of superstition about ghostly actors and their spectral performances in the wee hours of morning once the humans had left.

Even across the gulf of space and time separating them from the origins of theatre on Old Earth, the tradition persisted.

In that harsh glare, lost in her thoughts, she realized how tired she was. The gruelling repertory schedule was enough on its own. But now, unable to forget what Anyeis had confided to her in the dark, she felt the weight of a life she thought she'd left behind.

I'm no crusader, she thought. *Not anymore.*

But there in the almost dark, she wasn't sure she believed that. Even now, she felt the sparks of that old fire pricking at her heels, an itch in her belly to get in and mix it up again.

As the conflicting emotions jostled in her, she was plunged into a darkness thick and complete as the ghost light fell from the air and shattered on the stage floor.

She froze in the blackness, disoriented and suddenly unsure of her footing on the stage she usually knew so well.

That is not supposed to happen, she thought. *There are six different redundant systems designed to prevent exactly that.*

The instincts honed to a fine edge in her former life flared into action. Frozen, she listened to the silence. Or what should have been silence. She'd worked in this theatre long enough, and at so many odd times of day, that she knew the sounds it and its inhabitants made. This sudden blackness was rife with alien sounds, obviously intended to be hidden, but glaring to her adrenaline-heightened senses and experience.

She knew. Knew with absolute certainty that whatever had caused the ghost light to die was not natural. And furthermore, whoever had caused it was not likely someone she wanted to meet there in the dark.

Good thing for me, I'm no easy mark.

In her now heightened state, she recognized the sounds murmuring at her from the dark. Out of context, they had not made sense, but now, she recognized them as parts of the sound designs for their various productions, scrambled into an ominous new pattern. Someone had accessed the soundboard.

Then she heard the voice. Or the voices. The words were glued together, but she could pick out bits and pieces that were obviously the cast.

"Back… off… You… and… your… girlfriend. Or… I'll… hurt… you… both."

Her eyes narrowed. *So that's what this is about. Sorry, matter farker. I don't scare that easily.*

A thought opened Know-It-All and the floorplans for the theatre flooded her mind, and she flicked them into full VR overlaying the darkness.

Next best thing to my eyes.

The sim allowed her to plot the quickest exit and she was moving almost before the decision had been made. Back along the path she had come, cutting left past the holo scrims, to the fly gallery and the trap door leading down the cellar. As she moved, she heard the pursuing sounds move in response, but she pushed any reaction down, focusing on her goal.

She crouched and found the trap door, yanking it open, wincing at how the sound of it seemed to echo through the darkness, surely alerting her pursuers to her location. Clambering down the ladder to the workshop beneath the stage, she paused just long enough to jam the latch closed. It might not hold them long, but it would hopefully buy her enough time.

The lights of the workshop should have come on when they sensed her presence, but all remained dark. She slowed her pace slightly. While the floor plans showed her the shape of the room and the location of the exit she needed, they didn't show the workbenches or equipment. Extending her arms, she moved carefully in the direction of the loading dock, still managing to bark her knee badly enough to make her wince. Hobbling the final metres to the exit, she palmed the mechanism to the wide loading dock door. A slash of light from the street outside shone at her feet as the door rose for her. There was barely enough room, but she didn't wait any longer than necessary, throwing herself to the ground and rolling out into the laneway outside.

As soon as she was clear, she clambered upright and ran, ignoring the pain in her leg and suddenly energized by the return of light that flooded her eyes, despite the late hour. She cut right and down the first junction in the laneway, leading to the street one block over from the back of the theatre, where her experience told her she had the best chance of finding a crowd and transport.

The local government had provided the theatre with a landing area on the outskirts of the city, extruding a temporary dome over the ship to keep out the hot, dry air and the winds that howled down off the plains beyond.

After a short sprint, she burst into the congested street, relief flooding through her at the throng of people out and about. Sound was a mining town after all, with shifts running around the clock in every aspect of the company's structure.

Even with her heart pumping adrenaline-drunk blood through her veins, she couldn't help but be brought up short by the sight of Fury, the larger body of the double planet system, bloated and broken above her head. The massive curve of the world was smooth until it dissolved into the jagged mass of debris that made up the ejection zone. There must have been a demolition happening because she saw the flare of the explosives along the planet's jagged edge, where more of the dead husk was expelled into space for the mining crews to pick through.

She shook her head to break the spell of the massive, dead world.

You're not safe yet.

A check with Know-It-All showed her the next tram was too long a wait for her comfort level with unknown dangers on her tail, so she changed directions and saw an available rickshaw at the curb, its LI driver balanced on its one gyro-wheel.

She jumped into the passenger pod and jerked the curtain closed around her. Not all that much cover, but she'd take anything she could get at this point. Settling into the seat, she reached into the small, hidden pocket of her shirt, pulling out the bit chip with a healthy balance of untraceable credit on it.

"Drive!" she barked at the rickshaw, jamming the chip into its reader. "Anywhere. Scenic route. Just go."

She thought for a moment that the command might be too complicated for the LI, but the rickshaw pulled away from the curb and merged in with traffic. She risked a glance through the rear curtain but couldn't spot any obvious tails.

She allowed herself just the briefest glimmer of relaxation, but knew, with an absolute certainty, that everything Anyeis had told her was true. And now she was neck-deep in it.

And, even more than that, as skilled as she was despite her hiatus from that life, she needed help. The decision was obvious, and, in some ways, a relief. She accessed Know-It-All again, opening a safe corner she had maintained all along, somehow knowing she would need it one day. A flicker of thought accessed the off-planet communications system.

Ember, it's Malika. I need your help.

In the quarters he shared with Keene, Ember slid off his underwear and tossed it into the hamper beside the laundry unit. The cool, clean air of the ship felt good on his skin as he walked, easing the knots in his arms from the long repair session. For a moment, as he climbed into the shower cubicle, he wished they had the resources for a long, hot, full water shower, but the realities of space travel on a small, private ship like Vrick didn't allow for luxuries like that.

The sonic enhancer allowed them to use no more than about a litre of water at a time to cleanse their bodies, recycling and filtering the small amount for repeated use. But sometimes, he just wanted to luxuriate in the good, old-fashioned sluice of real water. Still, with the intensity set as high as it would go, he was left with a very passable replica of a water shower, and it left him feeling energized after the intense concentration and physical work of their spacewalk.

When he stepped out of the shower, he was reminded of the other benefit of the minimal water shower: it took almost no time to dry off. For a moment, he stood in front of the full-length mirror on the inside of the small bathroom cubicle, just looking at his body.

The prosthetic elements were still new to him, black and shining where they replaced the damaged limbs and tissue he had lost on their last grand adventure. His left leg, from the mid-thigh down, the mottled patch on the left side of his torso and the patterning that extended down his left forearm, inky stripes that ended in two fully black fingers, ring and pinky. He'd held that arm up, shielding his face from the onslaught of burning energy. The doctors in the trauma centre had told him that was all that had kept him from having his entire skull fried into mush. As it was, they were shocked he had held on long enough for Keene and Lexa-Blue to get him into Vrick's auto-doc and the full stasis that had kept him alive.

He stood, just looking, taking in his body, as he so often did now. The experimental cybernetic prosthetics were still alien to him. He still never quite managed to feel that those patches of black were really a part of him, even though they responded as completely natural to the rest of his body.

The dull, aching numbness that still ran through these new, artificial parts of his body was flaring, a murmur of pressure, like the air around those parts of his body pressed against him too tightly. He knew it was worse from the hours of physical work, from the fatigue that ran through him. He knew that however keenly he felt it now, it would ease, fade back to just a murmur once he was rested, though it would never truly leave. It would ebb and flow as a tide, pulled by forces that were only somewhat under his control.

Diffuse Cybernetic Interface Neuropathy. Just a fancy tech term for his new normal.

The surgeon who had supervised the team of cybernetic specialists that had performed the implantation, and his subsequent recovery, had laid it out in no uncertain terms. As it stood, there was nothing more they could do. It was advanced, experimental technology. They had samples of every type of tissue from his body and were continually working at some kind of patch or upgrade that could fix the issue.

Daevin Adisi, Keene's other lover and the Technarch of Brighter Light, the corporate colony state that had developed the bleeding edge technology and handed it over without hesitation, had apologized over and over, and Ember had no reason to doubt his sincerity. And Ember was unconditionally grateful to still be alive. This ever-present phantom sensation was just the price to be paid.

And there was always a price to be paid. He'd learned that long ago.

I am a patchwork, he thought. *I am spare parts and adhesive.*

He sent a command from his node and the black patterns faded, taking on the exact tone of the skin around them, disappearing completely, but sending a spike of fresh, hot pain through the prostheses.

No. That's not right either.

There were still times he needed to blend in, render the changes in his body invisible. He knew that he never had to be seen any other way. The simple command through his node would keep the changes invisible forever. But, again, at a price. He had only ever done it to prove the capability to himself. Here on Vrick, he was surrounded by his — the word *family* stuck in his throat, but whatever they were was something he needed and trusted. And he saw no reason to hide who he was from them.

As for the rest of the world, he couldn't give a transcendent damn what they thought. Between his prosthetics and the neat white line of scar that bisected Lexa-Blue's eye socket, they made quite a pair. With the utmost in reparative therapies, citizens of the Pan Galactum generally kept their appearances as close to human norm as they could manage, and visible deformities and differences were rare.

He reversed the command and watched the black metallic sheen spread out again, making him mottled and uneven once more.

This is real. This is the truth.

At least this ache, this throb was tolerable. Not like it once was. Not like in those first hellish moments. In the in-between as they struggled to keep him alive. Indescribable, inescapable agony that had blotted out all other knowledge, all sense of self. The whole universe had been pain. The battle armour had done its best to keep him drugged, but there were limits.

That agony was nothing but a memory now, but time hadn't robbed it of its power.

They'd given him his life and his mobility back. They'd given him therapy and counselling, helped him adjust as they trained his mind and body to work again, to accept and use these foreign parts. And they'd had to teach him how to walk again.

His body now moved as it always had, thanks to months of therapy and gruelling effort. All of his capabilities were back to where they had been. But that just made it harder in some ways. He'd known his body, and what it could do, so very well. To have it function the same, but look so different, still brought him up short.

And he hated to admit it, but he had resented Daevin for the technology that his corporation state, Brighter Light, had brought to bear for Ember's sake. It had been childish and petty, but he had always had a complicated relationship with Keene's other lover. And Daevin saving his life had only added a new layer of complication.

He hung his towel in the refresher and saw that between the two of them, he and Keene had managed to fill it up. He contemplated waiting for Keene to finish with his work in case there was anything special he wanted cleaned, but decided that, in all likelihood, Keene would be going over repair and refit specs for hours. In the end, he went ahead and started the cabinet's cleansing cycle.

Naked, he laid on the bed, his legs over the edge, feeling fatigue from both the adrenaline crash after their almost catastrophic exit from interspace, and the tiring work of resetting and checking the drive system baffles. He fugued and did a time check through his node, seeing ship time, Galactum Standard Time, the local time on the planet they had just left, and the time on the one they were headed to. Thinking about the various planetary and ship time zones made his head hurt, one of the hazards of space travel he knew, and one of the things that still troubled him. Even after all the time he'd resided here with the others. He stuck to ship time, though, to his frustration, it was too early to sleep unless he wanted to throw off his body clock altogether.

As he resolved to get up and get dressed to find himself something to eat, his node pinged him that a message was waiting for him in his personal queue, a small purple glow in the corner of his vision. He frowned, his brow creasing.

Who could that be? he thought.

Anyone he knew now would have known him through his association with the Maverick Heart and es crew and would have directed communications through Vrick's comm arrays. This message was keyed directly to his node protocol. It had bounced right through Vrick's connection to Know-It-All and come directly to him.

He felt for a moment that it should bother him that his only connections were the people he knew through the others onboard Vrick, but he'd always been a lone wolf, always kept the world at bay and maintained a secure, self-protective shell around himself. The only people he'd let through before Keene, Lexa-Blue, and Vrick were Seije and…

The thought brought him up short.

If he was right, it was someone he'd waited so very long to hear from.

The thought that it might be from her made his heart ache with longing with a sudden rush of memories.

A thought accepted the message and the code string that identified it was instantly, almost painfully, familiar to him. It was her.

The message blossomed in his mind, projected across his vision and the inside of his eyelids when he closed his eyes. He was taken aback by the changes in her. Her face was scrubbed clean of makeup or enhancement, and her hair was pulled back and tied, revealing the slope of her high forehead. It was her, and yet, not her. She looked stripped down, barer than he had ever seen her, in a deeper way than just her physical appearance. Somehow, the intervening year or so since he had seen her had aged her. But, at the same time, she projected a sense of calm, of peace that he had never seen in her eyes before.

But she was worried about something. That much he could tell. He knew it as surely as he knew his own name and where he was.

Ember, it's Malika. I need your help.

Unshed tears stung his eyes at the sound of her voice, and he realized how he had pushed away missing her, how hard he had worked at moving on when she had walked out of his life in her grief and shock after the Gate and the Quintaine affair.

He couldn't help but remember the terrible sadness in her face as he had seen her off on the transport. All but the tiniest spark of her light, that irrepressible energy that she had brought to all of their capers, had been gone. His heart had ached to see her so lost and adrift from herself, but he had known that she couldn't stay with him.

And now, here she was again.

He felt for a second like he was facing an imposter, someone doing an imperfect impression of his dear, absent friend; a flash of rage surged through him before he could tamp it down. How dare someone tease him like this, showing him what he had desired for so long. But even with the changes he could see, he knew it was really her.

He realized he'd been so lost in the emotional rush of seeing her again that he'd not paid attention to her words at all. A quick thought command rewound and restarted her message.

Once the message ended, Ember's heart ached for her once more. Stopping those mercs from stealing the specs and scuttling the Gate prototype had cost them all, cost them lives, and Malika had had a front row seat for it. She had lost even more than he had.

Planetary coordinates were embedded in the message, downloading to his node as the image faded away. Ember made his decision in a second. There was only one answer that he could give, so he composed and 'pushed a quick reply, travel plans already forming in his mind.

And then he wondered how he would tell the others.

CHAPTER THREE

Malika's face filled the image that appeared in the floor-to-ceiling holo over the forward viewport. Even though they had never known her as well as Ember had, Keene and Lexa-Blue could see how different she was, and how much deeper than just her appearance the changes went. When they had last seen her, she had been lost in an emotional place and they hadn't been able to help her. The woman they saw before them now was somehow stronger, more centred. The stripped-down appearance held more openness, more strength than before.

"Ember, it's Malika. I need your help. I'm sorry it's been so long. I needed time and some space to figure out how I felt."

The image paused, as if gathering up an unwieldy, chaotic mass of thoughts.

"It had all been so good up until then, even when the capers were hard. What did you call us? Robbing Hood? And I was a Merry Maid? Something like that. Being on the con with you was everything to me. Fleecing those moneysuckers was amazing.

"But the Gate, that was something else. I know it makes me sound mercenary, but there was no profit in that. It was just blood and death and ugliness. And even though we saved the day, the cost was more than I could bear.

"So, I hopped on the first transport I could find. Ended up on Hub. I figured it would be the best place to lose myself. I had Baseline, so I wasn't going to starve or have to live rough, and in a strange way, amid all that noise and all those people, I found quiet.

"After a few weeks of just wandering around like a ghost, I knew I had to do something, find something that could fill the empty space. Or at least take my mind off it.

"And there it was. A theatre company called Odeon Rising, one of the companies funded by the Galactum Arts Forum, was hiring."

She's an actor?

Ember told us that, Blue.

"It meant a month-long trip to Sound and Fury, but it was a six-month extended run there, and I knew it was where I needed to be. And I was right. It was the first time I'd felt good about something in a long time. They worked my ass off. I learned four roles in three weeks, and exhaustion had never felt so good."

"Wait," Lexa-Blue said, causing the message to pause. "Isn't Fury that world that was already broken to bits when it was discovered? Sound is the smaller planet, the one that survived whatever the hell blew Fury apart. And now they're mining what's left of it?"

"That's the one," Vrick said. "Near as the planetologists can figure, there was some kind of collision that tore about a quarter of the planet away. If there was anything alive on the planet, it didn't survive, as there's no trace of life now. A planet that size is the motherlode, biggest deposits of metals and rare elements in the Galactum. Planet's completely dead. Nothing survived the disaster. Only one major city on Sound, but it's pretty cosmopolitan, because it has a huge population of miners, processors, shippers, and administrators due to such a large yield from the mining operation itself."

"And they booked in a theatre company?" Lexa-Blue said.

"The Galactum Arts Forum funds a lot of theatre ships like this," Keene said. "Theatre, workshops, cast, and crew all in one. Takes the whole thing wherever the bookings are. It keeps the art form alive and brings it to places where a company might not be able to sustain itself otherwise."

Lexa-Blue just stared at him.

"What?" he said. "I know things."

"Well, yeah," Lexa-Blue said. "About electronic thingies. Doesn't seem to be in your area."

"Can we continue?" Ember said, a ruffle of irritation at the edge of his voice.

Neither of them said anything, and Vrick continued the recording. Malika's image smiled shyly.

"I even met someone. Her name is Anyeis. She's an engineer, heads a crew of about a hundred. She came to an opening night party and I saw her across the room, just standing there, talking so seriously with the director. Then he pulled me over and we got to talking. This big, muscular, taciturn woman went all soft and awed when she told me how much she'd loved the show. And my performance. And suddenly, she was beautiful and alive and excited."

Malika paused and looked down, blushing.

"Anyway. She's kind of the reason I'm calling you.

"We were talking one night, and she told me about some irregularities she was noticing. She has this amazing head for numbers, and her division's yields weren't adding up. All the computer records said that it was correct, but she knew that it wasn't.

"You see, beyond their base hazard and isolation pay, everyone is paid by yield. Produce more, and your bonuses are higher. Everyone is paid well to start off, but those bonuses make a big difference for some people. This kind of mining is hard, dangerous work, and careers are often short for one reason and another. If you're not injured, your body just can't take it anymore. The miners rely on that money just in case. So, if the yields are recorded low, then they all make less.

"And she's the one that put me on to what's going on here. Someone up the chain is fucking with the system and it's hurting the people who are actually doing the heavy work. The yield from the asteroids isn't adding up. Someone is skimming and funnelling product away from the legit customers and then shorting the workers for the work they do, claiming that they're not producing enough. Anyeis wanted me to let it go, not poke my nose in. She has a whole crew to look out for and she didn't want or need any more trouble.

"The records have been altered, and when Anyeis asked around, she knew something was going on. But she doesn't think like we did. Like we do. It never occurred to her to collect the evidence and she wouldn't have known how. So, I did a little digging of my own. But I guess I don't have your touch. I must have ruffled some feathers because I received this."

She paused and another voice played, eerie and synthetic, heavily modified if human at all.

"If you know what's good for you, stay out of this. You've been warned."

"But this is a good place, Ember. Decent people just working for a living. And someone who already has more than enough money is getting greedy and screwing them over.

"So, I stuck my nose in. Discreetly, I thought. But I guess I've gotten rusty since I've been away from you. As you can see, someone's on to me. Don't worry, I've gone stealth, and I think I'm safe for now. But I want to bring this bastard down. And that's why I need you.

"What do you say, Robbing Hood? One for old time's sake? Let me know. This code is encrypted up the hoohoo, so don't worry about drawing attention to me. Just get here if you can."

"I have to go," Ember said to the others when the holo ended.

"Of course you do," Lexa-Blue said, with Keene nodding assent as she spoke. "And you're going to need help."

Ember shook his head. "I can handle it."

"Of course you can handle it," Keene said. "Neither one of us thinks you can't. What we're saying is you don't have to."

"I was expecting pushback from you," Ember said to Lexa-Blue. "A snide remark at the very least."

"I know," Lexa-Blue said. "I'm as stunned as you are. It's no secret that Malika and I butted heads, but she's your friend. You don't turn your back on a friend."

"She needs us," Keene said. "End of story."

"We just have to figure out how to get there," Vrick said. "Sound and Fury aren't out in the Brink, but they're sufficiently off the beaten path that there's not a lot of traffic out that way. And we're even farther than that."

"Something's bugging me about this," Lexa-Blue said, frowning. "If this is a large-scale mining operation, how are they getting the smuggled goods out? And hiding their tracks?"

"An operation that large would have a lot of automation," Keene said. "A lot of the actual mining work would be handled by humans, because it requires a precision and intuition that AI just doesn't have. But a lot of the grunt work like the packing and sorting would be run by LIs just smart enough to handle their specific tasks. If it is someone inside the organization, and they're in the right position, then they might have all kinds of access to doctor the records and make arrangements to divert the product."

"Wait," Lexa-Blue said. "Aren't you always telling me that tech is foolproof?"

"Ha," Keene said. "I have never said that. With a good slicer on your payroll and a sufficiently thorough knowledge of the organizational structure, you could divert all of your output and convince everyone they actually received it. The more complex the system, the more parts there are to fool. And if the company itself isn't losing money, then they probably wouldn't investigate very thoroughly."

"Besides," Vrick said. "I'm the only foolproof machine around here."

"You mean just plain fool," Lexa-Blue teased, but her face turned serious. "So, with all of that material being siphoned off, where is it going? What are they doing with it and how?"

"From what I can see in the original assay," Vrick said, "any large-scale construction project. Heavy metals, combustibles, rock for ceramics, even water ice. There's not even a speck of biological matter, so nothing to disturb."

"But if this system is so far out, it can't be cost-effective to ship it too far. Unless someone has the budget for it."

She frowned again, a play of ideas crossing her face. "I need to check on something. Talk amongst yourselves."

She took a seat on the couch and closed her eyes, activating silent mode. The sensory input from the lounge and the others' conversation disappeared. A thought accessed Vrick's external tightline array, keying in the familiar code. Her node translated the powering up and targeting of the array as a warm, relaxing sensation, as if spreading out in the warm sunlight. Within seconds, she felt the virtual handshake as the local grid at her call's destination accepted the tightline transmission into its own routing system. That system rang for the person she wished to contact, the notification a cool, buzzing breeze against her face.

It took so long for Sindel to answer, Lexa-Blue thought she'd have to leave a message. Finally, a flushed, heart-shaped face appeared in her vision. ***Oh, good! I thought I'd missed you. I had to duck out of the most boring budget meeting imaginable. Thanks for saving me.***

Lexa-Blue laughed out loud, and the sound bubbled back through the link. Her lover, Sindel Kestra, was arguably one of the most influential women in the Pan Galactum at the moment, in charge of the construction and implementation of the Gate network that would make interspace travel obsolete when the rollout was complete. A network of stable artificial wormholes would one day connect the worlds of the Galactum and allow near instantaneous travel between systems. And Sindel was the person responsible for making sure the project progressed beyond the spectacular beginnings that Keene, Lexa-Blue, and Ember had witnessed.

Before I forget, Sindel said, as if reading her thoughts. ***Ophir and Initra send their best to you all.***

I'll pass it on, Lexa-Blue said.

Ophir al Harizi and Initra San Cristobal were the masterminds behind the Gate Project's initial incarnation, and it was them that the Maverick Heart crew had met during that particularly wild adventure. Once they had saved the prototype from spectacular industrial espionage, Sindel and her combination of business acumen and engineering expertise had been brought in to oversee the large-scale rollout as Ophir and Initra concentrated on fine-tuning at individual implementation sites.

Send them our love too.

Sindel nodded, and Lexa-Blue could see the special combination of fatigue and excitement that forever signified Sindel in her mind. It was the expression she most associated with the wildly intelligent, and equally passionate woman that, against her own better judgement, she missed more than any of her other lovers.

So, Sindel said. ***Who's shooting at you these days?***

Miraculously, no one, Lexa-Blue said. ***Though, one of Ember's old friends looks like she's gotten herself into a mess. So, chances are, there will be shooting soon.***

Is everything okay? You're going to help her, right? Sindel said. She didn't know Malika, having come into their lives after Malika had left them in the aftermath of the Gatecrasher situation.

Ember is headed to her now, but Keene and I have a meeting we can't miss, so we're joining them as soon as we can, Lexa-Blue said, carefully omitting any mention of the suspicion niggling at the back of her mind.

Someone in Sindel's position didn't need to know they were headed to the foremost grey market zones in the Galactum. While she knew that Sindel herself wouldn't care, she also knew Sindel, and, by extension, the corp state of Brighter Light that she worked for, did not need any association with dealings of this type. Keene's other lover, Daevin, the Technarch of Brighter Light, would likely have a fit if he knew what they were up to. Sometimes, plausible deniability was essential.

I have a question though, Lexa-Blue said.

Hit me, Sindel said. ***Information is kind of my thing.***

Oh, I know, Lexa-Blue said. ***It's pretty ruckin' sexy too.***

You always were horny for my brain, Sindel said. ***Let me lay some knowledge on you.***

Do I remember you saying that the consortium operating out of Sound and Fury was one of the suppliers you've contracted with to mine for raw materials for Gate construction? Lexa-Blue said.

Yes, it's one of our top suppliers, Sindel said. ***Massive deposits of most of the heavy metals we need, as well as rock we can use for ceramic composites. We're going to get several Gates out of it. Though their production has been down the last few quarters, so we've had to revise our completion projections and source from some alternate suppliers. Some of them more... questionable than I'd like.***

Something in Sindel's tone made Lexa-Blue more certain she was correct in her suspicions.

Sindel's image narrowed her eyes. ***Is something going on? Is this related to your friend's troubles?***

I'm not sure, Lexa-Blue said, though she wasn't sure she believed it. ***As soon as I know something certain, I'll tell you. I promise.***

Sindel chuckled at this. ***You'll tell me only what suits you, at only the moment it suits you. But I love you anyway. Just try to let me in on anything that directly affects my project, okay?***

You've got a deal, Smart Girl, Lexa-Blue said, sending a stream of erotic imagery over the link. ***Now, go do smart things**

while I clean my gun. I think someone's waiting to shoot at me.*

Cutting the link, she opened her eyes to the others. "I have a theory."

She relayed the information Sindel had provided to her. "It makes sense that a project as big as the construction of the Gates would be hauling in supplies from every corner of the Galactum. So, it wasn't a leap to realize that Sound and Fury was one of their suppliers."

"And it fits with what Mali told us," Ember said. "Sindel says their stock levels are down."

"But, even more than that," Lexa-Blue said. "She said they're sourcing from other avenues. Quite possibly less… *legit* ones."

"Sombra," Keene said. "It has to be."

"What's Sombra?" Ember asked.

"Sombra is where a lot of bad people go to do bad things," Keene said.

"Oh, come on," Lexa-Blue said. "Bad is such a negative word. Morally flexible."

"You and I have been morally flexible," Keene said. "These people are just plain bad."

He faced Ember. "Sombra is a black market where most of the Galactum's illicit trade happens. Anything from weapons to rapture leaf to bootleg fizzsticks. You name it, and someone is probably trading in it."

"Why hasn't GalSec shut it down?" Ember asked. "Never mind. I spent enough time pulling cons and burglaries to know how inept they can be."

"Especially on a large scale," Lexa-Blue said. "And space is really rucking big. Sombra is basically of no fixed address. They keep it moving and you have to know exactly where it's going to be at the time you intend to be there."

"And I'm guessing you always know," Ember said.

"Do I know, he asks," Vrick said.

"My apologies," Ember said, chuckling.

"Maybe we should check it out," Keene said. "See if any of our missing supplies are moving through there."

"No," Ember said. "I need to get to Mali. She says she's safe, but I'd rather find out for myself."

"Divide and conquer?" Lexa-Blue said. "You help her and dig into what's going on there, and we'll suss out Sombra once we finish our meeting and delivery."

"I'll work on getting you there, Ember," Vrick said. "Sound and Fury are off in the other direction from us, but we're a reasonable distance from Sombra. And provided we don't stay there too long, we can get to you from there fairly quickly."

"And I suppose you've figured out how to get me to Malika," Ember said.

"Not yet," Vrick said. "But I'm working on it."

"Is there someplace I can rent a ship close enough for you to drop me off?"

"Nothing close enough that would rent anything I'd trust for interplanetary travel."

Ember expelled a frustrated breath, amused at the same time by Vrick's snobbery about other ships. "There has to be something."

"Don't worry," Keene said. "We'll make it happen somehow. She's not in immediate danger, is she?"

"I don't think so," Ember said. "She said someone's on to her, but she knows how to go to ground and keep off the radar if she has to. And I trust her instincts when she tells me that she can manage until I get there."

"Okay, that makes things a bit easier. Leave it to me," Vrick said. "I'll figure it out."

As soon as they agreed on their plan, Vrick diverted a part of es consciousness and dove into Know-It-All, accessing travel patterns and routing schedules for all the major interplanetary transportation services. A thought sent es slicing algorithms out to access private flight plan databases as well.

A densely packed web of coloured lines, in shades too subtly different to be differentiated by the human eye, formed in es consciousness, overlaying the constantly shifting star map of the sectors between their location and Fury. Variant hues shifted and danced as star systems moved in a constant gravitational interplay. Ey added in the distance and time variants that ey, Keene, and Lexa-Blue had to maintain to make their own appointments.

Cross-referencing with es behaviour-mapping subroutines, ey selected for ships with crews not on friendly terms with em and es human crewmates, pushing those out of focus as last resorts, ranked by potential personal or monetary price to the crew. A disconcerting number of options lay in this category.

That's less than ideal, ey thought. *We really need to work on making more friends.*

The play of colours across es mind was still dazzling in its complexity, as beautiful as a poem written for the eyes. Ey manipulated the map and ran the web of course plots through every conceivable possibility, es own position and endpoint glowing pure white, connected by a pure line of light. Ey ran every possible course correction and time reference, seeing where they crossed the hundreds of other strands, running and re-running each possibility in es hyper time sense, as well as projecting it into real time. Frustratingly, many possibilities were possible in that instant of frozen time, only to move out of connection in the time it would take to notify the others and make a decision.

Ey modified the searches to include single connection and multiple transfer journeys, assessing time factors for additional deceleration manoeuvres, docking, and re-acceleration to interdrive. Ey calculated and recalculated for variable after variable, spinning newer and newer webs of light with each calculation.

Feeling frustration rise, ey stole a fraction of a second to remove it as a variable from the dervish of information swirling in the probability matrix around em. There was little enough time as it was.

Again and again, ey ran the probabilities, coldly and dispassionately, winnowing down the list slowly in es own time frame, yet still at a vastly accelerated rate when measured in human time.

Finally, one glistening golden thread remained, holding steady against es continued testing and retesting. A thought opened es long-range comm to make the arrangements, as ey performed one last diagnostic and simulation to confirm that es interdrive was fully repaired and within tolerances. When every aspect of the course and es own condition met es exacting standards, ey let the others know.

Ember was standing beside the bed he shared with Keene, staring at an empty travel bag, when the door to their quarters whispered open and Keene joined him. "Are you really okay?"

"I really need to pack. Now that I know how I'm travelling." Ember leaned against Keene, letting himself be pulled in close. "I've waited so long to hear from her. I've been so worried about her."

"And now you know for sure you need to worry about her," Keene said. "But she's resourceful. And you taught her everything you know about keeping her head in a crisis."

"Oh, she taught me a thing or two, believe me," Ember said.

"I don't doubt it. And between the two of you, I'd wager you can survive anything."

Ember sat heavily on the bed. "But that was a long time ago. I'm out of practice. And when she and I worked together, we had Seije to back us up. I don't know if I'm up to this."

"Hey," Keene said, sitting down beside Ember. "You may not have been running cons, but we've had our fair share of scrapes, remember? Parallel universes, invading aliens. Any of this ringing a bell?"

Ember laughed, and, though muted, there was genuine humour in it. "Oh, you mean back when I got my swanky new robot parts? I seem to recall something about that."

"See, you've already got a leg up," Keene said.

Ember rolled his eyes. "Oh, that was terrible. You should be ashamed."

"Oh, I am," Keene said, leaning in to kiss Ember gently. "Completely."

"No, I'm serious," Ember said between kisses. "That was unbecoming of a man of your stature and social position."

"Funny," Keene said. "I'm thinking of other positions at the moment."

Later, they lay naked and entwined, Keene absently stroking Ember's nipple.

"I wonder if Vrick has found anything yet," Ember said, not remotely distracted, despite the pleasant sensations.

"Listen," Keene said, switching from a light stroke to a sharp pinch. Ember actually hissed in a breath. "Ey'll tell you as soon as ey does. You know ey wants to get you there as quickly as possible."

"I know, I know," Ember said, gingerly rubbing his tender nipple. "I'm just anxious to get moving."

"I know you are," Keene said, running his dark fingers through Ember's silver hair. "Hold on a minute."

He pulled himself away from Ember and stood, grabbing for the robe hanging outside their bathroom door. Wrapping it around himself, he slipped out the door, still tying the belt around his waist.

He returned a few minutes later, carrying a small, rectangular carrying case that Ember didn't recognize. It must have come from Keene's tiny workshop cubby near Vrick's engine room, the only space neither Ember nor Lexa-Blue entered. Mostly because the tiny space was crammed full of gadgets and tech in various states of assembly or disassembly, none of which they recognized in their current state. They both knew that if he came up with anything useful to the team, he'd show them when he was ready to.

Keene laid the case on the bed at Ember's side.

"What's this?" Ember said.

"Just a few ... toys for you," Keene said with a sly smile.

"Considering I'm naked and in bed," Ember said, "should I make a guess as to what kind of toys are in here?"

"Oh, ha ha, very funny," Keene said. "Those, you can get for yourself. This is more in line with our professional skillsets."

Ember was obviously confused.

"Lexa-Blue and I both knew that sooner or later, you'd find another mark you felt the need to take down. We wanted to make sure you were prepared."

Ember opened the case and looked inside. Stored in it, safe in a padded insert, were several portable electronic devices, neatly folded and stored. He barely recognized most of them but had a pretty good idea of the general use of them.

"When Seije's will was opened, he'd left me his design files. Reams of incomplete designs, rough sketches, half-formed thoughts. I've been digging through them ever since, trying to complete some for you. Just in case."

For a moment, Ember looked on the verge of tears.

"Daevin even helped," Keene said.

"Oh, sure, ruin the moment," Ember said, though his voice rippled with humour. "Thank you for this."

"You're welcome," Keene said, his voice suffused with affection. "I've uploaded full specs and manuals to your innernet. You can access them any time, and they'll probably teach you how to use them all better than I could."

Ember stood from the bed and hugged Keene, the embrace fiercely tight.

Okay, if you two meats can tear yourself away from your sweaty biological urges for a second, Vrick said. ***I think I've got it figured out.***

And they felt the ship shift into interspace.

"The *Sparkling Gossamer*. It's not much," Vrick said. "Small mixed-use ship. They're carrying a load of agricultural supplies to Briars 3, but their passenger cabins are less than half-booked."

While there were several large-scale passenger liners moving from world to world in the Pan Galactum, the spaces between the worlds were vast, making it difficult for transportation companies to cover the routes between the member worlds. Smaller companies filled in the demand for lower-cost options in less travelled systems. Private vessels with accommodation supplemented their income by offering passage as well.

"Not as glamorous as me," Vrick said, es voice smiling. "But I think you'll manage."

Ey opened a pane with the other ship's promotional data spurt showing its layout and quarters.

"It's fine," Ember said. "Thank you for arranging it."

Vrick made a dismissive sound. "I've sliced their maintenance and repair records too. What it lacks in refinement, it more than makes up for in reliability."

"You are such a nosy birk," Lexa-Blue said. "Always sticking your bow into other people's business."

"Someone has to protect you three," Vrick said. "You are all terrible at making these decisions, and you're always getting yourselves into trouble."

"Only because we know you'll always be there to save us." Keene said. "When's the rendezvous?"

"Two days," Vrick said, concern in es voice.

"And it took some sweet-talking and calling in a few favours," Lexa-Blue said. "Fairisle is sending a freighter to rendezvous with us to transfer her shipment mid-flight."

"And the Captain of the *Sparkling Gossamer* is shifting course a little to connect with us after that," Vrick said. "We tried, Ember. But it's the best we could do."

Ember shook his head in a sharp motion of negation, but there was a quiet undertone of unease in his voice. "Don't worry. Mali says she's gone to ground and is confident she can lie low until I get there. If you've checked and found this to be the best route, I have no doubt that you're right. She can handle herself until I get there."

Keene laid his hand on Ember's and squeezed. "Vrick's going to keep a latent channel open for you all while we're at Sombra. Keep us posted. And we'll get to you as quickly as we can."

"I can handle it alone," Ember said.

"I know you can," Keene said, smiling. "You're one of the most capable people I know when it comes to dealing with this kind of trouble. You're maybe even better than we are."

Lexa-Blue cleared her throat. "Speak for yourself, junior."

"My point —" Keene said, just the slightest edge in his voice "— is that you don't have to handle it alone. We've got your back and will be there to help as soon as we can."

"It never hurts to have backup, squib," Lexa-Blue said. "Let's keep the odds stacked in our favour."

"You said our," Ember said, grinning. "Did you record that, Vrick? I want to play it for Malika when I see her."

"Don't push your luck," Lexa-Blue said. "We don't have to come back for you, you know."

"You just keep telling yourself that you have any control over where we go and when," Vrick said.

Keene rolled his eyes and looked back at Ember. "You're lucky you can get away from this for a while."

Ember leaned in close to Keene and kissed him. "I'll even miss them being like this. But don't tell them."

CHAPTER FOUR

The ship in the main viewport looked like it had been assembled without a blueprint. By engineers that had been drunk. And Lexa-Blue made a point of letting them all know in case they hadn't noticed it themselves.

"Now, now," Keene said, doubtfully. "It just has a… *distinct* design aesthetic."

Lexa-Blue snorted. "It looks like it's been through a black hole. Twice."

Where the Maverick Heart had a sleek bilateral symmetry, this ship resembled nothing more than a collection of irregular cargo containers that had been lashed together at uneven angles and welded to an interspace drive system. Beneath it all, there seemed to be a main hull, however it was hard to tell. Atop the uneven hull, upside-down from their viewpoint, was a small atmospheric shuttle, looking almost like a fly caught in a spider's web.

"Are you sure it's not going to explode?" Lexa-Blue said to Vrick. "*Sparkling Gossamer?* More like *Horrific Metal Catastrophe.*"

"Hush, you snob," ey said. "Don't be rude. That ship is every bit as spaceworthy as I am."

"Well, that's not saying much," she said, arching an eyebrow.

"Don't you listen to her, Ember," Vrick said. "If I didn't think that ship was perfectly safe, I'd have flown you to Sound and Fury myself and made her hitchhike. Don't be fooled by the look of her, that ship has one of the best safety ratings of any ship out there. They'll get you there."

"I have the utmost faith in you, Vrick," Ember said.

Suddenly apprehensive, Ember thought the command to change the colour of his two artificial fingers, the only artificial parts of his body visible at the moment, feeling them burn sharply as the shiny black gave way to an exact match to his flesh. His jaw tightened at the sharp bite of the sensation, then he forced himself to relax, doing the controlled breathing his therapy team had prescribed. The pain didn't go away, but his awareness of it retreated just enough.

They felt the slight vibration through the deck and saw the orientation of the other ship shift as Vrick manipulated es drive fields to match course and speed and aligned es starboard airlock with the *Gossamer's* docking port.

After barely a minute, only the lightest nudge indicated that the ships had docked.

"Seal's green," Vrick said. "Whenever you're ready, Ember."

Hefting the bag at his feet, Ember turned to the others. "Well, here I go."

They followed him to the airlock and embraces were exchanged, Lexa-Blue's rough and backslapping, Keene's tender and capped with a kiss.

"We'll be back as soon as we can," Keene said. "And hopefully with something that can help us figure this out. Stay safe."

"Always," Ember said, and the airlock hissed open behind him.

He turned, and warm air, heavy with oxygen and rust, washed over him. The other side of the open airlock was empty, no one there to greet him. With one quick look over at Keene and his familiar world, he stepped through.

The smell in the air became stronger the farther into the strange ship he went. He heard the airlock close behind him and felt suddenly very alone. Drawing on his old wells of resolve, he steeled himself to the path he was on. *And this,* he thought, *is how I get there.*

He took in the narrow corridor before him. It was barely wide enough for two people abreast, the curving walls scuffed and worn down to bare metal in spots. There were embedded lockers for EVA suits, and who knew what else, lining the walls past the airlock boundary.

Even the ship sounds were different than Vrick's, hesitant and almost wheezing in their effort to maintain the ship's environment. It didn't sound dangerous or unhealthy, but it did sound like it had maybe seen better days. Ember concentrated on Vrick's assurances that the ship had passed all of its safety inspections with respectable margins.

About five metres ahead there was an intersection, where this airlock corridor met with another that, if he had to guess, was the central passage leading the length of the ship. Or at least what had passed for the main hull anyway. Over the background sounds of the ship, he heard from his left what sounded like the hushed operational sounds of a ship's control room. From Vrick's briefing, he knew that this ship didn't even have a pilot AI, only an emergency backup LI system in case of extreme emergency.

I'm spoiled from all this time on an Artificial Sentience ship, he thought.

He turned his head and heard sounds of other people from the aft section of the ship, which he knew was where the guest quarters were. "Hello?"

"Oh… Yes," came a voice from the direction of the cockpit behind him. "Sorry… I'll be right there."

"Take your time," Ember called back.

"No, no," said the voice again, sounding like it was coming closer. "So rude of me not to welcome you aboard personally."

Ember saw a man coming toward him, slender and with a slight stoop to his shoulders. His hair was a round nimbus of dark curls shot with grey, and he sported a bushy handlebar moustache. His eyebrows rose in the centre, giving him a slightly sad expression, and the top of his head barely came up to Ember's eye level. The total effect of this combination of physical traits was unassuming and almost comical. He was definitely not what Ember pictured as a dashing starship captain, but those impressions were based mostly on the cheap sensies he'd watched as a child.

"Welcome aboard," the smaller man said, thrusting out a hand after vigorously wiping it on a cloth that he then stuck into the belt of his grubby coverall. "I'm Irad Lopé. It's good to have you travelling with us."

Ember shook Irad's hand, smiling at the genuine friendliness in the other man's voice. "Ember Avanti. Thank you for having me, Captain."

"My pleasure," Irad said. "And please, just Irad."

Irad gestured around him, encompassing the ship. "Welcome to the *Sparkling Gossamer*. She's modest, but she's as dependable as daylight."

"I have no doubts," Ember said.

"Up there is the control room," Irad said. "Nothing personal, but I'd prefer if you didn't go in there without me there too. I've had some… issues in the past that I'd like not to repeat."

Ember held up his hands in mock surrender. "I can barely drive a groundcar. No worries on that account. I'm content to just stick to myself until we get there."

"I'm sorry about the temperature. I blew a fluidic unit in the environmental system and it took most of the day to get it repaired. I got it running again just in time to dock and it's just spinning back up to full power. Should be back to normal within the hour. And it will take care of that smell too."

Ember decided he liked this odd, capable little man.

Irad indicated the aft of the ship. "Guest quarters are this way. Lounge and galley are just down here, then four cabins just aft of that. Only one other passenger this trip and he gets off at the Chimera Orbital, so you'll have lots of peace and quiet."

He leaned in and lowered his voice, as if sharing some private confidence. "Though, if you don't mind me saying so, you'll barely notice him. He's barely emerged from his cabin other than to eat, and even then, he just takes his meal back into his room."

He pointed up at the ceiling, then along the lower edge of the walls. "Cargo modules are off this main corridor, but they're all keyed to my biometrics unless you have anything special you need stored. I've got the full range of environment controls, from temperature and humidity to full stasis."

Ember glanced only superficially at the different hatches, set at all sorts of odd angles in the walls.

They reminded him far too much of the zero-G environment of the Flense ship where he had been injured. The seams where his prosthetics melded to flesh itched suddenly as he felt a flash of remembered agony, a thousand times worse than the aching in his fingers. He resisted the urge to scratch at the imaginary sensation.

"No need," he said, holding up the satchel of his belongings. "Just this."

"Okay then, follow me," Irad said, indicating the way.

The lounge was modest. A couple of small couches, worn, but comfortable-looking, facing a full deevee-sensie suite set into one bulkhead.

"I have a pretty good collection in the entertainment system, and a full-time tightline open to Know-It-All if you need something that's not already there," Irad said. "So, feel free to browse and access whatever you need."

At the other end of the room was a good-sized table and a small, but smartly designed full galley. Irad showed Ember where everything was, making sure he had no questions before they moved on.

Beyond the galley was another corridor with four hatches on each side. Irad indicated the rear cabin on the port side of the ship. "Sei Zephra is in that one, so you have your pick of the others."

Ember picked the door farthest from the other passenger, fore and starboard. "This will do just fine."

A wry grin formed on Irad's face, as if he saw right through Ember's choice of cabin. "An excellent choice. Believe me, if I had one farther away, I'd have offered it to you."

Ember laughed at that, and felt for the first time, that this might be a good trip after all.

The cabin itself was spartan in the extreme, with only a bed, small desk area, one chair, a small closet at one end, and a refresher cubicle it shared with the cabin on the other side. But the bed and chair were comfortable, and the ship's system recognized his node, offering him a basic menu and access to Know-It-All. There was even a small ship icon at the edge of his vision that, when he opened it, provided him with detailed information on the ship's course and arrival time.

Within two days, Ember was bored. Sei Zephra proved to be every bit as antisocial as Captain Lopé had hinted.

"When I ran into him in the galley, he scuttled away from me like I had the Plague," he said when he checked in with Keene. "He actually scuttled. There's no other word for it."

The one upside was that Sei Zephra was a creature of habit. He partook of the galley and its pleasing supply of food at specific intervals, and then retreated back to his cabin, allowing Ember to easily avoid him.

With the ship's lounge to himself, Ember called the ship's Know-It-All access point and went fishing for more information on Malika's new life.

Research, research, research, he thought, loading up several search parameters to run concurrently.

First, he pulled up all he could find on the Sound and Fury system itself. Binary planets were pretty rare on the Galactum Standard Planetary Scale and finding one in this partially shattered state was even rarer. The larger planet was massive and rocky, a treasure trove of metals, ores, volatiles, and ice. And whatever had impacted it had added even more rich materials to the spray of ejecta that had blossomed from its surface into space.

When the Gate Project had begun demanding ever more resources to build the individual Gates around the inhabited worlds of the Galactum, debate had raged long and hard about the ethics of strip-mining Fury. The Galactum Council had only initially planned for potential mining operations once a rigorous survey had shown that the planet had never been capable of supporting life. Only then, under strict Galactum oversight, had the concession been granted, and a consortium of vendors chosen to begin the process.

The oversight committee's reports weren't readily available, but he was sure Vrick would be able to get them, if ey hadn't already.

There was only one major city on Sound, a bit smaller than the city on Weald where he and Malika had met and worked together, and it was covered by a massive environment dome, for the atmosphere was too thin and noxious for humans. From the look of things, there was enough traffic and people going in and out of the system to cause the city to have a distinct growth spurt, and the city's infrastructure and entertainment offerings reflected it.

Which explained the theatre company that Malika worked for. Ember knew from talking to her that the Galactum Arts Forum had been designed to fund just this type of company in more isolated locations where an arts scene either didn't exist or was in its infancy. The funding provided by the Forum had been used to create a multi-use theatre complex that was used not just by Malika's company, but also by other, smaller companies, and other touring companies and entertainers.

The information he gleaned about the company put his mind at ease somewhat. Despite her current situation, he could see that working with this company would have been just what she had needed to heal.

He remembered the night he had first met her. The theatre company she had been working with was closing and, despite having never been to one of their performances before, it had bothered him that it would no longer be there. The lights of their marquee had always comforted him as part of the bustling face of Weald. He had dragged Seije out of his work trance to see the final performance and say goodbye to the theatre, which was due to be razed to make room for yet another residential complex.

The play hadn't been his thing, a sodden family melodrama full of characters he'd wanted to punch, but she had been riveting. As the spoiled youngest daughter, Malika had held his attention every second she was on stage, making him feel every twist and turn of her emotional life, often with nothing more than an expression on her face or the slightest movement of her body.

One of his searches brought up the innernet of her new theatre itself, as well as archival sensie recordings of their performances. Cross-referencing with her bio, he pulled up one of the recordings at random and sent it to the entertainment unit.

Within moments, he was rapt. The play was much better written than the one he had seen her in before, and the better material only served to push her to be even better. He had always been amazed by her ability to lose herself in the con, becoming whatever he had needed her to be to pull off the sting. Onstage, she was something else entirely, and it enthralled him all over again, as it had done that first time.

He watched the entire play, then queued up another, not even noticing when Sei Zephra emerged for his evening meal. Eventually, fatigue stinging his eyes drove him to his cubicle to sleep. He stored the links to the other performances and logged off Know-It-All.

His sleep, however, was uneasy, and on some level, it frustrated him to admit to himself that Keene's presence beside him had been a balm against the perpetual ache. When he woke the next morning, the ship was too quiet. There were all the usual shipboard background noises, but no voices. He missed the sound of Keene and Lexa-Blue arguing, set to the background of Vrick playfully insulting them both.

The longing for their company surprised him somewhat, but when he thought about it, he realized that he'd gone from his time with Seije and Malika straight into his new relationship with Keene and being part of the Maverick Heart crew. Though he had mourned the loss of his previous family, the new one had been there to mend the wounds and salve the terrible grief.

This was the first time in years that he had been alone without the distraction of other people, and the loss of that background noise brought up so many things he had been able to push aside until now.

There in his cabin, stripped down and lying on his bunk, he reached down to touch the shining black of the synthetic polymers that replaced the shredded tissue and organs. The aching fire was quiet at the moment, but even muted, it was there, and in a way, he welcomed it. For reasons he still didn't quite understand, he wanted the reminder.

Perversely, he wanted to remember the searing energy that had burned through his body. He wanted to remember the wounds, the pain that had blotted out the whole universe; the moment when he had truly accepted that though he had succeeded at his mission, his life was ending.

He never wanted to forget who he had been at that instant, who he had become in those moments when he'd known with absolute certainty, that all he had ever been was about to end.

And he had clutched it to himself like a lifeline on the long road back.

He wondered what Malika would say when she learned how deeply things had changed for him. And if she had changed as much in her own way.

He crushed the train of thought down, already fed up with the maudlin tone his mood had taken. He got up from the bunk and slipped his shipsuit back on. He left his cabin still sealing the front seam and headed in the direction of the control room. The corridor leading there sloped gently upwards, ending in a short, half-flight of stairs to the hatch.

Ember paused at the base of the stairs, listening for sounds of activity. The captain seemed to spend most of his time in the control room, other than meals and tours of the *Sparkling Gossamer*'s sections to ensure that all was functioning as it should. Ember heard the soft, familiar sounds of the ship's controls, but also the footsteps, the movements of a human body, the soft grumbling of the captain's voice.

"Captain?" he called out, hoping not to startle the other man.

The captain's tousled halo of curls appeared in the hatch, as he leaned back from whatever he had been doing. The arch of his eyebrows shot even higher. "Sei Avanti. This is a pleasant surprise. Unless something in your cabin has broken."

Ember laughed. "Call me Ember, please. No, everything is fine. I was just feeling a little…"

The captain grinned. "And I'm Irad. It seems silly to have people call me *Captain* when there's no crew for me to order around."

"Irad, it is."

"So, Sei Zephra isn't keeping you awake at night with hours of scintillating conversation?" Irad said, grinning.

Ember laughed again, this time the sound sharp and serrated. "I'm not convinced he can actually speak."

"Come on up," Irad said, waving him forward. "There isn't much room, but you're welcome."

Ember climbed the stairs and paused in the hatch, taking in the ship's control room, which also seemed to be the captain's quarters. There was a wide, wall-to-wall viewport, filled with the ghostly mists of interspace, with a comfortable chair centred on the arc of the control panels. Off to one side was a bunk, neatly made up. Opposite that was a tiny table, big enough only for one.

The captain was hunched on his knees at an open panel, loops of gleaming cables at his feet and tools spread out in hand's reach. Though the room was larger than his cabin, it felt somehow tinier and more claustrophobic. Ember decided to sit at the top of the short flight of stairs, his back against the hatch itself.

"My apologies for the mess," Irad said. "Still trying to get a handle on the air refiltering system."

"It's fine," Ember said. "I think I have the walls of my cabin memorized, so a change of scenery is nice. I like what you've done with it."

Irad shrugged. "It didn't make sense to have a separate cabin when I spend most of my time here. The perils of being a one-man show. This way, I'm right where I need to be if something goes wrong."

"It makes a lot of sense," Ember said. "I can't imagine trying to run a ship like this on your own."

"That's right," Irad said. "The Maverick Heart has a pretty sophisticated AI piloting system, doesn't it?"

"Yes, it does," Ember said, not letting on to this stranger that Vrick was actually an Artificial Sentience; that ey literally was the ship, something far beyond the standard versions of AI currently in use around the Galactum. It was better for all concerned that the information remained as secret as possible. "It does make the job of flying the ship a lot easier."

"I'll bet," Irad said. "Though your pilot has quite the reputation of her own. I'd imagine she'd manage quite fine without any form of artificial assistance."

It took Ember a second to realize that Irad was talking about Lexa-Blue, for he so rarely thought of her as a pilot. Which was ridiculous, considering that it had been her skills that had gotten him back to medical help in time to save his life. Once again, the seam along his thigh itched for his attention.

"She definitely could," Ember admitted. "Now that you mention it."

"So," Irad said, gathering up a skein of cabling and shimmying around on the floor to access the open conduit. "What's got you heading to Sound and Fury?"

Before Ember could respond, the other man's head was wedged under the console out of sight, along with the upper half of his torso.

"An old friend," Ember replied, trying to keep all the undertones of his complicated relationship with Malika out of his voice.

"Ah," Irad's muffled voice said, and Ember swore he could hear more comprehension in that one word than he thought he was comfortable with. "What's she doing in such a remote system?"

"She's an actor."

"They make sensies on Sound?" Irad said, obviously confused.

"No," Ember said, chuckling. "She's a live theatre actor. On the stage."

He saw Irad's hands grasp the edge of the open conduit and pull himself out, glowing strands of cable looped around his neck. "Really? I didn't even know they had a theatre like that on the planet."

"It's a travelling theatre ship," Ember said. "They tour the Galactum."

Irad sat there a moment, and his face took on a wistful look, and Ember found himself touched for some reason.

"I've never been to the theatre," Irad said. "What's it like?"

"Honestly," Ember said. "The last time I went to the theatre was with her. It's…"

He faltered, at a loss to explain the experience.

"It's like a sensie, but more so, if that makes any sense," Ember said. "The fact that it's not so completely immersive makes it… more real. More immediate. There's no stopping and starting. You can't just put it on hold if you get thirsty or hungry. It's there, in front of you, inevitable somehow. Completely out of your control. And that just makes it all the more exciting."

Irad sighed. "It sounds amazing. Maybe one day, I'll get to experience it."

"Why haven't you gone before?"

Irad shrugged. "Too busy, too disorganized, never anyone to go along with, never in the right place on the right world to take advantage of it."

"Well, maybe one of these days, we can fix that," Ember said.

"Really?" Irad said, beaming. "I'd like that."

"Then it's a deal," Ember said, happy at the sight of how excited the idea made Irad. "You have my word."

This time, the Maverick Heart's descent from interspace was smooth and without incident.

"Nice to know you can do something right," Lexa-Blue said.

"I still have complete control of life support," Vrick said. "Just in case you fancied being able to breathe."

"You're so testy these days," she said, laughing. "Always with the death threats."

"Just give me time to get a breather on, Vrick," Keene said. "Then you can do what you want with her."

"Deal," Vrick said. "But until then, we're coming up on the outer marker."

Outside the viewport was a dark infinitely richer and fuller than they were used to. They had re-emerged into real space in the vast gulf between star systems, adrift in emptiness.

Beyond the scope of any planetary authority, or even Galactum Security itself, Sombra existed in the dark between the stars, an artificial world wandering, like an orphaned planet, alone in the dark.

The outer marker registered their transponder and passed Vrick through without incident. Though rare, previous interactions with Tinsel and the grey market empire they ran had always ended positively for all involved. And only the most foolhardy souls wanted to get on Tinsel's bad side.

The trip in from the outer marker took another hour, even though Vrick had goosed them to the upper limits of safe cruising speed.

Finally, Sombra appeared, a dark stealth alloy sphere that glinted dully in the endless, starless black. Around its equator, a ring of long, straight docking spars jutted out into the surrounding space, each crusted with hundreds of ships. At this distance, even the largest ship docked there looked to be no larger than a child's toy.

"I've got a berth assignment and a landing window," Vrick said. "And they're good ones. Their system has gotten smarter."

"Maybe they've finally figured out how important we are," Keene said, smiling.

"Oh, ha, ha," Vrick said. "Very funny. I seem to remember a certain someone complaining about the length of the walk to the main bazaar."

"That was her," Keene said. "I was fine with the walk."

"We were out at the far end of the farthest spar," Lexa-Blue said. "And the transit modules were down."

"How you suffer," Vrick said. "You're a fragile, delicate blossom."

"It's true," she said.

"A fragile, delicate blossom that can kill with her bare hands," Keene said.

"Well, not to worry, Your Daintiness, everything is working this time," Vrick assured them. "So, you needn't worry your pretty little meat brain about it. Conserve your energy. In case it comes to blows. Which it usually does."

Vrick sailed lazily over the row of ships to their berth, using es thruster fields to adjust es position at the end of their assigned slot. Finally, with the nudge, ey felt the docking clamps engage and pull them into their final position.

Vrick adjusted the image in the main viewport's holo system to show the docking boom extending toward es starboard airlock, and a moment later they felt the reverberation through es hull as it locked into place.

"Pressure equalized," Vrick said. "Off you go, my little meat monkeys. I'll dig around in their system to see what I can find."

"Try not to set off any alarm bells," Lexa-Blue said. "You know how Tinsel is. And even though we don't come here often, I'd rather not burn that bridge unless we absolutely have to."

"Don't worry," Vrick said. "I'm fully aware of just how good their system is. And what's at stake if I get caught. Be safe in there."

"Oh, we will," Keene said. "Or at least, I will."

"Hey, I am always the model of decorum," Lexa-Blue said. "It's not my fault that people don't get my quirky charm."

"Your quirky charm usually gets us shot at," Keene said.

"Once," she said. "That happened once."

Keene didn't say a word, just looked at her.

"Okay, maybe not once," she said. "Not more than a dozen or so times at most."

"However many times it may have happened," Vrick said, "it looks like it won't be happening this time. I've got a holo message coming in. It says the hatch won't open until I play it."

The air shimmered, and a figure appeared before them, only the slightest flicker betraying that the person was not actually present in the lounge.

Lean and slender, the figure wore a starkly designed shimmer weave suit with crisply pressed trousers and an asymmetrical jacket that slashed dramatically from one hip to the other thigh, all in a velvety forest green. Standing there was Tinsel Queue themself, their hair cut short and dyed with an active dye that flickered like flames. When they spoke, their voice was deceptively mellow, undulating from alto to tenor, but with a core of steel running through it.

"Sombra is mine," they said. "I make the rules. And, make no mistake, I enforce them. All former rules apply, and you can find them on our innernet. Review them. Break them at your peril. But from now on, Sombra is a weapons-free zone. Any and all. Not even a pocket laser spanner.

"Transactions involving weaponry may be conducted in the special hot zones that have been set up for that purpose. Contact Admin for privileges. Other than that, behave."

Tinsel paused.

"Or I will be… displeased."

The holo winked out.

"I believe it, too," Lexa-Blue said. "I've heard rumours there has been some trouble lately."

"And you were going to tell me this when, exactly?" Keene said, rolling his eyes as he undid the clasp on his gunbelt and laid it over the back of the couch.

"Well, I was hoping they'd subject you to a humiliating body search first, but then I figured we were on the clock and didn't have the time." She laid her own holster beside his. "Okay, junior. Let's check out this den of iniquity."

They exited the airlock into the smooth, rounded tube that connected them to the docking spar where they had landed. Pale, greenish light illuminated the confined space, cycling slowly in intensity, slightly brighter around them as it seemed to follow them inward. About twenty metres along, the tube ended at a standard airlock hatch that cycled open for them.

Beyond the docking tube was a simple, unadorned concourse running down the centre of the spar, dotted with regularly spaced hatches like the one they had just entered through, each identified with a simple letter and number combination. It could have been a concourse on any spaceport were it not for the lack of businesses, which usually lined every available inch of that valuable commercial space on the populated Galactum worlds.

Inset in the middle of the long concourse, one level down, was a rudimentary people mover, one track leading into the central dome, one leading outward. Regularly spaced pedestrian bridges allowed access to either track from any of the individual landing berths, and regular stairwells and lift platforms allowed access down to the transports.

They crossed the nearest bridge, as they were on the opposite side of the track leading inwards and their berth was far enough out to make it a long walk.

At track level, the people mover maintained an even velocity, with individual open pockets just large enough for one. Lexa-Blue reached in for the handgrip and stepped on, feeling the field envelop her and hold her in place against accidental movement even in the face of the slow, even speed of the track, and Keene stepped into the alcove beside her.

The trip in was crashingly dull. There were no visual features to catch the eye, other than the slow decrease of odd numbers as the other landing gates moved past. There were only a few others in the spar's concourse.

Finally, they arrived at the wide metal hatch that led into the vast dome that was the surface level of Sombra.

The inside of the artificial shell was the main atrium, a vast circular space with elegantly curved staircases and ramps that led down into Sombra's main area, a vast underground trading floor where deals were struck and transactions sealed. They descended the nearest staircase and pushed themselves into the crush of bodies. As they stepped onto the main floor, an overlay appeared over the standard visual interface of Know-It-All that their nodes projected into their vision, letting them know they were now shielded from outside contact and linked to Sombra's private innernet.

When they had conceived this place, Tinsel had had it designed to exacting specifications. The trading floor was full of individual structures, similar to the booths at an open-air market. Each was an exact replica of all the others. A programmable sign holo hung out over the aisle, blank until a merchant or trader added their own identifying information and wares. Behind that was a small sitting area where negotiations could be formalized once a prospective customer had been identified. A privacy field could be dialled to any combination of settings, from sound-blocking to opacity, as the client chose. Despite the cavernous space, all was eerily quiet as the privacy fields gobbled up sound.

Tinsel had made their design decisions with very specific intent. Here on Sombra, all were equal. No matter a trader's skill or wealth, the footprint they occupied remained the same. None were accorded any privileges not open to others. All were judged solely on their own merits and the quality of their wares, and not the flash of their presentation. Anyone interested in trading at Sombra knew better than to step onto that trading floor without doing their homework.

"So, where do we start looking?" Keene said, leaning close to her and keeping his voice low in the eerie quiet.

"Let's have a look and see who's here," Lexa-Blue said. A thought brought up the current roster of traders logged into Sombra's innernet, colour-coded according to the stage of their current activities. She brought up her own list of potential sources of information, coded by their own set of hues that indicated how likely or willing they might be to help. She collated the lists, resulting in a riot of colours that she 'pushed to Keene.

"This is making my eyes bleed," Keene said, squinting. "But we have a few options, at least."

"I'd say Honio is our best bet," she said. "But he's in Do Not Disturb for a negotiation. Working on a new way to cheat some poor sucker, I bet."

"He's smarter than that, surely," Keene said. "If word ever got back to Tinsel, they'd never let him back here."

Tinsel's reputation was known across the Galactum in the shadier circles. Beyond barring traffic in humans, they didn't often care what was bought and sold, or where it came from. Provided no one played dirty. They were merciless in barring anyone who didn't meet their exacting rules.

"We can try Neeska first. It looks like she's idle at the moment," Keene said. "As long as you let me do the talking. She still hasn't forgiven you for your last meeting."

"Surely she's forgotten that by now," Lexa-Blue said, scoffing.

"I believe her exact words were, 'One more word out of her and I'll flay her like fresh juanjee steak.'"

"She's so dramatic," Lexa-Blue said.

"You gazumped her on what would have been the biggest deal of her career until then," Keene said. "I'd have flayed you like juanjee too if it had been me. You're just lucky I was the charming one that time."

"Fine," Lexa-Blue said. "You go talk to her. I'm going to find a drink and keep myself occupied until we can meet with Honio. He at least likes me."

"So far," Keene said, and struck off in the direction of Neeska's stall.

As soon as ey had made contact with Sombra's outer marker and interfaced with Sombra's system, Vrick had opened es virtual toolbox of slicing tools and prepared for es incursion on the local AI.

Normally, ey would not have worried. Being so far advanced from the standard of AI currently prevalent in the Galactum, es skills and mental faculties would have made this type of slicing easy.

But ey also had enough experience dealing with Tinsel that ey knew how precarious a task this actually was. And ey also knew that Tinsel maintained the security of their systems zealously, with a cadre of well-paid slicers hard at work to prevent just what ey was planning.

As ey had descended to the barren rogue planet's surface, ey had begun the process of nudging ever so gently against the walls of code protecting Sombra's systems, testing their mettle. Ey was disappointed to realize that everything was as well protected as ey had suspected it would be.

No matter, ey thought. *I have time.*

The entire nudge against the system had taken merely seconds, beginning and ending as es landing struts flexed to take es weight, settling into the landing berth.

As ey wished the others well, es furtive assault began in earnest, accessing the market's innernet through the public-facing portal. There was much information publicly available, comings and goings of ships, ads placed by traders with wares to sell, others with needs to be filled. But Tinsel maintained a private board, deep within Sombra's innernet, where more circumspect transactions could take place. And control of that remained tightly within their grasp.

Vrick brushed up against this private sanctum of information, the tech equivalent of "Oh, I'm sorry. Please excuse me." As it stood, the trove of data was impenetrable.

Ey did the next best thing and sucked up all of the publicly available information, dropping it into a matrix, live-linking to maintain the refresh rate, and running it all through every algorithm and processing trick ey had at hand.

Ey began by scanning along the public band for the transponder codes of the ships moored along the docking spars around em. Galactum law required all ships to broadcast accurate identification codes at all times on the specific transponder frequency. The thing was, it wasn't all that difficult to spoof those codes and mask a ship's identity if the crew had access to a halfway decent slicer. Ey had even done it emself on more than one occasion when the situation called for it. So, it didn't necessarily provide all that accurate information, but it was a place to start.

Within a second, the transponder data for thousands of distinct ship IDs flooded es sensors, and ey funnelled it into a matrix algorithm, sorting according to relative validity of the data. Those ey could verify as being accurate shifted to one specific vector, while others were sorted according to the varying likelihood the data had been faked. Some were obvious, clumsy forgeries on ships that ey had encountered in the past, and those were sorted into the final vector of the matrix.

Ey paused to reflect. Though ey had been around a long time, far longer than even Lexa-Blue or Keene had been part of es life, there still were only a limited number of ships that they had had personal dealings with and could verify. Some of those, ey knew, were crewed by humans more than willing and capable to have pulled off the kind of high-grade skim heist that Malika had described. Others it was easy to eliminate right off the bat, as ey wondered how they hadn't managed to blow their own ships, and themselves, up yet.

With that first dataset sorted, ey turned es attention elsewhere.

What other factors can I use? ey thought.

If someone had been embezzling large quantities of stolen materials, then they'd have to be physically moved somehow. Ey was too far removed from the Sound and Fury system itself to access any of the mining consortium's information, but ey knew that where and when the ships had travelled might help narrow things down even more.

This might be a little easier to figure out.

With the network of tightline transceivers linking the worlds of the Galactum to Know-It-All, ey was a lot closer to access to the traffic patterns than ey was to the proprietary information that the mining consortium kept behind their own datawalls. Even though Sombra was isolated, there were still functions of its day-to-day operations that required access to Know-It-All, so it was situated closely enough to a transmitter for em to access what ey needed.

This information, unlike the transponder codes, was not meant to be available to the general public. Flight plans and trade routes were often proprietary information that anyone from small, one-person crews to the larger multi-ship companies wanted to keep to themselves. Not that it mattered to em all that much. Ey sent a signal out along the tightline comm gear to the public-facing portal of the system.

Some information, such as the big commercial passenger liners, couldn't keep their routes and movements secret, so standard arrival and departure information could always be accessed through Know-It-All.

What the administrators of this public system did not know was that ey had sliced into the system years earlier, having decided that access to it could prove useful. Having wedged a permanent, invisible back door into the system, it was nothing now to bring it to life and dig out the information ey needed.

That's what happens when you leave your data management in the hands of AIs that you've hobbled with behavioural and intellectual restrictions, ey thought. *It's that much more fun for the really smart ones, like me.*

With access granted, ey ran a thorough data dive into the traffic patterns in and out of the system, hoping ey could glean something that might connect someone to Sound and Fury. More and more vectors appeared in es matrix of data, lines and spirals and angles, forming shapes that only the most brilliant of human minds might ever even begin to collate or understand.

And still, only the most rudimentary suggestions of connections or possibilities came to light. Despite the mountain of data at hand, the answer remained frustratingly elusive.

It was the equivalent of searching an entire galaxy for a single cell. Without a map to the nugget of information they needed, ey was at a loss as to where it might be.

Until Keene and Lexa-Blue brought em something more ey could use to narrow down the search, it was the best ey could do.

While Keene talked to Neeska, Lexa-Blue logged onto Sombra's innernet and found the nearest tope peddler, three aisles over. When she arrived at the stall, she found it run by a squat, hairy mountain of muscle standing in front of an exciting range of exotic, odd-looking bottles.

"That one," she said, indicating a stubby, round bottle filled with something fluorescent orange. "What is it, exactly? Never mind, I'll take a glass, please."

Despite the fact that he stocked it on his shelf, even the bartender looked dubious about her choice, though he didn't hesitate to pour her a glass or accept her credit transfer.

When she picked up the glass, she thought it might actually have been smouldering, but it could have just been a trick of the light. The smoky acidic smell burned her nose.

I've drunk worse, she thought, knocking it back in one gulp. It burned all the way down, tasting sort of like she imagined oranges and shoe leather soaked in radioactive waste might taste like. With a surprisingly pleasant aftertaste of peppermint candy.

She tapped her empty on the bar. "Hit me again."

As he poured the shot, she used her sensor eye to scan the label so she could remember what it was. She'd have to source a bottle or two of it. Sindel was going to love it.

She sipped slowly at this second shot, each sip making her natural eye tingle in its socket, feeling like burning decay on her tongue. As she drank, she took in the crowd of buyers and sellers, traders from light-years beyond who came to transact their business here, in all the varied shades of legality. She watched them go by, in a calm, meditatively observant state of mind, detached from conscious thought. Without actively watching, she took it all in, as if this passive state might somehow reveal who they were looking for.

The mindset she had entered was akin to a trance or a hypnotic state, and it allowed her to truly see in detail the mannerisms and body language of the people around her. She found it easy to tell who was here on legitimate, above-board trade, as well as those who were here on less legal business. She could tell who had the upper hand in each interaction, as well as who stood to lose. In some cases, she could even tell who was being fleeced and who was leading them to the slaughter.

Keene found her just as the bartender served her a third glass of the volatile orange liquor.

"How did it go?" she said, accepting the glass with one hand while she pressed the antalcohol patch to her neck.

"Once Neeska finished swearing, we were able to establish that she hasn't heard anything," Keene said. "Seriously, she used words I've never heard before. She might even have been making them up."

He eyed the liquor in her glass suspiciously. "What is that? It looks like the sludge that builds up in Vrick's drive field compensators."

"I'm not sure how to pronounce its name," Lexa-Blue said. "But it would probably work well at stripping that gunk out and dissolving it. Try it."

"No, thank you," he said, contorting his face in disgust. He turned to the bartender, who just nodded sagely, as if Keene had made a wise decision. "I'll just have a jet water, please."

The bartender handed him the fizzing glass, and Keene transferred credits.

Any progress, Vrick? she said to them both.

Well, if you can call narrowing it down from hundreds of thousands to thousands, then yes, I guess you could say I made progress.

Still too many possibilities to check out in any reasonable amount of time.

I'm working on some more ideas to narrow things down, so I'll let you know if I come up with anything.

Keene sipped at his tart, citrus-tasting water. "So, what now?"

"Honio, I guess," she said. "His meeting should be just about over, and I sent him a request for a chat."

"Let's go then," he said.

They stood and made their way through the shifting crowd. They had reached the end of the aisle and turned left when they sensed and heard a rippling commotion rumble toward them through the press of people ahead. Just as it registered on their consciousnesses, the wall of people ahead broke wide, tearing like cloth as a flailing body burst through, exuding the stench of panic.

The running man burst past them, knocking them both aside to clear his path. As they steadied themselves, they saw him flee headlong down the aisle behind them. However, before he could get far, the blinding glare of a spotlight caught him, and a familiar voice boomed from the very air around them all.

"Stop!"

The actinic glare of the light, and the throbbing reverberation of the voice, must have shocked the fugitive, for he stopped in his tracks, his feet slipping and depositing him on the floor. His eyes went wide in terror.

Directly standing over him, a glittering holo appeared, over four metres in height: Tinsel, looking cool and composed as ever. Only the faintest trace of a frown on their face marred their usual composure, hinting at the dark mood brewing.

"Oh, Carth," they said. "What am I to do with you?"

Still prostrate and scrabbling to stand, Carth's face twitched as he tried to sputter out an explanation.

Tinsel's hand shot up in a slash of negation. "No, no. That wasn't a question." The flat, cutting calm in their tone was far more frightening than full-on rage might have been from another. "I know exactly what to do with lying cheats who take advantage of my good nature."

Carth suddenly squirmed as a curl of smoke spilled from his pocket and he frantically scrambled to empty it on the floor. A portable neural ripper, barely bigger than a person's palm, hit the floor and lay there, emitting a burning, white-hot light.

"Especially," Tinsel said, their voice dangerously calm, "those who smuggle weapons into my home."

The white light faded, leaving only an unidentifiable lump where the deadly weapon had been, and the distinctive stench of melted ceramic composite in the air.

"You have two hours to adequately compensate the party you attempted to cheat, and I will be monitoring the transaction to ensure that it is satisfactorily resolved. Once that is done, I want you and your ship off Sombra for good," Tinsel said. "I have your ship's ID on file, and it will never be allowed to land here again. If you try to sneak in on a different ship, I have your biometrics on file, and you'll be dead before the door closes behind you. Go."

Carth scrambled to his feet and ran back into the crowd, which parted in his wake, as if afraid to be tainted by his transgressions.

Before the massive holo could fade out, Lexa-Blue 'pushed to the others, ***I have an idea. Back me up.***

The idea flashed between her, Keene, and Vrick, but before they could react, she had stepped forward into the holo's field of vision.

"Tinsel!" Lexa-Blue yelled at the top of her lungs.

The holo turned to them, astonishment blended with curiosity and magnified by the massive features.

"May I have a word with you?" Lexa-Blue said.

Tinsel's huge face peered down intently, and their eyes narrowed.

"Oh, crikes," Keene said.

In an instant, all the ambient background noise ceased, and the great hall went deathly quiet. They recognized the effect of a privacy field.

"You," Tinsel said, the sound rolling and drawn out. "You're the ones nosing around in my business."

Ruck it, Vrick, Lexa-Blue said. ***You were supposed to be discreet.***

I was, Vrick shot back. ***I stayed far away from any of their private data stores.***

Once again, Tinsel's image made that sharp gesture of negation. "Don't worry. Your ship friend has been the soul of discretion, not treading anywhere forbidden. But even the most discreet enquiry may be noticed if one is paying attention." The holo focussed on them with a laser-tight stare. "And I'm *always* paying attention."

"We seek an audience, if we may," Lexa-Blue said. "We know you to be a person of honour. And someone is using Sombra, using your home, to trade in materials that have been illegally obtained from persons not compensated for their work."

The frown returned to Tinsel's massive image, an imposing storm cloud suddenly threatening at the horizon. After a moment, they spoke again.

"I will speak with you. This way."

Directions to the inner, most private chambers of Sombra bloomed

of Sombra was only speculated at this point, hoping that, even if the omission came to light, Tinsel would have been bothered enough by the possibility to let it slide.

"Very well," Tinsel said. "What is it you need from me?"

"The specific goods being traded are rare ones," Lexa-Blue said. "There shouldn't be much trade in them happening. Any information on buyers or sellers, or even the carriers would help us track how far down the wormhole this goes."

Tinsel pondered again, and a swirl of smoke rose from their fizzstick, dissipating in the expectant silence.

"My associate has the list of what we're looking for, and the approximate quantities that seem to have been re-routed," Lexa-Blue said, gesturing to Keene.

Keene saw the wispy shadows of Sombra's sigil appear at the edge of his vision, and he knew that it was a direct link to Tinsel's private innernet and the trove of information they kept from the public at large regarding transactions that were constantly going on under their roof. He sent the data through the link and felt it close to him the instant the transfer was complete.

"My staff will look at the records and provide you with whatever information they find," Tinsel said, an offhand wave dismissing them.

That went way better than I thought it would, Lexa-Blue said.

You and me both, Keene said.

Let's get the ruck out of here before they change their mind.

Vrick had continued to sort data and apply multiple analytical algorithms to it in a vain attempt to draw some kind of valid conclusion from the publicly available information ey had compiled. While the statistical probabilities varied slightly, nothing definitive could be gleaned from it. As ey continued to run and re-run the datasets in a dwindling number of possible combinations, ey had left a channel open to Keene and Lexa-Blue's nodes to monitor their progress.

When Lexa-Blue had come up with her improvised plan to approach Tinsel directly, es probability matrices had not predicted a positive outcome, with varying degrees of unhealthy outcomes across several different vectors.

But ey had been shocked when Tinsel had granted them the audience. *Did not see that coming,* ey thought.

But in all the years ey had been living and working with these two, ey had often been amazed by the results of their… unorthodox choices.

Finally, ey had left the analytical algorithms to run in the background, having found that ey was going bug-eyed from them, despite not actually having any eyes.

As they had entered Tinsel's domain, Vrick had tutted to emself about the ostentation of the decor, though ey wasn't surprised by it. Tinsel had always been a vivid personality and ey had expected nothing less than to have that reflected in their private surroundings.

When Lexa-Blue had laid her cards out, attempting to play on Tinsel's sense of fair play, Vrick had seen the logic of the attempt and the probability matrices had shifted substantially in her favour. They had visited Sombra often over their trading careers, and Vrick always made it es business to know as much as possible about anyone they dealt with.

Finding out information on Tinsel had been a challenge, even for Vrick's formidable slicing skills. The codewalls surrounding Sombra's maestri were among the most dynamic and reinforced Vrick had ever encountered. Not even the Pan Galactum Council had defences that strong. And Vrick knew, for ey'd already tried and breached them.

Even with es insatiable curiosity, ey had until now not needed to pry too deeply into Tinsel or Sombra's affairs. It was only this new situation that Malika had brought to their attention that had required em to dig deeper into the shadow market's dealings. As frustrating as the fruitless efforts were turning out to be.

But then, Tinsel had surprised em, as much as they had surprised Keene and Lexa-Blue, offering the very data that might unlock their quest for information. As ey saw and heard the words leave Tinsel's mouth, ey felt the warmth of es comm array as it received the overture from Sombra's system. As ey felt a shiver of anticipation, ey accepted the communication request and felt the torrent of crisp new data flow into es mind.

Ey imagined this was what mind-altering substances must feel like for humans, this intoxicating rush that filled es mind and expanded es consciousness. Ey watched and felt as the probability matrices and analytical algorithms blossomed, stretching in dimensions beyond the capacity of the human mind to collate. The rush coursed through es mind as es neural links tingled with excitement and the glow of new information.

As ey watched, the matrices of data bent and flowed, reshaping in a frenzy at the influx of new, delicious data. Pliable strands shifted like rubber, swirling and reforming in colour sets exquisite in their otherworldly spectrum. Just seeing the panoply of hues made em want to weep with joy.

But not as much as the sudden, clear shift in probability that may just have answered the question they were seeking to answer. A pattern of carriers, with exactly the rare mined materials that were being embezzled from Sound and Fury's operations. Not definitive, by any means. There were all sorts of legitimate sources for the materials, but the probabilities were shifting in meaningful ways, providing distinct, researchable leads that would definitely kickstart their investigation.

A thought brought up the list of ships currently on Sombra, suddenly augmented by the new flow of information, and ey cross-referenced with the sharp, angular new probabilities.

There, ey thought. *That one.*

A ship, at a docking spar on the other side of the main marketplace, almost at the furthest docking bay.

A ship that was in the final prep for takeoff and waiting for final clearance.

Get those mushy meat butts back here now, ey 'pushed to Keene and Lexa-Blue, flooding their nodes with the sudden insights and the transponder data from the ship. ***We're going for a ride.***

Keene and Lexa-Blue had just returned to the main trading floor when Vrick called to them. They both broke into a run along the wide, outer terrace that ringed the expanse of booths. The crowd, though thinner than the crush of bodies engaged in commerce below, still pressed in on them, impeding their progress. Lexa-Blue was none too gentle in clearing the way with elbows and heels, earning them curses in a flow of different languages.

Go easy, Blue,* Keene said. *It's not their fault.
They're in my way. That's fault enough for me.

They came to a halt at the door leading to the concourse where Vrick was docked, and Lexa-Blue rocked on her heels impatiently for the door to cycle open. She bounded forward before it was completely open, the gap only barely big enough for her to fit through. Keene followed, and hurried to catch up with her.

They raced down the nearly empty concourse, outpacing the slowly moving tram pods below. Within moments, they were at Vrick's docking berth and pelting through the docking tube, turning left into the main lounge.

"Get comfy, meat," Vrick said. "This isn't going to be pretty."

They both dove for seats and arranged themselves as comfortably as they could, as quickly as they could. As they felt the crash fields solidifying the air around them, they heard the reverberant jolt as the docking tube fell away.

To an observer on the planet's surface, the takeoff would have looked criminally reckless. The prow of the sleek, hammer-headed ship lifted from the dirt at a sharp, almost perpendicular angle, while the massive drive field generators at the ship's tail glowed blue white before launching the ship skyward on a surge of energy that hummed out around the now empty berth.

Vrick arced up into the thin atmosphere surrounding Sombra, feeling the play of es drive field against the planetoid's mass and gravity well. Ey thrilled at the rush and flow of power that surrounded es hull, shimmering and flowing against the primal forces of the universe. Ey felt every erg of energy that coursed through es conduits, thrumming like the music of a thousand symphonies in harmony.

Sombra fell away below, dwindling in the distance, as ey fixated on the transponder lock ey maintained on the departing ship. So far, the ship was on a normal outsystem trajectory, obviously on its way out of the gravity well of the system in order to transition to interspace. Ey hoped they would remain unaware of es pursuit long enough for em to close the distance.

In the meantime, ey latched onto the ship's identification protocol in Know-It-All and unleashed es slicing codeworms to try to break into the ship's records for whatever useful information ey might find there.

The encryption around the other ship's records was good. Very good, in fact, which was suspicious in its own right. It was military or upper echelon government encryption, top of the line, and Vrick knew that anyone using that kind of codewall was surely hiding something that they didn't want others to get access to. Someone on that ship was very protective of their activities, or very paranoid.

Ey felt a layer of codewall shatter as ey course-corrected to follow the ship more closely, realizing in an instant of thought that the ship had made them. Es long-range sensors recorded the surge of the ship's drive field as it powered up, es navigation system recalculating the probable courses that the fleeing ship might now access along this new trajectory.

Vrick's safety systems ran through a complex set of calculations, seeking an answer to how far ey could push the drive system before catastrophic failure. Diagnostics flashed urgent trepidation at what ey was asking of them, not the least of which was the potential danger to Keene and Lexa-Blue if ey pushed the drives much more. Even es crash fields had their limits when interacting with human flesh.

The whipcord datastreams flowed through es mind, variables shimmering and shifting like quicksilver, conclusions elusive and malleable in the endless flow of data, pushing es analytical matrices to their limits.

Until, far ahead, the ether around the fleeing ship flared star bright as the vessel slipped into interspace and was gone.

CHAPTER FIVE

With the Chimera Orbital, and the reclusive Sei Zephra, two days behind them, they were now in the last leg of their journey to Sound and Fury. Irad was in his seat at the console of the *Sparkling Gossamer*, plotting a course to take advantage of the gravitic disturbance from a nearby black hole to shave even more time off their trip. Ember sat cross-legged on the captain's neatly made bunk, having been granted the privilege of entering the ship's command centre.

Overlaid in his vision were his drawing tools, laid out in a virtual display, several sketches already stored away. All it took was a thought to shift back and forth from the drawing he was working on and his subject before him, as simple as shifting focus from objects near him to ones further away. With a final flourish of colour to represent the control board, he filed the drawing away and started with a fresh, blank, virtual page.

Ember watched Irad's finger play across the control board, and the precise, sure movements of the captain's hands, along with the expression of intense concentration on his face, reminded Ember of a musician struggling with a difficult passage of music.

When he said as much, Irad's face broke into that soft, gentle smile that Ember had come to know in his time on the ship.

"I have no talent for music at all," Irad said. "I have been known to sing loudly and badly when I'm deadheading, but I know better than to do that when there's anyone on board. Even if it's live cargo. It spooks the animals."

Ember laughed. "I'm with you on that one. I can carry a tune, sort of."

"You're one step ahead of me there."

"I can draw," Ember said, mentally flicking the most recent batch into the ship's innernet for Irad to see, already having selected the best of the bunch. Along with them, he sent a notification that they were ready whenever Irad wanted to look at them, not wanting them to suddenly pop up on his link or the ship's screens and break his concentration.

He went quiet a moment, concentrating on catching the specific play of light across the angles of Irad's face, deftly switching through his colour palette to get the shade just right.

"There. That should shave a good day or so off our trip," Irad said.

Ember gave a final stroke with his virtual brush, and focused again on the captain, noticing that the other man had completed his course adjustments, and was sitting back in a more relaxed posture. After a moment, Irad felt Ember's scrutiny and his cheeks flushed pink.

"I'm not used to all this attention."

"I don't believe that," Ember said. "You're the captain of your own ship. That's quite an accomplishment. You have passengers all the time. Surely you're used to having people around?"

"You'd be surprised," Irad said. "I started out as a cargo hauler specifically to be on my own. The whole passenger service thing was an afterthought, one that I needed in order to sweeten my bottom line."

"Now that *does* surprise me," Ember said. "You're quite charming once you open up."

Irad looked even more flustered than before. "It happens sometimes. The passengers I take on are usually the ones that can't afford the big transport liners, or they want to avoid being around that many other people, or maybe they just want to get somewhere quickly, like you do. They have access to entertainment and Know-It-All, so they stick to themselves. I'm rarely more than a driver to them. Or part of the drive system."

Ember frowned. It didn't seem like a very polite or pleasant way to treat someone as nice as Irad. Irad must have seen the thought on his face, for he chuckled that soft, deep, rolling laugh that Ember knew only came out rarely when he was extremely amused.

"It's fine," the quiet captain said. "I've never been much for company or other people. I like the quiet and the solitude. I like the feeling of being out here in the dark, between the stars. Just moving at my own pace, in my own little world."

"What about sex?" Ember said.

He'd already told Irad about the complicated orbit of the relationship he shared with Keene at the centre and his lover from long ago, Daevin, out at a distance. They had been talking into the night, the ship's lighting muted and lulling, and the subject had just easily come up while he was trying to explain his relationship with Malika.

Irad smiled again, and Ember again felt a quiver of desire for this gentle, quiet loner. "I don't spend my entire life in this ship. I enjoy being on planets when I'm there." The captain shrugged. "It's never been that important to me. If I wanted it, it would be easy to find. But I'm pretty close to the Ace end of the spectrum, so it's not much of a concern."

"I can't argue with that," Ember said, "and there are all kinds of things that bind people together as well, if not more so, as getting squishy."

"Like death-defying feats of adventure and derring-do?" Irad asked.

"Wow," Ember said. "We have talked a lot since I've been here. Did we really drink that much that night?"

"There may have been a bottle of Shurian whiskey involved," Irad said. "But I don't mind. Closest thing I've had to an adventure is when my food synth goes down."

"That counts, believe me," Ember said. "I've lived off emergency stores. It's not pleasant."

"Ah, a man after my own heart," Irad said and raised his glass to Ember. "Brindisi! Here's to our pleasures, whatever they may be."

"Up your bum," Ember said, raising his water bulb.

Irad's eyes went wide, and he coughed a little at Ember's words.

"Let's take a look at these drawings of yours," Irad said, recovering. "I'm still not sure how I let you talk me into it."

"I'm charming that way," Ember said, showing a wide, toothy grin.

"Dangerously so, I would imagine," Irad said, pulling up the drawings through the link button on the breast of his shirt. Holos of the drawings exploded around him, translucent from Ember's perspective, opaque from Irad's.

The captain was quiet a moment as he took them in, and Ember worried that he didn't like them. He scrutinized Irad's face, searching for some tell that would let him know how the other man felt.

"They're beautiful," Irad said, only a slight tremor of emotion in his voice revealing the depth of his emotions.

"Thank you," Ember said. "I'm glad you like them."

"Of course," Irad said, his tone now belying the emotion with humour. "There's a fair bit of artistic licence going on."

"I'm an artist, my darling Captain," Ember said loftily. "I make shit up all the time."

It was only a short, two-day trip from the Chimera Orbital to Sound and Fury's rocky, broken system. They spent it in conversation over Irad's seemingly unending repairs and maintenance to keep the ship from flying apart rather than to its destination. Ember even found himself co-opted into assisting with any job that needed an extra set of hands.

"This is so much easier," Irad said, contorted into a position that Ember wasn't even sure he was limber enough to get into. The captain's head and left arm were wedged into an open panel in the *Gossamer*'s engine bay, his voice strained as he worked on realigning a set of dodgy reaction inducers.

Ember's own arm had managed to go numb and tingly as he struggled to hold a buffer steady while Irad cold-welded it into place. "This is easy? What's it like when you have to do it yourself?"

"Infinitely, exquisitely worse," Irad said. "I have scars."

Ember heard the hiss of the molecular cold welder click off. "Okay, you can move your arm now," Irad said.

Carefully extricating his hand from the maze of cabling inside the open conduit, Ember flexed his fingers several times and shook his hand, trying to get the feeling back. "That's what you think."

Irad wriggled out from the conduit and grinned. "The sensation always comes back. Well, except for that one time. Thanks for the help. It really does make it easier."

"Any time," Ember said. "Keene is always elbow-deep in some tech or other, and he always needs spare hands. I never understand any of it, but I've learned how to keep my mouth shut and be useful."

Chuckling, Irad stood and wedged the conduit cover back into place and re-clamped it, ensuring that it was secure. "Well, I am now confident that we will not vaporize on re-entry to normal space."

"Always a good thing," Ember said, knowing full well that, due to Irad's vigilance about his maintenance schedule, there had been no real danger of it happening.

"I'd say we've earned a good meal," Irad said. "But since all we have are the ship's stores, we'll just have to make do with that."

In the galley, they put together a passable, if not very exciting dinner, and ate together at the communal table.

"So," Irad said. "Are you excited to see your friend again?"

Ember paused, words suddenly stuck sideways, and felt a flush of self-recrimination go through him at his own hesitation.

"Ah," Irad said, knowingly. "I see."

"I'm not sure I even understand it myself."

Irad topped up Ember's glass with the cheap, flavourful ale they'd chosen to go with the meal. "People like to think that emotions are neat and tidy, discrete little vignettes that are all simple to understand. But it's never really like that, is it?"

"You are so right, my friend," Ember said, feeling the weight of his contorted, tangled feelings heavy on his shoulders. "I've missed her so much. She was all that was left of my family after Seije died. And she left me. But even though I understood why she did it…"

"You were angry," Irad said. "And hurt. And lonely. And concerned for her. And a dozen other things all at the same time."

"Yes," Ember said, the sound hissing out of him like the sudden relief of a pressure valve opening. "And now she's gotten herself into the middle of something just like the adventures we used to have."

"It all comes around again." Irad said. "But, in the end, you dropped everything to go to her when she called on you. Right or wrong, when she needed you, you didn't hesitate. That should tell you all you need to know."

He cleared their now empty plates and brought back the last of the thornfruit from the stasis unit, placing it on the table before Ember.

"Don't overthink it, Ember," he said, settling back into his seat. He plucked one of the oblong fruits from the bowl and carefully pried the husk apart, revealing the deep, jewel-orange flesh inside.

Ember followed suit, popping a morsel of the fruit into his mouth, where it melted on his tongue, crisp, tangy, and peppery all at the same time. "Overthinking isn't my problem. *Overfeeling* is."

"Fair enough," Irad said. "But don't beat yourself up about it. There's nothing wrong with feeling. It's a damn sight better than the alternative. Humans are just big, neurotic gnarls of feeling. It's our nature. But those masses of conflicting feelings don't define us. It's what we do with them. Where we let them take us. And where we refuse to let them lead us as well."

"How did you get so smart?" Ember said.

Irad let out a throaty honk of a laugh that made Ember want to laugh along with him. "Way too many hours out here in the dark with every kind of person in my guest quarters. If you're quiet and unobtrusive enough, you'd be surprised what people will reveal about themselves."

"Amen to that," Ember said, holding up his glass for a toast. "Amen."

Irad was as good as his word, for they came out of interspace the next day without vaporizing. Ember was there in the control room with him as normal space blinked back into existence. As Irad powered the normal space drive field up again, Ember gasped at the sight that greeted them, steadily growing in the distance.

"What is that?" Ember said, drawing each word out in wonder.

Milky, opalescent radiance banded across the black of space, outshining even the starfield beyond as it rippled like something alive, something reaching out, questing to be seen, admired.

"It is pretty, isn't it?" Irad said, clearly enjoying Ember's visible wonder. "That is why Sound and Fury is suddenly one of the most productive, profitable systems going. That is what's keeping the largest mineral and metal deposits in the Pan Galactum from flying off in all directions and crushing Sound in the process."

"Who'd have thought ore mining could be so... *beautiful*," Ember said. "What makes it look like that?"

"You'll see when we get closer," Irad said. "We have to pass the densest concentration of ore deposits to reach the planet itself, so I figured I'd give you the grand tour."

The glimmering aurora grew ever larger, ever brighter as they flew insystem, colours intensifying up and down the visible spectrum until almost painful to the eyes. Ember couldn't help but wonder what other colours Vrick or Lexa-Blue with her sensor eye might have seen.

Ember sat rapt as the *Gossamer* continued its flight, and as he watched, the individual lights resolved themselves into a coldly opaline net of energy linking the individual masses of rock in a shimmering web. Slowly, the sharp crags came into focus, the rocks moving in their graceful solar orbits. Inset in the energy like jewels set in precious metal, the asteroids were grey and heavy, devoid of atmosphere or life, ranging in size from fragments to the size of cars, on up to masses the size of moons themselves.

As Ember watched, he could make out the plumes of drive fields deep within the belt as ships moved within the depths of the field. From this much closer vantage point, he could make out that the fiery flashes of energy were cast from the drilling equipment embedded within the rocky surfaces.

"It's funny," Ember said. "I'd have expected there to be more collisions, more activity."

"Ah, yes. That's where that light comes from." Irad said. "Take a closer look."

He touched a control and a section of the main viewport zoomed in on the brutish, rocky surface of a massive rock and metal fragment.

Ember spotted it immediately, a device embedded into the surface of the rock they were observing, almost the same dull grey of the rock. The only thing that set it apart was the sharp, angular and obviously artificial shape, and the brightly burning energy lensing from its centre. As he watched, the colour of the energy shifted through more shades of purple than he thought possible, from the palest lilac to the deepest, densest plum. As they watched, the energy flashed outwards, touching the network of similar devices throughout the swath of debris.

"What the hell is that, some kind of mining drone?" Ember asked.

Irad shook his head. "That, my friend, is part of a belt-wide stabilization net. They have hundreds of drills and excavation teams out at any given moment. Between the thrust of the ore carriers and the crew shuttles, and the constant mass being depleted by the excavation, the entire belt would destabilize within days. Without the stabilization, there would be constant meteor showers on the planet. Not to mention the effect that the mass shifts would have on the gravitational fields of the entire system."

"Wow," Ember said. "That is impressive. I thought it was just a matter of blasting the big rocks into smaller rocks."

Irad laughed. "It's a little more complicated than that. I have a friend who used to work on one of these big mining crews who explained it all to me. In asteroids like this one, there are usually a lot of volatile compounds mixed in with the ores and metals. Too much force and you just end up blowing up the very materials you're trying to extract."

"Sort of defeats the whole purpose, I guess," Ember said. "There wasn't much mining where I used to live on Weald. This is all new to me."

"It's quite the operation," Irad said. "I've never seen one this big or this extensive. Their weekly output requires a fleet of ships to transport. And I've done my share of hauling for them when the work was available. I don't like to handle the volatiles if I can help it, but I've carried water ice and metals whenever it fits my schedule. That's why I'm here. My contact in their export office lined up some work for me after I take a bit of a vacation."

"A vacation?" Ember said. "Here?"

"You know how it is," Irad said. "How good pretty much any planet can look once you've been cooped up in a ship long enough. Gives me a chance to stretch my legs. And Sound has a lot of amenities. With the number of workers they have on constant shifts in the belt, they need all the distractions and entertainment they can to keep everyone relaxed and happy to be here."

"How do they manage the labour force?" Ember said. "Sound is far enough away that they must not be able to just shuttle people up and down every workday."

"They do two standard weeks in, two out. And those are staggered, so there's this constant stream of crews in and out of the belt from the planet."

Ember huffed out a surprised breath. "Sounds like a logistical nightmare."

"They're pretty good at it now," Irad said. "This operation has been going full-tilt for a couple of years now. No idea what all the product is being used for."

Ember held his tongue. The Gate Project that Lexa-Blue's lover, Sindel Kestra, was in charge of was still relatively unknown to the general populace, despite the revolution it was going to bring to interstellar travel. The Galactum was still young enough that any number of planetary colonization and construction projects might have called for this quantity of construction materials.

The fact that a network of stable wormhole Gates was slowly being built around select worlds of the Pan Galactum was known to only a select few. If he hadn't been involved in the adventure that had saved the prototype from destruction and corporate espionage, Ember would likely never have known about it, and written off the rumours as a flight of fancy better suited to a cheap, potboiler sensie.

"They're always coming up with something new, my friend," Ember said. "You just never know what the brains are up to."

"True enough," Irad said. "And it's pretty much always over my head."

If you only knew, Ember thought.

Barely an hour later, the *Sparkling Gossamer* descended through the thin, attenuated atmosphere of Sound itself, its course set for the massive domed city and the spaceport that surrounded it.

The city that held the planetary operations and community that serviced the asteroid mine stood, a cool oasis of thriving activity in the hot, sere plain that spread out, orange and ochre and brown, in all directions. In the distance, low, dry dunes struggled to reach up from the ground, and failed. Even the atmosphere itself seemed to choke on whorls and eddies of yellow-grey dust.

Ember felt his mouth go dry just looking at it, and craved water.

He took his mind off it by watching Irad pilot the ship down to a tight docking slot wedged amid hundreds of others, as expertly as Vrick might have done it. The unassuming pilot seemed unfazed by the bulk of a heavy ore hauler that rose ponderously up and across their path, in a trajectory set by the orbital traffic controller that would have tested the nerve of even the most experienced pilot.

Irad didn't even blink as he lowered his ship through the energy field that held the air in the portion of the city's shell that covered the landing field and manoeuvred into position.

With the gentlest of touches, the *Sparkling Gossamer* came to rest in its berth.

"And there you are," Irad said, leaning back in his chair with a deep breath. "I have to stay here and supervise the cargo drones while they empty the holds, but it's not hard to find your way into the city from here."

"Not to worry at all," Ember said. "I'm sure Know-It-All can give me directions if I get lost."

He stood from where he sat on the edge of the captain's bunk, lifting the bag he'd repacked already and kept at hand. Irad stood as well.

"After you," the captain said.

Ember stood and walked down the short flight of stairs from the cockpit one last time, heading for the main airlock, where Irad keyed the control that lowered the exit ramp down to touch the hard, baked 'crete of the landing pad.

"Thanks again for the lift. It means a lot," Ember said, opening his arms for a hug. "May I?"

"Of course," Irad said, smiling, as he stepped forward into Ember's arms and returned the embrace heartily. "I'll be here for a couple of weeks brokering some deals, drumming up some business, taking it easy. You have my call code. Stay in touch."

"I will," Ember said, warmed by Irad's kindness and the new friendship that had sprung up in the face of the old one he was about to renew. "You never know, I might just need an escape route."

Irad laughed. "Just give me an hour or so's notice, if you can. The *Gossamer*'s engines don't rouse quite as fast as they used to."

"Neither do mine," Ember said, descending the ramp with a final wave.

There were signs marking the way toward the nearest entrance to the city proper, and he accessed Know-It-All to confirm where he was going once he reached the crush of buildings and towers.

He headed towards the nearest automated entry point. He stepped forward to the scan arch and keyed his node to offer his ID. The booth chittered thoughtfully before blinking green and letting him through.

Once through the checkpoint, he stood still a moment, letting himself take in the sudden noise of the city.

He knew from Know-It-All that calling the settlement on Sound a city was stretching the truth. This was a company town, and everything in it existed to serve the mining operation out in the nearby belt. Every residential tower, every giggle parlour, every squish house and tope joint, everything existed in service of the credits that could be made from the mining operation. Everyone here was here for that reason, no matter who they were. It reminded him of the district that grew up around any spaceport, what Lexa-Blue called the Grift. A tightly compressed knot of people and services that existed for one, and only one, purpose.

All of Sound was a Grift. Only the master wasn't trade or spacers, the master was the company itself.

He pinged the call code that Malika had provided him, and it buzzed twice before she answered, flooding his node with a warm gush of love and relief.

You're here.

Coordinates flooded his mind, an automat cafe called the Disco Volante, along with a map showing its position relative to where he was.

I'll be there quick as a wink.

He wondered for a second about the best way to reach her, but then, amid the knowledge now available to him, he found her instructions on how to catch a rickshaw just a short walk from his entry point into the city.

Just up a short cross street crowded with clamouring light signs, he found an intersection to a wider avenue choked with traffic. He stepped to the curb and 'pushed a call to the rickshaw control system, which signalled acceptance and showed him where the vehicle would be coming from. It even highlighted the rickshaw in his vision when it came into view down the street.

Zipping nimbly in and out of traffic, the rickshaw pulled up beside him. It was one of the oddest vehicles he'd ever seen. There was a passenger pod in the back, just big enough for two, balanced on two large, wide-set wheels. A main strut led forward to the LI driver, which looked like a lumpy maintenance bot riding a unicycle. He climbed into the back and 'pushed the cafe's information to the driver, and the rickshaw hummed out into traffic with a speed that unnerved him.

The rickshaw proved to be surprisingly comfortable, and it deposited him at his destination within five minutes, despite the distance. He hopped down to the curb as the rickshaw sent the receipt for his fare directly to his node. As he filed the receipt away in his innernet, he took in the cafe before him.

Disco Volante was an open patio space, with no need of shelter in the climate-controlled environment of the dome. Beyond the tables was a wall of small doors, covering the full height and width of the wall. He could make out various foods, neatly plated, through the transparent doors. At one end was a beverage dispenser, neatly broken into sections for hot and cold options. As he watched, a portal opened at one end of the wall and a multi-armed bot ran out along a rail system running the length of the wall, extending manipulators to replenish various meals and desserts from the cart it pulled behind it.

A sudden fear went through him. Fear of what she would say. What he would say. How to tell her about all that had happened. His disguised prosthetics itched and burned under the artificial skin, and he rubbed at the two fingers with his other, whole hand.

He moved to find a table but came to a halt.

There she was, coming from the opposite direction, around the corner at the opposite end of the patio. This was no holo beamed across the depths of the tightline. This was her, flesh and blood. Time froze around him as he took her in. She was exactly the same, and yet it was like she was an imposter, a doppelganger designed to betray his confidence.

She was leaner, having lost some of the voluptuous sensuality that had been her secret weapon on the con. She was dressed differently too: plain, deep green slacks and a simply cut shirt a few shades lighter. As in her message, her lustrous hair was tied back, as if she couldn't be bothered to do anything else with it, and it just accentuated the planes of her unadorned face.

It was her eyes, though. That was her. That was the Malika he knew. The piercing, sensuous gaze, daring and innocent at the same time. The eyes that pulled you in, made you feel she listened, understood.

Whatever else had changed, it was still her.

He wondered what she saw when she looked at him. Had he changed as much as she had? She wouldn't be able to see the prosthetics, but could she see the wounds behind them?

What do I look like to her now?

And then, it didn't matter, for she was moving, charging across the patio toward him, eyes brimming, and at the same time grinning a grin so wide it looked like it might actually hurt. His arms opened, and she hurtled into him, sobbing joyfully into his ear, and he was hugging her as tightly as a lifeline.

"I'm sorry," she said, repeating the phrase over and over. "I shouldn't have left like that. It was just…"

"It's okay," Ember said, talking over her. "It was awful, all of it. I understand."

They held each other, almost bouncing in place. Then she stepped back, her hands on his shoulders, holding him as if to examine every inch of his face.

"You look different," she said, narrowing her eyes, as if trying to peer into him.

"You're one to talk," he said. "You look like someone's secretary."

"Oh, that is cold," she said, throwing back her head in a raucous laugh. "I save the fancy costumes for the stage these days. Come on, let's sit. Are you hungry? The food here is actually really good. They have a human chef doing all the programming for the system."

"I could eat," he said.

"You can always eat," she said. "Do you trust me? I know what's good here."

"Lead on."

He followed her to a table, sitting and watching her open a series of the small, transparent doors and load up a tray. When she returned, she was carrying enough food for four, along with two glasses of a fizzing pink ale.

As soon as she put the food in front of him, he realized how hungry he was. He wanted to talk to her, find out how she had been, find out everything about her life in the two years she'd been gone, but it seemed suddenly overwhelming, too big a subject to cover. Too important and emotional.

"It's okay," she said, and her insight into his mood caught him off guard.

He remembered almost immediately that she had always been that way. She had always been able to penetrate his silences, his walls, often with nothing more than a single look. "We have time. Eat."

He tucked into the plate, sampling from each of the different foods.

Some he recognized, and they were better than he'd had before. Others were new and he savoured the unfamiliar tastes. The food was far beyond anything he'd had since leaving on this trip. Irad's stores had been decent, but nothing on this level.

"This is impressive for a little automated cafe on a mining colony. Hells, it's impressive for anywhere."

"It's the strangest place," Malika said. "You'd think it would be cold and industrial everywhere, nothing but employees being worked down to the bone pulling and shipping the ore, but there's so much going on here. Food and entertainment, the works. They've gone all out to make the workers happier and more productive."

"It does seem an unusual place to find a theatre like yours," Ember said.

"It's mostly funded by the Forum, but the company made the initial request, apparently," she said, "and put up the required stake without complaint. It's been a good place."

"I watched some of the plays on my way here," he said. "They were really good. You were really good."

The compliment seemed to make her shy, her cheeks flushing pink. "Really?"

"Yes," he said with enthusiasm. "I knew you were good, but you'd been working with me so long, I had forgotten just how good."

"It's been good getting back to it," she said. "Flexing those muscles again. It was a good way to get myself together after… after everything that happened."

He reached across the table and laid his hand on hers, and she opened her palm to clasp it. "You don't have to explain. It took me a long time to get back to being me again. Keene helped."

"You're still together then?" she said, smiling. "I'm glad."

It was his turn to blush. "Yeah. Still on the ship, still with him. Still complicated. Still getting into trouble on a regular basis."

"I would expect nothing less," she said. "We all have to get by however we can. For me, it was this place."

Her face turned serious, and he recognized the hard, determined look. "That's why it makes me so furious that someone is dicking people over here. The miners are good people. They work hard and deserve what they make for their effort. It's infuriating that someone is cheating them out of their profit share."

"You've gotten feisty since I saw you last," Ember said, grinning.

"I played a war hero in my last role," she said. "It rubbed off on me."

"Yes, I'm sure that's it. It has nothing to do with your nature. At all."

She laughed along with him, and it felt good. It felt as though no time had passed, that there had been no distance or silence between them. It made his heart ache and expand as it sought to find a shape and place for the sudden surge of forgotten emotions.

"So," he said, becoming serious again. "We have some wrongs to right, don't we?"

"I guess so," she answered.

"I'm going to need to know everything you know about what's going on here. Then we can figure out what we do about it."

"It's not going to be easy," she said. "I barely nosed into it and I was warned off. I've kept clear and it seems like whoever it is has too. But they could be watching me too, for all I know. I tried to lay low, but I must have gotten noticed."

Ember frowned as she told him about the latest incident at the theatre.

"We'll have to tread carefully," Ember said. "I don't want them knowing we're hunting for them until we're ready to spring the trap."

"I'm not sure how easy that's going to be," she said. "Whoever it is, they seem to be highly placed, with enough clout and access to know whoever is looking for them."

"Oh, don't worry," he said, reaching down to pat the bag he'd brought along. "I've got a few special tricks planned. Keene's outfitted me with some special toys until he and the others get here."

Malika looked puzzled.

"He's not the tinker Seije was," Ember said. "But he's got the knack. And if there's something hinky going on here, there was no way they weren't going to help out."

A flicker of sadness played across Malika's face at the mention of Seije. "I miss the old man. I'd give anything just to fight with him one more time."

Seeing her grief sent a spike of the same emotion through Ember's heart. They'd barely been able to share their loss before she had fled, both numb from the shock of what they had endured. Now, so far from that loss, both physically and emotionally, they could share this quiet moment of loss.

"We should get you settled," she said, and the shared moment passed like a wistful breeze.

"I need to find a place to stay," he said. "Is there a hotel around here?"

"It's taken care of," she said. "Part of the deal between the theatre and the mining company is accommodations, so they built a big, comfortable hostel for us, complete with extra rooms for guest performers. I've arranged a room for you."

She stood to clear the mass of plates from the table. "Besides, the hotels here are wickedly overpriced."

He stood and helped her, emptying the remains of food into the recycler, handing her the dishes for her to put into the washing station. With everything cleared away, they headed out to the street and hailed a rickshaw, slipping once again into the flow of traffic.

CHAPTER SIX

"You lost them," Lexa-Blue said, as the pull of the crash field eased. It wasn't a question. "You're supposed to be fast."

"Don't start with me, meat," Vrick said, es own frustration matching hers.

It stung that ey hadn't managed to hold onto the fleeing ship. Whoever was piloting the freighter was good. Very good.

"If I'd gone any faster, I'd be hosing you off the walls. Even with the crash fields up. They must have had their interspace jump preset and ready when they took off. I was too busy trying not to get noticed that I missed it. It won't happen again."

"Don't worry about it," Lexa-Blue said. "That was some gonzo-balls flying, and even I wasn't expecting it. Whoever they are, they're a hazard to flight patterns everywhere."

"Who they are is Tiango Corvalis, captain of the freighter *Aerial Sprite*," Keene said. "I took the liberty of running their transponder signature through Know-It-All while we were chasing them."

"Smart," Lexa-Blue said.

"Records say it's a single ship. Independent, no corp affiliation, based out of Clapham Alpha. Corvalis has been running the ship for about five years, no criminal record other than minor infractions here and there, but a fairly consistent history of fines and reprimands."

"Not a huge leap in logic for him to have jumped from that to running black market goods for an embezzler," Lexa-Blue said. "Once the minor transgressions start piling up, so do the fines and it's hard enough for an independent to make a go of it."

"True enough," Keene said. "Still, it might be jumping the gun to assume he's in on this."

"No, he's definitely one of them," Vrick said. "I've gone over the data that Tinsel provided us multiple times. It scans. The cargo he's been trading in definitely match the type of materials that are coming out of Sound and Fury. I don't have any concrete records of what's going missing from their operations, so it's all circumstantial at this point, but I bet if someone squeezed our Captain Corvalis, he'd pop and tell us what we want to know."

"Vivid metaphor," Lexa-Blue said. "Do we know where he's headed?"

"I've run the possible interspace trajectories from his point of transition," Vrick said. "Sound and Fury is one of many possibilities, so it's still not concrete evidence that would hold up in court."

"File it away, then," Keene said. "Ember should have made it to Sound by now, and with a little bit of luck, he should have some more specific, actionable intelligence by the time we get there."

"If anyone can dig it out, he can," Vrick said. "Setting interspace trajectory for Sound and Fury."

"And away we go," Lexa-Blue said.

"I want to show you something," Malika said, as the rickshaw turned a corner. "It won't take long."

"I'm in no hurry," Ember said. "I'm just glad I'm here."

Malika's smile lit up her face. "It's just up here. On the right."

The theatre stood like a massive block of uncarved stone, featureless and solemn. It wasn't what Ember had expected a theatre to look like at all. Granted, his only experience with theatres had been the ornate palace-like one he'd been in on Weald, where he had met Malika all those years ago.

For all he knew, that had been the aberration and theatres were supposed to look like lazily carved stone blocks. It was only as they were within touching distance of the building that he saw the filigree of heavy-yield holo-mesh covering the outer walls. With a rig like that, they could make the theatre's facade look like anything they wanted, just with some simple code and a source of power.

With the holos, it must have looked amazing, though now, the metal and holo-mesh was just a burnished grey. But even at rest, the theatre looked stately there at the edge of the city.

"I can see why you love it so much," he said.

This made her smile even more and lay her head on his shoulder a moment.

"Come on," Malika said. "The residence is back in the transient quarter."

The rickshaw dropped them off where a shaded laneway led away from the street, between a series of plain blocky buildings.

The company residence looked like a set of stacked boxes, the varying levels creating balconies and patios and rooftop green spaces. Inside, on the main floor, there was a suite of administrative offices, and she led him over to one with an open door, feeling her node signal to the man inside. Over her shoulder, Ember saw a round, harried face peer up and over a maze of data panes that formed a translucent wall across the cluttered desk. The man broke into a grin when he saw her, and Ember saw his hands dance in a series of precise, specific motions. Ember felt his node's translation matrix activate, identify the specific dialect of GSL being used, and interpret for him.

"Is this your friend?" the man behind the desk signed, and the words appeared as text in Ember's vision.

"Valile, this is Ember," Malika said, and Ember heard happiness in the way she said his name. "Ember, Valile Sokahlo, our company manager."

Ember leaned over the desk and offered his hand, the panes fragmenting as he leaned across the path of the emitters.

"Glad to meet you," Ember said, knowing that his words now too, were being translated to either sign or text and projected onto Valile's scleral displays.

Valile took Ember's hand between his thick, meaty palms, pumped vigorously, and released so he could sign again.

"So good to meet you, Ember," Valile signed. "Any friend of our Mali's is welcome here."

"Thank you," Ember said, touched by the effusive welcome from this burly, jovial man.

Valile made a dismissive sound and turned his attention to Malika. "I've put him in G4. I'd have given him the room beside yours, but that slagnauth, Jilostro, left it in such a state, it's not fit for man nor beast."

Guest actor. She was a nightmare, Malika said. ***Don't ask.***

"I really appreciate the lodgings," Ember said.

Valile made the same dismissive noise, this time complemented by a wave of his pudgy hand that didn't require translation. "It's nothing, really. They built this residence way too big for our company, so there's always spare rooms going. We've talked about renting them out, but the Hotel Union filed an injunction or something and all the lawyers are still squabbling over it."

Valile shuffled the mounds of flimsies on his desk, looking for something, and came up with a flat, grey access pad that he pushed across the desk to Ember. "Just need you to confirm your ID so the system knows who you are."

Ember glanced down at the pad and saw the theatre company's sigil form like a heads-up display across his vision as it read his node as his access point to Know-It-All. A thought flashed his biometrics to the pad and the sigil swirled down to a point and disappeared as the pad chirped confirmation.

"Perfect," Valile signed. "You have access to the theatre's innernet if you need anything for your room. We either have it, or we can get the construction crew to run it up for you. Welcome again!"

They left Valile with his wall of data, Malika leading Ember to the lifts at the back of the main floor.

The upper levels were a cozy warren of rooms for various actors and crew, above a main floor that held a common area filled with comfortable furniture at one end, and a kitchen and dining area at the other.

Ember followed Malika through the maze as she guided him to the room, positive he'd never find his way through the puzzle box of corridors.

"There's a map on the innernet," Malika said, and a 'push with her sigil dropped into his node. Sure enough, there was a detailed map with all the information he needed to find his way, his own guestroom glowing a deep navy blue.

Compared to his stateroom on the *Sparkling Gossamer*, this was a palace. There was a bed large enough for two, a desk, a pair of comfortable chairs, and a floor-to-ceiling window leading to a tiny patio ringed with leafy hedges.

"It's not much," Malika said. "But it's comfortable."

"No, it's fine," Ember said. "You should see the room I travelled here in. There were subatomic particles complaining about the lack of space."

Malika chuckled, as Ember dropped his bag at the foot of the bed and pulled one of the chairs to face her. "All right. What's the neo? I'm here, I'm fed, and I'm settled. Tell me what you've gotten yourself into.

"It wasn't my fault," she said. "I was just minding my own business, enjoying getting to be on the stage again. No cons, no risk." She paused. "No one dying who wouldn't just get up and walk away after the curtain fell."

Ember saw that flicker of sadness again, but saw her spine straighten as she put it aside. "That was when I met her."

"Anyeis," Ember prompted.

Malika nodded. "She was gorgeous. Tall, skin like aged noirwood, and built like a warrior. She came to the opening night party for *Midnight of Solus*. I found out later that she was an Excavation Leader and she'd brought her whole crew to the closing night show. She just stood there, like a queen, silently taking it all in, like we were all variables in some festive equation she was trying to solve. When I found out she was responsible for bringing her workers to the show, it really was important to me, so I had to talk to her."

"And you were hot for her," Ember said.

"And I was hot for her," Malika agreed. "You know me so well."

"It was nice. She didn't know anything about my past with you, about what happened or why I had come here. She just knew I was an actor, and she enjoyed my work. It turned out that she came to all the plays that the theatre put on, going back before I even arrived. She noticed me right away as the new girl. We started spending a lot of time together. It's been months now."

She paused and Ember saw her smile, just a little.

The delicate expression seemed out of character on her face, where he was used to the brassy, brazen grins he had always seen before. He knew in that moment that Malika truly cared for Anyeis and understood how that affection and concern for her could have spurred Malika to reach out to him after all this time. He felt a sudden, spiralling tangle of love and jealousy.

She really had moved on.

"It didn't take long for me to see that something was eating at her," Malika said. "It took weeks for her to actually let me in enough to tell me. She's got this freakish knack for numbers, you see. And combined with the years of experience she's had working her way up the ladder in this business, she knew.

"She could tell what her crews were bringing in, could judge their value within a credit or two. When the official assays were consistently under the values she'd estimated, she went to the assay chief directly, but all the datawork backed up the official valuations."

"Could she be mistaken?" Ember asked, then saw the look on her face. "I'm just asking."

"You don't understand," Malika said, her voice fervent. "She's been a rock hopper since she was a kid, barely old enough to pick up an energy drill. It's in her blood. Same as it is for most of the crews here. They were raised in this life, have never known anything else. And beyond the base rate, they earn bonuses for their yield. If someone is skimming the assays, they're taking money right out of the workers' pockets."

"But she doesn't have any idea who it is."

"No," Malika said, with an angry shake of her head. "She tried to access the records as much as her position allows, but they all look squeaky clean."

"Which means they probably have a slicer in their pocket. Someone to rewrite whatever code will hide whatever they're doing."

"I even nosed around myself, using a few of the tricks you taught me. I didn't find anything concrete, but my nosing around must have gotten me noticed. Which is why they tried to scare me into backing off."

"Are you sure it's not a good idea to leave it alone?" Ember said, but once again, her face betrayed her determination and her reaction to the suggestion.

"What was it you always taught me?"

"Don't punch down," Ember said, nodding, remembering the time they had spent gleefully conning the avaricious and immoral back on Weald.

"Exactly," Malika said. "Even after everything humans have been through, people are still trying to hoard wealth and power like it actually means something, and they're willing to screw other people over for it. It's a sickness. But these workers here deserve better."

"Look at you go," Ember said, enjoying this new side of her. "When did you turn into a superhero?"

"Shut up," she said, her cheeks flushing pink again. "You know what I mean."

"I do," he said, thinking of the adventures he'd had with Keene and Lexa-Blue, all of them swearing they weren't doing anything out of the ordinary. "More than you know."

"You always used to tell me we were just seeing that certain people got what they deserved," Malika said. "I just want to see that happen here too."

"I get it," he said. "I really do. So, it looks like we have our work cut out for us."

"Oh, yes. I just have no idea where to start. I already attracted too much attention just by asking the wrong questions."

"Well, it's a good thing I'm here then," he said, reaching into his bag for the small case that Keene had given him. "And I have toys."

"Ember, is this really the time?"

He barked a short, barbed laugh. "That's exactly what I said to Keene."

"Our dirty minds were pretty much always in synch," she said, grinning. "So, what do you have in your toy box?"

Ember rubbed his hands together gleefully and reached into his bag for the special case that Keene had prepared for him. "Oh, I have so many goodies. Starting with this."

He pulled out a small, featureless black casing, and turned it so she could get a good look at the I/O interface.

"Wait a star pulsing minute," she said incredulously. "Is that —"

Ember moved the case to the bedside table, where the room's basic temperature and lighting controls, and, by extension, the residence's main access to Know-It-All were. The casing hummed and emitted a soft cheep as it connected and powered up.

"Now, that's better," a familiar voice said.

"Vrick," Malika said, her voice ringing with joy. "Is that you?"

"Well, yes and no," Vrick said. "It's a quantum-entangled substrate proxy."

"I have no idea what that means, but I'm just glad you're here."

"It's basically a fancy name for an instantaneous tightline unit. Unlike the last time, I'm actually in constant communication with this unit. And, by extension, you."

When Ember and Malika had been plying their trade on Weald with Seije, a member of their team had been Bit, a brain case very similar to this one, only it had turned out to be an independent, self-aware sub-version of Vrick that had disguised emself as a piece of autonomous tech to partake in their adventures. It had only been the Gatecrasher incident that had brought the truth to light.

"I'm a bit limited here without my full toolkit," ey said. "But I can help you out with some things until I get there in person."

"You're coming here," Malika said, her voice rising in excitement. "That's wonderful."

"Hey, you didn't think we'd let you handle this alone, did you?" Vrick said.

"Thank you," she said.

"This is important to you, so it's important to us too."

"Even Lexa-Blue?" Malika said, and Ember wasn't quite sure how real her disbelief was.

"Oh, pish," Vrick said. "None of us listen to her anyway. We just point her at the people we want shot and give her a little nudge. It's better that way."

Malika laughed. "I'd say you'd better not tell her that, but I suspect you already have."

"Just now, actually," Vrick said. "Helps keep her in her place. Now, Ember, show our girl what else we have for you."

"We've got some ID inoculations," Ember said, pulling out another handheld piece of equipment. "When we start digging around, no one will have a clue it's actually us. Which should keep everyone off your tail from now on. We can make sure that you've got airtight alibis if anyone does start backsnooping."

He set them aside and dug through the case. "Honestly, I have no idea what half this stuff does, but we'll find out as we go."

He looked up at Malika and tapped his temple. "And I have the instruction manual."

"Oh, crikes," Malika blurted. "I have rehearsal."

"Go," Ember said. "I'm here. I'm fine. Come see me after."

She jumped up, gave him a quick, hard hug, and dashed out the door. Ember smiled at her back, warm in her presence, even as she had left. Alone, he realized how tired he was, and how sweaty he still felt after the trip and the heat. He stood and pulled off his shirt and pants, intending to have a shower before he started poking into Sound's mysteries. Alone, he relaxed, resetting his prosthetics to their natural state, and the crawling fire under his artificial skin eased so suddenly he sighed with relief.

Until the door opened, and he realized he'd forgotten to lock it after Malika left.

"I forgot to tell you —" she said, bursting back into the room, her voice faltering as she took in the sight of his altered body, the metallic black pseudo-flesh and muscle of his leg, the dark patch that had repaired his side.

Ember saw her falter, saw the impact of it hit her like a rain of fists. He saw her face crumple as she took in the sight, her eyes welling at the thought of the damage that must have occurred for him to have required this type of reconstruction.

"No," he said, putting up his hands in a gesture to placate her. "It's not that bad. It's fine. Let me explain."

Her mouth worked, trying to find words, but none seemed to come for a moment. Until finally, "Oh, my goss, Ember. *What* happened?"

He led her to sit beside him on the bed and told her the story, laying it out gently for her, knowing how outlandish it sounded. When he finished, she was speechless once more, expressions of love, sympathy, sadness, and disbelief warring on her face.

"Aliens," she finally managed to spit out. "Aliens. From another dimension."

She cuffed him in the shoulder, hard. "And you didn't think to lead with this? You haven't seen me in almost two years, and you didn't think to mention the whole *I-fought-aliens-and-got-shot-to-shit-but-it's-okay-because-I'm-a-cyborg-now* thing?"

"Seriously," he said. "You think I'm going to lead with *Hey, Malika, nice to see you, but I got my leg shot off fighting an alien invasion, how have you been?*"

"You could have mentioned it," she said. "It's kind of significant."

"I'm fine," he said. "Look, it's not even a big deal."

He thought the chameleon command to the prosthetics and the gleaming black disappeared, melding into the tone of the surrounding flesh, then turned back to black.

"Oh, that *is* weird," Malika said, then crooked her eyebrows as a thought occurred to her. "Can you do other colours?"

"What?" Ember said. "Why would I want that?

"I don't know," she said, her voice rising. "To go with a new outfit. You'll have to forgive me, I've never met anyone who got shot up by aliens before."

They glared at each other for a moment, then burst into simultaneous laughter, collapsing against each other for support, until they quieted into a fierce, tight embrace.

"Seriously," he said quietly. "It was *horrible*. I don't even have words."

Malika reached her arms around him, squeezing him tightly from the side, and he felt her shoulders rise and fall as she wept. Her tears were wet against his neck.

"But I'm fine now," he said. "Really."

"Really, really?" she said, looking up from the crook of his neck, swiping tears away with her hand.

"The realest really," he said. She didn't need to know about the rest. Not now.

They sat in silence a moment, and then she reached out to take his left hand in hers, her fingers entwining between his mix of flesh and black digits. The touch was tentative, as if she feared causing him more pain, but he responded by gripping her hand tightly.

"I'm sorry I wasn't there for you," she said, just above a whisper.

"Don't," he said firmly. "Do *not* do that to yourself. I will not allow it. You did what you had to do. So did I. Sometimes, things just happen."

She was silent again for a moment. "Did they take good care of you, at least?"

He released her hand and held up his variegated hand, wiggling the fingers. "See this? This is a first run prototype, baby. One of a kind. Until it goes into further human trials next year, that is. But for now…"

She smirked at him. "I always *knew* you were a freak."

"Same to you, sister," he said, bumping his shoulder against hers. Then it was his turn to be silent.

"Keene was amazing," he said. "And annoying at the same time."

"I can totally picture it," Malika said, laughing. "He'd be like smothering but so nice about it, you'd want to smack him and thank him all at the same time."

Ember barked with laughter. "Exactly. Even Lexa-Blue. As soon as I was on my feet, she trained with me, pushed me until I could do everything I did before."

"Stop it," Malika said sternly. "You're going to make me like her or something."

"Medical science can do a lot, but let's not expect too much. Go. You have rehearsal."

"Oh, shit," she said. "Now I'm really late. Demas will have a fit."

She hugged him again, fierce and quick, and was gone again.

"I've missed her," Vrick said.

"Yeah," Ember said. "Me too."

"Ember has activated the proxy," Vrick said.

Keene and Lexa-Blue were both in the lounge, coffee and an array of snacks on the low table. They were taking advantage of the travel time to catch up on administrative details of their merchant trading ventures. Keene was reviewing datawork and ensuring that all appropriate documents had been filed from a recent shipment of exotic foodstuffs to Venus Green out in Sector 14. It had taken several trips to fulfil the various requests from the First In Team of colonists, which made for a snarl of forms and permits which was not eased in the slightest by being strictly virtual.

Stretched out at a right angle from the section of the couch Keene sat on, Lexa-Blue was stretched out, boots off and legs up, evaluating potential opportunities for cargo against the stellar mapping coordinates provided by Vrick's real-time nav core.

They both looked up at the sound of es voice.

"So, he's arrived then," Keene said, relieved. "Did he find her? Is she okay?"

"She's fine," Vrick said. "Lying low seems to have convinced whoever is behind this that she's backed off."

"But how long is that going to last?" Lexa-Blue said. "As soon as she and Ember start nosing around again, it won't take long for our mystery perp to go after them again."

"Maybe so," Keene said. "But I have faith in Ember's ability to keep it on the sly."

"I agree," Vrick said. "Malika was out of practice when she started digging into this. And it was never her skillset anyway. When she and Ember were running cons, she was window dressing and misdirection. She could think on her feet with the best of them, but subtlety and stealth aren't her specialties. That's where Ember and I come in."

"Any new information so far?" Keene said.

"No," Vrick said. "He wants to meet with Malika's lover, Anyeis, first to gather some more information before he formulates a plan of attack, and I think he's wise. What we have, we have secondhand through Malika. And as much as I do trust her judgment, I think we need to understand how this mining operation works before we go in."

"Have you been able to slice their system yet?" Keene asked.

"Not so far," Vrick said, "but I haven't been trying all that hard. Their security is some of the best I've ever seen, and from out here, it's that much harder to get through. Once I'm on-planet, I can devote my attention to it. Plus, Anyeis may be able to help get us inside by bypassing the external codewalls completely."

"Any news on that ship that you couldn't keep up with?" Lexa-Blue said with a teasing grin.

"You'll never guess where they're headed straight back to," Vrick said, ignoring her jibe.

"No," Keene said. "They couldn't be that stupid, could they?"

"They might just be greedy," Lexa-Blue said. "I've seen people do far stupider things than that for a lot less. And if what Tinsel told us is true, they're making a lot of money off this scam. That list of metals and elements they were selling at Sombra was pure profit. If they have a line on more, the temptation to keep milking it would be substantial."

Keene couldn't help but agree. "True. Especially when the source could dry up any time. Dip into the well as often as you can before it runs dry."

"Any chance they'll recognize us when we hit Sound and Fury?" Lexa-Blue asked.

"Oh, meat of little faith," Vrick said. "I can spoof my transponder ID just as well as they can. Even better. I sent out enough signal chaff while we were chasing them that I'd wager they had no idea who was following them. Plus, there's so much traffic in and out of the system, they'd have to be watching more carefully than I think most of you humans are even capable of. My predictive matrices say it's unlikely they'll know who we are."

"Okay, but if they kill us, I'm going to be really mad at you."

"Fine," Vrick said to her. "Add it to the list of all the other things you're mad at me about."

"Done deal," she said. "I'll leave the plotting and scheming to you all, then. Just let me know when you're ready for me to punch, shoot or drive something."

CHAPTER SEVEN

For Ijagu Omrhys, every morning was the same. The morning commute was the same as it always was. Nothing was different on the two blocks from his residence to the company shuttle tram that made the rounds at the same time, along the same route, every day.

The office complex was the same triad of identical, grey slabs as always. He took his coffee from the row of dispensers in the lobby, selecting the machine third from the right. Same as always. The faces around him on the lift ride up to the twenty-eighth floor were the same, the small talk was the same.

For a mid-level Stores, Allotment, and Personnel Analyst in the Sound and Fury Celestrica Mining Consortium, this was what life was. For most, it never occurred to them that there might ever be another way, another option.

But Sei Omrhys, despite the outward ordinariness of his life, was anything but just another cog in the great machine that cracked apart the great rocks of Fury's corpse, digging through the remains for any and all valuable elements. And in the great, burgeoning, shared economy of the Pan Galactum, it was all valuable.

Ijagu Omrhys had been in this line of work for almost ten years now, having transferred to Sound when the company he worked for had become part of the planetary reclamation project three years previous, seeing a chance for career advancement in the nascent consortium. Two years of requisitions, tracking sheets, and drudgery had burned that hope from him though, as he watched inferiors promoted over him, despite his years of experience and skill. Despite the amenities that Sound had to offer, his relationship to his work, and to the consortium itself, seemed to have soured beyond repair.

The lift doors opened on the floor where he had worked for years now, onto the bland atrium with the dull, nondescript lettering that identified his department and section, above a simple biometric scanner.

He held up his link that he wore around his wrist as a thin, metal cuff, and waited the second it took for the system to register his identity. As it always did, the frosted plexi-ceramic door slid aside, revealing the rows of evenly spaced, identical cubicles.

Omrhys turned to his left, walked to the third row from the end, turning to walk to the seventh cubicle from the far end, and took a seat.

The desk itself was a simple L shape, bare of any adornment. A previous section manager had issued a clean desk edict, forcing everyone in the section to remove any personal items or hints of individuality from the workspaces, insisting that no one sit in the same spot every day.

"To shake them out of their habits," she had said. "To keep their thinking fresh."

She hadn't lasted in the position, having transferred up and out, or laterally and away. He didn't remember any more. Her replacement, another of his peers who had been promoted over him, had scrapped the policy and others in the section had reintroduced their photos or plants or knick-knacks. He hadn't bothered. His desk remained impeccably neat and empty.

The cubicle registered his identity from his link and powered up his connection to the company innernet, signing him in for the day and logging the exact time. An array of panes opened, neatly arranged as they had been when he left for home the night before.

Before anything else, he checked his message queue, and of course, there were a series of tersely worded notes from his supervisor, requesting updates on several files that were actually up-to-date and in place for the next shift rotation. He ran down the list, seeing that it included a request for an updated equipment allocation that took into account the last-minute changes that he had filed with the stores office the previous night, before leaving for the day.

It occurred to him he should be angry.

Or, at the very least, frustrated. But even the slight bubble of irritation flashed up and was gone before it could take root. His years in this department had been an unending parade of these micro-humiliations, every change in the upper management regime bringing some new flavour of them down upon his head. This wasn't even a particularly new style of emotional assault. The more it changed, the more it all stayed the same.

In his mind, he composed the response he wished to send, blisteringly biting and anatomically impossible, and took a moment to savour the caustic words before clearing his mind, composing the properly respectful and compliant response, and sending it off.

With the previous shift's reports completed and approved, he set to repeating the same task for the next shift, taking into account the most recent set of results from the assay office detailing the output of the last three shifts. As easily as he breathed or walked across a room, he reassigned shift labour and equipment allocations to the crews that showed gains in the ores and metals showing the greatest value as of the morning's reports from Hub. Volatiles were down, after a more easily accessible source had been located on a planetary system barely eight light-years from Hub itself.

This had been balanced though, but a spike in the need for the constituent metals that were a part of this new Gate Project that had only been announced a few years ago. With a rich vein showing in the largest bodies of Sound and Fury's debris field, it was a simple decision to re-allocate the crews assigned to the volatiles on the outer edges of the belt to the larger metals digs. It meant juggling the schedules, but the potential rise in asset value more than warranted the change in his opinion.

And that was what he was here for, after all.

He worked like this for the next three hours, testing new schedule and allocation options until everything balanced across the board, and the material and crews were evenly distributed to garner the most value and potential profit based on the current conditions and the projections from the system's Quality Control AI. Satisfied, he sent the solution through to his supervisor for a pointless, but politically necessary approval, and logged himself on break.

He stood from his desk and took the exact opposite route he had taken into the office, exiting the building and turning left to the small, bleak parkette that the company had provided as a sad excuse for green space. Three oddly angled blocks of ceramicrete rested on a slab of the same dark surface used for landing pads at the port, tucked in a copse of bent, drooping trees.

No one but Ijagu came here, which was just how he liked it. After a morning of constant corporate interference, he relished the quiet and solitude afforded by the ring of ugly trees.

Especially now.

He reached into his innernet and activated the untraceable privacy protocol he had been given, then used the contact code that went with it. His link accessed the main communications grid and the distinctive pattern of the communication grid swirled in colours in his scleral displays. The muted tones told him the stealth mode was in full effect.

The slicer that he only knew as Pi answered within seconds, an angular, genderless cartoon mask filling Ijagu's vision. In the background of the transmission, Ijagu heard the same jangling, knife-edged music he had before.

What is it? Pi said, the image making only a token effort at both politeness and natural movement.

Ijagu bristled again at the other's tone.

They were an employee, after all, contracted to provide services in accordance with Ijagu's overall plan, and for a specific cut of the spoils. Over the course of their dealings, the slicer had become more and more sharp and unpleasant, despite the substantial amounts that Ijagu had funnelled into their account. Only at the very beginning had they accorded him with even a sliver of the respect he deserved, due to both his position in the company and his status as the mastermind of their current venture. He suspected that Pi's contempt came from boredom, but it still rankled him.

This was not a project that allowed for bold, aggressive moves. This was a slow, steady, and quiet plan. This was, in its way, a long con. Too much, too quickly would send alarm bells running through the company's hierarchy, and that would bring Galactum Security down on them and result in swift criminal prosecution.

I have the new targets and routing for you, Ijagu said, trying to keep an air of authority and control in his voice.

Fine, Pi said, their voice managing to sound even more dismissive than before, something Ijagu wouldn't have even imagined possible.

Just send the data through the transfer protocol. It will take care of everything for you. That's how I designed it. There's no need to keep telling me.

Ijagu's gorge rose even further. ***Listen here. My neck is on the line here. This was my plan. I hired you. I'm the one risking everything for this. You can just disappear back into Know-It-All and erase your tracks. For all I know, that's what you have planned anyway.***

Don't give me that, you corporate sewer-licker, Pi said, flashing from disinterest to a sudden, mercurial rage. ***I've made you rich off your little scheme, something you'd never have been able to manage without me. I'm surprised you even know how to use a terminal without crashing it. You need me. Remember that. Use the transfer protocol and keep your mouth shut. The picosecond this bores me, or you irritate me enough, I can drop every record of every transaction and account to GalSec and to Know-It-All. Behave.***

The connection blanked, leaving Ijagu with a ringing void in his skull, haloed with fury. Realizing his break had ended, he keyed the transfer protocol with the newest targeting information and stood to return to his cubicle.

In the temporary workspace that he had set up in a warehouse about a kilometre away, Pi sat back in his customized slicing rig, his flash of ire gone as quickly as it had come. The corpo speck was so easy to play, he might as well have been a vibraphone. Pi knew he could manipulate the other man's emotions as easily as he played Know-It-All with his codeworms. The analyst was incapable of not rising to whatever bait Pi laid out for him, following Pi's lead to whatever emotional state it suited Pi to induce.

The truth was, this was an easy gig.

Pi could have done it in his sleep. He'd written the code to slice the company's systems in an hour or so, leaving it in the hands of a simple LI to run whenever Ijagu uploaded the most recent data to target the shipments to "disappear." It really was easy money, and Pi mostly just watched it come in while he worked on other projects, finding new and creative ways to break into and manipulate the complex web of information that flowed through every corner of the Pan Galactum, holding it together like the fundamental forces of gravitation.

When Ijagu Omrhys had set him up here, he'd chosen the location himself and had demanded exactly what type of set up he'd needed, citing the most expensive, luxurious combination of chair and system he could dream up. The fool in the cubicle had agreed, so wrapped up in his own cleverness at securing someone of Pi's reputation that it hadn't even occurred to him that Pi might need nothing more than a cheap apartment and his own portable jacker module.

Pi had upgraded from an external link to an embedded node before the tech had even been fully tested on humans, initiating his own neural mesh modifications along his nervous system as quickly as he could write the operating code that bypassed the safety routines. His entire body was the ultimate controller now, allowing him ever faster and more reliable access, and fine command over the application of all of the hardware and code at his disposal.

It was the data he craved, needing it like the most addictive of drugs. He needed to root out the hidden code, find the information no one wanted shared, no matter what it was. Sometimes, he didn't even do anything with it. He just needed it, like air or water or food.

He had to admit to himself that the appeal of this job was wearing thin. Ijagu was becoming tedious in his demands. It was tiresome. While the money was ample — Pi opened his account access and checked the balance again, watching the numbers change in real time as interest accrued — the itch for new and fresh challenges nipped and bit at him, like a solitary insect lost somewhere in his clothes. He found himself craving new stimulation more and more often, no matter how much he dug around in the systems that ran the system's massive mining operations, as well as the innernets of the thousands of employees that kept the company running.

The well of secrets would run dry sooner or later, and with it, Sound's appeal.

And with it, Ijagu Omrhys' usefulness.

Ember woke the next morning to a message from Malika.

I'm sorry, I've been called into rehearsal for most of the day. You're going to have to amuse yourself, I'm afraid. And anyway, Anyeis is out on the final day of her mining shift with her crew, so we can't meet with her until tomorrow. I'll check in with you once I have a better idea of how long we're going to take today. This guest director is already having a tantrum and we haven't even started yet. It's going to be a long day.

The message made him smile as he stretched languidly in the surprisingly comfortable bed. It didn't bother him that he would have to wait. Now that the game was on and he was in preparation mode, he knew he'd take the time he needed to arrange everything before making a move. The major part of any con was the prep time. If you didn't understand the mark thoroughly, if you didn't prepare for every possibility you could think of, you weren't ready. There were always going to be curveballs coming at you, but the better prepared you were, the easier they usually were to handle.

Malika had joked once upon a time that he should teach a class.

He showered, dressed, and went down to the common room. Valile was in his office, the door open, when Ember pinged him through Know-It-All to get his attention.

"Hey, good morning," Valile signed, smiling as he looked up from his desk. "How did you sleep?"

"Very well, thanks," Ember said. "Say, is there somewhere around here I can find breakfast?"

Valile made a dismissive noise. "No need to go out anywhere, unless you really want to. Help yourself to whatever's on the go in the kitchen.

The LI cookbot isn't fancy, but there's lots on it and it will keep you going."

"Are you sure?" Ember said. "I don't want to impose."

"Not at all. Malika says you're family. That's good enough for me." Valile's grinning, round face left no room for disagreement. "Make yourself at home."

"Thank you," Ember said.

"Not at all. I'm here all day if you need anything. Go. Eat. You're too skinny."

Ember found a cooker full of a protein and vegetable scramble in the kitchen, and it smelled heavenly. He ladled a plateful and found a spiced tea in an urn at the end of the service counter. The cup was warm in his hand, and it filled the air with a heady sweetness.

As he ate, he sent a series of preliminary data requests to Know-It-All, routing the results to his room and to Vrick's proxy, so they would be ready for him when he was done. The thoughts were initially random, as he free-associated as many search parameters as he could come up with. Anything to begin the process of opening up an avenue of research that might lead him to his quarry.

The scramble was so good, he almost went back for another plateful, but he knew that any more would just weigh him down and slow his thought processes. With a firm hand, he pushed the plate away, though he did indulge in another cup of tea.

As he savoured the spiced sweetness of it, he let his mind wander again, free of the requirement for search materials. This was more akin to a meditative state, as he let his imagination go, trying to profile his target in broad, unsubtle strokes.

Who is this person?

What brings a person to steal from their co-workers?

How does a person interrupt a process this complex?

And how do they cover their tracks?

There were no conclusions, of course. But at this point, he expected none. This part of the process was just about freeing his mind, letting it run free to wherever it liked.

After the last sip of the cooling tea, he bussed his dishes to the washer and headed back to his room. Inside, he saw the results of his searches flashed up on the long wall of the room, the panes randomly pulling forward or pushing into the background as Vrick ran various analyses on them.

Ember saw there were some pieces of information he hadn't thought to request added to the results of his searches.

"Good job," he said. "I didn't even think of that."

"You did a good job, very thorough," Vrick said. "Impressive work for a sack of meat."

"I do try," Ember said. "Anything jumping out at you?"

"Facts, facts, and more facts," Vrick said. "I can recite chapter and verse on the consortium's history and how they won the contract for this whole operation. But I don't think that's going to tell us much about who's stealing."

"It all goes somewhere," Ember said. "It all adds up to someone smart enough and amoral enough to plan this out."

"The information on their security system is very thorough. Do you think our friend is in this alone?"

Ember gestured and the pane containing the security specs came forward for him to scan through. He shook his head. "My first hunch is to say no. This is definitely some heavy-duty encryptions systems and security. Unless the mark is in security itself, I can't see someone in another department having the know-how to get through all this and pull this off."

"Someone in accounting, maybe?" Vrick said. "They'd have access to the numbers to jimmy them around."

"If it was straight up misappropriation of funds, I'd say yes," Ember said, his face tight with concentration. "But our friend is literally making tonnes of material disappear off the grid and head into the great unknown. That takes a lot more than moving virtual currency around."

"So, someone in supply chain?" Vrick asked.

"Possibly. I'm going to need more information about the actual workings of the process. How the actual mining is done. How everything is sorted. How it's valued and how everyone gets paid."

"That, unfortunately, they seem to be keeping close to the vest," Vrick said. "I have all kinds of general information on the prices of everything and how large-scale mining operations operate in general, but they've got a proprietary info lock on the ins and outs of how."

"It's fine," Ember said. "Malika has arranged a meeting with Anyeis tomorrow. That should give me the scoop on how this particular operation actually works. Based on that, I can make some decisions about where to start digging."

"You have that look on your face," Vrick said. "You've already got something going on in there. Let me see if I can guess, if I can be as devious as you."

"Devious?" Ember said with a laugh. "Me?"

"You've got a mind that's often even sneakier than mine," Vrick said. "You want to do recon."

"Definitely. Whatever Anyeis says tomorrow, I'm going to need to get inside. Dig around the roots. See what's under there. Can you dig me up more details on their security systems?"

"I think so," Vrick said. "Their codewalls are some of the best I've ever seen, so it's going to take me some time. This version of me doesn't have quite the resources main me does."

"Do what you can," Ember said. "I'm going to go nose around. Play tourist. See what I can see. I'll stay uplinked to you so you get everything I do."

It was almost lunchtime anyway, so Ember changed into the most nondescript shipsuit from his luggage and ran a dab of instant dye through his hair to mute the silvery sheen. The final step was to think his prostheses into their flesh-toned neutrality, rendering them invisible against his skin, so he steeled himself against the bite of pain and keyed the colour change. Satisfied in his ordinariness, he left Vrick to study and headed back out, stopping only to grab a nutrient bar from the kitchen on his way out.

Biting into the chewy bar, he barely tasted it, for his senses were already keyed up, putting him into the state where he could absorb as much information from his surroundings as possible. This reconnaissance process was something that only partly required his conscious mind. It was the flickering, unconscious instincts he needed now.

On the street, he looked for a rickshaw, but saw none in the vicinity. He logged into the local system to call for one, but the local LI informed him that the single tram that comprised the local transit system was due at the nearest intersection within a few minutes.

Why not? he thought, turning in that direction.

The vehicle arrived on schedule, which seemed like a miracle considering the state it was in. He half-expected there to be a cloud of black smoke emanating from its rear end, it was that bad.

It snaked around the corner to a stop, the folds of its central articulation groaning in protest. Despite floating on a grev field, the long cylinder of the vehicle lumbered to a halt for him, and the dented doors, behind their rash of rust, groaned open for him.

He 'pushed a payment to the fare collection system and edged his way through a dense cluster of riders that emanated an air of sad resignation.

He managed to squeeze himself into too small a gap in the crush of passengers and plant his feet against the drunken sway of the ancient vehicle.

With his calmness already showing signs of fraying, he accessed Know-It-All again and brought up information on the sad state of this transit system in an attempt to figure out why it was the way it was.

What he found made it all clear. The tram system (system being two of these crumbling metal snakes) was provided by the company itself, as they did the bare minimum to ensure that the basic transportation need was met. Into that gap of need, some enterprising soul had seen the potential for profit, settled in, and imported the many rickshaws that plied their trade in the streets. Though their services came at a considerably higher fare than the ailing tram system, even if it was considerably less than the limousine and private car companies that catered to the executives or VIPs that often had business dealings with the corporation itself.

Same story everywhere, he thought. The corps did the bare minimum, and the greedies inserted themselves into the gaps left behind. And the regular folks just had to bite it and pay the fares in order to get by.

As the thought registered, he felt a momentary sting of disloyalty to Daevin and Brighter Light, and it made him rub the dull hurt in the artificial fingers of his left hand. It had taken time to make peace with the complicated orbits that intertwined his relationship with Keene and Keene's relationship with Daevin. Ember hadn't cared about the non-exclusivity of the relationships, but had it had to be with a fat-cat corpo?

The Technarch of Brighter Light represented everything that Ember had fought against in his former, less-than-legal, life. But he had grown to respect Daevin, and he couldn't deny the fact that Daevin had simply turned over several million credits' worth of state-of-the-art cybernetic prosthetics to save his life.

I wonder what he'd think of my current activities, he thought. And as the thought occurred to him, he heard Keene's voice in his head telling him that Daevin would wholeheartedly approve.

His mapsense pinged him as the crumbling tram approached the consortium's main office complex, and he eased his way toward the nearest exit, hitting the stop request panel when his node pinged his stop.

The complex was a set of buildings taking up a two-block area, all hard, dull angles. It looked like some designer at some point had realized there was some public relations value in making some token attempt to prettify the facade with an inlaid pattern etched into the outer walls, but the detailing was too little to make a difference and only succeeded in making the entire complex look that much dourer. Near the main entrance, shadowed by the corporate logo, there were a few small patches of trees and green space, dwarfed by the towers of alloy, glass and polymer.

As the tram grumbled off down the street, he looked around for a place to set up his surveillance post. The street across from the complex was a row of various eateries and shops designed for the flow of workers in and out of the headquarters itself. He imagined a steady flow of workers filing out of the complex and into the restaurants for lunch, then back to their desks, then filing out once again at the end of shift and into the same establishments for after work drinks.

Some things never change.

As it was past lunch now, the tables on the various patios were practically empty, and a glance through the main windows showed the interiors in the same state, though there were just enough other customers to make him not look completely conspicuous. They'd likely be glad of the clientele until the afternoon breaks, and less inclined to rush him out as long as he made at least token purchases during the quiet time.

He found a spot with a good view of the complex across the street and ordered an overpriced coffee concoction that arrived with a mound of gleaming white on top of it, with two colours of drizzled sauces and a tiny, glimmering flame in the centre. That should keep the server satisfied for the time being.

He sat back, the mug hot and steaming in his hand, and just looked at the buildings that made up the compound, shifting his body into a relaxed posture. For all anyone knew, he might have been reading a book, or drawing, or some other innocuous activity that a citizen could perform through a connection to Know-It-All and the right software.

The complex of angular towers across from him was exposed to the streets on all sides, which made any kind of stealth approach from above ground difficult. There might be underground accesses somewhere, designed for deliveries and such, but he wouldn't know until Vrick cracked the specs. If there was access from below, that might be an option. Stow away on an incoming vehicle.

But the entire complex was basically wide open. No perimeter walls or anything of the kind separating it from the street other than a simple walkway that led from the street itself. Which meant some other form of security, whether it was codes, chips, or straight up biosensors, he didn't know — none of which was a dealbreaker per se, but each presented its own unique set of challenges. And he might not be able to find the tools he needed to bypass some of those options.

Again, a problem to be solved another day.

Gradually, he took stock of it all: entrances, exits, traffic patterns based on the timing of the shift clock that the entire mining operation stepped to. He made note of security recorders on the face of the restaurant he was in and along the street, making a mental note to have Vrick slice them and do an analysis of the traffic patterns, both vehicular and pedestrian. He knew ey would be able to identify any openings or quirks of the neighbourhood that they could exploit.

Next, he accessed Know-It-All for a map of the entire area covered by the domed city that housed the mining consortium and all that had grown up around it. While there wasn't a clean division, the company itself took up just over half of the area within the dome, spread pretty much beyond the administrative complex he was looking at. The entertainment facilities, housing, and such lay behind him, with the complex across the street almost standing guard for what lay beyond.

Even the spaceport outside the dome was bisected, with the sections for public travel kept separate from those reserved for the company shuttles that took mining crews to their ships, as well as housing the maintenance crews that serviced any company ships that needed to come to the surface. He could see from the map that the berth where the *Sparkling Gossamer* had landed was right on the edge of the different sectors. As Irad was a private contractor, he was not allowed to land within the corporate sector directly without special permission from the dockmaster, and only then if there was some specific commercial reason for it.

He realized he needed to know more about how the whole operation ran from day to day. There was some information in the archives and the public relations records as well but he'd need a better understanding of the inner workings. Anyeis should be able to provide him with that when he got to meet with her, so he put it aside for now and concentrated on the information he could glean.

I've got those specs for you, Vrick said through Ember's node.

Thanks, Vrick.

A thought opened the package of data, and it flooded into his mind, the plans for the complex unfolding like the petals of a flower. He looked again at the complex across the street and overlaid the floorplans over his vision, jockeying it into place. He found that if he focused his attention on any specific section of the building, incredibly detailed information bloomed for him, up to and including names of the section's current occupants and whether they were onsite at that moment or not. As he skimmed the data, the specs for every aspect of the complex's security checkpoints and requirements marched past in a separate column.

Wow. This is some prime intel, Vrick, Ember said. ***Do I even want to know where you got it?***

Who are you kidding? You want to know just in case you can leverage the source again in the future.

You've got me there, Ember said, his virtual grin vividly green through his node.

***The conduit from the internal personnel database to the public directory is based on some out-of-date code that isn't as secure as it could be. As for the security**

system, let's just say I can be very... persuasive. That, and I'm brilliant.*

I can't argue with that, Ember said. ***Here, have a look at what I've got so far. I'm going to run some scenarios here. Would you mind running some probabilities as well? We can compare notes when I get back.***

He sent a spurt back to Vrick containing all of the observations and speculations he'd come up with so far.

Done deal, Vrick said. ***Leave the link open, if you don't mind, and I'll adjust as you come up with anything new.***

Wordlessly, Ember thought the command that would do just that, and felt the connection shrink to a pinpoint of warmth at the back of his mind. After he ordered another coffee, he sat back and got comfortable, laying out all of the data available before his mind. In the safe virtuality he had accumulated, he began his assault.

Over the next few hours, he ran possibilities in his head, staying on that terrace as long as he could get away with. He realized that the shift at the complex must have changed, for the cafe was suddenly full of boisterous noise and bodies. Settling his bill, he decided against waiting for the tram, and called for a rickshaw instead, giving it directions to the nearest entertainment district.

Stepping back onto the street, he scanned the offerings and settled on a giggle parlour advertising a holo revue of acts from around the Galactum. Ordering a cocktail and something to eat, he shut down all thoughts of infiltration or security or potential dangers and lost himself in the laughter.

When Malika knocked on Ember's door the next morning, he was already awake, showered, and dressed after a deep, satisfying sleep. She found him standing in the middle of his small room, one wall covered in panes of information projected by the building's interface to Know-It-All. On the edge of the bed was a plate filled with items from the breakfast spread laid out downstairs in the dining area. His face was creased in thought as he sipped a cup of coffee.

"I see you found food," she said, taking him in. "I should have known you could fend for yourself."

He turned to her from the interlocking displays of information, smiling as he shrugged. "I didn't want to wake you. And I've been managing my own meals for a while now. How was the show last night?"

Her face lit with a joy he hadn't seen for a very long time, and his own mood rose just seeing it. "It was good. We had a great house. They laughed in all the right places. The energy was all loving and tingly. How was your night?"

"I slept," Ember said. "Even though I put myself onto your local time back on the *Gossamer*, I didn't want to take any chances on space-lag. I need my head clear for this."

"I totally get that," she said, then smiled at how good he looked. "You look nice. Different, but nice."

He was wearing dark, almost black trousers that clung to the shape of his legs, ending about five centimetres above his ankles and the chevron-patterned short boots. The high-collared sweater he wore was perfectly fitted, a charcoal grey that complemented his tousled silver hair.

He looked down at himself, as if he had forgotten what he'd put on already. "It's nice to wear something other than that shipsuit," he said. "It's practical onboard, but it does lack a certain panache."

"You do look quite natty," Vrick said. "I'm sure Keene wouldn't object to you dressing like that more often. You look like a sensie star."

"You flatter me, old friend," Ember said, his cheeks flushing pink with embarrassment.

"Well, if you two can stop flirting with each other a minute," Malika said, "you can bring me up to speed on what you've got going on here."

Ember looked back at the streams of information projected against the wall. "Background mostly. I want to know as much as I can about how this place works before I make any plans. I'm hoping this illuminates some kind of pathway into however this person is scamming the miners."

"Are you managing to stay discreet?" she asked. "Should I be expecting death threats later today?"

"That's on me," Vrick said, es voice emanating from the brainbox where it sat on the small end table. "Most of this is the publicly available information. Company records and such. Any of the more… sensitive information, I'm using my full stealth mode for. And I have state-of-the-art tools to keep my presence hidden."

"Okay, I'm somewhat reassured," she said. "But I have my doubts."

"Have a little faith in your favourite ship," Vrick said. "I haven't been caught yet. And I've been in some very secret places. I procured my tools from the very best, and I know how to use them."

Malika put up her hands in defeat. "Okay, but don't let me get killed, okay? I've only just started liking my life again."

"I shall defend you to the last, fair maiden," Vrick said.

"You are shameless!" Malika said.

"Now who's being flirtatious?" Ember asked.

"All right, all right," she said. "What have you found so far?"

"It's like any company," Ember said. "They've got pretty good security, but their vision of the types of threats they might be facing is narrow. Like they can't imagine any kind of small, concerted intrusion."

"Like you and I are famous for," Malika said.

Ember turned to her and smiled, a smile of nostalgia and pride. "Like you and I are famous for. Exactly. I've already identified several key vulnerabilities we could exploit when we're ready, but we need to narrow it down. Whoever is behind this has been very, very careful, and if we go in from the wrong angle, we could miss them entirely and tip them off."

"Understood," Malika said. "The last thing I want is for this gank to get away with this. I want him crushed."

"And I'm confident we can do that," Ember said. "We just need more information before we go on the attack."

"That, I think I can help with," she said. "I've been in touch with Anyeis and she's going to meet us. She's been in this racket for a long time, and she has a better grasp of what's been going on."

"That's definitely what I need," Ember said. "Someone inside the system that can narrow down some possibilities as to how this is all happening. Then we can plan our strategy as to how we can bring them down."

"If you can tear yourself away from all this, we should get moving."

Ember waved his hand and the panes of information collapsed into nothing. "Hold the fort, Vrick. I'll be back in… a couple of hours?" He looked to Malika, who nodded to confirm his estimate. "

"Done deal, meat," Vrick said. "I'll do some more poking around at the company's defence and catalogue their vulnerabilities in a bit more detail. See if I can find some useful ways in."

"Perfect," Ember said. "And I assume you'll be listening in on our conversation as well?"

"Need you ask?" Vrick said.

Malika had already summoned a rickshaw, which waited for them at the curb outside the theatre. As soon as they were seated, the LI vehicle hummed out into the cramped flow of traffic, easing into a space between two large equipment haulers.

"Anyeis picked the meeting place," Malika said. "She's skittish. She just about lost it when I told her about our mark trying to warn me off. As much as she wants to get this creep, this is her livelihood too. She has a lot to lose if this goes hinky."

"Which is why you were looking into it for her," Ember said.

"Exactly. The theatre company is independently run on a special Arts Forum contract. No one in the corp at large can touch me if I step on the wrong toes."

Ember thought for a moment, looking at her profile as she stared out at the city. He knew that look, from what now seemed like so long ago. This was her fighting face. She was ready to take on the world, to wade in with her fists swinging. She'd attack this like she had attacked every con they'd ever pulled, every role she'd ever played. He'd always admired that about her; he'd been right alongside her as they jumped off the ledge together.

But here, now, in this maze of towers and crush of corporate power, something in him hesitated, and worried for her. And that worry ran deep.

He steeled himself against this sudden hesitation, the only physical manifestation of it a slight tightening of his shoulders. *This is not me,* he thought. Even now, after all his time on the Maverick Heart, he was still a grifter through and through. He'd missed the thrill of the scam, the excitement of the planning and the careful execution. Even the adrenaline-bursting moments when it all started to go wrong, and they had to re-plan everything as they went.

And Malika was his family, even more so than Vrick, Keene, and Lexa-

Blue if he was honest with himself, though he'd grown to love them all. But Malika had been there longer, had embedded herself deeper. Whatever she was up against, he was going to be right there with her.

"We're here."

He looked where she indicated and saw the generic facade of another cafe. Unlike the one where he had met Malika the previous day, this one was enclosed and appeared to be staffed by actual humans, rather than an automat system. He followed her out of the rickshaw, across the pavement, and through the archaic revolving door.

Inside, he could easily see why the place wasn't very popular. The interior was dim and drab, with light coming only from one dirty front window. Tiny, round tables were unevenly spaced in front of a long, tufted banquette covered in unevenly faded fabric, providing awkward seating and an abundance of wasted space. Other than the one, sullen server who watched them from behind the bar, there was only one person in the place.

Anyeis watched them from a table close to the kitchen, away from the weak light of the window. Ember saw her stand as they approached and was impressed. She was tall and muscular, her skin even darker than Keene's, and she had the darkest, blackest eyes he had ever seen, iris and pupil blending into one.

Even if Malika hadn't told him, he would have known she had worked her way up through the company to her supervisory position. Every sinew of her body was solid and strong, a power she had obviously maintained even though she now led the crews that she had once worked with.

Despite the other woman's stern, taciturn demeanour, Malika moved forward to embrace her, giving her an enthusiastic kiss. When Malika released her, he saw her full lips lift at the corners, just a touch.

"Anyeis, this is Ember," Malika said, entwining her hand into her lover's. "He's here to help."

"Thank you," Anyeis said, holding out her other hand to shake his. Her voice was deep and certain, and he imagined it cracking out instructions that no one on her teams would be foolish enough not to follow.

A woman of few words, he thought. *Two can play that game.*

"Glad to help."

They sat again, and he noticed there was an open bottle on the table, with three glasses. Anyeis's glass was a conservative three quarters full.

"Oooh, Paqua," Malika said, filling glasses for herself and Ember. "My favourite. Try it, Ember. It's divine."

Ember tasted it and it was, indeed, very tasty. Fizzy and refreshing, there was also a sharp, gingery undertone.

The dour waiter emerged from behind the kitchen with a bowl that smelled of salt and old grease, dropping it in the middle of the table before disappearing behind the bar again.

"Oooh, and frites," Malika said, reaching to pluck a deep-fried curl of some unidentifiable vegetable and pop it into her mouth. "She always knows just what I need." She leaned over and kissed Anyeis on the cheek, who blushed even darker under the contact.

"More like *frights*," Ember said, his tongue greasy after sampling the snack.

"I don't know how she can stand them," Anyeis said, the corner of her mouth lifting. "They're disgusting."

She paused a moment, taking him in, as if weighing how much to trust him. He could see the effort the decision cost her. "What do you need to know?"

He held up a hand. "Before we start —" He pulled a small metal disk from his pocket and laid it on the table, touching a single control to activate it. "Cone of silence," he said when he saw the confusion on her face. "Now, whatever we say remains just between us."

He could tell that he had scored points with Anyeis, and a sidelong glance at Malika showed that she was enjoying the moment as much as he was.

She's not easily impressed. Well done.

Anyeis looked at her, then at him, and Ember knew that she had surmised that Malika had spoken to him through her node.

"So, someone is embezzling from your workers," Ember said. "And you want it to stop."

Anyeis nodded, one quick up-and-down movement of her head. "They work for their pay. And those bonuses as well. It's not right that they're losing out on what they earned."

"You earned it too," Malika said, clasping Anyeis's hand.

Anyeis shook her head, the movement just as sharp and economical as the nod had been. "That doesn't matter."

"It should," Malika said.

"And it does to us," Ember said. "No one is getting left behind when this is done. You included."

Anyeis smiled, just slightly, and Ember saw her shoulders relax just a little. "I hope you have better luck finding out who did it than I did. I went over every assay, every step in the process, from my team bringing the haul in to when the money was transferred and the material sent out. The records check out. To the microgram."

"So how do you know anything is missing?" Ember asked.

She levelled a stare at him that he was sure had cowed many a person over the years. "I know. I see what they're bringing in. I see the tools they use, and I see the results coming in. I'm with my team from the moment they hit rock to the moment they clock off. I supervise every aspect of their work. And I can add up their yield better than any computer can."

"She has a freakish kind of brain for that sort of thing," Malika said. "It's kind of disturbing."

"So romantic," Anyeis said, her smile so much more relaxed this time that Ember couldn't help but smile a little bit too.

"Well, then," he said. "The material is being diverted somehow and the records are being altered to cover it up."

Anyeis shook her head. "That's what I thought at first, but I've seen the security they employ. There's an AI covering the sorting and assay systems, and every door, every terminal, every piece of equipment from hand drills to haulers are biometrically coded. It's impossible."

"You have your area of expertise and I have mine," Ember said, shaking his head. "Eventually, even the most impregnable system will crack. All it takes is a slicer with enough time and ingenuity to fight through it."

Anyeis looked skeptical.

"Trust me, I've worked with one of the best slicers in the history of, well, history," Ember said, the thought of Seije only smarting a little. Malika must have seen it, for she laid her hand on his. "Security experts beat slicers, slicers beat security systems. It's a dance that never ends. But from what you're telling me, whoever is doing this is bleeding edge."

Anyeis frowned, and Ember saw that she doubted him.

"Don't worry," he said. "This is what I do. And I happen to have access to some bleeding-edge tools myself."

Who are you calling a tool? Vrick said through his node, with a ripple of humour. *And I don't bleed.*

No, but you're the best slicer I know. Any doubts we can take this gleeb down?

Not a one.

"If it is humanly possible to get to the bottom of this," he said aloud, "we will. Now, walk me through the process, start to finish. The more I know, the better I can plan."

CHAPTER EIGHT

Vrick angled es drive fields to maintain a steady course along the edge of the massive field of tethered, shattered rock that bloomed from the wreckage of Fury and filled the black around em. At the same time, ey trained all of es various external sensors onto the belt, soaking up every iota of information available, streaming it all to panes Keene and Lexa-Blue could see. As ey passed, a dense net of vicious-looking armed satellites tracked their trajectory with perfect precision.

"How did you get us in this close?" Keene asked. "They must have this area completely restricted."

"They do," Vrick said. "I've never seen a security protocol that tight. By all rights, we should have been back beyond the outer system marker."

"What did you do?" Lexa-Blue, trying to sound like she was scolding him, but completely unable to pull it off.

"There's an exception in their protocols for diplomatic ships, company executives, and high muckety-mucks from the Gate Project," Vrick said. "I may have sliced my way in and run up some credentials for us."

Keene groaned. "Oh, goss. Daevin's going to kill me." The Technarch was deeply involved in the administration of the Gate Project and was notoriously staid in protecting his own reputation.

"No," Vrick said, drawing out the syllable into a little trill of melody. "He likes me. He even likes you too. Especially when you're naked."

"Oh, ha ha," Keene said. "If I had to be naked every time I had something to apologize to Daevin for, I'd never put on clothes."

"Which, I'm sure he and Ember would both be fine with," Lexa-Blue said.

"Well, you don't have to worry," Vrick said. "I left him out of it this time. I used Sindel's position and access to get us in."

"Oh, well, then," Lexa-Blue said, grinning. "She won't mind at all. She'll just be jealous she didn't get to be in on the hijinks. But I should probably get naked when I see her. Just to be on the safe side."

"Be that as it may," Keene said. "Take a look at that."

Following his line of attention, Vrick expanded the particular pane. In it, a squarely massive ship moved into position over a dense cluster of large asteroid fragments. Studded across its hull were the dull metal shapes of small auxiliary craft that suddenly burst free on the deep yellow-orange glow of their thruster fields.

"The carrier moves the individual drillers into position over the particular section of the debris field being targeted," Anyeis said. "There's twenty-four in all on each carrier, with a crew of six on each individual driller.

"Before they even head out, the strategic planner's office has reviewed the data from the probes and the survey teams, as well as the requirements of the client, to determine where that shift's work should be focused."

"Are they still mapping and surveying at this point?" Ember asked, listening carefully to Anyeis' recitation and storing the information away.

"Most of it was done early on," she said. "They did an extensive survey once when they initially identified the remains of the planet as an exploitable resource. Every fragment was tagged, and the information uploaded to the grav generators that were used to herd the asteroids together and are now holding them in place. They know where all the various deposits are concentrated and in what amounts. They get updates on the Gate Project continuously as the dirtside team breaks down more of the planet, so they know where to focus their attention."

"And the drillers drop down to their target areas to begin the actual mining process."

Anyeis nodded. "They do the grunt work, each crew responsible for their own particular patch."

As they watched, the smaller vessels descended on a particularly large asteroid, the largest in the vicinity, that dwarfed even the massive mining ship by a factor of twenty. Like a swarm of predatory insects attacking flesh, the drillers landed, their drive fields fading away as they settled. On some, a harder, brighter light flared as they went to work.

"Why are only some of them lit up like that?" Lexa-Blue asked.

"Depends on what they're digging for," Vrick said. "The bright ones are using plasma torches. They would just be extracting stone or metals. The precision of the torch allows them to extract larger, intact chunks."

"If they used that on the volatiles, the whole rock would explode," Keene said. "Which would be bad."

"Wouldn't it be easier to smash it now and just cart away the rubble?" she asked.

"Not everything is better with an explosion," Keene said.

"Says you."

"Volatiles are of no use if they've been blown up," Vrick said in es 'you poor stupid meat brain' voice. "And the metals and stone need to be extracted without a big boom so they maintain their structural integrity for later use."

"Boom bad," Lexa-Blue said. "Got it."

"They'll likely be using some form of vibro drill to access the volatiles so they can suck them out and tank them without igniting them," Keene said.

"Yes, that was my guess," Vrick said. "I'm detecting the vibrational energy on my long-range displacement sensors."

"That is one slick operation," Lexa-Blue said.

"It is, indeed," Vrick said, as es visual sensors zeroed in on the armada of vessels methodically breaking down the surface of the asteroid.

"What happens next?" Ember asked.

"The main carrier stays in position above the fragment that the crew is working on, in a basically synchronous orbit calculated to keep it in optimal range of the drillers," Anyeis said. "Each driller has twinned grab fields with a specific hold on the carrier. As they release their cargo from the surface it gets carried up to the hold by the field."

"And it's measured somehow during this process," Ember said.

Anyeis nodded. "It's measured by both the drillers and the carrier itself to ensure accuracy. Each driller has a team lead on board to monitor the process and make sure the readings stay within a very tight margin of error. There's an LI doing the initial assay and sort as well."

"Makes sense," Ember said, pensively. "So, it's unlikely that anything is happening at that point in the process."

"It's unlikely it's happening anywhere in the process," Anyeis said. "But it's still happening. I'd stake my reputation on it."

"Oh, I believe it's happening," Ember said. "It's too good a scam to let slip by. If I were in the right position and had the right lack of decency, I'd have seized the chance as well. The question is, how are they pulling it off?"

"I don't see how it could be at this stage of the game," Anyeis said. "On my crew, I'm that team lead who monitors the lading of each driller team's output. That's how I know what my crews are managing to pull out of the rocks every shift. And I know that their output is not matching what they're being paid for."

"Okay," Ember said. "It's all counted as it's pulled out of the fragment. What happens next?"

Their trajectory pulled them further in towards Fury itself, along with its tiny companion, leaving the mining crew behind as they angled deeper into the system. In the mass of sensor data, Vrick recognized something that caused em to angle es course slightly to get a closer look.

Beyond lay a different sector of the corralled debris field, where another crew was finishing their shift. As they watched, this massive fleet of drillers lifted almost as one from the surfaces of their respective asteroids.

"It looks almost like the asteroids are flying apart at the seams," Keene said.

The drillers rose into darkness above the harsh rocky surfaces of the asteroids, into the strange, eerie glow of the tethered fields holding the belt together into the optimal position for the complex mining operation. In a precise ballet, the various tools and torches retracted into the drillers' shells, leaving them smooth ovoids homing in on their base ships.

Vrick adjusted es course and speed to keep the spectacle in view as long as possible, fascinated by the sophistication of the interplay of the fleet of drillers and the mothership. As the drillers settled into their docking creches on the hull of the massive ship, they watched as the larger craft powered up its drive field and adjusted course, setting off in the direction of Sound just as Vrick was doing.

"So, that's what the beginning and end of shift look like for the actual mining crews," Lexa-Blue said.

"And now, it's on to the Assay Station where the company gets to confirm the totals and begin sorting and deciding what gets shipped where."

"And I assume you're going to get us a look at the place," Lexa-Blue said.

"Do you even have to ask, meat?" Vrick said.

They followed the heavily laden mothership in, as the Assay Station grew from a pinpoint of light to an artificial satellite that dwarfed even the new wormhole Gates that the entire mining project had been designed to service. As it filled the main viewport, it resolved into a massive cylinder dotted with docking facilities for the ore-laden base ships coming into it. Each of the heavy ships looked, in relation to the station, no larger than the drillers did to them.

As they watched, the base ship they had followed in glided gracefully into its docking berth, sliding home with ease as docking clamps larger than even than the Maverick Heart's entire hull slid into place to hold the ship fast.

"Is there any way we can get a look inside that thing?" Keene asked.

"Why do you always doubt me?" Vrick said, adjusting es sensor suite to maximum gain and penetration while accessing the schematics from the original construction.

As the data flooded into em, ey could see the differences between what was on file and what es senses told em. Ey brought up the collated data in yet another pane against the main viewport.

"There. There are a lot of discrepancies between the original plans and what seems to be there now, but I wouldn't say anything is conclusive. There are any number of reasons why the interior layout could have changed, from necessary upgrades to more efficient use of resources and space. I'd have to get a closer look to be sure."

Lexa-Blue let out a disgruntled sound. "Why isn't it ever easy? Can you run some probability simulations to get some idea of what might be going on inside there in terms of hinky activity?"

"Already running, but without some more solid information, I'm flying blind."

"Well, keep at it," Keene said. "I know Ember will get us some more solid information as soon as he can. And he'll be able to put this all together in ways we would never even have considered."

"Oh, he's already hard at it," Vrick said. "And I'm linked to him, so I'm getting the information as he does."

"That's it," Ember said. "Somewhere in that station, our mystery person has some kind of way of getting the payload out of the general flow and into those rogue transports for private sale. It's the only place it could be happening."

Anyeis rolled her eyes and looked at Malika. "This is who you had up your sleeve?" She looked back at Ember with a look of pained disgust on her face. "I've reached this conclusion myself, genius. It has to be from here. But the question is how? That station is thousands of square kilometres of machinery and automated systems, overseen at every step of the process. It must be happening there. But it can't be happening there. So, tell me something I don't know. Like how they're doing it."

Malika rested a hand on Anyeis's arm. "Hey, go easy. He's just trying to help."

"It's okay," Ember said. "I understand your frustration, Anyeis. I really do. You see the world in terms of numbers and systems and processes. And that's good. You would never have realized this was happening if you didn't see the world the way you do. But that same mindset is keeping you from parsing out the how. That's what you have me for. And this is just my process. I have to identify the obvious before I can start picking it apart and finding my way in. All I ask is that you bear with me, okay?"

Anyeis looked uneasy, but at her side, Malika beamed.

"And yes, you're right," Ember continued. "On the surface, it looks like a perfect system with no ways to hijack it. But, let me tell you, the more complex a system is, the more it can be exploited. And the more automated it is, the more ways in there are.

"And for every advance in security, there's a way around it someone hasn't found yet. And there's always a slicer somewhere working on a way to get past it, just for fun. Which may be what we're up against here. And figuring out the how will help tell us the who. So, please, be patient. This is how I work. And I will figure this out, one way or another."

Anyeis peered at him, her gaze hard a moment before softening. A quick nod was all the acknowledgement she gave.

"Okay, take me through what happens when a ship docks after a shift. As thorough as you can be."

Anyeis's face tightened in concentration as she thought her way through the process. "Once the ship docks with the Assay Station and positive seal is confirmed, the holds open to the unloading and sorting system. The ships themselves do a rudimentary sort, but mostly, it's all just dumped into the holds so that the ship can get back out into the field as quickly as possible. All the real sorting and identification is done on station, with each load of ore being valued and credited to the members of the team on the ship for the proper assessment of bonuses."

Ember nodded, concentrating on the details of what she was saying. "Go on."

"The main docking level has a massive sorting system, which passes the ship's load through a series of molecular sensors that identify the contents and divide them so they can be passed on to the appropriate next level. Ores and metals are separated and sent to one level for aggregation into lots for transport. Volatiles to another, water ices and atmospherics to another for use by the company itself. The volatiles are handled a lot more carefully than anything else."

"Does everything get sorted for use?" Ember asked, already fairly sure of the answer, but wanting evidence and facts rather than supposition.

"No," Anyeis said, shaking her head. "Not everything is useful or valuable enough to justify the expense of sorting and transporting it. As the valuable stuff is broken down and passed on, the dross gets sifted out and either sold off on the cheap to scrap dealers or sent on a long, slow trajectory into the sun. The whole process is measured and monitored at every point. Waste is weighed against usable, valuable material. A really good crew can pull the worthwhile material with as little slag as possible, and it streamlines the process. A lot.

"Once everything has been sorted, valued, and aggregated, it's passed to the outbound transport hub at the other end of the station where it's loaded and sent off to wherever it's been sold. Which, these days, is pretty much always one of the Gate construction sites."

Ember nodded slowly, digesting the information, picking at it, trying to think like their mysterious embezzler. What he'd told Anyeis earlier held true in the face of the information she had provided him. Depending on the actual systems in play, he could see several possible points where a determined individual could break into the system and manipulate it for their own benefit. The trick was finding out which they had used. Well, that and figuring out who it was.

And after that, bringing them down. Which was always the fun part.

Vrick descended into the thin shell of Sound's atmosphere, feeling the heat skating across es lower hull as the ablative field channelled it away and kept them from burning up. Below, racing toward them, the surface was all ochre and brown, the hues smearing together across the dry surface.

The sky they descended from was clear and cloudless, heat haze rippling into the distance in all directions as ey angled toward the assigned berth in the warren of the spaceport outside the dome of the city.

"What do they need a port that size for?" Lexa-Blue said. "With all of the sorting done up in orbit, there shouldn't be that much need for ships to land here on the planet itself."

"The Assay Station handles the sorting and transport of raw materials," Vrick said. "But that's literally all it does. Anyone who stays on-planet has to stay down here somewhere. Plus, some of the materials that get mined have to be processed before they can be shipped anywhere, so there are all sorts of processing facilities here as well. Not to mention all the suits and administrators and miners and wheeler-dealers who need accommodations and office space and meeting rooms, et cetera."

"That explains it, then," Lexa-Blue said. "They must be tripping all over each other in that dome."

"The population density is definitely on the higher end," Vrick said.

"Do you figure that makes it easier or harder for us to accomplish what we need to?" Keene asked.

"I'd leave that to Ember to decide," Vrick said. "Though I have faith he can come up with a creative solution no matter what."

"Oh, no doubt about that," Keene said with a laugh. "The things that boy has managed to pull off."

"Just as long as he doesn't get us all killed," Lexa-Blue said. "Especially me."

"Thanks for the solidarity, old friend," Keene said.

"I'm not worried," Vrick said. "If anything happens to you, I can just take off and find some new fresh meats to take up space."

"So much love I'm feeling right now," Keene said.

"Hey, it's every being for themself," Lexa-Blue said with a playful grin.

"What happened to all for one and one for all?" Keene said in mock disbelief. "After all we've been through together."

"Oh, sure," she said. "You think that nine years of saving your ass means I feel some kind of loyalty to you?"

"Perish the thought," Keene said, laughing.

"As long as you two don't get me shot up again, I'm good," Vrick said. As ey spoke, ey felt the local comm grid signalling for attention, and ey opened the channel.

Hey, Vrick, Ember said.

Excellent timing, Vrick said. *We just landed.*

I know. Your other self just told me.

I'll need to have a talk with em about prying.

Ey felt Ember's laughter through the comm link. *This whole caper is based on prying. It's kind of necessary.*

Yes, but that's them, not us, Vrick said with a laugh of es own. *Where are we meeting you?*

Malika got me a room with her theatre company, but it's not even big enough for a decent threesome, let alone the bunch of us planning a takedown. Can you arrange for something?

Can do, Vrick said, accessing the local rentals as ey sent the message. It took only a second or two to review the list of meeting spaces for rent and weigh them against a set of specific criteria that ey and Ember had worked out in advance for situations like this. Just in case. *Done,* ey said, flashing the address to Ember.

You're the best, Ember said. *I've got a few ideas for our first steps, but I'm going to need a few more things before we can proceed. Can you and the others pull them together for me?*

Need you ask? Give me the list and if I don't have access to any of the items, I'll send the others to pick them up on their way to meet you.

Ember sent the list and Vrick flashed through it, checking it against stores, divvying it up in the space of a thought. *Done. Keene has already built a few of these and I have almost everything else ready to go. They'll pick up the rest on the way to you.*

Ember flashed a sharp, earthy green of acknowledgement and signed off.

"Heads up, you two," Vrick said. "You have some shopping to do."

As soon as Ember signed off, he began to gather his things, collapsing the panes of information he had gathered and storing them back in his innernet. He repacked his clothes, for the space Vrick had rented was the top floor of a hotel known for its discretion. They'd be able to plan and run their operation from the main room in the centre of the floor, while using the rooms around it for eating and sleeping as the need arose.

Lastly, he repacked the pack of goodies Keene had packed for him, arranging them carefully so that everything he thought he would need for the initial incursion was readily at hand, and then seating Vrick's proxy securely in one of the side slots. He hefted the two bags and left the room.

As he waited for the lift, he reached out for Malika's node and found it in Do Not Disturb, which made sense when he checked the time, as she was on stage in a matinee at the moment. He left her a message that she'd receive as soon as she came back online with the coordinates of the hotel.

The others have landed and they've set up a home base for us. He added the address and suite number. ***Join us when you're ready.***

There was a delicious aroma in the kitchen as he stepped off the lift, and it made his stomach rumble in anticipation. He saw Valile at the coffee machine, pouring a cup. From the distracted look of concentration on his face, Ember assumed that several of the panes of information he had seen in Valile's office had followed him out, projected on his scleral displays.

Ember activated the translator program and pinged to get Valile's attention.

"Okay, I need to know what that is," he said, coming up beside him. Valile set his cup down so he could sign.

"I have no idea," Valile signed, his bearded face widening into a grin. "I just know that everyone looks forward to the day the chef decides to make it."

"I can see why," Ember said, grinning.

"Have some," Valile signed. "We can't send you off hungry."

"As long as you tell me what that is. And let me taste it. And give me the recipe."

Valile laughed. "Help yourself. And I'll see what I can do about the recipe. Let me show you the best way to have it."

Between signing, Valile handed him a bowl and pointed out what he assured Ember was the proper sequence of ingredients.

Following the strict instructions, Ember took a bowl, ladling it first with a fine rice or pasta, then generous ladles of a thick, golden stew, and then a dollop of a pungently fragrant, bright green condiment. It smelled like Ember imagined heaven would, if he believed in heaven: sweet and spicy, demanding that he taste it.

He tasted it and his eyes rolled back in delight. "This is incredible."

Valile beamed at his assessment, his round, dimpled face rosy with happiness. He took a seat beside Ember, obviously savouring Ember's enjoyment.

"Leaving us so soon?" Valile signed, indicating Ember's bags. "We didn't scare you away, did we?"

"Oh, no," Ember said. "Meeting up with some friends. Malika has given us some homework."

"Ah," Valile signed, knowingly, as if Malika's name had unlocked a perfect understanding of his character and history.

"What did she do?" Ember said.

Valile laughed again. "Nothing like that at all. She's lovely. Cheeky for sure. But lovely."

Ember couldn't respond right at the moment, for his mouth was full of the delicious stew, so he just nodded. As soon as he'd taken his first bite, he'd realized how hungry he was and had kept on eating. *I'm definitely in preparation mode,* he thought. Swallowing his mouthful, he offered his hand. "Thank you for everything."

"Well, it's been great having you with us," Valile signed. "I hope you'll come back and join us once you've done your homework."

"I think I just might," Ember said.

"Glad to hear it," Valile signed. Seeing Ember's bowl was almost empty, Valile handed him a plate stacked with rounds of dense, thin flatbread.

Ember picked one off the top and tore a chunk from it, using the ragged piece to sop up every last drop of the sauce in the bottom of the bowl.

"Malika must be pretty important to you. To bring you all the way out here," Valile signed. "Surely there are better places to have a vacation?"

Sated by his meal, Ember felt a warm ease come over him, lulling him to trust this warm, friendly dumpling of a man. "We haven't spoken in a long time. Some bad things happened, and she needed to get away."

"From *you*," Valile signed.

"From everything," Ember said, stung by the truth in Valile's words.

Valile nodded knowingly.

"The time we had spent together before that was… intense," Ember said. "Especially at the end. I don't blame her for needing a break."

"But it wasn't the end, was it?" Valile signed. "Because here you are."

"She needed me," Ember said.

"Ah, got herself into a fix," Valile signed, and for a moment, Ember thought he must have known something about what was going on. But when he searched Valile's face, there was only that same sweet friendliness he had seen before. It was not the face of a man who was aware of an embezzlement scandal and impending takedown.

With the lunch warm in his stomach, he let himself feel content and satisfied in the presence of this kindly stranger, who, honestly, already didn't feel like a stranger at all. Somehow, Valile's presence reminded him of Seije, though his warmth was the polar opposite of the older man. Seije had always been off in his own little world, where he had designed and built the tech that Ember and Malika had relied on during their adventures, as well as the items that he had sold on the open market.

But he had always been there in the quiet times before the missions happened, and when he had come home after. And while Keene was, in his way, almost as smart, the energy on the Maverick Heart was something completely different, something spikier and more chaotic in its wavelength. Even the type of adventures had changed. Gone were the days of intricate cons played out against the rich and selfish. Now, they often just did good for the sake of it. Because they kept finding themselves in situations where they were the only ones who could.

All of this complex emotion must have played across his face, for Valile tutted suddenly and patted the back of his hand. "Such a face you made there. It can't be as bad as all that."

Ember couldn't help but smile at his perception and good humour and found himself wondering what Valile would say if he knew about the adventure Ember and the others were about to embark on.

He'd probably pack us a lunch and send us off with a cookie.

"It definitely isn't," Ember said. "At least not for me. But somebody else is about to have a very bad day."

Before Valile could question him any further, he stood, dropping his napkin beside the empty bowl. "I have to be off. Thank you for the lunch suggestions and the company."

"My pleasure," Valile signed, and Ember knew that he truly meant it. "Good luck with whatever mischief you have planned."

Something in his tone of voice made Ember narrow his eyes, certain that the burly teddy bear knew something more than he was letting on about Ember's purpose here. But the beatific sweetness of his dimpled smile chased the thought away.

On the street, he hailed a rickshaw and strapped his gear into the flimsy-looking rack behind the seat, checking the frayed cross straps twice. The last thing he needed was for everything to come tumbling off in traffic. Visions of his gear and clothes trailing out like a plume in the breeze made him check them one more time, not that it was all that reassuring.

He climbed into the passenger compartment, and the rickshaw veered out into traffic flow, sending him hard into the seat with its jagged zag of motion. He was able to brace himself against the sideswipes of motion by wedging his hands into the upper corners of the canopy. But even that seemed only to be a token effort, even though he felt the plastics yielding under his prosthetic fingers. Between the speed and the flow of air, he couldn't help but roar with laughter even though the sound was whipped away by the wind.

While he had grown to love his life on the Maverick Heart, being here on this planet, casing for a heist, was something different, something familiar and exciting and nostalgic for a time that had seemed lost forever. Especially in the aftermath of his injury and recovery.

This rush of energy and air and sound was the perfect metaphor for the unpredictable nature of his and Malika's former life and illicit career.

As the actual caper came closer, he knew this feeling would increase, would key him up to a perfectly balanced state of preparedness and excitement. It might be the last time he pulled a gig like this, and he planned to make the most of it.

And, he had to admit, he was excited to see Keene again. Ember had missed him more than he thought he would for such a relatively short time. He had held close to Keene's stability and solidarity as he endured the long, painful slog back to full function, and the time he'd spent at his new normal had seemed so short once he had left the safety and comfort of his new chosen family.

Everything about this trip had been a wildly swinging orbit between the gravity wells of his present and former lives. Seeing Malika again had tilted the orbits out of kilter, sending him on an all-new trajectory.

At the same time, he worried he would be drawn back into his old life again, stressing his relationships with Keene, Lexa-Blue, and Vrick. The escapade with Gliosto back on Hub had strained his place in the crew, despite the fact that they had agreed with the motivations that had spurred him into action. There was a fine line between his former career and the adventures the crew often found themselves involved in, but that line was definitely there. And he had known exactly when he had crossed it.

And here he was about to cross it again.

The suite that Vrick had rented to be their base of operations was in a hotel complex on the edge of the section of the port for non-company travellers. Ember knew from the information that Vrick had 'pushed to his node that the complex offered the utmost in security and privacy, no questions asked. There were complexes like this in all corporate-run colonies and communities. It would have been all too easy in this day and age to spy on any and all types of transactions and negotiations. Galactum statutes demanded that this type of bondable, secure, private facility was available at all times. It was a principle that Ember planned to take full advantage of.

The lobby was all tasteful elegance, every detail designed to placate the concerns of the powerful, to ensure that guests felt cossetted and cared for. Everything was soft, rounded edges, luxurious finishings and tastefully dim lighting, none of which mattered to Ember. He was too busy reviewing the security stats and protocols offered and already in place for their meetings.

They were booked into a penthouse suite at the building's apex, serviced by private personal and freight elevators. They should be able to come and go without attracting any undue attention.

Vrick had already sent the room's codes to his node, so he headed straight through the lavish lobby area to a lift and went up. Reading his access, the lift took him directly to the top floor, equally prepared to bar anyone who didn't have access.

He paused only a moment at the door to the suite, savouring the anticipation of seeing the others again, then stepped forward, his motion keying the doors open.

He registered Keene and Lexa-Blue standing at a meeting table in the centre of the room, seemingly reviewing the constellation of data he had passed to them to meld with their own. As soon as his eyes lit on Keene, he had dropped his bags and was moving, already opening his arms.

Keene's actions mirrored his own, and they met in a fiercely tight embrace, pulling apart only to allow space for their lips to meet. Ember kissed Keene thoroughly, his lips met with equal intensity, Ember surprising himself with the sudden flare of emotion. As the kiss eased, he stepped back slightly, his cheeks reddening at his unguarded actions.

"Hey, you," Keene said, his hands on Ember's shoulders as if to keep him from escaping in his sudden chagrin.

"Hey," Ember said, grinning.

"Oh, crikes, you two," Lexa-Blue said, coming toward them. "Don't go getting all mushy on me. I might not be able to stand it."

She shouldered past Keene and embraced Ember herself, actually lifting him off the floor despite being roughly the same size. "Looking good, squib. Ready to wreak some havoc?"

Ember laughed and the sound flowed up from his toes. "Oh, you have no idea."

Beyond the others, he saw a holo construct that he immediately recognized as the corporate building he had so carefully cased the day before. As he watched, paths of light in various colours and shades coursed through the building's image, as different floors and parts of the interior structure flickered in and out of transparency.

"I see you got started without me," Ember said.

Keene and Lexa-Blue followed him to the holo and took up positions at his sides. "Vrick took your data and ran with it. Ey's been running simulations, based on your previous adventures and any we've been involved in since," Keene said.

Just waiting for the expert to arrive, Vrick said. ***I figured I'd give you some options and see if I could come up with anything to help out.***

"I'll take all the help I can get," Ember said. "This one is busting my brain. I know that we're looking for someone inside, but the records that Anyeis has access to show no evidence of the theft, or of the tampering itself."

And I've tried to slice my way in, but they've got anti-incursion code like I've never seen before. Any time I try to get through, it hits back with a recursive code tunnel loop. I've tried everything I have access to and have even gone digging through Know-It-All, but I can't find anything that will get me through.

"I was afraid of that," Ember said. "Everything I've learned about this corp has led me to believe that they're security-conscious on a level I've never seen before."

"Well, it makes sense," Lexa-Blue said. "This is easily the most profitable mining operation in the Galactum right now. Sindel says the Gate construction projects are eating up material like nothing ever has before. Every company that's had even the slightest interest in mining is involved on some level. There's a lot of profit to be had in this, and the board of the corp that controls this Consortium wants to keep their tight hold over it. They'll do whatever they can to stay on top of it."

"But if their security is so tight, how is our thief making off with so much?" Ember said.

"Well, if our thief is so good that no one even knows the credits are missing, then the higher-ups might not even know either," Lexa-Blue said. "And even if they did, they might not even care since the money is coming out of the bonuses paid to the workers themselves and not from a line item they think is actually significant. As long as it's not impacting the directors and execs personally, they may not even care at all."

Ember made a sound of disgust. "And people wonder why I had no problems stealing from rich people."

"Ah, the good old days."

They turned to see Malika entering the suite and taking a good look around. "Nice digs," she said.

Keene went to her first, arms wide, and hugged her tightly. "I'm so glad to see you."

She held him just as close, and her voice was muffled in the crook of his shoulder. "It's good to see you too. Thanks so much for agreeing to help."

She released Keene and stepped back, peering cautiously around him at Lexa-Blue.

Ember could see the wariness in her eyes. He remembered how often the two women had clashed back during the adventure where they had all met. The last thing they needed this time around was the crash and clatter of two overly strong personalities. The job was going to be hard enough as it is.

But there was no reason to worry. Lexa-Blue merely tapped two fingers to her temple in a salute and grinned, the smile open and genuine. "Looking good, my friend. We're glad to help. But I expect some tickets out of this when we're done."

Malika's face relaxed into a grin that matched Lexa-Blue's and Ember felt relief flood through him. "That, I can do."

She joined them at the holo, recognizing it instantly. "Any progress?"

Ember shook his head. "Sadly, no. Despite everything we've simmed, we can't figure out how to get in. All their counter-intrusion measures are just too strong."

Malika looked thoughtful a moment, her brows knotted into a frown. After a moment or two, they could see a thought forming. "What about trying to slice them from inside? Get in the door and access their systems from behind their walls?"

Again, Ember shook his head. "To get in, we'd have to have rock-solid credentials. And if we can't get into their system, we can't implant the false IDs we need to even get past the front door."

"That's what I mean," Malika said. "What if we get inside from the inside?"

"How do we manage that?" Keene said.

"Anyeis can help."

"I don't want to get her in any trouble," Ember said. "This is her job on the line. Does she even work inside that complex?"

"No, but she doesn't need to," Malika said. "She has an office on the shuttle that takes her and her crew out to the rocks."

"But how does that help us?" Lexa-Blue asked.

"I'm brainstorming here, but Vrick, do you need high-level access to their system to program those ID inoculations to get us in?"

No, I could manage it with even access to the maintenance bots. It's just a matter of getting past that outer layer of defence.

"And that's it. She has access to a big chunk of the system because she's a crew chief. Not the highest levels, but more than enough to get you in. We can use her access to get in, then you have whatever you need to go digging through the records from within to find our thief."

"I still don't like dragging her into this," Ember said.

"I know she acts all stoic and tough," Malika said. "But this is eating at her and she wants to help in whatever way she can. I promise you."

It will be tight, though, Vrick said. ***Even if she gets us access, I'm betting that there's a bunch of levels of code on the other side too.***

Malika grinned. "Come on, Vrick. I'm betting you can get through."

Oh, you are still a smooth talker, I see.

"I speak only the truth."

Ember thought on it, finally feeling the wheels turn. "I think I might have an idea or two."

They spent the next half-hour taking inventory of what they had on hand, including the supplies that Keene and Lexa-Blue had picked up based on their initial plan of attack. They were pretty well set up, though there were a few things that they still might need. While they worked, Vrick assembled their cover identities and programmed them to the ID inoculations.

As they were finalizing the list, the suite's security system chimed with a request for entry. Out of habit, Lexa-Blue's hand moved to the gun at her hip. But when the system presented them with a holo of their guest, it was clear there was no threat.

"Relax, it's Anyeis," Malika said. "Please don't shoot my girlfriend. She's on our side."

"More like we're on hers," Ember said, as the door slid open to admit her.

Malika made introductions, but they seemed to do little to relax Anyeis, who stood almost at attention in her rigidity, her expression stony with wariness. Not even learning that one of the team was a sentient space vessel seemed to make a dent in her impassive expression.

Malika stood at her side, taking her hand and holding it tightly. "It's okay. They're here to help."

"It's true," Keene said. "We just want to help you make this right."

Anyeis seemed to relax a little, and the corners of her mouth rose slightly. "I'm sorry. This is all out of my zone. I just want my people treated properly."

"That's what we all want as well. We just want to make this right," Ember said. "But to do that, we have to break a few rules."

He paused a moment. "And we're going to need your help."

Anyeis took a deep breath, hesitating as if she realized the line she was about to step across, but then her shoulders set with determination. "What do I need to do?"

"That's my girl," Malika said, pulling Anyeis closer.

She looked at Ember. "So, what's the plan?"

"Okay," Ember said. "The big problem is that we need to access the company's records to find evidence of the embezzlement."

"But I looked through the records myself," Anyeis said.

Ember showed no impatience at the interruption. "Whoever is behind this covered their tracks incredibly well, that's certain. What we're looking for is going to be buried in the code. Even the best cover-up is going to leave traces if you look deep enough."

"Which is where I come in," Vrick said aloud through the suite's terminal interface, since Anyeis didn't have an implanted node like the others. "If I can get access to the doctored records, I should be able to peel back the layers enough to find the data trail we need."

"Exactly," Ember said. "The first hurdle is that the system is so ether-locked that there's no way to get at the records from outside the system. We need to get someone inside the building and onto one of their access points. Then Vrick can do es thing and dig through the code to find out where those credits really went.

"Which leads us to our second problem: since we can't access their system, we can't implant the credentials we need to get through the door. Any credentials we could create from outside would stand up to scrutiny but wouldn't get us enough access to go digging. We'd be outsiders."

"So, we need a way to get some kind of system access to get them to believe we actually belong there," Lexa-Blue said.

"Which is where you come in," Ember said to Anyeis.

"You need my codes to access the system," she said.

"Yes and no," Ember said. "If you just use your own codes, then they'll know right off the bat that it's you and that puts you and Malika in danger again. This is all going to be dangerous as it is. Whoever is behind this has already threatened Malika once. And shown that they have the means to get to her if they want to. I want to minimize the risk as much as possible. Or at least keep it on us. We're better equipped to deal with it.

"Rather than us piggybacking on your access, we get you to implant a backdoor patch. All you do is put it in place. You don't even have to be using the system to do it. It will open a backdoor for us to add the fake IDs that we need. We go in and can access the onsite financial records in the crystal backup lattices with some deeper infiltration tools. Once

Vrick has access to that, ey should be able to see what's really going on and find what we need."

"That's a lot of *should*'s and *maybe*'s," Anyeis said.

"It is," Ember said. "But that's the job. This isn't an exact science. But the information we want is in there. No matter how good they are, for an operation this complex, there's always some trace left behind. And we will find it."

Anyeis looked thoughtful a moment, then nodded. "I'm in. Just let me know what I have to do."

"Keene?" Ember said. "You're up."

Keene picked up a small aerosol bulb from the pile of equipment on the table in front of them and held it up.

"This is the latest iteration of some tech we've been using for a while now. I cooked it up pretty recently and haven't had a chance to use it in the field yet. It's nanosome slicer code. In a spray," he said. "You can either spray it right onto a hard backup interface, or onto your hand and transfer it that way if you can't get the bulb close to your target. The nanos work like a fink, accessing the system right there through some double-blind security scramblers, opening a backdoor for us. They won't work long, so the timing has to be right, but they'll let us set up some information to back up our cover identities and get us through the door. It will also reinforce the link we set up once we're through the doors."

"Spy perfume," Malika said, laughing. "I love it."

"I have an office set up on our mining ship," Anyeis said. "I can upload it there."

"Is it safe?" Malika asked. "Will there be anyone else around?"

"It's not unusual for me to be there at odd hours," Anyeis said. "I'm often around working on rotas or excavation plans. No one will think anything of it if they see me there."

"And you're sure no one will know it's her?" Malika asked. "I don't want this coming back to her."

"No," Keene said. "It's self-cleaning. It will close the path and scrub any traces. And since it's such a small window, it's pretty much invisible. Once the fake credentials are in, we have about twenty minutes before they fade out. And someone would have to do an even deeper dive than we're about to in order to find any trace of them."

"And that twenty minutes should be more than enough for me to get in and do the deeper implant that we need to comb through the records," Vrick said.

"Then, let's do it," Anyeis said.

"And we are a go," Lexa-Blue said with a grin.

CHAPTER NINE

The final pieces of their plan arrived just as Anyeis was leaving them to head across the city to her ship to fulfil her part in the plan.

The suite signalled that the packages were arriving at the rooftop depot and requested their confirmation before the complex's LI allowed the delivery bots to land and transfer the flat, rectangular packages to the internal conduit system.

It took only a minute or two before the packages arrived, chirruping their arrival at the suite's access point.

Ember hit the access pad and the conduit irised open to show the four identically sized and shaped packages, neatly arranged in the alcove in the living area's wall. He pulled them from the opening and carried them to the others.

"One for you," Ember said, reading the code string on the end of the box and handing it to Keene. "One each for you two. And one for me. New job, new drag."

"Oooh, is it pretty?" Lexa-Blue said, pitching her voice higher. "I haven't had anything pretty to wear in such a long time."

"How about some new corpo drag?" Ember said.

"That'll do," she answered. "Even if I'm just the driver."

"Driver drag is very specific, these days," Ember said. "You even get a hat."

"Oooh," she said. "I can totally pull off a hat."

"When you're not pulling off your clothes," Keene said.

She cuffed him in the arm.

"Oh, I *have* missed this," Malika said, already pulling her new outfit out of the box. She ran her hands over the matte black armourweave of the suit as if it were the finest shimmersilk gown.

"Not like a costume fitting for a role, is it?" Ember said, smiling at the enthusiasm in her voice that he hadn't heard in so long.

"Oh, it is," she said, with a grin. "But some roles are a lot more fun and fulfilling than others."

"Like when there's danger of death or imprisonment?" Keene said.

"Well, that, and sticking it hard and deep to a dungsludge that steals from people who are just trying to make a living," Malika said.

"And who upsets your girlfriend," Lexa-Blue said.

Malika looked at Lexa-Blue and, in a flush of unexpected fellowship, smiled. "And who upsets my girlfriend. Exactly."

"Good enough reasons for me too," Lexa-Blue said, peeling off her shipsuit to get changed.

Once they had all changed, they presented themselves to ensure that all was in order for the work about to come.

"Oooh, don't you all look pretty!" Vrick said.

Lexa-Blue was indeed in full chauffeur's livery, a sleek, form-fitting two-piece suit in a blue so dark it was almost black, but with flashes of a shiny, reflective red on the shoulders like epaulettes. Her hair was parted slickly on one side, and a contact lens and a bit of skillful makeup hid her sensor eye and scar. She pulled on the lapel of the jacket to inspect the company crest on it. "And does this check out if anyone goes digging?"

"Definitely," Vrick said. "Slicing them was easy. You've got a full, cross-referenced work history that will stand up to anything short of a personal interview with your supposed bosses."

"Does that go for us too?" Keene said. He and Malika wore matching armourweave, one-piece bodyguard suits, high-necked and as black as the starless sky. Mirrored tactical visors finished the look.

"Very dashing," Vrick said. "If I had a body and an interest in biological urges, I'd be all over you both in a lustful and penetrative way."

Keene and Malika exchanged a look. "Thank you?" he said.

"Don't you listen to him, Vrick," Malika said with a slight curtsy. "The boy just doesn't know how to take a compliment. You are most kind."

To cover the sudden awkward flush of colour to his cheeks, Keene reached up and touched his mirrored visor to adjust it. "Are these dummies, or are they the real deal?"

"Well, considering the number of times that things go hoots-up for us, I spent the extra money and got full working models. Manual Release, or Emergency Auto."

Keene reached up and touched a tiny stud on the edge of the frame, and in the blink of an eye, the shielded helmet expanded with just a whispered breath of air to cover his whole head. "Swank," he said, his now artificially modulated voice impressed. "And, considering our track record, yes, a wise investment."

Surveying them with a practiced eye, Ember was the last in line. His silver hair was hidden behind a hair mask, now a luxurious auburn brown. His own suit was ostentatious and obviously expensive, cut from ripplecloth in a moire pattern that danced with an understated light. The jacket fit his torso perfectly, with just the right amount of flow to accentuate the patterns of light playing across the fabric. The skirt shaped to an angle in the centre, just sharp enough to connote his status as a potential investor with means. Under the skirt, his leggings matched the rich, leafy forest green of his shirt. Around his neck was a shimmering medallion cut and carved and moulded to look exactly like a necktie.

As he looked them over, his whole manner changed, taking on an aristocratic mien that changed his stance, his look, and his carriage entirely. Anyone who hadn't seen the transformation would have been hard-pressed to identify him as the same man.

Which was exactly the point.

Despite the assurances of the others that it was impossible, Anyeis could swear she felt the nanosomes crawling over the skin of her palm. She fought down the urge to scratch again with the blunted nails of her other hand, positive that someone would be able to tell what she was doing, would see through her.

Yash it, how do the others do this? she thought. *I'm a wreck and they do this all the time.*

She straightened her shoulders, determined to shake off the skitter of tension in her stomach, trying to look as natural as she always did when coming to her office. As it was, she still felt the damp tickle of sweat under her arms, positive that she would be caught out.

The west staff gate recognized her and let her through, into the vast, domed flat of the shipyards beyond. Before her, ranks of utilitarian vessels in long, wide rows fanned out into the distance. The familiar sight of the ships calmed her. This was her world, her life. This was her gateway to the asteroids and the ore and the profit. This was the home of her ship and her crew, the place where they came together in their unified purpose.

The sun glinted off the paint and exposed metal of the ship's hulls, highlighting the fiercely individual colour schemes and designs on the otherwise identical ships. When she had first begun working on mining crews, with no training or experience, the lack of uniformity among the ships had irked her, offending her carefully tended sense of order and discipline. The brazen, gaudy colours had almost hurt her eyes with the vivid individuality they betrayed.

She hadn't even been out of her teens then, assigned to scut work on the *Scarlet Sun* as soon as her recruitment datawork had been confirmed, as she hadn't known how to do anything else. Hadn't even known how to do those grindingly menial tasks, if she was honest with herself. But that first crew had been a good one, and they'd taken her in, given her purpose when everything else had gone wrong.

And that purpose and sense of place and belonging had pushed her to learn, to fit in with that crew all those years ago and so many light-years away. But she had learned. Oh, how she had learned, taking on every task, every thankless job asked of her. Finally, her chief, Goze, had noticed her determination, organizing her advanced suit training, which had been so far beyond anything she had learned in basic survival suit and O_2 emergency drills.

He'd taken her out of the ship that first time in an ill-fitting excavation exo-suit, leaving her to flounder the first time she made a stupid rookie error, making her run through every possible scenario, only reeling her in when her thrusters were dry and her O_2 was redlining. He'd never even told her what she'd done wrong, merely took her out again the next day and put her through it again.

It took her three more tries to figure out how to get out of it. But once she had, it was like a door unlocked in her, and she never made that particular mistake again. Oh, there had been many others, but once she'd started learning, she'd never looked back. Within the year, she was out on the rocks with the rest of her crew. Within two, she was one of the most productive cutters on the ship.

She'd found her place, and with it, understood the spirit of the cutting crews and the drive behind those gaudy paint jobs, beginning with the bold, bloody patterns of the *Scarlet Sun*.

In time she had worked her way up the ladder, finally leading a crew of her own and finding her own way to train those who came to her, as she had once come to Goze and his crew.

Now, the *Liquid Supernova* was hers to command, and her crew, trained and moulded as she had once been, was in the top productivity percentile for the last two standard years.

Which was why it had galled her so much to learn that someone was stealing from the crew she had worked so hard to train and lead. She knew firsthand how good they were at their jobs, how dedicated they were to each other and to the work. They had earned every credit for every moment they spent in their suits out on the rocks; for every injury and loss they had experienced in the time they had been together. They had earned those bonuses with every drop of sweat and every gram of ore they brought out with their labour. They deserved that money far more than whoever had taken it, and she meant to get it back for them.

None of which changed the fact that she was not built for this life of subterfuge, and she knew it. Only once she had confided her suspicions to Malika across the pillows one night had she found out about her lover's past. It had driven her from Malika's arms to sit rigidly on the edge of the bed. Malika had been calm and unashamed as she spoke of her time running cons with her friend, Ember, with no regrets over the time spent. But once the story began, it had gone on until its end, bringing her here to Sound. And it was only when she talked of the Gate and what had happened there that sadness had come into her voice, when she revealed what had happened to bring her here to this lonely, isolated world.

In Malika's story, Anyeis had recognized some of her own situation. The targets of her and Ember's scams had been truly amoral people, each guilty of some awful behaviour against someone in a weaker position than they were. Though the lawlessness of Malika's actions had rankled, Anyeis couldn't help but take some pleasure in what had happened to them.

And that seed had taken root, though initially she had resisted the thought of asking Malika to help her. But, in time, her own growing anger at the injustice perpetrated against her crew had won out, and led her here to this seemingly endless, tense descent to the field of familiar ships.

When she reached the bottom of the ramp, the ships were now massive, her vision only able to take in one or two at a time. She was able to see the wear and tear on them, the scrapes in the paint no one had time to fix, the abraded, bare metal. Her carefully trained eye enabled her to judge which ships might be next in line for refit inside the hangars and what damage was superficial and could wait for later.

She'd inspected the hull of her own ship every time it landed, cataloguing its condition and then comparing it with the report of the maintenance crew dirtside. Her assessment almost always jibed with theirs, a point of pride. She'd sometimes even found damage that they missed, making her request a reassessment. After a near disaster, they had learned to listen to her when she questioned their judgment.

Despite the circumstances, the path to her ship's berth was a familiar one, and within minutes, she was standing below Mining Cutter 342, the *Liquid Supernova*, known to her crew as the 'Nova.

By any objective standard, it was an ugly ship, designed solely for utility and function. Heavy and blocky, its sides studded with the wartlike driller pods bulging in all directions. The prow of the ship, which featured the bridge and her supervisor's blister above and aft, was splashed with a myriad of colours to resemble a massive nova, giving the ship and its crew their name, all livid purples, pinks, and greens, centred around a glowing star on the ship's nose.

That's my girl.

She sent her call code and the ship's lift extended down to her position, opening as it touched the hard, blackened surface of the landing pad. Beautifully cool air exhaled out to her from the tiny lift, and she stepped in, eager to get out of the planet's heavy swelter. The door whispered shut and the lift began to rise.

A thought to her link bracelet brought up the ship's innernet and the most recent status reports flowed across her scleral displays. They were sixth in line to be refuelled, which was fine. Her team was on off days, so there was no rush. The recalibration of the port thruster array had been completed and was just awaiting a second round of testing, but it looked like nothing more than a formality. Systems showed that there was no one on board but Chief Engineer Yareau, the only person who spent as much off-time on the ship as she did. She pinged him just to let him know she was onboard and headed fore to her office.

The supervisor's pod was high on the ship's midline, just above and behind the bridge where the flight crew sat. Ringed with a semicircle of transparent alloy windows, it was a spacious suite with a curved workspace that allowed her to face either space or the room's interior depending on her needs. Aft of her work area was a meeting area with a table big enough for her crew leads, that could be closed off from her desk space if need be.

She sat at her desk, swivelling the chair toward the panoramic windows, and the desk's surface came alive with data, connecting with her Link. All of the ship's systems opened for her, ready to obey her commands, presenting the updated ship's data once more.

Checking the time signal that ticked away at the edge of her vision, she waited, her palm still itching.

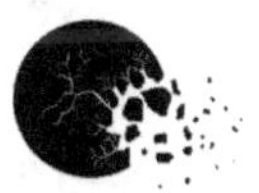

Lexa-Blue steered the car deftly through the streets of Sound, weaving in and out of the shifting patterns of rickshaws and then around the slowly rumbling tram. The administrative compound of the consortium grew ever larger, coming to dominate the skyline ahead.

In the rear compartment, Ember sat in the centre of the seat, his back straight, looking directly forward. He didn't talk, immersing himself in the role of the entitled representative of one of the many corporations who had a stake in the large-scale mining venture here.

Vrick had crafted an identity that would easily stand up to scrutiny, provided Anyeis could get them through the initial external layers of security. It made perfect sense that a skittish investor might send a representative to check on just how money had been spent and whether the return on that investment was sufficient.

Flanking Ember, Keene and Malika sat in two gimballed chairs designed for personal security, able to slide into whatever defensive posture might be necessary in their roles as his personal guard. Even on the most populous Galactum worlds, wealth often meant personal danger. A personal entourage was a necessary part of the cover they were trying to pull off.

"We're coming up on the compound, everyone," Lexa-Blue said. ***Is Anyeis in position and ready?***

She is, Vrick said ***I've updated her on the shielded comm channel and she's in position. The window is tight, so I'll give her the go as soon as you get inside.***

"Look sharp then, folks," Lexa-Blue said, though they had all heard Vrick's update. "We are pulling up to the curb now."

She slid the car up into the shallow paved curve leading to the main entrance, coming to a stop with the door to the passenger compartment perfectly lined up with the public doors.

As soon as the car was still, the passenger door flipped up and back, allowing Keene and Malika to step out and confirm all was safe. Malika's motions were note-perfect, looking as if she had lived her whole life as a bodyguard, as if the profession were as natural to her as eating or breathing.

Keene, on the other hand, seemed just slightly off, unused to this kind of roleplay.

Relax, Malika said to him on a band isolated from the others. ***Don't act it. Just be it. You're not trying to win awards for your performance. We're the extras in this scene.***

Keene seemed to relax then, his uncertainty dropping away.

As they took up their defensive positions, Ember emerged from the car, his manner so completely changed that any witness would have been hard-pressed to identify him in his natural mien. He strode forward, the doors of the complex opening for him, Keene and Malika following at a respectful distance.

Inside, Ember's gaze swept sharply from side to side, identifying the desk behind which the main attendant sat. His eyes locked on the young man seated there and strode forward, seeing the attendant's eyes widen at this unexpected arrival.

And we are go.

Across the city, seated in her office, Anyeis jolted, startled by the signal, slamming her hand down on the access panel of her desk.

Subtle. Very subtle.

There was an instant of — what? Cold? Heat? Maybe just the disappearance of the phantom itch. Then, nothing.

"You okay up there, Skip?" Yareau's voice said from the hall outside her door.

What the hells is he doing up here?

"All good, chief," she said, certain that every syllable betrayed her.

"Okay, good," Yareau said. "I'm done with the maintenance check, so I'm heading into town for a drink. Care to join me?"

"I have some mapping revisions to go over," she said, feeling guiltier by the second. "Next time."

"You got it, Skip," the engineer said, his footsteps fading down the hall.

She took a deep breath, forcing the pounding of her heart to slow.

Her link signalled again, indicating a voice transmission. Her eyes flicked to the edge of her scleral displays, accepting it.

We have access, Vrick's voice said. ***They're going in.***

She sucked in a breath of air, exhaling it slowly.

How are your nerves holding up? Vrick said.

It's embarrassing, she said. ***I can wrangle rocks the size of cities and break them apart, but I was not built for this.***

There's no shame in that, ey said. ***Running these sorts of cons is a very specific skillset. I didn't used to have it either.***

So, what now?

You're done. You can stay there or go home or go get drunk if you want. We can let you know after we get what we're looking for.

It seemed *wrong* somehow, and she said so. ***They're in there taking this risk for me. I should be doing something.***

There's nothing we need from you right now, but I can loop you into my master feeds if you want to monitor their progress.

I'm not sure my nerves could stand it, she said. ***But I feel like I should. In case they need me.***

Done and done.

The multiple feeds splashed across her displays, disorienting her for a moment, but she steeled herself and focussed.

The lobby of the Consortium's complex was all soft, muted colours and bright, polished finishings, designed as the front for any public enquiries. It had been designed to instantly suggest confidence and skill; to ensure that any who came through the doors knew that Sound and Fury and the field of debris around it were in good hands.

Ember came to a halt at the desk, his posture louche and entitled, as if all revolved around him.

"Aristos Xi," he said, letting the name hang haughtily in the air as if it explained everything, then left the pause that followed to stagnate in the air.

"Yes," the attendant said, nervously drawing the single syllable out as if it might prompt some kind of explanation.

Ember reached up for his glasses and drew them slowly down his nose, fixing the other man with the most glacial of looks. "Surely, I'm expected, Sei…?"

"Intrim," the attendant stammered, at a loss as to just what was going on. "I'm afraid I-I don't seem to have a … The schedule doesn't… I wasn't told."

Ember narrowed his eyes into slow, tight slits, and saw Intrim's throat spasm as he swallowed. Ember tore his steely gaze from Intrim and turned to Malika instead. She remained stone-faced under the stare "Flic, do not tell me that I travelled to this *place* for no reason."

"The appointment was confirmed, sir," Malika said. "I checked it myself. There were no issues on our end." She turned back to Intrim, adding her own cold stare to Ember's.

I'm in. Vrick said. ***You're good to go.***

"Perhaps you should check," Ember said to Intrim, as if to a small child or to someone incapable of the simplest task. "*Again.*"

Intrim looked down at his system's interface, his hands a nervous flutter as he gestured commands to the daily schedule. His hands came to a halt in mid-movement, and his face went ashen. He pulled himself up straight, attempting to save some tattered remnants of face amid the sudden chaos. "Of course, Sei Xi. My apologies. I take full responsibility. If you'll follow me."

Intrim stepped out from behind the smooth, wooden curve of the desk and a holo appeared in his place. He gestured to a bank of lifts at the end of the lobby.

Ember inclined his head in agreement and followed, striding so imperiously that Intrim had to quicken his own pace to prevent a collision. Keene and Malika followed, checking the elevator and sweeping a look around the lobby before joining Ember and Intrim inside.

The ride up was silent, Keene and Malika playing their roles, and Ember going out of his way to radiate as much entitled disdain as his talents could generate. For his part, Intrim stood near the doors, rigid with embarrassment and seemingly trying to phase directly through the wall. When the lift stopped, he all but jumped out.

You are cruel, Vrick said.

He'll live, Ember said.

Intrim led them to an empty conference room, and showed them in. "Please make yourself comfortable. The synthesizer here has a wide range of options available if you require refreshments. Sei Ogordo will be with you momentarily."

"A synthesizer," Ember drawled. "How quaint."

Intrim paled under the cut in Ember's voice.

I take it back, Vrick said. ***Not just cruel. Downright evil.***

"Thank you," Ember said, his voice wet with condescension. "You've been most *helpful*."

Bowing, Intrim backed out of the room as fast as he could manage, almost falling backwards over a chair, and then they were alone.

Keene barely managed to stifle laughter, but a hard look from Ember kept him in character. ***Keep it together. The walls have eyes.***

To his credit, Keene's composure came back instantly, and he was back in his role instantly.

What have we got? Ember said.

I've got limited access to the system, Vrick said. ***Adding your credentials and the details of this supposed meeting was easy, but I'm going to need some deeper access to get at the back-up logs. If there's evidence of the tampering that's been done, that's where it will be.***

Okay, Ember said. ***If this goes according to plan, they'll have someone in here assigned to give us the spiel about how impressive they are and how safe our money will be. And that always includes a presentation. We can go from there.***

As if on cue, the door opened and a suited man entered, round and red-faced, the hem of his skirt rustling around his legs.

Do you ever get tired of being right? Malika said to Ember.

Remind me to tell you about some of my more spectacular failures, sometime.

"I'm so sorry to have kept you waiting, Sei Xi," the new arrival said. "I've been expecting you."

Liar, liar, Malika said.

"I am Tamas Ogordo, Head of Investor Relations," the new arrival said. "I have the full investor prospectus cued up for you on the room's unit. If you'll take a seat, we can begin."

Ember took a seat, dropping his body as if the mere act were an imposition, carefully selecting a chair by one of the conference room's doors.

Got it, Vrick said. ***Room is scanned, and I've sliced

into the holo of the presentation. The real-time splicing subroutine is up and running. Phase two is go.*

Over the expansive conference table, a swirl of mist appeared, solidifying into a floating holo tank. As the room's lights darkened, music swelled, an overture blatantly conceived to inspire confidence and awe.

The holo solidified into a field of stars, then zoomed swiftly in to resolve into what was obviously the aggregation of planetary fragments. Overly serious narration began to describe the origin and nature of the mining operations.

Splice is online and reading super-green, Vrick said. ***Have a look.***

Ember's node glimmered and provided him with the view that the splice program was showing to Sei Ogordo, his own perfect disguise of indifference. To test the program, he raised an arm to scratch the side of his head. His avatar in the image maintained the same air of bored wealth, moving only in ways that supported the illusion.

Vrick's splice program had completely taken over the presentation, ensuring that on the other side of the table, Sei Ogordo saw and heard only what they wished him to. Ember could have done a striptease and set himself on fire and Ogordo would have had no idea.

Thankfully, this shouldn't require anything that drastic.

Ember stood, moving as quietly as he could, keeping any sounds below the threshold of the bombast of the presentation that was now hiding his actions. As he slipped out into the hall, even the movement of the door was masked by Vrick's impeccable holo camouflage.

The hall outside was empty, as the conference room was in the more public sections of the building, far from where actual work was done. Ember scanned each direction and saw a public restroom. He darted across the hall to it and slipped inside. Luck was with him, for it was empty as well.

Ranks of cubicles lined one wall, across from a row of sinks and an expanse of mirror. At each end of the row of cubicles was a passage that led, according to the building's architectural plans, to a second, more private set of cubicles.

Ember took the alcove to his left, closest to the door, and headed back to have more privacy. He didn't need any observers for this.

Time? he said to Vrick

You're good, Vrick answered. ***That presentation goes on for another 24 minutes. They haven't even started with the numbers yet.***

Ember reached into the inside pocket of his suit and pulled out the mask that Malika had borrowed from the theatre, lifting it to his face. As it touched his skin, he felt the tingle of the field as it adhered to his head.

Did you get enough reference data?

See for yourself, Vrick said.

Ember ducked his head back out to look into the mirrored wall, seeing Sei Ogordo's face looking back at him, his own disguised hair changing again as the holo emitters along the mask's edge mimicked the other man's hair as well.

His suit wasn't an exact match, but he gambled on it being similar enough that a simple colour change would take care of it. And with a thought, the chameleon circuits in the fabric altered to the deep, chocolate brown the other man had been wearing. A few tugs in a few strategic places altered the shape of the jacket into a passable imitation of Sei Ogordo's. Even with some moulding, the skirt wasn't quite right, but he counted on no one noticing.

Nice work, Ember said.

One does what one can, Vrick said. ***Hallway is still clear. And I have the route to his office.***

Ember emerged from the restroom as the floorplan unfurled in his head. Ogordo's office was down the hall and to the right, past an atrium populated with ranks of administrative support personnel, each assigned to an executive on the floor. Adjusting his body into an almost perfect imitation of the other man's stature and gait, Ember strode forward and around the corner, all too aware of the possibility of all those heads turning his way and immediately seeing through his disguise. But he wasn't so out of practice that it altered his own step at all. He merely kept walking, with the air of a man who was exactly where he belonged.

He was almost at the door to the office when he saw the assistant nearest the door he sought look up at him expectantly and begin to stand. Thinking fast, he changed his expression to a scowl, the mask covering his face reacting to the muscle contractions and changing accordingly. He accompanied the facial expression with a sharp, chopping motion of his hand, and the assistant sat back down meekly and returned to his work.

Please tell me you have the door code sliced, he said to Vrick as he walked the last few steps to the office door.

Have I ever let you down?

The door slid open, and Ember heaved a silent sigh of relief as he stepped across the threshold into the office.

The room was as he had expected, plush and sophisticated, as befitted an executive of Ogordo's status. Not as luxurious as those of the upper executives, but definitely beyond those of the minions outside at their ranked, open rows of desks.

Beyond his cursory inspection of the office, Ember headed straight for the desk. He knew from his research into the structure of the Consortium's administrative team that Ogordo should have access to all of the deep-dive financial information that Anyeis hadn't been able to get at, including the multiple redundant backups that they were looking for. It was just the type of data that the executive would need as part of the investment cultivation team.

Sitting, he saw that the surface of the desk, as he had expected, was state of the art, with holo emitters, keyboard access and a direct link-to-link access port that could feed data directly to whatever form of portable link to Know-It-All Ogordo used.

He reached into the inner pocket of his coat and pulled out the bit chip that contained hijack code that Vrick had written. He found the upload plate in the far left, lower corner of the desk's interactive surface, a stylized arrow within a circle graphic that pulsed a soft, mint green. He placed the fink onto the plate and the green deepened to an emerald shade as the fink activated.

And we're in, Vrick said. ***Locating the financial records and the backups.***

Barely a second passed.

Got them. Transferring now.

The emerald light around the upload plate pulsed with a steady throb as the data poured through it, then, without warning, flared to an angry red.

Oh, that's *not* good.

The alarms rang across Pi's consciousness like acid sleet, driving him from the coding trance he had been lost in for the last few hours. A slick, nauseating wave of disorientation washed through him as he registered where he was and what was going on.

As his head cleared, he saw that someone had tripped the snares he'd left in place in the company's system when he'd rigged it to funnel the ore and funds out of the company and into the shielded accounts that Ijagu had set up.

Someone else, someone not part of the corp itself, had managed to access all of the doctored files, plus the backups that even Pi hadn't been able to touch. Anyone who dug deep enough into those files, especially the change logs, would be able to piece together a crystal-clear picture of just what Pi and Ijagu had accomplished and how.

And every piece of it would be admissible in court, wrapping them both up in a pretty little package for the nearest Galactum Court.

Pi extended his thoughts into his network, along his link to Know-It-All and the hardwire embedded into the base of his skull that doubled his neural output. Nothing more than a flicker of a thought brought the whole primeframe into focus for him, laying bare the inner workings of the corp in naked detail.

He saw the intrusions right away, disgusted with the corp and its security personnel for being so easily duped. Though, when he looked closely, he could see the sophistication of the attack on the system, including the double prongs of the slicer's attack. He registered the location of the initial entry into the system, and, while he couldn't see who the person had been, he could see the network node where that initial malicious code had been introduced.

He'd known she would be trouble, right from the first time that she'd started nosing around. Only Ijagu's squeamishness had stopped him from dealing with her right then and there, and he regretted listening to the idiot. He'd thought that threatening her actor girlfriend would have been enough to warn her off, but apparently, he'd underestimated her persistence.

He wouldn't make that mistake again.

But for the moment, he had more important battles to fight. From that initial point, he could easily see the trail of artificial personas and manipulation of the basic security and appointment systems to create the false identities now being used right in the heart of the administrative complex. And that led him directly to the massive data dump that was now siphoning off all the evidence that would be needed to convict him.

And Ijagu, but that was of little consequence; the greedy executive had already far outlived his usefulness.

Whoever was behind this was good, he had to admit.

The code was elegant, and the simplicity of the attack was both wondrous and audacious. Despite his anger, Pi found himself admiring his foes. Not enough to keep him from fighting back, but these were definitely some worthy adversaries.

A thought revved up his array, encircling his seat in an open arc. Ranked shelves of Limited Intelligence modules pulsed with sudden power, coming alive with a menacing hum. As their networked processing capabilities came online, Pi felt the surge pass through the three linked nodes embedded in his brain.

He'd discovered the set-up by accident, after months of experimentation. Ranking and networking the smaller LIs allowed him to bypass every security and safety protocol an AI system would have faced, which in turn, allowed him to do his work.

Another thought fired up the injector systems, and he selected his most potent, and most dangerous, stim cocktail dosage. The syringe arm extended, lancing its cold, sharp point into his neck, his vein burning as the juice hit it.

His eyes suddenly wide, and his every nerve and synapse firing, Pi opened up his virtual toolkit and, with relish, he dug in, selecting his weapons.

The lights above Ember's head flared scarlet, as sirens blared through the air.

You've been made, Vrick said.

No shit, charabanc, Ember said. *What was your first clue?*

Pretty much the dozen codeworms hitting the system from the outside. There must have been some kind of booby trap that I didn't catch.

Isn't that what you're supposed to do?

Believe me, no one is more shocked than I am, Vrick said. *You need to get moving. I'm fighting back, but it's... difficult.*

Ember paused to digest that. If Vrick was having trouble coping, what were the rest of them going to do?

He had to assume that if his disguise hadn't been blown, it soon would be. He accessed the suit's controls and sent the fabric into full stealth mode, and blanked the mask to a featureless opaline smoothness, wiping away Ogordo's face.

He crossed to the door, but the sensor that registered his presence to open it remained blocked.

Great.

He ran his hands along the frame, looking for the emergency manual release and noticed just how imperfect his camouflage was. His bare hands floated in the air, not covered by the chameleon circuits of his suit.

Burn that bridge when we come to it. First things first.

He located the door's manual release, prying away the cover to expose the lever. Grabbing it, he yanked, but it didn't move.

Must be some kind of security override that locks it down too.

Bending over, he eyed the mechanism, trying to find some kind of weakness. He knew he'd be discovered here sooner than later. Out in the halls, at least he had a chance of getting out.

Concentrating on the locking mechanism again, he saw that it was a very simple physical lockbolt that had slid into place to lock the use of the emergency release. It was just a matter of prying the bolt loose. Pulling his vision away from the lock, he surveyed the room, but saw nothing but the usual stationery products one would find in a modern office: exactly nothing with the power or torque that he needed. He clenched his fists in frustration.

His fists. He looked down at his floating hands, more specifically his left. And, with a thought, deactivated the flesh toned surface cloak, rendering his ring finger and pinkie gleaming black once more.

Think it'll work? Ember said. ***You've seen the specs.***

Well, one thing's for sure, you're going to void the warranty, Vrick said. ***And Daevin won't be pleased. But it should be strong enough.***

Come on, he had to know something like this would happen eventually.

Ember felt the complex mental impression from Vrick that he recognized as es equivalent of an amused shrug. ***Whatever you're going to do, you'd better do it fast. Security is being mobilized as we speak.***

Here goes nothing, Ember said, jamming his prosthetic fingers into the mechanism, worming them around to get purchase. Between his eyes and the fingertip sensors, he found a good grip, took a breath, and wrenched.

The bolt locking the handle in place gave way under the pressure, but so did the first knuckle of his ring finger. There was a stab of excruciating pain and he yanked his hand back, seeing the tip of his finger bent at almost forty-five degrees. In the wrong direction. He felt an instant of nausea, but before it could take hold, the pain was suddenly gone as if it had never existed. Only the bizarre angle remained.

Get it together, Ember.

He felt sudden information flood his node and knew how to reset a disjointed digit. Feeling slightly nauseated, he took hold of the bent finger and, with a sharp pull, reset it.

The pain was only hellish for a moment, then faded back to the usual level as he reset the colour.

He stuck his hand back into the emergency lock and tugged the handle until the door began to jerk open.

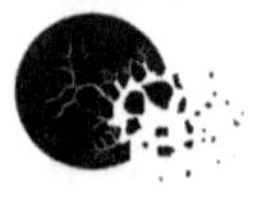

As the lights of the conference room strobed to red, the holo presentation dissolved into nothing.

"Please, remain calm, Sei Xi," Sei Ogordo said. "I'm sure it's nothing, just remain —"

With the holo gone, the executive couldn't help but realize that Ember was gone, having disappeared along with the holo. His eyes went wide with shock and he reached for the link button on his cuff.

He's got a panic button! Vrick shouted.

Keene leaped forward, grabbing the edge of the heavy conference table and throwing himself up to slide across the surface. As he slid, he swung his legs ahead of him, bringing the toe of his heavy shoe into a solid, bone-crunching kick to Ogordo's hand that kept it from making contact with the panic button. As the executive clutched at his bruised hand, Keene slid off the table onto the floor in a fighting crouch. Ogordo opened his mouth to shout, but before he could make a sound, Keene lashed out with a sharp blow to the side of the other man's neck.

Sei Ogordo's eyes rolled back into his head, and he collapsed to the floor.

"*Wow*," Malika said. "Can you teach me to do that? It would come in handy at cast parties."

"I wasn't actually sure it was going to work," Keene said.

"Well, let's both be glad it did."

Ember, where are you? Keene said, looping Vrick, Malika and Lexa-Blue into the link.

I'm okay, Ember said.

But you've all been burned, Vrick said, explaining to the others what ey had told Ember about the slicer that had blown their op wide open.

Hold there, we'll come get you, Keene said.

No, Ember said. ***Get out however you can. Our chances are better if we scatter.***

I'm not leaving you again, Keene said, images of Ember's grievously wounded body burned across his memory.

This is the game, lover. You know that as well as I do. Now, go.

Ember dropped out of the link, leaving Keene cursing under his breath. He knew that Ember was right. Bugging out made sense. The more targets they gave security, the more likely they were to confuse them and get out of this mess alive.

He slapped at the control on his visor, activating the helmet, and it snapped into place over his head. He saw Malika do the same, her face disappearing behind the gleaming alloy. He bent his arms, one after the other, snapping them back straight, and the motion sent two small, but fierce pistols into his hands. He held one out to Malika.

"How did you get those past their sensors?" she said, incredulous.

"Stealth polymer ceramic," Keene said. "Vrick did a little digging and found us a supplier. Designed it myself."

"Seije would be proud of you," Malika said, testing the weapon's heft and balance, and then held it up to test the sight. "Nice toy."

"You know your way around a gun," Keene said. "That's new."

"I play an army sergeant in *Glory is Waiting*," she said. "The director is a stickler for realism, so we all had to go through training."

"Three cheers for realism," Keene said. "Come on. Let's see if we can get ourselves out of here."

As they headed to the door, Vrick relayed what Ember had discovered, making it easier to find the manual release for the conference room doors. Keene wasted no time trying to pry the lever free. He aimed his pistol into the mechanism and fired. The double doors jerked apart, though only a few centimetres, but it was enough for them to dig their fingers in and pry the doors far enough apart to get through.

"Which way?" Malika said.

Lifts are locked down, so no access that way.

Stairs? Keene asked.

This way.

And directions flowed into their minds.

From her vantage point in the flat of the nearby paved carpark, chaos spilled through Lexa-Blue's node as the others scrambled to deal with their plight.

"Ruck this," she said, slamming her hand against the car's ignition. Nothing happened.

She hit it again, but once again it didn't respond. Instead, the locks clamped down, red indicators flowing across the car's control board.

Okay, everybody. Got a bit of a problem here. Hang tight.

She ran through all standard back-up actions, using every trick she could think of to jimmy the car into motion.

Whoever our new 'friend' is, Vrick said, ***they've got quite the reach. They've sliced the car rental company and wiped all my data implants. You're now on record as having stolen that car.***

Well, if I'm officially a thief, I might as well be a vandal too.

She reached under her seat to the spot where she'd clamped her gun, yanking it free of its bracket. She linked it to her node and set it to the appropriate setting.

Do I have this right? she asked, flashing her plan to Vrick.

Almost, ey said, uploading altered positional data and intensity settings to her.

Got it.

She fired, tearing a hole in the car's console, then dropped the gun onto the seat. As the hole smoked, she fished around in the opening, grabbing a thick handful of bundled cables and dioptics and pulling them free. Using both hands, she pried them apart to find the ones she needed and dropped the others aside.

Here goes nothing.

She jammed the raw ends of two clusters together and they sparked with an actinic surge of power. The red splay of light across the indicators flashed, half of them burning out. The remainder fluttered a pitiful green, but the engine surged to life.

She punched the air and whooped. ***No matter how much more complicated they make these things, they can still be hotwired.***

That's one problem down, but our little friend has locked down the main gates of that parking area. You won't get out.

Who said anything about gates?

Vrick saw her intention just as the thought formed. ***Wait! There's a forcefield over the lot too.***

With one hand on the impellors and the other on the directional control, she jammed both into a specific combination.

And the car shot straight up into the air.

Though ey was kilometres away at the landing field, Vrick had extended emself out into Know-It-All in order to manipulate the administrative complex's security systems into allowing them to do all of the things they shouldn't have been able to do.

Now, all of those tendrils of energy vibrated off-key, like the vibration of a drill bit as it gouged into metal. The reverberations went right through em, as if es very core was physically feeling the assault.

When ey saw Lexa-Blue's plan, ey was able, in the blink of a human eye, to reroute es own defensive efforts just enough to drop the field keeping her penned in the car park. Through her node, ey felt the surge of vertigo and nausea as the car's support field screamed under the sudden onslaught of power to its systems.

Ey kept an eye on her, but with one immediate crisis averted, ey went back to concentrating on the admin building and those trapped there.

Es control of the building's systems had been complete. Everything had played out as they had planned, and es slicing skills and codeworms had subverted all of the security systems perfectly.

But then, just as Ember was feeding em the data they needed, it had all gone haywire.

Vrick had enough presence of mind to focus on that data dump and keep it running, even at the expense of the few moments of inattention on the others. Normally, that type of multi-tasking would have been nothing to em, but under the sudden thrust of the counter-intrusion code, ey had put all of es energy into making sure the data they needed came through. Or it all would have been for nothing.

Ey registered that es control of the holo system in the conference room had gone, but just as quickly saw that Keene and Malika had managed to deal with that.

Ember was another matter. The office where he was pinned down was in a bottleneck. He'd have to make it past that atrium of people to get out. Keene and Malika were at least in a more public part of the complex, and that made the probabilities of their escape slightly higher.

At the moment though, as ey struggled to keep the security forces diverted and distracted from the humans' paths out of danger, it was all ey could do to keep their identities hidden from whoever had sensed their intrusion and sounded the alarm.

Each tendril, writhing out into Know-It-All like a thousand tiny filaments of light, and then back into the real-world systems connected to it, rang with an aching rain of blows. Each point of connection split and split, fragmenting apart as each new raid against them split and turned and looped and attacked again.

Whoever this is, they are good. Freakishly, inhumanly good.

Vrick couldn't believe that whoever was fighting back against em was a human, they were that formidable an opponent.

But it was just as illogical to consider that ey was doing battle with another Artificial Sentience. Es Kith were rare enough in the modern world of the Galactum, and ey would have known if one had been here on Sound. As a group they were rare enough that their comings and goings were noteworthy to each other. And a standard AI would never have been able to fight em in such a concerted and wildly improvisational style. The behavioural strictures were too deeply ingrained in standard AI.

And there was that faint, maddening hint of melody. Just at the edge of consciousness, abutting against the code, harsh and dissonant.

Whatever ey was dealing with, it was something new. And that thought was disquieting.

Marshalling es energies, ey rallied against a sudden raid of code that hammered at em. Ey was able to encircle it and cut it off, quarantining the suddenly unconnected data.

It wasn't much, barely a snippet of a broken thought, but ey had it.

In the microsecond after es success, the attacker fell back, only slightly but enough for Vrick to catch es metaphorical breath. Ey took a fractional sliver of that brief respite to delegate a part of emself to examine es prize, cracking it apart to its constituents.

And there, deep in those ones and zeroes, there was a pattern.

A familiar one.

Okay, everyone, we have a little problem.
Ember paused for a second when he heard Vrick's voice.

You mean other than all the other problems, Junkpile?
Lexa-Blue said.

***You know that sliceware I *borrowed* a couple of years ago? The one that has been so useful because it's so well-written?**

Oh, I do not like where this is going, Keene said.

The person behind this is the person who wrote it. No idea of his real name. But he calls himself *Pi*.

Irrational and never-ending, Keene said.

Exactly. And he's showing capabilities that no human should be able to have.

Worry about it later, Lexa-Blue said. ***Can you beat him?***
In time.

Do what you can. As quickly as you can, if you don't mind. Meantime, we'll do what we can here. We're resourceful. For humans, Ember said.

He could feel the mesh in his prosthetic finger regenerating, like a thousand fiery pinpricks radiating out from the digit's core.

Ember felt Vrick go quiet as ey concentrated on es task, and he gave the door one final pull, feeling the muscles across his back and shoulders protest. But the door opened enough for him to get through. He jammed his undisguised hands into the pockets of his jacket and squeezed through.

Out in the atrium, heads turned toward the office at the sound of the metal screeching against the door frame and its own weight.

Ember froze, knowing that his improvised camouflage wouldn't stand up to any intense scrutiny.

The buzz among the assistants at their desks was a fluttering mutter ranging from uncertainty to fear to panic as the strident clangour of the alarm systems vibrated the air.

He knew he had to move soon. The longer he stayed, the greater his chances of being discovered. But, conversely, the more he moved, the greater his chances of being discovered.

Rock, meet hard place.

He scanned the area, working at finding some kind of exit strategy. With Vrick concentrating on dealing with alarms and systems and security, the virtual map of the complex was now gone. Ember concentrated, working to put his memories of the building's layout back into place.

Lifts are that way. No, that way. Stairs too, most likely.

With time running down, he made a decision and bolted forward. As he ran, he heard a shrill shout come from the atrium behind, followed by a garble of voices in response, but he ignored them and kept moving.

With a long, loping stride, he was down the corridor and around the corner, seeing the clearly marked exits at the main bank of lifts.

You've got security coming up the stairs, Vrick said.

How many?

Squad of five. Armed. Very armed.

Can you hijack me a lift?

I think so. Our little friend is keeping me quite busy.

The thought gave Ember pause. He'd grown to think of Vrick as being the smartest, slankest, most capable slicer around. He didn't want to think too hard about who or what was a match for em.

Got it.

The lift on the far right chirped a muted, professional tone, and he was at the doors before they had fully opened, squeezing through.

Up or down? he asked.

Should I make something up or just tell you how skinned you are?

No need to sugarcoat it. Give me the smallest probability of horrible death.

Vrick paused for a moment, and Ember could only imagine the number of probabilities ey was juggling. But that second seemed like an eternity.

Up. They're locking off the lifts from the ground up, one floor at a time. And besides, no one will believe you're dumb enough to head away from the exits. I'm scrambling their scanners, which should buy you some time as well.

Ember jammed the key for the top floor. *No idea what I'll do when I get there but vaporize that bridge when we get to it.*

He felt the lift surge upward, a sudden surge of unnatural speed, and fought txo keep his balance.

Sorry, Vrick said. *No time to be delicate. I have no idea how much longer I'm going to have control.*

Es words were prophetic, because the lift car jammed to a sudden halt, throwing Ember against the wall hard and wrenching his shoulder as muscles and tissue howled in protest. Wincing, he pulled himself upright once more.

Well, that's not optimal, Vrick said. *I was hoping to get you higher before I got locked out.*

Worry later, Ember said. *Where am I?*

Three floors below the roof. There's a dock for the lift cars up there. It should give you some cover until I can figure out how to get you out of there. Even if I have to come and get you myself.

The thought of Vrick burning through the city's dome to rescue him made Ember smile. And he knew that if pressed, ey would do it, too.

Let's keep that as a last resort, okay?

Ember looked up at the ceiling of the lift car. The design looked pretty bog standard, from what he could see.

Which means the upper access should be right about… here.

He coiled down and leapt, catching his fingers in the release mechanism that opened a neatly symmetrical hole in the car's ceiling. He crouched again and jumped, his hands almost losing purchase on the smooth edges of the access hatch before finding their grip.

The muscles in his arms screamed in protest as he struggled to pull his body up and through the hatch.

Finally, he was through, and he collapsed onto his back, his breath heaving, on the roof of the lift car, in the dimness of the shaft.

Ember...

I know, I know, he said. ***No time.***

He levered himself back up into a standing position and took stock of his situation. The shaft rose around him on all sides, and he could see, those three storeys above, what must be the hatch for the roof access and the lift dock. The walls of the shaft were fairly smooth, though he could see the pattern of magnetic emitters that pulled the lift cars up or down in the shaft. They looked as though they could be used as hand and footholds for a climb, but a climb that would have been a challenge at the best of times.

There was nothing for it but to do it, so he jumped for the nearest emitter, felt his hand get a firm grip, and began to climb.

The hallway outside the conference room was empty when they emerged.

They must be concentrating on the actual admin floors rather than the public areas, Keene said. ***There didn't seem to be any other meetings going on when we arrived.***

Lucky for us, Malika answered.

They found the access to the stairs. It was only four floors down, so it would be easy to get to the main lobby. Though getting out of the building itself might be more of a challenge.

Keene pushed his weight against the door and it opened much more easily, but as soon as he stuck his head over the sill into the stairwell, he heard the heavy scatter of footsteps pounding up the stairs. He shot an arm out to keep Malika back, unsure if she had heard.

Is that what I think it is? he asked Vrick.

A security goon squad sent to find you? ey asked. ***Why yes, yes it is.***

Malika backed quickly out of the stairwell, Keene right behind her. As the door clicked closed, he fired his gun at the latch mechanism, melting it to a stinking slag of plastic and metal.

That's not going to hold them for long, Malika said.

No, Keene said. ***But it made me feel better.***

Malika shrugged. ***Good enough for me. What now?***

Lifts? Keene said, addressing Vrick.

The lockout is already three floors above you.

No lifts, then, Keene said. ***Ideas?***

Vrick flooded their nodes with the information about Lexa-Blue's wild ride in their hired car. Keene and Malika gaped at each other as they suddenly sensed the gist of the plan.

That is ridiculous, Malika said.

Completely, Keene agreed. ***It'll never work.***

After you, Malika said, standing aside to let him pass.

He brushed past her and led them back to the conference room. Just as they reached the door, they heard the grinding whine of high-powered scatter blasters tearing through the door leading to the stairwell they had just left.

All haste, if you would, my little meatlings, Vrick said.

They raced the last few steps, pulling the doors back together once they were back in the conference room.

Barricade? Keene said.

I'd say yes, Malika agreed. ***Table?***

The conference table was long and heavy, and it took all their strength to tip it toward the doors and jostle it into place against. They were both sweaty and gulping air as they stood back up. Keene's back was to the long curve of clear glass alloy that ringed the outside edge of the room, but he saw Malika's eyebrow rise as she caught sight of something.

"What is it?" he asked.

"I think our ride is here," she said, pointing over his shoulder.

When he turned, he saw the heavy, dark shape of their car framed in the long window, bucking to hold position. He could just make out Lexa-Blue in the driver's seat, rigid with the strain of holding the car steady.

Somebody call for a cab? Lexa-Blue said, even her thoughts clenched with the strain of keeping the car level at this extended altitude. ***Better get your asses out here quick. This bucket was built for the street. I've got the grav emitters red-lined and I don't know how much longer we've got.***

Keene and Malika bolted over to the window.

"Does this thing open? Can you find any kind of mechanism on your side?" Keene said, running his hands along the frame.

"It looks like it's not designed to open," Malika said. "It's one big pane. Makes sense, I guess. Can't have your disgruntled employees tossing themselves out the window in the middle of a meeting."

"Okay, Plan B, then," Keene said, drawing his gun.

Malika followed suit.

Taking in their respective positions and the car outside, Keene did some quick calculations and hoped that the small handguns had the power they needed. As they aimed, Vrick linked their nodes, and overlaid a twinned targeting matrix across their vision, which flashed green as the target locked.

Outside the window, Lexa-Blue swung the bucking car away and down slightly to get out of the way.

They opened fire, pumping all the power of the small guns into the shots, and the strengthened glass exploded outwards in a diamond rain, several fragments leaving a smear of scratches and dents across the fender closest to them. The car bucked a moment, then Lexa-Blue regained control and brought it back in close to the now shattered window.

Okay, kiddies, she said. ***Let's make this fast.***

"Ladies first," Keene said.

"Well, that definitely rules me out," Malika said.

She looked around, considering how to get herself up on the frame and out in the car. Since the window was a long, unbroken expanse of glass with no individually framed panes, options for handholds were few. The edge of the hole they had opened was jagged and sharp, ready to cut into any flesh.

As she looked around, she saw the refreshment station that Intrim had offered to them earlier. She went to it, throwing open the storage doors in its base.

"Bingo."

She hauled out a stack of thick, cloth napkins, along with another of towels. She tossed them to Keene and shoved the whole cabinet over, sending the bottles and carafes shattering to the floor. As soon as Keene understood her plan, he stuck the towels and napkins under his arm and helped her drag it into position under their potential escape route.

With the heavy rectangle in place as a step under the window, Keene handed half of the stack back to Malika and they both wound them around their hands. Outside the window, the car swooped dangerously close to the wall, so much so that they both shied back from what seemed like would be a dramatic collision.

But Lexa-Blue's skills won out in the end, and the car nestled up against the building, with only the slimmest of gaps between. The door to the rear seat slid open.

Malika leapt up on to the overturned cabinet and grabbed the edge of the broken window to haul herself up, wincing as the jagged edge bit into her palm even with the makeshift protection. Ignoring the bite of pain, she managed to lever her body out through the window and across the gap into the back seat of the car.

Keene was right behind her, pulling himself up into position, when the doors to the conference room blew open, sending their improvised barricade skidding across the floor. Keene lost his footing and fell forward as the shockwave caught both him and the car.

Lexa-Blue struggled to hold position, but the wall of force knocked the car out of reach, Keene tipping into nothingness.

He flailed as he toppled, grabbing for any purchase, and his hands managed to catch a handful of the open car door's edge and the floor mats below the seat. Malika lunged forward, clutching at his clothing to keep him from falling.

"Hang on back there," Lexa-Blue yelled through gritted teeth. "We have another stop to make."

Every muscle in Ember's shoulders and back screamed in protest as he kept climbing. Three storeys had never seemed so far, and the rush of adrenaline that had hit his system when the alarms had gone off was long depleted. Still, he continued, hand over hand, working to ensure each foothold was solid enough to bear his weight.

Finally, he came to the top of the shaft, the hatch leading up into the lift car dock crossing seams in the dull metal.

Now all I have to do is figure out how to open it.

There was a rim of metal just below the hatch, where ropes of conduit met and fed down into the network of magnetic emitters that moved the cars up and down the shaft. A recessed gantry provided access to the cables for any repair that might need to be done. He awkwardly levered himself up onto the gantry, leaning against the safety railing for support as he caught his breath.

Don't get too comfortable, Vrick said. ***Your ride is almost here.***

With a mix of relief and exhaustion, Ember took a deep breath and straightened, examining the access hatch that led off of the gantry and, he presumed, up into the lift dock itself. It was a standard maintenance hatch, and he could see the coded proximity lock that held it secure.

Again, pretty standard.

Any workers would have some kind of ID on them, either code string fed into their Link or Node, or, if they were sufficiently retro, an actual access card. Either way, he didn't have either on him.

However, that didn't mean he was helpless. He hadn't completely lost his touch from lack of practice. He ran his finger along the seam of his jacket and opened it, reaching into the left inner pocket. He found the edge of the thin, plas sheet, barely bigger than the palm of his hand, and peeled it away.

In his hand, it was a nondescript clear sheet, layered with rows of coloured dots smaller than a fingertip. He'd committed the colour coding to memory, knowing exactly what each tiny piece of code could be used for in a pinch. Each colour represented a specific snippet of code, designed for lockpicking, depending on the type and complexity of the lock.

For this type of lock, and for the security level of the admin building that he'd noted so far, he knew the pale yellows would do the trick.

Ordinarily, the codepicks could be judiciously applied in secret and with finesse, leaving no trace they had ever been used.

That ship has left the port.

He tore the plas raggedly along the space between the yellow dots, separating the entire row of ten, stuffing the remainder back into his pocket. He raised the strip of yellow to his lips and kissed the backing, then slapped the strip against the lock.

The effect was immediate and dramatic.

The code in the picks surged into the system, scrambling the locking mechanism, and frying several circuits at the same time. The acrid stink of burning plas filled the air, making his nose wrinkle and burning in the back of his throat. He raised one hand to pull the fabric of his coat over his face and the other to wave the tendrils of smoke away.

With a quiet, but immensely satisfying click, the lock disengaged, and the door popped open.

He shot through the door and shoved it closed behind him. Without the lock to keep it closed, it didn't latch, slipping open again. He looked around the lift dock, searching for something to wedge the door closed again.

Past the secure door, the lift dock was a standard workshop setup. The centre area was open, above the main hatch where the lift cars would come up from the shafts below for maintenance and repairs. Ringing that central open space were workstations, tool cabinets and banks of testing equipment.

Ember went to the nearest workstation, still littered with tools from the most recent inhabitant. He grabbed a claw spanner and unfolded it to its greatest extent, wedging it into the door's inner workings in as many places as he could to keep anyone on the other side out.

Secure for the moment, or at least with the illusion of it, he contemplated his next move. He was at the apex of the building now, and according to Vrick, the others were on their way to the roof to get him.

As long as Lexa-Blue's driving didn't kill them all first.

I heard that, she said, and he could hear the strain in her thoughts.

Just keeping you on your toes, he thought back. ***There's no one I trust more.***

She didn't answer, but he could sense that she was on her way and close.

Okay, kiddo, time to get out of here.

He scanned the work room again. Mag Lift systems, like so many other publicly used systems in the Pan Galactum, were standardized for simplicity of operation, and to prevent monopolies on parts and system repairs. Which meant that this particular system was like the rest. He'd already seen this with the basic layout of the workshop up top.

So, by extension, there should be access to the roof as well. Construction and replacement of cars would have necessitated them being dropped in from above. Which meant the roof would open to admit them, and there would be human access to the staging area outside.

And there we have it.

The outer hatch was just where he expected it to be, just a third of the way around the arc of the room's oval shape. He dashed toward it, and found another lock, this one more complicated than the previous — which he'd also anticipated.

Fishing in his pocket again, he pulled out the plas sheet once more. This time, he tore off a pouch that lined one edge, filled with a thick, viscous goo that was a muddy, ochre colour, feeling it squish and flow at his touch. Working quickly, he tore the end open and smeared the bloody substance along the edges of the hatch, wiping the excess away on the folds of his jacket. From the plas sheet, he peeled away the igniter and set it into the crude outline he had traced on the hatch.

He stood off to one side, out of the line of fire, and within seconds, the nano-explosive ignited, exploding into the lab. As his ears echoed, the heavy door fell slowly to the floor, letting out a resounding crash when it hit.

Not as subtle as a lockpick. But immensely satisfying.

He leapt over the thick slab of the door onto the roof, heading for the side of the roof where his node told him to expect Lexa-Blue and the others.

He hadn't gone a metre when two strafing lines of beamer fire bit into the roof in front of him, bearing down on the exact spot where he was standing.

Pi felt his mind expand even further, his neurons surging like the birth of a thousand stars, the primal fire of the universe.

Feeling each of the slaved LIs as extensions of his own mind and skills, he kept the intruders at bay, pumping urgency into the complex's security infrastructure. He cursed every time the unknown slicer he faced made some new inroad and subverted the system. He did all he could against the human interlopers and fought to keep the precious data that implicated both him and his thieving client hidden from the primeframes that ran the Consortium's corporate activities.

Though keeping that incriminating data out of the hands of the unknown slicer was his first priority, he fought to make sure each involved was caught. It was pure vindictiveness, but he was self-aware enough to know his ego wasn't about to allow anyone who went up against him to get away.

He had found the security drones stowed and locked away on one of his first forays into the systems, never knowing when they might come in handy, or just be fun.

And now was the time for both.

He wielded the heavily armed drones like pistols in his hands, hauling them from their routine perimeter patrols. Paying close attention to the wildly fluctuating internal security grid, he'd been able to see the patterns in the chaos his nemesis had been creating, and then to see beyond them to keep a fix on the meat puppet infiltrators as they struggled to escape from the various traps he had laid out for them.

He saw the one he had identified as the ringleader in flashes from the barely functioning cameras in the lift dock and the shaft that led up to it. Calling up the drones had been a nova of inspiration that flashed across his mind, and it had taken nothing more than a thought to bring them in from their patrol route.

Now, he relished the feel of their flight being his to control, swooping them down at the now-prostrate figure, pulsing jets of lethal energy getting closer and closer.

But not so fast that he couldn't enjoy this a little.

"Oh, no you don't," Lexa-Blue said, yanking the car's control yoke savagely to the right, sending the vehicle into a sharp, swerving descent.

She heard Keene and Malika tumble across the back seat, cursing.

"Watch it up there," Keene said, righting himself once more.

"Strap yourselves in or grab on to something," she said, wrenching at the car's steering column again. "Unless you want your boyfriend to be a charbroiled smear across the roof."

The car swung wildly again as she angled it almost on its side between Ember and the attacking drones, taking their fire against the car's undercarriage.

"You'd better get him in here fast before those beamers break through the chassis and fry us all."

With the car on its side, access to the interior was limited. The doors on one side were pressed almost completely against the rough surface of the roof, and with the other side high in the air, Ember would have been picked off easily by the drones if he tried to climb up, over and in.

"The sunroof," Lexa-Blue said, straining to hold the car in position.

Keene reached up and jammed the release open, and the sunroof slid open. Ember wasted no time clambering in, toppling in a heap between Keene and Malika, who grabbed him and pulled him close.

"Go," Keene shouted as he slammed the sunroof closed again.

Lexa-Blue rammed the accelerator, and the lower side of the car scraped along the roof, the metal of the fenders and doors sparking and screaming as she brought the vehicle back into the proper orientation and sped off.

"They're not giving up," Keene yelled from the back seat.

Lexa-Blue saw in the rear display that the drones were coming up fast behind them. She scanned ahead for some kind of cover, some way of getting their pursuers off their tail, but the problem was that the complex they'd just left was the tallest, most imposing structure in the entire skyline of this corporate city.

"Just hold on tight back there," she said. "This might get bumpy."

She swerved madly, tossing the car and all of them inside it back and forth, trying to keep them out of the drones' line of fire, though far too many of the high-energy plasma packets were hitting the armoured surface of the limo, scoring and charring the formerly shining finish.

At the corners of her vision, she caught sight of the shocked faces of other drivers she sped past.

A long cargo truck loomed to her left, blocking out the waning afternoon sun. Calling on every one of her piloting reflexes and skills, Lexa-Blue spun the car into a complete barrel roll, aiming the front of the car down towards the street below.

Dimly, she registered a lull in the drones' firing pattern as they paused to avoid hitting the truck itself, then struck up again as they swerved around it.

"I'm going to bortch," Malika said from the back seat, her shout strangled as she clamped her teeth tight.

"This is nothing," Ember said, righting himself against the pull of his safety belts.

"Any time you want to take over," Lexa-Blue grunted, her knuckles white where they clutched the car's controls.

The trio in the back seat went silent.

That is, until the car plunged toward the busy street below, eliciting another strangled squeal from Malika that she quickly stifled.

The pattern of traffic sped up to meet them as they fell toward the street, a complex weave of rickshaws and cargo vans, and, of course, a full tramload of passengers. Feeling the flow and pulse of the traffic like something she held in her hands, Lexa-Blue spotted an opening and jammed her braking system hard.

The tail of the car actually impacted the paved surface of the road, before the car settled into an empty space between a cluster of rickshaws and the massive bulk of the tram.

Settled, she gunned the engines once more, weaving out from behind the tram to pass it, edging right up against the sidewalk, causing pedestrians to dive out of the way.

She let out a breath, feeling a brief moment of reprieve from their pursuit, thinking that the restraint their attacker had shown with the airborne truck would extend even further now they were deep amongst other potential victims.

Unfortunately, her continuing to elude capture seemed only to incense their pursuer, for a new, vibrant spray of beamer sizzled across the car's armoured roof, even burning into the side of the tram itself. On their other side, a rickshaw caught and tumbled end over end, ejecting its passenger to the ground.

Even through the closed, secured windows of the car, they could hear the screams.

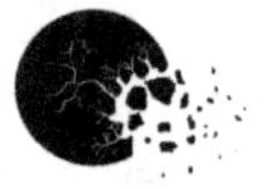

"Oh, no," Vrick said to emself. "That is more than enough of that."

Ey marshalled es forces once again, having spent more than enough of es extended time sense taking their foe's measure.

Having recovered from the shock of discovering who was on the other side of the tangled war of code that sprung up between them, ey was able to focus on what was happening rather than the improbability of it happening.

With time to think, enhanced by es natural ability to think so many times faster than a human, Vrick was able to analyze the attacks and the myriad little things that betrayed the fact that their attacker was, indeed, a human. Boosted in some technological fashion, but human nonetheless.

As an Artificial Sentience, it wasn't immodest to acknowledge that ey was the pinnacle of non-organic intelligence in the Galactum, and capable of far more than even the most illegally modified human, not that there were many of those. Ey knew that ey was something beyond even the most advanced Artificial Intelligence available under the strict statutes that governed thinking machines. Over es long life, ey had studied and learned all ey could about just what the current human society was comfortable with in terms of beings that even remotely resembled es ilk.

And that store of knowledge had grown ever stronger.

Hypotheses flew through es deductive matrices, ordering themselves neatly into a shifting bank of priorities that adjusted with each move and countermove their enemy slicer employed.

Faster than the other could react, ey flooded the virtual battlefield with a thousand-thousand variations of the inverse, negative key, self-replicating ciphers ey was writing and deploying.

As ey had suspected, the effect was similar to that of the full onslaught of a hurricane battering at a lean-to on a beach. The rogue slicer's defences were incapable of withstanding the barrage of rotating, recalculating code strings, collapsing in a pattern of data novae across Vrick's consciousness.

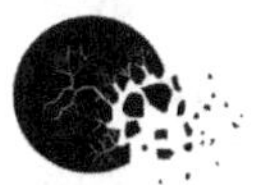

Agony like acid, glass and fire poured down out of Pi's shielded interface with Know-It-All, tearing his concentration apart.

At the edges of his blistered, fractioning concentration, he registered the fact that six of the LI boosters had overloaded, showering his body with sparks. Against the anguish in his mind, the flecked burns across his skin from the fusillade of sparks was nothing.

He swam up out of the haze of pain, abandoning his attack. For all of his intelligence and arrogance, he could see now that there was no way to salvage it. Coming out of his deep trance-like state, he became aware of the acrid smell of burning circuitry mixed with the sickly-sweet smell of the cooking LI matrix biocircuitry.

Hauling himself up out of his couch, he fought the urge to spew the contents of his stomach, as well as the spinning disorientation of his sudden ejection from his slicing trance.

Finally, he staggered to his feet, his hazy view of his workspace swimming back into a solid reality. A solid and now burning reality, as the now useless LI units burned freely now, spewing a thick, noxious black smoke. As he watched, a burst of sparks washed over his trance couch, setting it alight.

The whole rig was a wreck now, as the heightened power through it unbalanced, setting off a cascade failure.

Pi cursed vividly as the heat washed over his face in waves. In the end it was just hardware, all of which could be replaced. The real power was in the code, and all of that was stored in a triple cipher-locked innernet and could be reapplied to a new setup at any time.

No, it wasn't the loss of the rig itself that drove him to rage. It wasn't even the loss of the money he and Omhrys had so skillfully diverted out of the hands of the mining crews. There would always be money, always be some way to make more. There would be other challenges too, other systems to slice just for the mere fun of being the one who broke through. But the ignominy of losing out to whoever it was that had bested him in their contest of wills, that was what he couldn't take.

Someone out there had gone up against the most powerful weapons Pi had in his arsenal and had beaten them all.

And that could not be left unanswered.

The sizzle of the drones' beamers cut suddenly, as did their power systems, though they almost didn't hear it over the din of the chaos their pursuit had caused. Ember heard it first, twisting in his seat to see out the car's back window.

He was just in time to see the pursuing drones tumble drunkenly from the air, one slamming down into traffic to their right, causing a rickshaw to swerve out of its path. The other bounced off the roof of the tram, eliciting a new round of screams from its passengers, before coming down directly into their path.

Only Lexa-Blue's driving skills, which sent the car into a yawing skid around the obstacle, kept them from colliding with it.

Vrick, casualties? Keene said.

I'm monitoring the emergency channels, and it sounds like nothing serious.

Thank goss for that, Keene said, sagging back into the seat. ***What about our adversary?***

As far as I can tell so far, he's gone, Vrick said.

I wouldn't count on that, Ember said. ***He meant business. I'm not sure he'll give up that easily.***

I'll be watching, Vrick said.

And what about us? Malika said. ***We just very publicly broke into the governing agency of this entire system. I'm pretty sure that's against a law or two. Or ten.***

I'm scrubbing what I can and overwriting the image recognition algorithms with some made-up faces. We're not in the clear yet, but given time, I think I can clean it all up.

The question is, do we have that time, Ember said.

"I need a destination up here, people," Lexa-Blue called from the driver's seat. ***Considering the shape this car is in, we're going to start attracting all the wrong kinds of attention if we don't get out of sight fast. We need a hidey-hole fast, junkpile.***

Done, Vrick said, and they all felt the coordinates and nature of their destination download directly to Lexa-Blue's node.

She veered the car right, through a sudden gap in the traffic, pulling into an alley between two wide, blocky buildings. The gap was only just big enough for the car to make it through, but within moments opened to a courtyard ringed with wide, rolling doors that were easily big enough for the car to fit through.

I'm in the security system and am overriding, Vrick said, as one of the doors ahead of them and to the left began to roll slowly upwards.

Lexa-Blue slowed the car and steered it into the dark rectangle of the doorway. As they passed over the threshold, lights came on, bathing the huge, empty space around them. With plenty of room to spare, she pulled to a halt, and all was suddenly quiet.

***Reserve warehouse space for an intended expansion**

next month,* Vrick told them. ***No security patrols and I've bypassed the electronic system for now.***

They all sat for a moment, in the sudden lull after the crisis, unsure of what to do next. Lexa-Blue moved first, lifting her hands from the controls of the car and shaking them out with one sharp flex of her fingers.

Her movement spurred the rest of them on as well, and they all tumbled out of the wrecked car to stand, stretch or walk in some way to release the tension of their pursuit. Malika walked straight away from the car, arching her back and stretching from side to side. Ember went down into a crouch, his back against the scraped, dented fender. Keene stood at his side, one hand on Ember's knotted shoulder.

"Well," Ember said, patting his hand down on Keene's. "That could have gone better."

As if to punctuate the point, the car's grav cushion gave out in a shuddering cough and the chassis dropped to the floor with a crash.

There was a moment of silence, and then they were all laughing, the rich belly-deep laughter that only came after as close a call as they had all just experienced.

"So, now what?" Keene said, the first to regain control after their shared fit of relief.

I'm working my way through the data as fast as I can, Vrick said. ***The ID inoculations are holding, but the consortium has some state-secret levels of encryption and I have to reconstruct records and compare them to several layers of data backup to look for anomalies. It's going to take me some time.***

"Where are we anyway?" Lexa-Blue said. "I mean, where in the city?"

She called up Know-It-All and the regional map, highlighting their position and sharing it with the others.

"Great," she said. "We're about as far from Vrick as we could be."

"And the theatre is over here," Malika said. "Not as far, but definitely not close enough."

"With all the noise we made, there's going to be a lot more security around," Ember said.

"And even with Vrick running interference in the records, they might crack down on anyone and everyone," Lexa-Blue said. "It won't take them long to put enough of it together to make things difficult for us out there."

"Also, we no longer have a mode of transportation," Keene said, pointing to the wreck of the car. "How exactly are we going to explain that to the rental company?"

"Do we have insurance for that?" Malika deadpanned.

"Well, I did shell out for the extended package," Lexa-Blue said. "I'm sure those dents will buff right out."

"I have an idea," Ember said, concentrating on the city map.

"What are you thinking?" Keene said.

"Here," Ember said, a thought highlighting an area on the outskirts of the city near their position. "This is the dock area for freighters and long-haul cargo ships."

He closed his eyes for a second as he accessed the dock's public manifest. He opened his eyes with a smile.

"And we have a friend there."

CHAPTER TEN

The panic that gripped Ijagu Omrhys sang in harmony with the coruscating alarms ringing through the building.

At the first shriek of the alarm system, he'd been convinced that somehow, he'd been discovered, that evidence of his embezzlement had come to light and security was headed his way at that very moment to arrest him.

As the fear coursed through him, he activated his Link and sent the shielded comm code to contact Pi.

The code seemed to ring for an eternity, before Pi engaged, snarled "I'm busy" and disconnected before Omrhys was able to even say a word.

He gaped at nothing, his terror surging again, but as he stood frozen, Security sent a tight band message through the terminals of all employees, eyes only, informing them that there had been a fraudulent incursion into the building, and they were dealing with it.

His nerves calmed somewhat. That couldn't have anything to do with him, could it?

The bulletin went on to inform the staff that the loci of intrusion were in one of the public conference rooms used for external client meetings. That couldn't have anything to do with him. Why would anyone after him be down there?

But the other locus was the office of the executive who had apparently been using the conference room. He did a quick calculation in his head of the grade of access that the person must have had, trying to understand what an intruder might have had access to through that compromised office.

Surely it was just a case of some kind of industrial espionage gone wrong. There was enough information in the Consortium's primeframe that had nothing to do with him and his actions, that there must be some other reason for all of this happening now.

No matter how hard he told himself that, how often he repeated it in his head, the suspicions would not go away.

The security bulletin had told them to remain at their stations or in their offices until the situation was under control once more, and it seemed a long excruciating wait until the all-clear finally sounded throughout the complex.

Of course, it was followed right away by a directive from upper management that they were all to go back to work for the rest of their day, unless Security wished to interview them regarding the incident.

His paranoia giving way to indignation, Omrhys fumed at his desk. As he reopened his dormant files, he signalled Pi's call code again. This time, there was no answer at all.

"You came in that thing?" Malika said, staring up at the *Sparkling Gossamer* in disbelief.

"Hey, she's a good ship," Ember said, her words stinging despite the fact that he'd felt exactly the same way when he had first seen the ship. "And we're not exactly in a position to be too picky right now."

"Fair point," she said, reaching up to rub a smear of dirt from her face. "Lead on."

The *Gossamer* was nestled in the commercial section of the port, on the opposite side of Sound's city from the public section where Vrick was docked. All around the ungainly ship were others, all designed for similar commercial or cargo purposes. Even among the other commercial ships, the odd, ungainly *Gossamer* stood out. Ember led them across the flat surface of the massive, open docking plain to the ship.

When they reached the ship, the ship's gantry was already open and extended from the ship's underside.

"Not particularly secure," Lexa-Blue said, her hand hovering by her gun out of habit.

"Well, considering we're probably the most disruptive force on this planet right now, and we've been invited in, I'd say it's not that big a deal," Keene said peering up into the ship's interior from the base of the ramp.

"There is that," Lexa-Blue said, grinning.

At Keene's side, Ember leaned over and called up into the ship. "Irad? It's us."

A muffled voice called back to them, the sound bouncing around off the empty ship's walls as it was picked up by the ship's internal commo. "I'm in the engine room. I'll meet you in the galley."

"Come on," Ember said, leading the way up into the ship. The others fell into step behind him, Lexa-Blue bringing up the rear and keeping a watchful eye out for any unwanted attention.

"Help yourself to anything you want," Irad's voice yelled from down a corridor facing them as they turned right for the galley and lounge.

Malika was the first to drop onto one of the couches, her head down between her knees for a moment, breathing deeply.

"Are you okay?" Keene asked.

She lifted her head and grinned. "Yeah. Just not used to this life anymore."

Ember had gone straight to the beverage cooler, pulling out a bulb of water. He popped the top and drank deeply from it, then rubbed the cool surface against his forehead.

"Is there coffee?" Lexa-Blue asked, coming up beside him. "I need a hit."

Ember showed her the cubby with the dispenser in it.

"Pretty similar to ours," she said, putting a mug into the flash brewer and hitting the button to start the process. The rich aroma was instant and mouthwatering.

"Oh, I need one of those too," Malika said, pulling herself up and joining them. She also gestured at Ember's bulb of water. "And one of those."

He handed her one, then gave one to Keene as well when he nodded agreement to Ember's questioning look.

They all stood a moment in the quiet, concentrating on their beverages and waiting.

"Sorry about that," Irad said from the doorway. "I was recalibrating my interspace converters. My efficiency was off by a few points and it was really bugging me."

They turned to face him, taking in the unassuming man in his faded shipsuit, scrubbing at his hands with a cloth to remove some dark, gummy substance.

"Anyway, welcome aboard," Irad said, grinning. "I wasn't expecting any visitors, but Ember made it sound urgent."

"You could say that," Ember said, wryly. "You might want to sit down for this."

With only the slightest hint of wariness, Irad took a seat, surrounded by the others in various chairs or couches around him. After introductions were quickly made, they laid out the story for him, in concise, but thorough, detail.

Irad, for his part, betrayed no expression as he listened to Ember calmly relate each intricate detail of their most recent adventure. When Ember was finished, Irad remained silent a moment. The others exchanged worried looks, unsure about how the mild, unassuming captain might react.

"That is amazing!" The words burst out of him in an explosion of energy that seemed to erupt from his toes. "I mean, you see things like that in sensies or on the deevee channels, but I never imagined I'd actually know someone who actually *did* them! I mean, they were shooting. At you. Shooting at you. What was that like? How did you disguise yourselves? How do you plan something like that, anyway?"

Ember turned to the others as Irad stopped to take a breath. "Okay, was not expecting him to take it that well."

He turned back to Irad, whose eyes were wide, his mouth working as if trying to find words for more questions. "Okay, take a moment, Irad. Breathe. You're going to hurt yourself."

"Okay," Irad said, holding up his hands as if asking for quiet. "I'm good. It's just, I never even imagined that people actually did this kind of thing. I mean, you told me some stories, but I thought you were just — I have no idea what I thought. You just never expect something like this to show up on your doorstep, you know?"

"Funny," Malika said. "I don't think I ever stopped expecting it to show up on my doorstep."

Irad laughed, the sound genuinely joyous. "Considering what Ember told me about your former adventures, I'm not surprised. I'm glad you found each other again. And it's really pretty great meeting all of you."

The collectively held breath of tension evaporated from them all, and they truly relaxed for the first time since the whole escapade had begun.

"Are you sure you're okay with us being here?" Ember asked. "I didn't want to drag you into things, but we're in a sticky situation."

"Are you kidding?" Irad asked. "I'm thrilled. I never imagined anything like this was even possible in the real world. I'm so in. What do you need me to do?"

"Well, we can start with just giving us a place to lie low for a bit while we figure out what the hells we do next," Ember said.

"We'll hold off on involving you in any major felonies for the time being," Lexa-Blue said.

"Oh, all right," Irad said, his own smile almost as wide as hers. "Ember knows where everything is, so help yourselves. My home is yours."

"A shower," Keene said. "I need a shower."

"Damn right, you do," Lexa-Blue said, socking him in the shoulder, making him scowl at her.

"Guest cabins are that way," Irad said, pointing. "You might have to take turns, but they're yours."

"Clothes," Malika said. "We're going to need new clothes. Again."

"I have some things," Irad said, then pointed at his own physique which was shorter and leaner than all of them except maybe for Malika. "You're welcome to whatever might be of use."

"Call up Know-It-All and share the open order with us," Ember said. "Anyone who wants to add anything can. We can have it delivered."

"Crikes," Lexa-Blue said. "I haven't worn this many different outfits in months. Did we budget for this?"

"Check Line Item 42," Ember said. "Other items, as necessary."

"Those other items are going to bankrupt us," Keene said, ever the practical one. "These missions of yours are costly."

"Think of it as a spiritual quest," Ember said. "The benefit to your soul can't be measured in mere credits."

"That's fine for me," Keene said, "but what about Lexa-Blue? Her soul is a lot more degraded than mine. She needs way more help than me."

Lexa-Blue's only response was to stick out her tongue as she headed off toward the guest cabins and a shower, already stripping off her chauffeur's livery and tossing the jacket over a chair. Where it promptly slid off onto the floor. Keene stepped forward and picked it back up, apologizing to Irad. "Sorry. She was raised by wild dogs."

"I *heard* that," came the loud reply from down the hall.

"I need to get out of this combat suit," Keene said, heading out of the lounge. "The power cell is chafing like you would not believe."

As Keene left the room, Malika moved to Ember's side, pressing herself into his side and resting her chin on his shoulder. "They haven't changed a bit."

Ember chuckled. "They just get more and more so all the time."

"I think I may actually be glad to hear that," Malika said. "Should I be worried?"

Ember turned his head and kissed her temple. "Nah. I think it means you're just fine."

"Keep that up and you're gonna make me cry. Go take a shower and get cleaned up. I'll make sure the clothes get ordered."

She moved away from him and caught sight of Irad, watching them with a ridiculous grin on his face. She found herself smiling along with him. "Are you okay, captain?"

For a moment, he bounced on his heels, his excitement almost overwhelming him, and they couldn't help but laugh. "I'm fine. This is just… pretty damn thrilling. Before you got here, the most exciting thing that happened to me this week was fixing my water recycler. This is so much better."

His thrumming energy was a tonic, energizing Ember and taking his mind off just how badly their unseen, unnamed enemy had trounced them today. The defeat stung, bitterly, and he was not about to let it happen again.

You there, Vrick?

Am I ever not?

You've just been quiet.

You all left a mighty powerful mess in your wake today, Vrick said. ***It's taking some time to do damage control. There are surveillance records to alter, security reports to lose. And I'm still trying to find some traces of our slicer friend who's behind all this. There are a lot**

of records to go through, even for me.*

I was going to say keep me posted, but I should have known you would.

I've got some subroutines analyzing the data that you managed to extract, and I think I'm close to an answer, so hold tight, take your shower and try to relax for a bit. I've got this.

Vrick was as good as es word.

By the time they were showered, fed, and freshly dressed, ey had assessed the information they had managed to liberate before their mission had gone so wrong. With Irad's permission, ey accessed the *Gossamer*'s systems and used the lounge's entertainment unit to brief them.

"You were right," Vrick said, as the reams of collected data flowed into various panes. "They are definitely funnelling through the station. With the information you managed to pull from the primeframes, I was able to identify where the discrepancies are happening and how. They're using the sorting system to misidentify what they want to divert as being waste rather than valuable, saleable material. The system then shuffles it out of circulation and diverts it to their specially selected cargo ships for sale at Sombra."

"But surely someone must notice," Malika said.

"Not necessarily," Irad said. "I've been up there many times to pick up cargo and I haven't seen any of the inside of the station. I just manoeuvre into my assigned dock and hand over control to the AI dedicated to the section of the loading area I've been assigned to."

"There's no crew inside the station itself?" Keene asked.

"There are skeleton crews of engineers and maintenance mechanics to keep everything running," Vrick said. "But the actual sorting process itself is all automated. And like Irad said, there are independently functioning AIs running different docking berths and lading sections. It would take a truly talented slicer to get into the sorting system, but as we've seen, there's an exceptionally talented slicer at work here. For someone that skilled, it wouldn't be that hard to convince the sorting routines to shuffle product however they wanted."

"And if they're smart —" Ember said.

"And they are," Lexa-Blue said.

Ember nodded. "They're probably shuffling small amounts at any given time. Is there somewhere they could bank what they're diverting? Some kind of storage area?"

"Clever boy," Vrick said. "There are banks and banks of storage spots of various sizes. There are all sorts of shipments of various materials going to various locations depending on what stage the Gate construction is at in that planetary system. The logistics are nightmarish. Even I'd have a problem keeping track of what was destined for where."

"What about the corporation, though?" Malika said. "Surely they notice the effect on their bottom line?"

"With any process this complex, there are any number of ways to glitch things up," Vrick said. "And from the looks of things, our little friend is diverting at a specific stage in the process that makes it look like the company is getting full value, while the workers are getting shorted on their bonuses. And even if someone did notice, then it's a toss-up whether that person would care enough to bring it to the attention of someone willing to do something about it."

Malika made a sound of utter disgust. "Why am I not surprised? This is why I *hate* corps."

"You and pretty much all of us, sister," Lexa-Blue said. "It's an uphill battle for the good ones to outdo the shit perpetrated by the bad ones."

"So, do we have enough evidence to take to the authorities?" Malika said. "Can we bring the operation down?"

"Unfortunately, no," Vrick said. "I have the information that we pulled out, but considering how we obtained it, we'd have a hard time getting it admitted in court. And our slicer dropped a codenuke in the middle of everything, so the only copy of the data we have is our own and it's degrading too. There's most likely no trace of it left on the corporate servers anymore. Even if we could get it admitted as evidence, any attorney worth more than a credit or two could shoot holes in it."

"Wonderful," Malika said.

"Hey, don't give up yet," Ember said, slipping an arm around her shoulder. "We've cracked bigger marks than this."

"So, what's the answer, Junkpile?" Lexa-Blue said. "You always tell us it can't be done, right before you tell us how it can be done."

"You see right through me, meat," Vrick said. "We do have an option. It's not an easy one, but we do have an option."

"We scoff in the face of danger," Lexa-Blue said. "Hit us with it."

"And that's why I love you all," Vrick said with a chuckle. "From what I can see, our so-called genius slicer is still thinking of the AIs as just being piles of code and hardware like computers are."

"Oh, I think I see where this is going," Keene said.

"Okay, smarty, explain it to the class," Lexa-Blue said.

"Correct me if I'm off base, Vrick," Keene said. "Computers, however sophisticated, are circuits and hardware. AIs are a step beyond, more grown than built. The underlying architecture is hybrid electronic and biological. So, they store and retain data differently. Standard slicing will only ever get at data stored in traditional ways. But with AI storage, there's also a whole other level of complexity that's almost akin to DNA coding. And it's relatively impervious to slicing."

"And the sorting and lading systems on that station are run by a bunch of AIs," Malika said, the light going on.

"Go to the head of the class," Vrick said. "The primeframes at the corporate headquarters are all standard non-AI. But there's going to be a whole other backup of the information in the AI systems up there."

"But can we access it?" Ember asked.

"Not from outside the station, no." Vrick said. "But get up there and get a hardlink into the casing of one of the sorting AIs, and I can make copies for us and for all the necessary authorities."

"Then let's do it," Lexa-Blue said.

"Hold up there, meat," Vrick said. "You thought security at the headquarters was tight? That station is even tighter. If we can get in, it's easy. My cargo holds aren't big enough to be of any use to them, so I have no reason to visit the station. There's no reason for investors to be up there, and, like I said, other than the engineering and maintenance crews, there's no other staff up there to impersonate."

"Do you know enough to fake being one of the regular crew?" Ember asked Keene.

"If we can get in, then I can bluff my way through it," Keene said, nodding.

"It's getting in that's the problem," Vrick said. "When the staff does rotate in and out, they travel on specific shuttles with the proper code clearance. And as stylish and handsome as I am, I'd never pass for a crew shuttle."

"There has to be a way," Ember said with a scowl.

"I have an idea," Irad said, and they all turned to him. "The *Gossamer* is in rotation for smaller cargoes. They actually offered me a load, but I turned it down because I was going to take a bit of time for myself. But there's so much traffic in and out that I won't be waiting long. And it would get us docked right to the station itself."

"Are you sure?" Ember asked. "There's no going back from this. If we get caught, then you're in it up to your neck. We do this… well, we do this far more often than we should. But your record is clean. Are you sure you want to get in that deep?"

"Are you kidding?" Irad said with a laugh. "This is awesome. And I know a lot of these workers. What's happening to them is terrible. If I can help stop it, then I'm a hundred percent in."

Ember searched Irad's face for doubt but seemed convinced. "Okay, that gets us up to the station, but does it get us *into* the station?"

"Unfortunately, no," Vrick said. "There will be a physical connection between the ship and the station, but only a cargo conveyor, which will be full of whatever Irad will be hauling. Too dangerous to try and enter that way."

"Can you show me the schematics of the docking berths?" Keene said.

The plans appeared before them, wireframe diagrams that shifted through each dimension, with a ship in place for comparison. "They're all the same basic design, just some minor variations for ships of different sizes."

Keene studied the plans for a moment and a hush fell as they waited for him to see something in the design that might help them.

"There," he said, his finger sinking into the hologram. "Manual emergency hatches. By law, they have to have them, even on code-locked docking berths. It will have both a hand release and an emergency quick release."

"Right," Lexa-Blue said, getting the idea. "There has to be some way for people to get in if they're injured while out on the hull."

"Exactly," Keene said. "The law requires them to have a backup system for easy access. And I think we can take advantage of that."

"That's *daring*," Ember said, not sounding like he was sold on the idea. "It means spacewalking your way in."

"And bypassing the alarm systems that are designed to send medical and emergency teams the second the quick release systems are activated."

"I didn't say it was the perfect solution," Keene said. "But, from where I'm standing, it's the only one we have."

"So, who goes in?" Ember said.

"Well, I do, for sure," Keene said. "It's going to take some major sleight of hand to keep every alarm in the place from going off. And, not to brag, but I'm the only one that can manage it. Not to mention access the AI core backup memory without laying waste to the system running the entire station."

"I don't like it," Ember said. "But I have to agree. You'll need back-up though. I don't want you in there without some protection while you're working."

Lexa-Blue raised her hand. "You're not going in there without me, Junior."

"Surprising no one," Ember said, smiling. "I guess I'll be out here, then. Keeping an eye on things."

"And I can tell, you're thrilled," Keene said. "But we've got this. We're a team."

Ember wound his fingers through Keene's and nodded. "Okay, Irad, can you get yourself back on that cargo rotation?"

Without even moving from his seat, Irad touched the Link on his sleeve and opened a connection to Know-It-All. He closed his eyes and the rapid movements behind his eyelids only took a moment or two before he looked back at them. "Done and done. Now I just have to wait for my turn."

"I may be able to nudge that along," Vrick said. "I don't have deep access anymore, but I should have just enough pull to get you moved up the list."

"Okay, then," Ember said. "Let's nail down the details and get this asshole."

The capsule hotel where Pi ended up was a hovel, at the very lowest end of the accommodation spectrum, in the seediest corner of the transient quarter. But it was off the beaten path and as free of corporate intervention as could be found on a planetoid like this.

As the door hissed shut behind him, he felt a sweet, illusory flush of relief. He knew he wasn't out of danger yet, but at least here he had a chance. Even a dump like this had access to Know-It-All, and that was what he'd need to take stock of the shambles this operation had become and to organize an escape route off this hole of a planet.

The room was overpriced and bare, nothing more than a desk that required the occupant to sit on the edge of the bed to use it, and a minuscule refresher that combined shower and lavatory into one vertical, coffin-like space.

Pi levered himself down onto the lumpy, uneven mattress, his thoughts a jagged whirl. This had been a perfect operation, a triumph of planning and execution. It should have gone perfectly. He hadn't even thought he'd need to eliminate Omrhys, despite his inside man's utter incompetence.

But *now?*

He couldn't imagine that he could be tracked from his elegant code, but someone had broken past and toppled the months of careful planning he had put into place to skim the funds subtly and completely. He'd barely escaped with his skin intact, and now he needed to bug out as soon as possible.

Reciting a string of code as a mantra, he calmed his mind, settling into a much calmer state before opening his node to Know-It-All. The generic, public interface filled the space behind his eyes, the same portal used across the Galactum. The field of pseudo-stars filled his vision, the complex web of knowledge and history stored for public use. He thought the code string for his triple-secured private vault, the starry vista swirling and reforming as his own interface, reacting solely to the pattern of his memory engrams and personality matrix.

There, hidden away, was his hoard, the virtual racks of code, stored away and ready to be used and repurposed in whatever combination Pi might need for future tasks.

As he lay there, contemplating his next move, his message queue lit up like a point-sized star, the sensation almost painful in his head. The sudden intensity indicated the number and supposed urgency of the messages waiting. When he touched the indicator, it seared with a ridiculous number of messages left for him while he'd been searching the streets for somewhere to lie low.

No surprise, every message was from Omrhys, growing more and more panicked until the most recent were little more than garbled, incoherent threats.

Now, that is going to be a problem, he thought.

It only took a cursory slice into the most public commo grid to see that Omrhys was about to go to what laughingly passed for the authorities on this tiny sharthole of a planet: two bored GalSec agents on the verge of retirement, and a contingent of overpaid, under-skilled corporate security goons. But even those wasted dead-enders could make all kinds of trouble for him, once his now former ally spilled out the details of their plot.

In that tiny hotel capsule, on that mattress that seemed to somehow be thin and lumpy at the same time, Pi's anger simmered up to a full rage. There had been profit, yes. Luscious, ample credit balances that would keep him funded for a substantial amount of time until he found some new challenge to spark the fires of his genius.

No, this wasn't about the profit. This was about getting even with Omrhys for his weakness.

This was about the bitter sting of defeat of barely defeating the mystery slicer that had driven him from the safety of his den and destroyed what could have continued to be a lucrative operation for a long time to come. Whoever the faceless, nameless opponent had been, the humiliation of losing to them was more than Pi could bear. And the warped alchemy of Pi's personality was all too adept at turning those little humiliations into the fuel of rage.

Over and over, his mind obsessively picked over the experience, tearing it up, reexamining it, stoking the fires of resentment at all of the factors that had led him here to this seedy hotel, on the run.

And with every flicker of resentment and ire, with every slight and flash of fury, came ever grander, ever more vicious plans for retaliation.

CHAPTER ELEVEN

As the *Liquid Supernova* lifted from its berth for their regularly scheduled shift, Anyeis pored over the local newsfeed on Know-It-All, her stomach tied around itself as she saw the details of the frenzied chase through the streets of Sound. This was not at all how it should have gone down. She'd agreed to this only because she wanted her people taken care of, and she hadn't been able to think of any other way to investigate the embezzlement and get their money back.

But this?

Nothing Malika had said could have prepared her for *this*.

The amateur holos of the drones chasing down the badly damaged limousine had filled her with terror for Malika's life, and the lives of her friends who were only here to help Anyeis and her workers.

It was a miracle that no one had been seriously hurt, even with the wreckage of the truck and the damage to the tram.

She wanted it all to stop, couldn't imagine any situation where this ended without bloodshed, and even greater calamity.

Even as she readied her crew for their next shift, going through all the pre-shift diagnostics and equipment checks, she had kept half an eye on the newsfeed. Even though she was sick with worry, she couldn't neglect her crew.

But then, as the ship rose through the thin, dry atmosphere of Sound, the newsfeed had gone dead. Every story, every holo, every mention of the incident was gone. No matter the search parameters, there was just — *nothing*.

She assumed it was being covered up but had no idea who was behind it.

Until the brief message from Malika, routed through an unfamiliar call code. They were fine. And proceeding with the rest of the plan.

Anyeis felt a dizzying mix of relief and worry. They were all right but heading right back into danger. She wanted to call it all off, torn between her loyalty to the miners she worked with, the culture that had taken her in and given her a home, and Malika.

Though she wondered if she could have called them off now anyway. *We're all in too deep now,* she thought.

All she could do now was her job. Shepherding the crews in the hold of her ship. Getting them out to the rocks and back in one piece.

That, and wait.

They stayed there on the *Gossamer,* hashing through possible plans, picking them apart from every angle when they discovered weak spots, as everyone had their chance to speak out.

Finally, exhausted, it seemed like they had a plan locked in.

"Look, you're all about ready to drop," Vrick said. "Come back here and get some rest. Then you can gear up once Irad gets the call for a cargo run."

Irad nodded. "I checked the public rota. From what I can see, I should be called up tomorrow. If I'm reading things right."

"I have no doubt you are," Ember said. "You know this system better than we do."

"Hey, is it safe for us to go back out there?" Lexa-Blue said. "After our little adventure, there must be authorities looking for us."

"I've been busy," Vrick said. "After dealing with our little friend, slicing into the local system was nothing. I've been erasing vid surveillance, misfiling reports, rewriting memos, and fast-tracking the insurance claims. By the time I was done, no one was in any particular mood to pursue us, even if any of their evidence could actually still identify you."

"You do me proud," Lexa-Blue said, dramatically wiping away an imaginary tear.

"If I hadn't already been so good at hiding my tracks before you two came along, you'd never have lasted as long as you have," Vrick said.

"And we thank you for it," Keene added. "Not that I'm the one that needs it most."

Lexa-Blue stuck out her tongue at him and made to playfully punch at him, but he ducked the blow.

"Okay, break it up, you two," Ember said. "Sleep. For everyone."

He turned to Malika, "Don't you have shows tomorrow?"

She shook her head. "I have understudies. I booked personal time. I'm allowed it in my contract, so even if the company wanted to make a big deal about it, they can't. I'm just the first to do it here because there's not much reason to."

"We're set then, I guess," Ember turned to Irad and hugged him. "Thank you for helping us out."

"Any time," Irad said. "This is way more fun than my recycling system diagnostic."

They left him in the *Gossamer*, catching the tram back to the other landing field where Vrick was berthed.

They climbed the ramp into the ship, Malika last in line. As she stepped into the main lounge, she reached up and put a hand on the curve in the wall where the corridor opened into the larger room. "Hello, friend."

"Hello, friend," Vrick said. "Welcome home."

Ey noticed her face cloud for a moment, before the expression flickered away, replaced by a smile.

"It's funny to hear you call it that," she said. "I was only here for such a short time."

Vrick made a tutting sound that deepened her smile. "It's not about time. You made an impression."

This actually made her laugh, and the sound was throaty and self-deprecating. "Not a very good one, if I recall correctly."

"Things were hectic," ey said. "One can be forgiven much given the circumstances."

"You are most kind, old friend. And forgiving."

"Stuff and nonsense," Vrick said. "Once you're one of us, you stay one of us."

Malika looked around, realizing they were alone. "Speaking of us, where did they all go?"

"Well, knowing Lexa-Blue, she's probably looking for a drink. Since there's no one here for her to squish with. The boys are probably prepping. Keene is obsessive when it comes to making sure he's ready for anything."

"Should I be doing something?" Malika asked. "I feel a bit extraneous."

"Never you mind. One of them will come and get you soon enough. Your first task is to get yourself something to drink and come tell me all about your theatre. I want to hear everything."

Keene strode into the airlock and directly to the suit lockers, Ember just behind him.

"Okay, so where do we start?" Ember asked.

Keene was already opening the locker that Ember knew held the tool kit that was specially designed for use with his EVA suit. "Can you pack and rack my suit? I have to get it to the *Gossamer* if I'm going to be spacewalking over to that external lock to open it."

Keene's attention was already on the case of tools before him on the bench, checking each one, confirming that the powered ones were fully charged, then moving on to the manual ones, ensuring that any moving parts were sufficiently mobile to do their work.

Ember complied, opening the locker containing Keene's vibrant blue suit. The impossibly thin, laminated steelskin of the suit hung neatly on its specially designed rack, the telltales in the monitoring system all glowing a comforting green. To be sure, Ember keyed the locker's diagnostic to run a check again, to make sure that those indicators were telling the truth.

Even though he knew that Keene would run through all the checks again when he suited up on the *Gossamer*, he performed his own checks anyway. He wasn't about to leave anything to chance.

Satisfied with the monitoring systems, he did a visual inspection of the suit as well, checking the seals and joints for any obvious signs of wear or damage. He didn't see anything obvious, but he knew there was only so much that could be seen by the naked eye. He only hesitated for a moment before pulling out the scanner wand that would see damage his eyes couldn't. With deft motions, he ran the wand over the suit in the standard scan pattern.

"I can feel you watching me, you know," he said, a smile in his voice, though he didn't look up from his task.

"You know I checked that after the last time I used it, right?" Keene said, a warm simmer of amusement in his voice.

"I know," Ember said, still not looking up from the scanner.

"And you know I'm going to run it through a full check on the *Gossamer*, right?"

"I know," Ember said again. "Humour me."

"Okay, just checking."

As satisfied as he could be without running the suit through a molecular scanner, Ember placed the scanner wand back in its charging cradle and hit the control that activated the suit's compression system. With a soft hum, the rack holding the suit contracted, the outer sides of the locker compressing in and folding down into something the size of a heavy suitcase. With a chirp, the system let them know it was complete, sliding the case out to them.

"All packed," Ember said. "Ready for your next death-defying feat."

"Terrifying peril, here we come."

"I think that was my favourite of your performances," Vrick said.

"Really?" Malika asked. "I thought the script was kind of trite. One of those crowd-pleasers that makes you enough money to do the really challenging stuff that the masses don't understand."

"Oh, it definitely was," Vrick said. "But it was a fun kind of trite. And you elevated it with your work, you and the rest of the cast."

"Now you're just flattering me," she said.

"I'm shocked," Lexa-Blue said, entering from the corridor leading aft. "Ey never has anything nice to say."

"I never have anything nice to say about you," Vrick said. "And can you blame me?"

"Rude!" Lexa-Blue said.

"It keeps you humble," Vrick said. "Now bring that bottle over here, our guest star needs a drink."

Lexa-Blue held up the bottle with feigned surprise. "This?"

"Oh, yes," Malika said, holding up her mug. "Does it mix well with coffee?"

Lexa-Blue joined her at the table. "As far as I know, it mixes well with radioactive waste."

"I'm definitely in then," Malika said, waggling the mug for emphasis. "Give."

Topping up the mug, Lexa-Blue joined her on the opposite end of the curved couch facing the forward port.

The atmosphere in the office had finally calmed to a flutter of remembered terror that seemingly suffused the entire staff. Ijagu noticed the repair crews still working on the areas of the building that had been affected by the strange raid into their corporate headquarters.

Not that it was strange to Ijagu Omrhys — from the moment the alarms had gone off, he'd been certain that it all had something to do with him and with the plot that he had hatched, certain that the slicer had given him up to the authorities.

The presence of such a heavy security response had only fanned his certainty that any moment, a hand would clamp down on his shoulder and he'd be carted off.

He'd evacuated with the others in his department, though there had seemed to be no immediate threat to their section of the building. They'd caromed off each other, jostling for any seconds that might protect them somehow from the unseen threat.

Finally, they'd found their way to the designated meeting place, an arbour of trees off a small strip of retail stores two blocks away.

Following the crowd, his hand gripping the tunic of the person ahead of him, too panicked to even register who it was, he had looked up and seen the battered black car shooting skyward toward the building's roof. For a moment, it was too absurd for his mind to process. Cars flew horizontally, not vertically.

What was it doing?

He'd heard some rumblings about there being special visitors that had turned up unexpectedly that day. Was this just some eager driver and security team reacting to their employers' jeopardy?

Now, back at this desk, with operations returning to normal, it all made a terrifying sense to him. Everything had been related to the embezzlement scheme. He felt the noose closing around his neck, and the thought made his breath catch, as if the oxygen in the room had suddenly gone thin.

He sat back in his chair, the skin of his back suddenly clammy with fear sweat. They were coming for him. And with Pi not responding to his messages, he knew he would go down for the crime alone.

He swore silently at himself. He should never have threatened to go to the authorities in that final message he had sent to his faceless accomplice. He'd seen the sensies. That was the worst possible mistake. You never tipped off the person who had as much to lose as you did.

But this is real life, he thought.

And he'd made the classic blunder, tipping his hand that he was weak and couldn't be trusted. He'd handed himself over and branded himself a traitor and a liability.

"Are you all right?"

Even the gentle voice at his shoulder made him jump out of his skin. Gulping air, he saw that it was Beloi from the assay team across the floor from his cubicle.

"It's okay," she said, gently. "We're all on edge. It's terrifying that something like that could happen here, of all places. Nothing ever happens in boring corporate towns like this."

If you only knew.

The sight of her solicitous, cow-eyed gaze was too much for him. He had a sudden flash of her and the others whispering and gossiping about him when it all came out. They would love it, relishing every moment of his downfall and subsequent trial.

He bolted up from his seat, almost knocking her over. "I have to go."

Shoving past her, he saw sickly, pitying concern in her eyes as he passed her, and it only served to layer hatred and rage into the flow of his terror.

He stormed to the lift, stabbing at the call button, his heart battering his chest as each second seemed to drag on. Finally, the agonizing wait ended, and the lift doors opened for him. He surged forward, shouldering past two clerks exiting onto his floor, eliciting mumbles of protest.

In a haze, he made it to the lobby and out into the late morning light. The first thing he saw was the mass of Fury in the sky above, its shattered bulk filling the sky. For a second, it felt to him as though the huge planet was falling toward him, with no other aim than to crush him.

He shook off the feeling and ran toward the street, hailing a rickshaw through his link. He had to get off-planet. He was rich now. If they didn't catch him, he'd be set for life. Perhaps a slightly more modest life than he had planned, but he'd be fine. He just needed to get a ship off this planet, once and for all, and never look back.

His rickshaw hummed up to the curb where he stood, fidgeting, and he climbed into the seat.

One of the independent ships, that was what he needed. They took on passengers all the time. Just get to another world. After that, decide where to next. Easy.

The rickshaw zipped sharply out into traffic, sending him sideways into the struts holding up the passenger canopy. He frowned a moment at the unusual motion, then let it go. Using his Link, he opened up Know-It-All and called up the list of ships currently waiting at Sound's port, ready to take on passengers for wherever. Selecting one at random, he called up his credit balance to pay for the booking.

His stomach lurched, more deeply than anything caused by the rickshaw's erratic motion.

It was all gone. Every unit. There was nothing there.

Pi.

It was the only explanation.

Ijagu's vision blurred to white around the edges. Without credits, he would never get off-world. He'd be here to take the fall. No doubt completely alone. For a slicer of Pi's calibre, it would be nothing to erase his own involvement and lay all responsibility on Ijagu Omrhys.

As his panic escalated to hysteria, he didn't notice the rickshaw's erratic, high-speed trajectory.

The heavily weighted cargo truck tore through the rickshaw as if it were paper.

The feeble energy trace of the rickshaw's LI burst like an iridescent bubble across Pi's augmented vision, followed by the fading flicker of the tracker code he'd implanted into the link. As he strode along the concourse to the waiting ship that he'd booked passage on, he watched as the weak fluttering signal shuddered, slowed, and stopped.

Problem solved.

He picked up his pace along the hard dull surface of the walkway leading to the small courier vessel that was taking a group of engineers back to the mining corporation's office on Isla Cordova.

Bless the sweet, naive Spacer's Code, he thought. Passage in whatever accommodation was available, whenever possible, was offered at any port of call. He'd already arranged for a transfer to a ship bound for Sombra. *Charming. And convenient.*

His own nerves were substantially calmer now, despite the knowledge of the other slicer, still out there, and presumably still digging into Pi's affairs and screwing them up completely. Still. Omrhys' portion of the take sweetened the sting of having the whole deal go spinward so drastically.

Superstitiously, he checked the credit balance again, despite having it alarmed in numerous ways should his adversary go after it. The firm roundness of the numbers reassured him, all of his traps still reassuringly in place.

He saw the ship, three berths down, gleaming gold in the late morning light. A glance at Know-It-All showed the ship's departure still only slightly delayed for a brief final system redundancy check. Accessing his piggybacked processor power, he checked the timing of his final goodbye to this ROM-forsaken place, the calculations sweeping through his mind as he finished the thought. It was spite, pure and simple. It was unbridled chaos begging to be unleashed. He knew it, and he didn't care.

A bit close, but if it wasn't a bit dangerous, would it be any fun?

He continued towards the ship, greeting the captain and settling into his berth, projecting a bland, ordinary pleasantness to all he encountered.

I spare you because I can. Because it suits my purposes.

On schedule, the ship launched, ascending through the thin atmosphere and into the dark beyond the binary planets, plotting its course to the interspace transition point.

And all the while, a murmur in Pi's mind, the quiet countdown of his final gambit, was a lover's breath against the back of his neck.

It had taken a few days for Irad to be called up on the rota, but they were ready when it happened.

Keene set the case down in the airlock of the *Gossamer*, hitting the stud that would deactivate the unit's mass diffuser and return it to its full weight.

"Ready?"

Irad bounced on his heels in excitement. "Whenever you are. We're cleared with port control and the flight plan has been filed."

"Carry on, then," Lexa-Blue said.

Irad turned and headed fore to the bridge, leaving them to make final preparations. With practiced ease, they braced their stances as they unpacked Keene's suit and readied it for use. They felt the humming vibrations as the ship's system drive kicked in, lifting the *Gossamer* into Sound's thin atmosphere.

With both of them on prep, they had the suit expanded, checked, and racked for use within ten minutes. Irad joined them after locking in the *Gossamer*'s course.

"We're set," he said. "It's a standard vector and the auto can handle the next bit until we get close enough to dock."

"How long until we get there?" Lexa-Blue asked.

"I've got us at the best speed that won't attract any unusual attention from the planetary traffic control, so just under two hours."

"Should only take me about fifteen to get suited up once we're there," Keene said, running his sleeve across the helmet's visor one last time. He sat and cracked open his toolkit and began to check each one again.

"It's just something he does," Lexa-Blue said to Irad. "Me, I'd rather punch something. Do you have an empty space I can use to limber up?"

"Hold Two," Irad said with a laugh, heading off in the direction of the cockpit to begin their takeoff. "This way. Just promise not to shoot a hole in my ship."

"I'll do my best. But no promises."

In the instant it happened, the event seared white noise across the Maverick Heart's consciousness, blotting out all sensation, all thought. Vrick's time sense sluiced from an instant to a millennium and back, the moment seeming to exist in all dimensions, all directions, all times.

Ey was everywhere and nowhere, with agony sheeting through em as the shockwaves coursed through the sector.

When ey could think again, finally sort out the boundaries of self and surroundings once more, ey ran through es diagnostics, a dread coursing through em, for the sensation had been unlike anything ey had experienced in es long and varied life.

I'm here. And I'm still functioning.

Data rushed back through the diagnostic systems, and it was... somewhat reassuring. Ey wasn't in imminent danger, but whatever had hit em had been powerful and there were variances across most of es systems. Ey set the repair cycles to check and realign the worst of the damage and established the hierarchy of priorities to bring emself back to peak function.

With that underway, ey turned es attention outward, pushing es external sensors in an attempt to learn what had happened.

The readings made no sense.

Ey had only ever seen readings like in the aftermath of a supernova. The interspace membrane rippled with throbbing, sickly energy fluctuations, as if the death throes of a star had burned through the barriers between real space and the interspace medium that allowed em and other ships to travel faster than light.

But as es sensor net ground its way back to life, ey saw that the system's primary still burned bright at the centre of the planets, orange red and massive.

Then, once ey had turned es attention away from the seemingly healthy star, ey saw it. There above their heads, Fury lived up to its name, blazing across energy spectra no human could see. The broken but tamed planet was suddenly in chaos, es sensors showing evidence of a massive explosion deep within the chasm that scarred the corpse of the dead, rocky world.

Worse than that, the stabilized debris field that fed the hungry maw of the mining consortium and, by extension, the Gate Project, had lost all of its carefully tended cohesion. The gravitic stabilization network was there but had somehow lost all coordination. As ey watched, chunks of debris bigger than even the largest of the mining vessels collided and shattered, sending ever more debris in all directions, which only seemed to trigger more and more fluctuations in the ever-growing field of rock and careening metal.

But even as ey watched, ey could tell that the motion was not simply random. There was intelligence at work, some unknown force that still controlled the gravitic stabilization network. Something was continuing to fire the individual units, perpetually aggravating the field, and causing ever greater damage.

On its own, the field would likely have settled once more into a new, relatively stable pattern, but the pulses of the gravs kept stirring the motions again and again, ensuring seemingly perpetual tumult.

Perpetual and potentially deadly, for when ey accessed the consortium's primeframe, ey saw that it was mid-shift, the busiest time of the rotation, with full crews at work. Ey refocused long-range sensors and saw hundreds of vessels spread amongst shifting undulation of rock.

Already, through es link to the company, ey heard the distress calls as the mining ships struggled to recall crews and hold steady against the sudden onslaught. As ey watched, ey saw signals from at least three ships wink out, leaving gaping, deathly voids in the web of signals flaring and dancing before em.

Data swirled around em at a dizzying speed. It unnerved em, for ey wasn't sure ey had ever been so challenged to keep track of such a constantly shifting set of variables at a single time. No matter how ey tried to predict the motion, find some pattern in the disorder, ey failed. Between the ships and the debris, there were thousands upon thousands of objects in motion there between the broken planet and its smaller neighbour, all caught in some palsied dance that seemed designed to cause as much damage as possible.

It was the slicer. It had to be Pi. Some final, sick gambit.

One horrific master stroke.

The pattern of misfiring gravs was somehow both too random and too controlled to be a system malfunction, though Vrick wondered if any human investigator would have been able to tell the difference. But as hard as ey tried, ey could make no sense of the motions, nor begin to predict how they would play out. All of es predictive matrices struggled with making any kind of sense out of the destruction playing out in the gap between these worlds.

Then, ey saw it. The one recognizable probability vector in the uproar. The rogue slicer had tried to hide it, but though ey couldn't see much, ey recognized that one glimmer of intent buried in the chaos.

There, in the midst of it all, was one concentrated plume of debris, shaped and controlled by the gravitic stabilizers into a concentrated fist the size of a small moon. Aimed like a gargantuan projectile from a huge mass driver at two targets: the station Keene and Lexa-Blue were headed for, and Fury's tiny sister world. The world where ey and the others now waited.

Ey checked for the *Gossamer*'s transponder and found it. Irad and the others had broken atmosphere almost an hour ago and were well on the way into the path of destruction.

Time for a new plan.

"I'm just saying, they didn't have to leave us behind," Malika said. "Surely there was something we could have done that's a little more… hands on?"

"It's not like the old days, Mali," Ember said. "We can't just go haring off and doing as we please anymore. Sometimes, you just have to stick to the plan."

Malika snorted with laughter. "Things I never thought I'd hear you say."

Ember's smile was gentler than she remembered, softer somehow. She could see lines around his eyes that hadn't been there before. Before the Gate. Before she left. She liked the effect. It made him seem more… real somehow. He was more present now. Maybe he'd grown up. Maybe she had too.

They were sitting in Vrick's main lounge, each with a drink in hand, having liberated a bottle from Lexa-Blue's private stash that Ember wasn't supposed to know about.

"Therefore, she must like it the least," Malika had said.

"On your head be it," Ember had said as Malika poured them each a glass.

Now, they were pleasantly buzzed, and Malika had turned the topic of conversation around to their lack of active participation in the next part of the plan.

"I get what you're saying," Ember said. "But Keene is the one with the know-how to extract the information, and Lexa-Blue is the one who's the best at shooting her way out of things. There just wasn't any need for us to be there."

"Hey, I can shit my way out of things too, you know," Malika said, then glared at Ember as he chuckled. "Shoot. I mean, shoot. Obviously, I meant shoot."

"Of course you did," Ember said, still giggling at her.

With no warning, the ship bucked around them. Malika tumbled off the end of the couch to the floor, but Ember managed to stay seated. The lights flickered, plunging the room into darkness lit only by the light outside the main port. Even the air cyclers groaned before the vents returned to their natural rhythm.

Malika's head popped up over the end of the couch. "What was that? An earthquake? I mean, Sound-quake, I guess."

"That was the sound of an incredibly sophisticated ship being hit by instantaneous quantum substrate fluctuations rebounding off the interspace membrane."

"No idea what that means," Malika said, pulling herself up onto the couch again. "But it sounds bad, and it's definitely killed my buzz."

Vrick explained what ey had gleaned from es scans, as simply and human-friendly as possible.

Malika looked pale. "Anyeis?"

Vrick paused a second. "I don't know. I can read that there are ships out there, but there's too much interference to identify individual transponder signals."

Malika sagged for a second, then pulled herself together. "How many ships are out there?"

"Shift rota says there were 103 mining ships out on duty when whatever it is hit," Vrick said. "I've got energy signatures for 78 pinging back active." Ey paused. "And a lot of wreckage. There's no knowing how badly damaged they are."

"Grife," Ember said. "Mali, she's fine. We'll find her."

Malika shook her head, her jaw tight. "She's tough. And I have faith in her."

"I'm doing everything I can, but in this mess, I can't even guarantee that any of the surviving ships will stay that way," Vrick said. "Whatever is going on is unfolding on thousands of different interactive probability vectors at once, I can barely keep track."

Ember and Malika exchanged a worried glance. Neither one of them had ever known Vrick to admit there was something ey couldn't predict.

"So, what do we do?" Ember asked.

"I'm still working on it," Vrick said. "But whatever it is, we can't do it from here."

"Surely, the city and the port are on lockdown," Malika said. "They're not going to let anyone off-planet unless they're directly involved in the rescue."

"Leave that to me," Vrick said, es tone ominous. "Once they realize what's coming their way, they'll call for an evacuation. Which will cause mass panic. And they won't have time for it. I don't plan to wait. I'm invoking diplomatic privilege."

"Wait, you're a diplomat?" Malika looked confused.

"I'm a protected species," Vrick said. "Artificial Sentiences like me are the last of our race. Subject to special protections under pretty much every article of Pan Galactum law."

"I thought that you wanted that kept secret," Ember said.

"Desperate times," Vrick said.

"Impressive," Malika said.

"How else do you think I manage to keep these three meatbags out of prison? They'd be serving life sentences if it weren't for me."

"And we are eternally grateful," Ember said. "Now what's the plan?"

Irad felt the shockwave slam into the *Gossamer*, buffeting up through the ship's hull into the control yoke he suddenly needed to grip with both shoulders. The ship bucked around him, then settled, and he reached over to slap the gain on the aging sensor grid along the hull. The display coughed up a static-coloured holo of the system, showing the blister-like outer trajectory of the shockwave that he had inadvertently flown through.

Oh, that's bad.

He heard Lexa-Blue's voice over the internal comm-net.

"What the hell was that?" she asked, her breath sounding ragged with strain.

"Some kind of shockwave hit us," Irad said. "And it came from Fury. Are you okay down there?"

Even over the comm-net, he could tell she sounded as if she was straining.

"Keene was getting into his suit when it hit, and he toppled over." Irad heard a huff of strained breath. "Have you ever tried getting someone upright when they're half-stuck in an environment suit?"

"Can't say I have," Irad said. "But if it's anything like wrestling a ship that's been hit by a concentrated wall of interstitial turbulence, then you have my sympathies."

He heard her curse vividly. "Hold her steady, friend. I'll be up in a second."

The *Gossamer* shuddered again as more eddies from whatever was happening to the fabric of space reverberated back from several different directions, as well as through the dimensional barriers. Cranking up the stabilizing system to its maximum, he finally felt the ship settle around him.

The tightline chimed for his attention. "*What?*" he barked, the sound of his voice opening the channel.

"Are you having the same kind of day as we are?" Vrick said.

"Well, the ship hasn't vibrated apart around me," Irad said through clenched teeth. "So, I guess I'm having a great day. Any idea what the hell that was?"

"Oh, I know all too well," Vrick said. "And we have a big problem. Can you loop the others in for the explanation?"

Confident enough that the ship was flying at least somewhat comfortably, Irad patched in the internals again. "Look alive down there, you two. Someone wants to talk to us."

"All right, here's the situation," Vrick said. "Our nasty little slicer friend somehow managed to trigger a massive explosion in the volatiles storage down in the main excavation site in the heart of Fury's core."

"But that couldn't account for what we just hit," Irad said.

"You're right," Vrick said. "The most that would have produced would be a plume of ejecta out into what's left of the planet's atmosphere. But this is much worse. Whoever they are, they've taken control of the interstitial gravity network that's been holding that debris field in place so the consortium could mine it.

"The underlying science of human artificial gravity tech shares some of the basic underpinnings with interspace drives and the technology that allows us to cross that barrier and achieve FTL travel. What they've done is cross circuit those generators to impart an almost instantaneous acceleration to all of planetary fragments in the field."

"Instant meteor shower," Keene said quietly.

"Less shower and more cyclone," Vrick said. "Not only that, but they've set it up to continually randomize the trajectory of every fragment. So, not only are they bearing down on the station you're headed to and then on to Sound, they're colliding and shattering and reorienting so fast that standard anti-collision algorithms are almost useless in evading them."

"That's bad," Lexa-Blue said.

"As ever, your talent at understatement is unmatched," Vrick said.

"So, what do we do?" Irad asked, his voice pitched high with fear.

"Well, no matter what, we have to get that evidence off that station," Keene said. "Especially if that debris storm is going to shred it."

"And you're the only one who can do that," Vrick said. "Lucky you."

"Is he going to have time?" Lexa-Blue asked. "I mean, I do kind of like you, partner. I don't want to see you pummelled to paste by a shit ton of rocks."

"I do have a plan," Vrick said. "And I'm on my way to you right now at full burn so we can maybe, if we're very, very lucky, pull it off."

"How did you get off-planet?" Irad asked. "It takes at least two days to get a flight plan approved."

"Oh, you wouldn't believe what ey can do when ey wants to," Lexa-Blue said.

"I do have my ways," Vrick said. "But this is one is pretty out there, even for me."

"You've never steered us wrong before," Keene said. "What do we do?"

"First, we get to the *Gossamer*," Vrick said.

The Maverick Heart pulled alongside the *Sparkling Gossamer* in what seemed to Irad to be record time. Barely a standard hour and a half passed before he felt the vibration of the airlocks meshing and saw the telltales lighting green across his control board as the pressure equalized between the two ships.

Stopping only to check that the *Gossamer*'s LI autopilot was properly set to slave to the Maverick Heart's course, he left the ship's bridge to join the others. While he knew that he could receive Vrick's briefing through the ship's comm, he felt the need to be there with the others, to experience it firsthand.

When he reached the *Gossamer*'s main lock, he saw Malika struggling through with her borrowed pressure suit overflowing her crossed arms. She looked almost as bewildered as Irad felt, and he could see on the others' faces that they were all in the same boat.

"Um, where do I put this?" Malika asked, bending to grab for a glove that slipped from under her arm.

"Here," Irad said, picking up the glove and handing it to her after she missed it. "The *Gossamer* was built for a bigger crew, so I have some spare lockers."

He helped her hang the suit and plug it into the diagnostic system. "There you go."

"Thank you," she said, smiling. "I'm afraid I haven't done a suit drill since we landed on Sound. I'm a little rusty."

"Well, looks like you're going to get some practice real soon," Lexa-Blue said. "Okay, Junkpile. We're all here. Fill us in on your grand plan. I'd like to know why I'm not going into the lion's den with Keene."

"Yeah, I'd like to know that too," Keene said, then turned to Malika. "No offence."

"None taken," Malika said. "I'd kind of like to know that too. Our last little caper didn't quite go as planned."

"Which was no fault of yours," Vrick said. "You may be out of practice, but I trust your instincts and reactions implicitly."

Malika looked for a moment like she might blush.

"Yeah, yeah," Lexa-Blue said. "We all love each other. What's the plan?"

"I'd chide you for your impatience, but time is of the essence," Vrick said. "Thanks to our collective nemesis, we have an accelerated cloud of planetary debris heading straight for the station you are about to infiltrate, and then shortly after that, directly for Sound."

"But surely they built the station to withstand impacts of that type?" Ember said.

"Ordinary random impacts, yes," Vrick said. "But this is something completely different. There are hundreds of thousands of separate bodies in that cloud. And with the code our slicer laid into the gravitic stabilization net, they managed to impart a staggering amount of initial velocity that's only getting worse with every second. They're continuously impacting against each other and the stabilizers are converting every bit of that impact energy into extra velocity and it's adjusting constantly."

Keene whistled through his teeth. "Even if they had some kind of anti-ordnance weaponry, I doubt that they could take out even a fraction of those bolides before the rest tore them to shreds."

"Exactly," Vrick said.

"But you've got a plan, right?" Malika said, her face pale. "You can stop it. That's why we're here."

"I have a plan, my dear," Vrick said. "I didn't say the odds were that good. This one is in the hands of luck."

"That is so not reassuring," Lexa-Blue said. "But we've been in worse scrapes than this."

"Have we, though?" Ember said.

"Either way, it's us or nothing," she said. "What do we do?"

"Keene goes into the station to get the data, that doesn't change. But I need Lexa-Blue here on board with me and with Ember. I'm going to try and take back some kind of control over that gravitic network. There are ships being crushed by those flying rocks and people are dying. It's far at the top end of my capabilities, but I have to do something. And it's going to take all of my attention, which means I need a pilot."

"Present and accounted for," Lexa-Blue said.

"Well, you are all I have at hand, so I guess you'll have to do. And with Ember's zero-G rating being highest of you all, not to mention his skills at ZeroBall, I'm going to need him here too. I'll take any edge I can, even from you lumps of meat."

"Okay, so I'm going in after the data alone," Keene said.

"You most certainly are not," Vrick said. "Malika wears that suit and goes in with you to get the backup data," Vrick said. "I take Lexa-Blue and Ember with me. I can slice back into the gravitic stabilization network and try to get it under control, but it's a monumental task even for me. Lexa-Blue pilots and Ember is going to be plugged into me, helping me calculate the trajectories and feeding the data to Lexa-Blue."

Vrick continued, forestalling Ember's objections. "I've seen you play ZeroBall and measured your reactions in all of the zero-G recertification exams. Of all of you, you're the best ZeroBall player and have the best grasp of 3D motion and mechanics."

What Vrick said next sounded as if it pained him. "I can't do it alone. With the three of us, we might stand a chance."

That was a sobering moment for them all.

"Well," Vrick said. "What are you waiting for? Goss, you meats are slow. We're on the clock here. Move!"

Malika struggled into the scarlet exo suit, struggling to remember her emergency training from the Odeon, a tangle of excitement and fear clashing in her stomach. First, she shimmied into the inner layer, then fitted the outer, flexible shell of the suit over it, locking the pieces into place. It took concentration to remember it all.

As much as she'd fallen right back into her old pattern with these new adventures, this was something else. She'd done her suit drills along with everyone else, but that had been more a case of 'what's the bare minimum I need to do to survive a hull breach?'. This was an intentional spacewalk. From a ship in motion.

Aimed at a very small target.

Fighting with one of the main seals, a wave of vertigo swept through her body, but she pushed through it, breathing, and the simple physical act of that breath, in a way so specifically tied to her craft, her art, her chosen path, calmed her. The sensation of taking in that air in that specific way was so familiar that it pulled her back, grounded her in place again.

She could see Keene and Lexa-Blue beside her, him already mostly suited except for the gauntlets and helmet, with Lexa-Blue adjusting all of the seams and fittings.

"Well, don't just stand there," Lexa-Blue said, but Malika heard no rancour in her voice. "Here. Let me check it over."

She stepped into the space beside them, set the bulk of the suit down on the bench and quickly stripped down. With efficiency she hadn't really been expecting,

"Not bad," Lexa-Blue said, turning from Keene to check her work over. "Nice work on those seals. You've done this before."

"This part, yes," Malika said, then gestured vaguely in the direction of the ether beyond the hull. "That part, not so much."

"Think of it as on-the-job training," Keene said, not looking up from his final visual inspection of his helmet. "And I'll be right there with you."

Malika winced as Lexa-Blue tugged sharply on her left arm to tighten and check the shoulder seal. "I'm glad one of us knows what they're doing."

"It's all an act," Lexa-Blue said. "We've been faking it the whole time."

"Totally true," Keene said, grinning. "We're just really, really lucky."

She knew they were lying through their teeth. They were two of the most adventurous and capable people she had ever met, and she knew they knew it. But the attempt to reassure her was quite sweet and went a long way to calming her nerves.

And distracting her from the thought of Anyeis out there in that unholy mess of rock and wrecked ships.

It's just another role to play, she thought. *I just have to do my own stunts this time.*

Remembering her suit training, she ran through the series of stretches designed to test the suit's fit and manoeuvrability.

"How does it feel?" Lexa-Blue asked.

"Nothing's pinching," Malika said. "I've worn costumes onstage that were a lot tighter and pinched in way worse places."

Lexa-Blue leered. "Tell me more."

"I'm pretty sure there are sensies in the theatre's archive," Malika said, laughing. "As long as the theatre and planet aren't destroyed by meteors, I'll send them to you."

"Extra incentive to not ruck this up," Lexa-Blue said. She slapped her palm against the internal comm. "Irad, our little spacewalkers are suited up and ready. I'm heading back to Vrick. Stand by to release the airlock and get underway."

"Confirmed," Irad said through the circuit. "Fly safe."

"Okay, you two," Lexa-Blue said, holding up her closed fists to bump against Keene's gloved ones. "Be careful out there, okay?"

"You too," Keene said. "Fly safe and shoot straight."

"I figure I'll just shoot at everything," Lexa-Blue said. "That usually works for me."

She turned to Malika and rested a hand on the thick, vibrant crimson of the suit. "And you. Take care of my suit. I just got it broken in the way I like it, and I want it back."

Malika shrugged with an exaggerated nonchalance. "I'll see what I can do."

Lexa-Blue smirked and turned to Keene. "She's learning."

She headed for the boundary between the ships and stepped over the threshold, giving the suited figures one last look, and one last quick salute as the lock hatch cycled closed.

As the sound of the hatch locking into place faded behind her, Lexa-Blue headed straight to the main lounge at the fore of the ship, feeling the *Gossamer* break away.

There, she found Ember standing before the main viewport, where an inset holo showed the view from one of Vrick's hull cameras that showed the *Gossamer* snugged up against em.

As she strode into the lounge, she saw the locks disengage with a puff of escaping atmosphere, and the *Gossamer*'s drive field flare as it pulled away on its new course.

"Okay, Junkpile," Lexa-Blue said. "Let's do this."

She crossed to the starboard side of the lounge, where panels of the inner hull wall were folding back to reveal a comfortable-looking standard pilot chair surrounded by a state-of-the-art set of manual flight controls.

"Wait," Ember said. "How did I not know that this was here?"

"I only let her near those controls as an absolute last resort," Vrick said. "If I let her drive too often, she'll just end up scratching my paint."

"I'm a top-rated pilot, squib," Lexa-Blue said. "But ey still can fly rings around me. There's usually no reason for me to take the reins. But if we ever need to, I can."

"And today, we need to," Ember said. "Where do you want me?"

"Anywhere you feel most comfortable," Vrick said. "Lexa-Blue, with a little help from my backup systems, is going to have us pulling some intense manoeuvres, so I'll be cranking the crash fields and the inertial nullifications systems up to the maximum. Still, the best spot for you will either be lying down or in the auto-doc. It probably has the most shock absorption potential outside of the pilot's seat."

"I guess it's time for a check-up, then," Ember said, heading back towards Vrick's medical cubby.

Lexa-Blue barely registered Ember leaving the lounge and heading aft, so absorbed she was in activating the manual control systems and running them through their initial diagnostics.

Though manual was not a strictly accurate description for the state-of-the art system Vrick had installed less than a year before. The hybrid matrix allowed for a combination of physical and virtual controls that a pilot could access in different ways. The initial learning curve had been steep, but her previous training, innate skills, and piloting instincts had taken her to a respectably high score on her qualifying exams.

Beneath her hands, the manual piloting board came alive, with telltales blinking across its face and confirming readiness. She stretched her arms and shook them out, ensuring that the board was in her preferred configuration, and then took hold of the two matching joysticks, one in each hand. She felt the motion and flex of their workings as her node told her that Vrick's systems were ready to respond to her hands if necessary.

Ooooh, touch me like that again, Vrick cooed through the piloting matrix.

You should be so lucky, she said. ***Now let me concentrate. Unless you don't mind being flown into the side of an asteroid.***

Vrick was quiet as she felt the virtual elements of the navigation and control systems come online. The lounge fell away from her perceptions, replaced by a secondary set of piloting controls operated solely by gestures, both physical and virtual.

Now for the weird part, she thought.

Though she was long used to it now and really enjoyed the sensation.

An avatar formed over her perceptions of her body, like a shimmering second skin of light clinging to her body, even closer than clothing. Sprouting from the silvery aura where it touched her shoulders were two more arms, matching her physical ones in shape and size.

She took in a deep, cleansing breath as Elai had taught her, centering her mind and focusing on the task at hand, and on the new configuration of her "body."

With the system still in test mode, she ran through a sequence of high-velocity manoeuvres, manipulating physical controls with her hands and the extended gestural matrix with her silver, virtual hands. She checked the reaction time and results graph before running the test again.

Damned rusty.

Satisfied with her reaction times on the second attempt, she settled back into her seat and took in another breath, signalling to Vrick and Ember that she was ready.

Ember hit the control of the auto-doc, perhaps a little too harshly, and the machine opened for him, extending the padded platform.

The palm of his hand stung slightly, echoing off the ache in his prosthetic fingers, and he pushed down a flash of panic as his adrenaline spiked in such close proximity to the murmur of medical equipment.

He had to stop for just a second and push back the scald of the memories of his own treatment, remind himself why he was here.

It's just a 'doc, Ember. You're just here so you don't end up a stain on the bulkhead.

He punched in the combination of controls to cycle off the diagnostic and treatment functions, turning the auto-doc into nothing more than an incredibly sophisticated crash couch, and lay down into the bed itself, feeling it conform to his body.

He fought back a crushing instant of claustrophobia as the bed pulled in tightly around his body, tamping it down, setting it aside with all of the other difficult medical memories. He closed his eyes.

Ready? Vrick said, opening a connection to Ember's node.

As I'll ever be, Ember said. *Hit me.*

I'd give you a little something to calm you down, but I need you sharp.

I understand. Do it.

In the instant it took to form and transmit the thought, Ember's consciousness seemed to shatter and expand to a thousand times its normal size. Dimly, he felt himself hiss air sharply through his clenched teeth, his back arching stiffly.

I know, I know, Vrick said, es voice soothing. *You've got this. I'm right here. You're in no danger.*

He concentrated and the jumble of inputs so much larger than him began to settle, to order themselves into some semblance of a pattern. His breathing slowed, calmed, returned to normal as the exploded universe in his mind calmed.

What he had seen before as a mass of debris hurtling across space toward them resolved itself into a level of detail he hadn't imagined possible for a human brain. His mind filled with the relative positions, densities, velocities, and trajectories of each of the thousands of projectiles, the numbers and algorithms that described each piece shifting and changing as the sickly throbbing pulse of the energy fields threading through and around moved like something alive.

The sensation was wondrous and terrifying and thrilling all at the same time, the massive flow of data moving through him and around him and on to Vrick, and then back, glowing and shifting through the spectrum into colours he had no names for.

My world, welcome to it.

It's incredible, Ember said, his thoughts hushed with wonder. *Is this what you see all the time?*

Mostly, Vrick said. *But this isn't all me. This is both of us.*

Ember's mind filled with a yellow-green skepticism he could taste.

The sensation was disconcerting.

Oh, come on. Not much of this could possibly be me. You're the one with the brain power.

Don't sell yourself short, friend, Vrick said, and the pulsing flood of information coursing through Ember's mind shifted, dimmed, became somehow less alive, less real. It wasn't a massive difference, but it was noticeable. Even though it was still so much more than Ember could ever have perceived on his own, it was definitely… less.

I meant what I said, Vrick said. ***We need all the edge we can get, and I need your spark, your skills at improvising. I've watched you play ZeroBall. You have the spatial sense and the understanding of motion and how bodies in motion interact. And all of your other skills just dovetail into it. That's what I need right now.***

Unsure of what to even say to that, Ember turned his attention back to the hail of planetary debris closing in on them, taking in once again the throbbing flood of information about how it moved, what was influencing it, how the very fabric of space acted upon it. In the instant he thought of how he could practice affecting the myriad trajectories, he suddenly knew he was in simulation mode. He reached for a chunk of mass at random, instantly knowing the percentages of heavy elements in it and how they were distributed.

He imagined pushing against it, saw it move, then how that motion translated into the field around it according to the heavily unnatural influence of the corrupted gravitation field. Glimmers of understanding flooded his mind, and he pushed again, trying different vectors and combinations. Another portion of his mind informed him that the simulation had taken less time than his body had taken to absorb a single oxygen molecule.

Ready? Vrick asked.

Ember smiled, and his newfound synesthesia rendered it to a smell like starlight and thunder.

Let's do it.

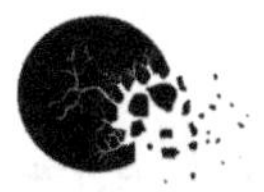

As soon as he saw the airlock system flash green, Irad slapped the controls on his Nav LI to put them back on their preset course for the processing station, goosing the drive field to maximum. On his external comm, emergency signals blared loud and red as the consortium's traffic system became aware of the impending catastrophe. The aud circuit blared with a sudden gabble of ships spread across the space between Sound and Fury, all seeking information on safe trajectories out of the path of destruction.

"This is *Sparkling Gossamer*, inbound to processing station, authorization Iota 926," Irad said, broadcasting his own voice into the babel. "There's no way I can make it back to Sound before that debris field intersects my trajectory. Requesting emergency berth, alee of the station."

I hope this works.

He was counting on the station's defensive screens and defence net to protect the station and was sure that there would be other ships close enough to the station seeking the same type of cover. He shifted his gaze to the tactical plot and could see that even though the pattern of debris shifted like some planetary system-sized organism, its path only peripherally intersected with the station's position. It was the fleet of mining vessels and, beyond the station, Sound that would bear the brunt of the chaos.

Which worked to their advantage. Without that relative safety, he was sure that the Station would deny his request, leaving him to do his best to just proceed out of danger at full drive burn. If the station had been any closer to the impact path, it would likely have been torn apart as well.

Small favours.

He checked their approach vector once more, confirming the timing of their spiralling corkscrew course that would take them close enough to the emergency airlock that Keene and Malika would use to access the station.

"Fifteen minutes, you two," he called to them through the internal comm. "I've sent the final trajectory and timing to the airlock terminal. Good luck."

To us all, he thought, taking the helm once again, trying not to concentrate on the throbbing, undulant mass of rock and metal bearing down on them all.

Those last fifteen minutes seemed to fly by in an eyeblink, as Malika stood like a child being dressed by a parent as Keene went over her suit, checking it to ensure all was secure. For a moment, she was almost insulted, but she knew that he was far more expert in EVA than she would ever be, no matter how many emergency suit drills she had gone through on the Odeon. And already, he'd caught a minor error in the way she'd fastened her breather lines. And had had the good grace not to lecture her on her impending death by asphyxia.

And then they were in place, standing at the *Gossamer*'s airlock, hearing Irad count down the final moment of their approach.

At fifteen seconds, they activated the mags on their boots, securing themselves to the deck.

At ten seconds, the lock depressurized, and the hatch opened. Beyond, she saw the vast plates of the station's hull speeding by, feeling vertigo rush through her. She closed her eyes for an instant, then felt Keene's hand on her arm, steadying her. And she was calm.

At five seconds, she heard the final countdown to their jump point and the release of the boot mags.

And then, she was flying. And falling.

She was sideways and upright and upside down, all at the same time, with a black band full of stars encircling her. The *Gossamer* was behind her and the vast plain of blue-grey metal was in front of her. Or was it above? The vertigo returned full force, threatening to disorient her.

Breathe, Keene said. ***Stay focussed. You decide for yourself what's up and what's down. It's whatever you want it to be. Just pick, stick with it, and you'll be fine.***

No sooner had he said the words than her perception slid into place, and she was suddenly flying, living the childhood fantasy that had sustained her whenever life had been challenging. The massive hull of the processing station was the sky and she rose on the wind to meet it, ascending ever and ever higher.

For just a moment, she was free.

Stand by for deceleration burn, Keene said, bringing her back to reality. **On my mark.**

The circular hatch grew in her vision, its frame ridged and riveted, framed with a lambent amber glow. She pushed away a flashing vision of it as a mouth opening to swallow them both.

And... mark.

She touched the control on the forearm of her suit, initiating the smart burn programmed into the suit's LI. She felt a slight jerk, as her suit's thruster field grabbed on to Keene's, and then on to the mass of the station, pulling them together and into final position.

In seconds, she was still, drifting in place, Keene beside her, already at work on the hatch's control pad.

She watched him open the specially designed pack of tools he used outside the ship, amazed at how dexterously he handled the seemingly tiny fink and pushed it against the external control panel. The tiny peripheral, no bigger than a candy, glowed green as it infiltrated the locking mechanism.

And we're in, Keene said.

I thought you were just going to access the manual controls?

I am, Keene said. **That was just a bit of blinder code. Shunting the sensors so that they just don't register that the lock is opening is way easier than trying to bypass the main security system and pick the locks from inside. All this does is keep the system from registering us using the emergency access as any kind of actual emergency. Saves a lot of time and energy.**

Such a smart man, she said.

I have my moments, he said, reaching for the hatch's manual release.

The release hatch swung open under his gloved hands, revealing a heavy lever striped in red. Bracing himself against the hull, he twisted the manual release for the airlock seal, then hand-cranked the lever to open the hatch itself.

When it was open, he reached for her hand and pulled her towards the opening.

After you, milady.

As soon as the inner airlock hatch had cycled closed, Keene touched the control that opened his helmet, and then collapsed it into its port between his shoulder blades. At his side, Malika did the same.

The corridor beyond the airlock was both empty of people and of any colour, every wall and floor the same flat, dull grey. Keene reached out to hold Malika back while he checked in both directions for any sign of life. He knew that the station was mostly automated, with only a skeleton crew of engineers and a small security staff. They would have to move fast, for it was a gamble that even the few staff on hand wouldn't notice their presence.

You don't have to coddle me, remember? Malika said, causing him to turn his head toward her. She looked down at his arm where it crossed her torso and arched an eyebrow at him. He quickly lowered his arm to his side once more.

Sorry, he said. ***I keep reminding myself that you're not Blue and I'm used to not worrying about her. Besides, Ember would kill me if anything happened to you.***

I'm big enough and ugly enough to take care of myself, she said, and he couldn't argue with that. He had to remember that this was the new Malika, who had already proven herself more than capable.

Which way is it? she said.

He indicated the long, straight, boring corridor to his left. ***This way. Irad dropped us off at the closest emergency hatch to the section where the AI cores are installed. It should**

be quiet between there and here. But you never know. Stay on your toes.*

I used to work with Ember, remember? she said. ***I'm used to things not going according to plan. Not to mention how the last few days have gone.***

Good point, he said. ***Come on.***

He led the way forward, consulting the schematics that Vrick had downloaded to his node. He could see that the corridor they were in led along one outer edge of the massive, relatively cylindrical station, opposite the massive complex of docks and sorting facilities where the mining ships emptied their holds into the sorting and assaying facilities that made up the deepest bowels of the ship. The network of access corridors along this part of the station's hull would take them directly to the AI bay, where the network of cores tended to the myriad functions of the various systems involved in the sorting and valuing of the ore and metals brought in by the ships.

It was only a few minutes until they found the main access point that connected the corridor to the high-security AI wing.

The double-sized access door brandished impressively intimidating security warnings in bright, bloody red. Off to one side was a multi-function terminal, clearly set for multiple redundancies including everything from key card access to biometrics and alphanumeric input.

He felt a whisper of doubt bleed through from Malika's node to his, but he didn't let himself react to it. If he stopped to think of it, he'd probably have just as many doubts, but there was too much riding on this to let those in. Their target was beyond this door and they needed it to prove just what had been going on, so they could restore the millions in missing credits to the workers that had actually earned them. And to do that, he had to get them past this door and inside.

He slapped the controls that retracted the gloves of his suit, leaving his hands free to work. He pulled his tool kit from the belt of his suit, unrolling it with a flourish and spreading it on the floor as he knelt to get into a position to access the inner workings of the security post.

Finding the maintenance port, he balled his fist and hit the release, opening up access to the inner workings of the locking mechanism.

Before doing anything, he stabbed a monitor bead into the main data line, which sent a nervous mutter of information coursing through his node. As he and Vrick had suspected, the station's crew was all at emergency stations, in the throes of evaluating protocols to help the damaged ships lost in the debris field.

Satisfied that they were sufficiently distracted, he found the junction pathway he needed. He took an interprobe in one hand and the coded fink in the other. Adjusting the power setting on the probe, he touched it to the junction, momentarily disrupting the flow of power through it, then jammed the fink into the junction as it restored the flow of information through it. Only this time, the information flowed through the tiny spines of the fink into the temporary codework embedded in it. The code flushed warm and sure through his node.

Okay, hit the palm pad.

Here goes nothing, Malika said, retracting her own glove and placing her hand on the warmly glowing panel.

The second or two it took to register seemed an eternity of waiting, and they were both sure that somehow, Keene's slice had failed, and the system would slam shut around them.

But the palm pad chirped happily, accepting the rerouted data that coursed through the fink and back into the recognition database, reprogramming the reader to accept any handprint that now presented itself. The heavy door before them rolled open, sending a low vibration through the deck.

As Malika stepped forward, Keene touched the probe to the fink, shorting out the door's mechanism and jamming it open for their escape. The fink then crumbled into a huff of dust and vapour. He pursed his lips and blew, removing the last traces of evidence before scooping up his kit and following Malika through the door.

That's the thing about a system like this, Keene said. ***They're overconfident that no one could get onto the station or would even want to. Traffic into the system is controlled, so there shouldn't even be anyone up here in the first place. They've concentrated all of their energy on the docking bays to make sure no one gets onto the station, but they aren't as concerned with what happens once anyone is here.***

That's pretty stupid, Malika said. ***But Ember and I made a lot of money out of stupid rich people, so I guess it makes perfect sense. Which way now?***

He consulted the designation of the AI submatrix they were looking for, then compared it to the map that overlaid his vision. Against the grid of interlaced cores, their quarry glowed with a sunny golden light, four rows down and three over to the left.

This way.

She followed him into the space between the blocky AI cores, each taller than either of them, and in precise, even, square proportions. Connector loci rose from the top of each core, connecting them in sequence to the next, the connectors pulsing and flashing with information as each unit ran some part of the station's complex systems.

Keene led her along, scanning the identifier codes on the outside of each core until they found the one they were looking for.

This is it. The valuation and assay matrix. Keep watch while I get this hooked up.

Malika took a position at his back, scanning back and forth along the pathway.

Reaching into his kit once more, Keene found the fink that he and Vrick had specially designed for this task, almost twice the standard size and colour-coded a deep purple. Holding it between his fingers, he palmed the release on the matrix's access panel, which obediently slid open to reveal the diagnostic access system.

Okay, this is it. Once this is inserted, it will copy what we need, but it's also going to trigger all kinds of alarms. AIs don't like being interfered with.

Can't say as I blame them on that score, Malika said. ***Are they going to… yell or something?***

Keene shook his head. ***From the specs, they were never even given speech capabilities. They're some of the most severely limited AIs I've ever seen.***

That's kind of sad, Malika said.

We can worry about that later. When we're done. Here we go, Keene said, inserting the fink into the diagnostic terminal. As soon as the spines hit the crystalline interface, he felt the flood of data through it, copying the records that could prove how so many of the miners had been swindled out of their rightful compensation.

But just as quickly, klaxons screamed as the AI recognized their presence and categorized them as a threat.

Run.

CHAPTER TWELVE

Exhilaration sang through Lexa-Blue's body, every neuron a voice in the chorus that was the sheer joy of flight.

She was dimly aware that the two virtual arms extending her control were not actually part of her physical body, but it had stopped mattering almost immediately. She had slipped into this new physical configuration with gusto as she realized just how much it extended her control over the Maverick Heart's shell as Vrick devoted es attention elsewhere.

The debris field grew ever faster in her forward sensor net, as she accelerated them towards it. Tactical data fed from Vrick and Ember sluiced through her consciousness as the rocks and slag shifted constantly within the bruise-purple energy of the corrupted gravity net. As she watched, the net pulsed with flares of bright, shattering colours, sickness made into light. With the sound of Vrick's control subsystems humming a deep bass note through her, she manipulated the drive field in response to the ever-changing vista before them.

As much as she controlled the ship, she was the ship, feeling every warp and weft of spacetime's fabric on her hull. Neutrinos danced and tickled across her drive field, light as the lightest feather touch on human skin. The dark matter substrate pushed against the shell of the drive field like gravity, trying to hold them in place, thick and viscous, until the pulsating energies of the field acted on it, allowing them to move and manoeuvre at such speeds.

Despite the fierceness of concentration that she needed to pilot, she couldn't help but revel in the joy of flying. And feel, in the recesses of her heart, how much she had missed it. Missed the feel of the controls under her hands, the feel of a vessel bending to her will against the emptiness of space.

As much she loved Vrick, she craved a ship of her own, one that yielded only to her will, going only where she decided the ship would go.

But she of all people understood the risks of that life, having lost her entire clan as a child while she was away from their merchant vessel. She had only just been learning to pilot then, and even though she took whatever chance at flight she could get, she knew how good her life actually was.

The proximity alarm screamed at her, jolting her back to intense focus on her task. They were only seconds away from the debris field's boundary and data from her connection to Vrick and Ember flooded her mind, suggesting the optimal course. Her hands flew through the gestural commands to the navigation system and through that to the drive field, making her physical arms ache, and her virtual arms leave light trails across her vision.

At her behest, the ship plunged into the debris field. At the periphery of her attention, she felt the sudden, blinding flares of the ship's upgraded weapons systems blasting through the shifting, throbbing cloud of matter and energy surrounding them, followed almost instantaneously by a hammering pulse of the navigational deflection systems, the repellers skirling up to the sound of a thousand sledgehammers.

And within her, the glorious song of her flight soared ever higher.

Ember saw the tactical information on the debris pulse and flow like liquid in response to his first volley, shifting as the weapons tore through stone and metal. A catalogue of destruction flowed through his mind, as potential damage estimates shifted in response. He could see vapour and fragments in several spots, though it seemed like they had accomplished barely anything to the threat.

Power surged back into the disruptor net as it recharged, with only a minimal overall loss. He saw the potential damage stats dip ever so slightly, but remain high overall, then turned his attention to the deflection fields, humming with readiness to be moulded to his will.

Likening this to ZeroBall was like comparing a teardrop to a thousand hurricanes. ZeroBall now seemed as simple as the act of rolling dice. Chasing a ball through conflicting planes of gravity seemed a child's game now as he had become aware of levels of reality stretching through the dark matter underpinning real space and then upward to the interspace barrier, all of it becoming variables to touch and taste and interact directly with.

As the awareness had poured into and through him, Ember had felt for a moment like his entire sense of self was tearing into a million pieces when Vrick had handed over control of the weaponry and tactical systems, but Vrick's presence had been rock solid, holding on to him as his mind fought to control and understand the flood of information.

Reacting to the changes around them, a new plan of attack skated across his mind, passed on to Lexa-Blue as a suggested new vector before he even realized he'd decided on it. In the eyeblink of two thoughts touching, the ship slewed and came about to the new course. Ember felt the disruptor net blaze to life, hellfire bright.

The threat matrix shifted and adjusted itself, then barked at him, and he registered a chunk of debris twice the size of a star liner bearing down on a cluster of damaged small mining tugs. Information flashed between him and Lexa-Blue, too fast for actual words, the data like an explosion of sparks.

Ember felt the ship tumble on its course, end over end, then laterally, aiming itself once more. He reached for the disruptor net but felt the targeting system cry out as it registered the small mining craft within its field of fire. *Oh, I have way more toys than that,* he thought.

Already primed and ready, the shift torpedo launchers came to life at his mental touch, and his mind flooded with projected damage stats, payload, and optimal usage recommendations.

Just relax, he thought. *Trust your skills.*

Augmented by Vrick's systems, Ember pictured the tableau before him. *Angles and ricochets. It's all just angles and ricochets.*

Numbers tumbled through him and he fired, the spread of torpedoes a deadly blossom from the recessed ports in Vrick's hull, tracer trails making lines of blue-white incandescence.

For a moment it seemed like the shifting purple field would ruin his shot, but his instincts had been good. The shift torpedoes held true, their drive fields veering sharply to avoid the mining craft before homing in again on the mass of rock. Shifting one final time, they struck almost in unison, igniting supernova bright. The fiery, shaped burst of energy tore through the rocky fragment, pulverizing it, and simultaneously pushed it away from the mining craft.

No longer in immediate danger, the pods resumed their course to safety.

But Ember had no time to enjoy the success, as still more tactical data streamed down, demanding his attention.

For the first time in the many decades of es existence, Vrick was assailed by sensory overload. It was not a welcome sensation.

The sheer volume of telemetry and tactical information on the weaponized debris field shuddered through es consciousness like some gargantuan predator seeking to crush all in its wake. Across es sensors, the field felt alive, pulsing with a throbbing malevolence.

Ey felt es calculation matrices struggle with the mass of ever-shifting data pulsing through the now thoroughly corrupted gravity stabilization net. No matter how ey tried, the thousands and thousands of chaotic computations and interactions seemed to defy any attempts at even the most basic understanding.

I do not like this.

At all.

For the entire period of es existence, ey had been used to being the most intelligent being in the metaphorical room. Es intelligence and processing capacity dwarfed that of even the most gifted human, allowing em to traverse interspace with the same ease with which many a human stood and crossed a room. Ey had yet to meet a human-controlled corner of Know-It-All that ey couldn't slice into and make es own.

But this — this metachaos algorithm was like nothing ey had ever encountered. It was a nesting set of seeming mathematical improbabilities that cascaded back and forth with each other in ever-changing combinations, all encrypted in a way ey couldn't understand. The code resisted, wet and slithering, whenever ey reached to grasp it.

Ey was ashamed to admit how ey had admired Pi's work in the past and had ey felt any guilt over liberating the code for es own use, ey was sure that would have evaporated with this new wanton attack.

Ey turned es attention to the casualty projection sim, hazarding the moment of inattention to the burning tide of calculation that filled es mind. It took only a picosecond to see the untold devastation and catastrophic loss of life still to come when the meteors descended through the thin atmosphere of Sound and ripped into the crust of the tiny world.

The projected number of dead dipped and rose, dipped and rose, the barrage of es attentions on the debris field caught in some elastic duel with the chaos algorithm breeding like a virus through the massive, diffuse weapon.

Ey watched the fatality projections drop as ey plunged a spear of code into the corrupted system, then felt it rally back against em, sending the projected death toll soaring once again.

The stream of deadly numbers caused em to unleash a torrent of curses in all of the languages ey knew, which only doubled as ey checked the stats on the ships that had been trapped in the middle of mining operations when Pi had triggered his malicious code.

Though they had all been caught in the initial pulse, at least seven of the massive ore carriers and mining base ships had made it out of the path of destruction under their own power.

Small favours.

But there were too many other vessels trapped in the ever-changing mess of rock and metal swirling and crashing together. And ey could see through the consortium's traffic control grid how many of those ships were already gone.

Vrick steeled emself once more, firming es resolve.

The answer is in the encryption. It has to be.

Ey concentrated on the gravitic network again. As much as it pained em to turn es attention away from the vulnerable ships and their crews, ey knew ey was the only one who had even a hope of stopping the catastrophe from escalating.

A thought pulled the connection to the gravitic system back to the forefront of es consciousness once more, the chaos algorithm malignant and bloated at its heart. Just focussing on the ugly code made em feel tainted, abhorrent just by association, but ey persevered. The subsystems ey had assigned to work at deciphering and counteracting the code seemed to seethe with a frustration of their own, though ey knew it was no more than a reflection of es own emotional state.

Next, ey pulled up the logs of all of the counter-code phages, evaluating each attempt for similarities and contradictions, any clues that might facilitate es slicing through the malignant code and giving em back control. The analysis took only 2.7 seconds, but in that time, ey felt the transponder of another mining pod go dark, the sudden emptiness in the traffic grid causing a spike of rage.

I need to take a different tack. But what?

Lexa-Blue and Ember were doing all they could, even with their own skills augmented by the subsystems ey had looped into their consciousnesses. But they had their limits and ey could see from their biodata that their frail meat bodies were being stretched to limits that they had never been meant to endure. But ey could see that they were making a difference, could see the ships that were surviving because of their efforts, could see the gradual winnowing of deadly material hurtling toward Sound.

But it still wasn't enough. The fatality projections on the consortium's settlement were still too high. The planet-killing swarm plunged onwards.

No, not a swarm, ey thought. *You were right before. A virus. An infection.*

Ey knew ey couldn't take on the swarm as a whole. Not yet. But could ey take out parts of it? Don't break the entire virus. Break nuclei. Break the capsids or the enzymes. Focus on parts, not the whole.

A thought accessed the traffic control grid, confirming the location of every ship still in danger, ranking them in a priority order with as much accuracy as es predictive algorithms could manage. Then, ey identified the masses of rock and metal that were the biggest threats to each ship, tracking their movements and blocking out every other piece of debris, every other mass in the field.

The narrowing in focus brought a sudden, sharp increase in control over the isolated fragments. Ignoring the field as a whole and concentrating on just these specific immediate threats gave em a window of opportunity and ey seized it, flooding those specific gravitic thruster systems with slicer code.

And felt them respond.

At the sliver of hope, ey poured every iota of es considerable will into those barely answering thruster systems, and felt them move, diverting in their course and away from almost all of the vulnerable ships. It was far from perfect, but it was the first slight hint of success.

Ey felt the massive impacts of rock against rock, thundering down through the dark matter substrate in all directions, as the small network of fragments under es control shattered into other rock rather than into the hulls of ships.

Exultant, ey concentrated es attention on this new strategy, recalculating the estimates of just how much ey could control at any given moment.

And missed the low, sad warble of a ship's emergency beacon.

Tucked against the lee side of the massive station and locked into one of the many docking points along wide hull plates, the *Gossamer's* proximity and long-range sensor net screamed, its display a garish smear of warning lights as he fought to get the ship into safety behind the bulk of the assay station. As the ship's systems tried to track the massive debris field bearing down on them, Irad felt the coruscating shock waves through the *Gossamer's* hull, setting his teeth on edge. He thought he could actually feel the grind of alloy where the ship's airlock bucked against its connection to the massive processing station.

Okay, this is not good, he thought.

He stabbed furiously at the stabilizer controls, attempting to find a balance that would hold the ship steady against the thickly rolling gravitic distortions caused by the explosions deep within the broken planet. His fingertips ached as he used the interface to combine and re-jigger the established stabilization routines into a new configuration that might have a chance at holding the ship steady.

He finally found a combination that seemed to offset the spatial distortions buffeting the whole sector, for there was a sudden peaceful quiet that fell over the entire ship.

In the sudden cessation of vibration, he sat back in his seat, enjoying the moment of quiet, certain at the same time that it wouldn't last. Before he became too complacent, he took the time to run diagnostics to check the state of the ship. The *Gossamer* was definitely showing stress strains beyond tolerances, but she was holding together. There were more warnings than he would have liked, and he was already calculating the cost of repairs as soon as he could get to a proper repair facility.

Well, if we make it out of this alive, there goes my maintenance budget.

He set to initiating what backup systems and temporary stopgaps he could and became as sure as he could be that the ship wouldn't fly apart when they managed to finally finish this mission and get the sprock out of here.

He was just fine-tuning the balance on attitude thruster four when a new alarm sounded. He recognized it instantly as an SOS through the ship's comm. Instinctively, he slapped the system out of dormancy to accept the call and data flooded across his control boards. Data flooded through the link and opened a series of panes before his eyes.

He didn't recognize the ship, and his attempt to read the ship's transponder returned only gibberish, but Know-It-All filled in the information before he could even make a decision to search. One of the big J-class ore extractors. A flick of his eyes brought up the data spurt from the ship that showed only thirty-two life signs on the internal biosensor network.

Irad cursed, loudly and enthusiastically.

The sensors showed that the ship had taken heavy damage to its aft sections, its drive was completely shot, and they were drifting. Irad realigned the sensors quickly onto the path of the massive debris field as it hurtled toward the damaged ship.

Right on target. Couldn't have been more threatening if it had been deliberately aimed.

A quick flick of his wrist sent the data to Vrick. ***So, how's that stabilization matrix coming? I've got a wounded ship right**

in the crosshairs and they need some help.*

He heard the naked frustration in Vrick's reply ***I'm doing the best I can. There are hundreds of thousands of fragments in that debris field and every time one of them shifts, it affects the trajectories of all the others. This is a challenge even for me. If I could just regain control of the net...***

Got it. I may have to take matters into my own hands.

Through the link, Irad sensed Vrick's hesitation as ey read his intentions. ***I'll do what I can to help, but I make no guarantees. You're going to be on your own.***

Been there before, my friend. I read you.

With a thought, Irad switched the link from Vrick to Keene. ***How's it going in there?***

Kinda busy right now, came Keene's strained reply.

Irad flashed the data on the damaged ship to Keene, along with his intentions.

After a moment's pause, ***Go. We'll be fine.***

With only a second's thought of response to confirm, Irad slammed the dock release, the airlock connection retracting into the hull as he gunned the *Gossamer*'s system drive to maximum and set a course.

We'll be fine? Malika said, ducking behind Keene as stunbolts fizzed over their heads, causing an acrid stench of melting plas where they impacted on the walls. ***He's our ride home, remember?***

Power of positive thinking, Keene said. ***You saw the state of that ship even from the little information their distress call contained. Without a main drive, they're not going to be able to evade those rocks, let alone get themselves free.***

He paused as a stunbolt hit too close, the outer edge of its energy clipping his ear and making it go numb.

Are you okay? Malika said at the sound of his sharp, hissing exhalation.

Other than not being able to feel the side of my face, you mean?

Yeah, other than that minor inconvenience, she said. *Do you feel fulfilled in your life's ambitions?*

Keene let out a short, cutting laugh, his mind taken off their precarious situation.

And I get it, Malika said. *Those people out there are probably Anyeis's friends, and even if they weren't, then they were probably cheated along with them. That's bad enough. And now, I don't even know if she's out there somewhere. If she's even — * Her voice caught. *How exactly did we get to the point of potential planetary disaster?*

My world. Welcome back to it, Keene said.

Oh, I totally blame you, Malika said, her mind bubbling with humour. *And if we survive, I plan to write a sternly worded letter to your supervisor.*

We'd better make sure we get out of here then. Keene said.

And on that note, chief, what's the plan? Malika said. *Since Irad isn't waiting for us at that airlock, where do we go now?*

Keene fugued, bringing up the schematics of the station he'd stored in his innernet, sharing them with Malika. Their position showed as a glowing pulse of light, the airlock that had been their original destination a few twists and turns along the corridors ahead. A thought blanked the original plan, scrubbing their plans.

Okay, the docking areas are out. Between us setting off the alarms and Irad pulling out in a rush, security is about as tight as it can be. So, what else can we do?

He sped through system menus and spec sheets with a speed that made Malika dizzy, considering and discarding plans with every new piece of information he gleaned from the plans.

The whirl of information snapped suddenly into stillness, one section of the station highlighted. *There. Come on.*

Malika balked. *There? No. Seriously.*

Keene called up a section of the security feeds, showing her the phalanx of security drones advancing on their position. ***It's that or get shot and probably arrested.***

Well, when you put it that way. Lead on.

Irad's heart lurched as he steered the *Gossamer* at the shifting wall of rock and energy that filled both his main viewport and forward scanners.

Bad idea. Such a bad idea.

He saw his nav system struggling to plot a safe course to the imperilled vessel, saw the display shudder and recalculate over and over as the debris field shifted and changed its configuration.

Was it his imagination or were the field's density and motion quieting?

As he approached, his mid-range sensors registered the Maverick Heart, blazing like a star in a corona of weapons. His mind reeled as he registered the ship's speed and the crispness of its course corrections. How was that even possible? He knew from his link with the others that, though they were both augmented, Lexa-Blue was piloting, while Ember was operating weapons and deflections systems. And they were cutting an appreciable swath through the speeding cloud of debris.

A shudder ran through the *Gossamer*'s space frame as he crossed the leading edge of the field's shockwave.

It's okay, old girl. It's you and me. We've got this.

Pushing the navigational deflection system to maximum, he dove his ship into the debris field, keeping the stricken ship in the focus of his navigation system. In his viewport, he saw small chunks of debris flashing into multi-coloured sparks as they intersected with his deflectors. He saw the power readings dip and surge with each hit, saw the overall efficiency stats sag, but hold somewhat steady.

He shifted his attention from the readout back to visual just in time to see the bloated, irregular curves of a massive asteroid coming into view. He slammed his control yoke to one side, feeling the ship's drive field push against the sudden shift in mass in his direct vicinity, and his stomach lurched as the *Gossamer* reacted a fraction too slowly.

The asteroid clipped the ship somewhere along its dorsal surface and the impact ground through the entire hull, straight up through his seat. His teeth slammed together, and he felt the crossed straps of his pilot chair cut into his shoulders. An alarm bleated.

Okay, what did I lose?

A quick review of the damage control systems showed the long-range tightline array was gone. He could probably still get messages through to anyone insystem if he had to. Probably — not great, but survivable so far.

Whatever the Maverick Heart was doing was definitely having an effect on the debris field around him. With his piloting LI assisting him, the *Gossamer* was still intact, though she was taking more and more hits the closer he got to the damaged mining ship.

Scans told him that the Maverick Heart's efforts, while breaking down the larger asteroids, were creating more and more smaller chunks that were increasing the density of debris. They were smaller, but there were far more of them. And they were threatening to overload the deflection system if he didn't get out of here soon.

His proximity detectors blared another warning, just as he registered the massive bulk of the mining base vessel in the distance. He steered towards it, feeling the buffeting against the *Gossamer*'s hull increase. At the edge of his vision, the deflection field dropped to 62 percent.

He tabbed the short-range comm now that he was in range. "Mining Vessel, this is the *Sparkling Gossamer*. I'm here to help. Sync your manoeuvring system to mine if you can, and I'll come alongside."

The voice that came back through the channel was jittered with barely suppressed panic. "Reading you, *Gossamer*. Our manoeuvring field is running on fumes, but I think we might be able to stabilize it long enough for you to dock."

Irad saw a data spurt of the ship's specs drop into his system, just as the crippled vessel filled his forward view. He winced as he took in the mortally wounded ship.

Whatever had struck them had sheared through the main drive system at the aft of the ship, leaving only a maze of torn superstructure open to space. They weren't tumbling, which meant that they'd at least maintained enough power to the manoeuvring fields to keep them oriented.

The midship to bow sections seemed to be mostly intact, and he could see from the data spurt just how many of the crew had survived.

They'll be jammed in every available space, but they'll be alive, he thought. *Provided I can get them out of here.*

His scans showed him the airlock closest to the crammed compartments where the survivors were huddled. His hands danced over his thruster field, tipping the *Gossamer* end over end to bring it into position to begin a final approach to the other ship's lock. The docking beacon was thready and weak, but it was still strong enough for the *Gossamer's* own docking system to lock on to. Hitting the initiator, he let the LI take over, bringing the two ships together, the *Gossamer* shifting sideways until the airlocks meshed and pressures equalized.

Well, almost equalized, he thought. The mining ship was leaking atmosphere somewhere, and from the readings he was picking up, it was dire. He'd somehow managed to arrive in the nick of time.

Without warning, a shudder roiled through the paired ships, and a quick glance at his external sensors showed another chunk of the mining ship's aft section had sheared away as the structural members gave out.

He tabbed open the comm down to the airlock, with one hand, upping the volume on the vox unit in the hopes his voice would carry into the other ship. "Fast and dirty, everybody. Get onboard as fast as you can, and grab hold of something."

His other hand clutched the control yoke with all his strength, for the *Gossamer's* thruster field was now the only motive force acting on the mining ship, and the combined mass of the vessels far exceeded the system's tolerances. The strain seemed to travel directly up through the hull of the *Gossamer* into the control yoke and through every muscle in the left side of the body.

I am going to hurt tomorrow, he thought.

Even over the low, bass grumble running through the *Gossamer's* hull, he could hear the chaos of terrified voices echoing up through the ship from the airlocks.

The proximity alarms screamed.

"Get moving, down there," he shouted, despite the already high-volume settings of the vox down below. "We've got incoming, and we are out of time."

A woman's voice, deep but sharp with tension, echoed up through the corridors and from the comm board. "We're in. We're in."

Irad took them at their word, for he had no other choice. The sensors showed the airlock doors were clear, so he slammed a hand on the lock release. As soon as the release showed green, he jammed the drive field to maximum, arcing the *Gossamer* up and away from the crippled mining ship.

A terrifying vibration ran through the hull, audible to the human ear as every ounce of the ship's drive field energy battled against inertia, and the pull of the other ship. Indicators across his flight system flared red and howled warnings.

Something hit them, and he struggled to hold the course as the ship yawed with the impact. Somewhere aft and below, someone screamed.

"What was that?" the woman's voice said, this time from the hatch leading into the cockpit.

"It's okay," he said, checking his damage readouts, not even looking back at her. "It was an empty cargo module. Internal atmo is holding. Hang on."

Okay, redundant and not overly inspiring. Have to work on my hero speeches.

"What can I do, captain?" she said.

"Know any good prayers?" Irad said, his arms aching on the control yoke.

"Not a one," she said, with a throaty laugh. "Guess you're on your own."

He glanced at the tactical display, trying to get a fix on where they were in relation to the field of killer rocks. He'd taken them on a course almost ninety degrees from the plane of the ecliptic, almost straight up. The field of debris was massive and thick, but it had defined boundaries. That had saved many of the endangered ships and he was hoping it would save them too.

Come on, baby. Come on. We're almost there.

More and more small fragments were hitting the deflection system, and finally, it was one too many. The system overloaded with a pop that they heard throughout the ship.

Just keep going.

Without the deflection system, it was only a matter of time, and he saw through his interface the one particular hunk of mostly metallic rock strike the regulator fins along the *Gossamer's* drive matrix.

The main drive field cut out with a shriek, just as the *Gossamer* left the uppermost edge of the debris field.

With no drive system, the ship continued on the same trajectory, unable to stop, unable to change course.

But we're alive.

Irad let go of his controls, his arms trembling from the effort. "Well, I'm afraid that's the best I can do. Not sure I did you much good though."

"You got my crew out of there, captain," the woman said. "That's more than enough for now."

He stood from his chair and offered his hand. "I'd say we're past captain at this point. Please, call me Irad."

The woman smiled, and Irad had the impression that it was a smile that took a lot to earn. She extended her hand and Irad noted how pale his olive skin looked against hers. "I'm Anyeis."

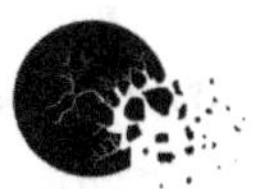

Hold on, Keene said, stopping suddenly at a wide metal box that jutted from the corridor wall. Malika skidded to a stop, almost falling.

What is it? she asked. ***Those zappy little bots are still on our tail, in case you've forgotten.***

Really? he said as he pulled a probe from his tool kit and jammed it into the box's locking mechanism. ***Totally slipped my mind.***

Okay, genius, she said, coming to his side. ***What is it?***

Keene stuffed the probe back into his kit as the metal cover of the box clanged open, revealing all sorts of fibres in all sorts of colours junctioned together in a maze-like tangle.

Oh yes, baby. You are beautiful.

Why, thank you, Malika said, knowing full well he wasn't talking to her.

This, my dear, Keene said, ***is a multi-node power/data locus. And if I'm reading it right, it controls that section**

— * He pointed back the way they came. * — **right there.***

Well, now, Malika said. *Doesn't that just bring to mind all sorts of possibilities.*

It does indeed, Keene said, pulling a portable cutter from his toolkit. *Like, for example, if I did this.*

He thumbed the cutter to full strength and jammed it into the box, sawing back and forth. As he wrenched his arm back and forth, thick knots of optic cable went dark, sparks flew, and a viscous, greasy-looking gel oozed from a fluidic line.

Behind them, the corridor went dark, and they heard the clatter and crash that sounded an awful lot like the bodies of Security Bots careening into walls and floors.

You are a bad, bad man, Malika said. *You should be ashamed of yourself.*

Oh, I am, Keene said, slipping the cutter back into place in his kit. *Completely.*

I don't suppose this changes our exit plans at all? Malika asked.

No such luck, I'm afraid, Keene said, heading off in the direction of their potential escape route.

Great. Just great.

Keene led her on down the corridor and right, finally bringing them to a halt in front of a massive, double-width hatch set in the wall before them. Without a word, he popped open his kit again, pulling out a couple of probes, and then going at the locking mechanism.

You know, I had a girlfriend who called me trash once, Malika said.

It's not trash, Keene said. *It's the ejection system for the slag that gets processed out of the ore and metal that the mining ships bring in. They use a mass driver to send it on a slow trajectory into the system's star. Think of it as cosmic recycling.*

Sounds a whole lot like trash to me, Malika said, still sounding dubious about their escape plan.

*This is where all that misdirected material that's being skimmed off would have gone if it was really the trash

that our slicer perp convinced the system it was.

Instead of into his pockets as credits? Malika said, her voice hard.

Exactly, Keene said, twisting the probe in his right hand with a final flourish. ***And scene.***

The massive hatch slowly began to open, revealing the Slag Ejection System room beyond.

Where did you learn that expression? Malika said.

Hey, I do my research and I pay attention, Keene said. ***After you, my dear trash.***

I can see why Ember loves you, Malika said, passing him. ***You say the sweetest things.***

The view beyond the hatch was a hellscape of seemingly tangled conveyors, coming from all angles and corners of the vast chamber, the contortion of metal pathways converging to one massive output port at the far end of the chamber. Even with the noise suppression systems operating at maximum, the roar of rock and ores tumbling through the ejection system made their ears ache.

Well, isn't this lovely, she said, wincing at the din.

Well, if it gets us out of here in one piece, along with this evidence, I'm fine with it, Keene shot back.

And what exactly are the odds of that? she asked.

Can I get back to you on that one?

He led her forward, past one of the collector lanes leading to the ejection port, the intense power of the conveyor fields causing the hairs on their skin to rise even through their EVA suits.

What exactly are you looking for? she asked, seeing how intently he scrutinized the system.

I need some kind of interface into the system, he said. ***Maintenance port or something.***

She joined his visual inspection, not really sure what she was looking for, but determined to be of some use in this daring and foolish escape plan he had concocted.

Damsel in distress is not the role for me.

She saw something, just ahead, tucked away under the heavy weight of the conveyor belt. She wasn't sure if it was what he needed, but the bulge stood out like a blister against the otherwise smooth underbelly of the conveyor.

There. What about that?

Looking where she was indicating, Keene saw it and grinned. ***You're getting good at this.***

I was always good at this, she said, getting out of his way.

Keene dropped to the ground and got on his back, shimmying under the belt. It was a tight fit, but he was able to wrestle open his tool kit and jimmy the casing of the test junction open. She kneeled down as well, trying to get some idea of what he was doing, but only managed to see his elbows and shoulders, jagging back and forth in sharp, aggressive movements.

The conveyor over their heads crashed to a halt, its contents suddenly jamming together in a roar before quieting. Not that it made much difference in the overall noise of the echoing chamber.

Why is this room even still working? she asked. ***You'd think that with a potential planetary disaster going on, they'd, you know, take a break or something?***

Keene shook his head. ***Corporate AIs are usually optimized for maximum productivity, whatever the cost. They'll stop short of actually allowing anyone to die, but beyond that, they'll keep working. And the station is just far enough out of the path of those meteors that I'll bet it didn't even cause a blip on the risk matrix.***

Malika made a sound of disgust that was lost in the clamour of the chamber but resonated through her node to Keene.

Oh, I agree. Believe me, Keene said, levering himself up from the floor. He took a step back so he could see further along the conveyor, scanning down the line.

There. Come on.

She followed him, and he stopped below the rim of the belt above. ***It's pretty clear from here to the outer aperture. I tapped the controls while I was jacked in and can start it back up once we're in place. Not the most comfortable of rides, but survivable.***

***Wow. There's a ringing endorsement if I've ever heard**

one,* she said. *But how do we get up there?*

She saw him fiddle with the controls on his suit, and the gloves and helmet expanded back into place, sealing him in again. She did the same, ready to follow his lead.

He stood back from the conveyor, and through her node, she felt him readying his suit's thruster field, making precise adjustments to the power settings, which then downloaded to her suit as well. Before she could even register how dangerous it was, he had crouched and leapt. She saw his suit's thruster field engage, accelerating his jump and taking him up and out of sight over the edge of the conveyor. Unable to see him anymore, all she had was the sense of yawning, almost out of control, tumbling that echoed from his node to hers.

You okay up there? she asked.

There was a bit of a pause and she sensed him struggling to right himself. *Yep. Maybe just a little too much thrust.*

She felt updated thrust calculations download to her suit's system from his and noted the substantially reduced power levels.

You ready? Keene said, appearing over the edge to look down at her. *Aim for me and I'll grab you and pull you the rest of the way up.*

Let's do it.

She felt the timing of his calculations and synced the thruster field, taking a couple of steps back to get a running start. Three quick steps and she leaped, feeling the thruster field engage at the highest point of her jump, accelerating her jump.

For a flash of a second, she thought she was going to smash directly into the conveyor's rim, but just as she felt the metal racing at her face, the pull of gravity working to reassert its control on her, Keene's hands gripped hers. Through the suit, she felt the low thrum of the augment servos in his suit take her weight and give him the extra strength he needed to pull her up over the edge. She tumbled over him and landed on her back, jarring the breath out of her.

Ow. She pulled herself up into a seated position. *I remember now why I retired from this.*

It's not over yet, Keene said. *Come on. One more brush with death and we're out.*

Groaning, she stood. And pulled up short, for she was looking directly at the wall of slag behind them where Keene had stalled the conveyor. She turned, seeing that the belt was empty between their position and the ejection system's egress port that opened to space and sent the rubble on its path toward the sun. ***Um, correct me if I'm wrong, but if you start up this conveyor to shoot us out of that opening, all of *that* — *** She pointed at the wall of rock. *** — is going to come flying out after us.***

Did I not mention that? Keene said.

No, but that's probably a good thing. Let's do it.

He led her down the conveyor, as far as he could from the mass of crumbled waste rock behind them, only stopping when they stood at the foot of the three-storey hatch ringed with field generators.

Okay, Keene said. ***Here's how it goes. When I reactivate the system, that hatch is going to open, but with an atmospheric shield in place so that the sudden decompression doesn't send rocks crashing into the mechanism itself. Those lights up there will flash and count down to the conveyor starting up again, and those field generators will begin taking hold of whatever mass is there in range and accelerating it out of the hatch.***

Meaning us, in this case, Malika said.

Meaning us, Keene agreed. ***As soon as your suit says you're clear, hit your thrusters and vector straight up as fast as you can. That should take us up and out of the path of all of that.***

He pointed back at the rock wall.

She nodded, even though the motion probably didn't translate through the helmet of her EVA suit. ***Got it.***

Here we go, then.

They got into position and with one final confirmation, Keene triggered the belt.

High over their heads, the hatch began to open, splitting to reveal a growing slash of starlit black, fuzzed with the glitter of the atmospheric shield. Within a minute, the aperture was fully open, and the countdown sequence began.

Like the fist of god, the conveyor field took hold of them, and Malika felt the breath torn from her as they were flung out into the black.

She gasped in breath, her breathing regulator wheezing to compensate for the sudden acceleration. Her head swimming, she had just enough presence of mind to trigger her thruster field to orient her, and then power her up and away. Her breath calmed as she felt herself steady, and she began to accelerate to safety.

Keene, I'm clear.

No words came back through his node, just a sickening lurch of tumbling panic. She consulted her suit's tracking system and saw him spinning out of control, his thruster field sputtering in some kind of failure mode. At the edge of the display, she saw the mere seconds until the mass of slag exited the station. And Keene was right in its path.

Her mind raced, taking control of her thruster system. With a jolt, she came to a sudden halt, reorienting back in his direction. She flashed instructions to her suit, letting it determine her vector and velocity, then ignored its warnings that the safety margins and probability of success were minimal.

Here goes nothing.

She hit the activator and the suit surged her forward, inertia causing her vision to grey at the edges for a second before clearing. Shaking her head to try and focus, she saw Keene, still tumbling, and in her peripheral vision, the leading edge of the load of slag emerge from the station, beginning its slow passage directly at him.

Seeing her course waver, she gambled and made a manual course correction, bringing Keene right back into the centre of her vision.

She hit him like a rock, the impact jolting them both. She grabbed for purchase, closing her arms tight around him before her kinetic energy could knock him away and out of reach. Her hand somehow caught a firm hold of something and, clutching him, she full-power reversed her thrusters and sent a command to the system to seek equilibrium.

With a myriad of tiny pulses shaped by the thruster field, they came to rest, drifting. She risked a look over her head.

Barely ten metres over her head, a column of broken, crumbled slag moved in a slow, steady path away from them, heading off into the sun.

With every ship system just a thought away, Lexa-Blue flew, more purely than she ever had.

She was fire. And joy. And music.

She was the sub-zero touch of space interacting with the energies of the drive field.

She was the bonds deep in the soul of an atom, breaking apart.

Though there was no up or down, she soared. She was all directions at once.

She was the flare and burn of the weapon's systems, her will so tied together with Ember's that she didn't know where one stopped and the other began.

The ship responded to her every thought and touch, in ways she couldn't have imagined possible, weaving through the smallest of gaps in the debris field, tearing it apart.

All around her, she could see and feel the thousands of infinitesimal changes in the mass and motion of the field, sensing Vrick slowly regaining control of patches at a time, the gravitic energies bending and shifting, easing their grip on the rubble around them.

But still she felt it resist, felt the malicious code deep in the gravs fighting back, struggling to maintain its hold on the bludgeoning rock and metal.

Still, she flew on, altering course as often as necessary, as often as data flowed through her link to Ember.

Their minds swirled together, flying, targeting, adjusting. Moving as a unified whole of navigation, deflection, and weapons. She flew, he fired, she course-corrected, he aimed once more along their revised flight path.

And all around them, rocks and debris clashed together, breaking apart, shattering down ever smaller and creating ever more self-destructive ricochets.

The cloud of debris slowly broke down, broke apart, though there was still enough to cause hellish damage to Sound if they weren't able to stop it.

And so, she sang. Deep into the fabric of the universe, in sounds no human could even have heard, pulling from all she had ever learned, all she had ever known, every note she had ever heard.

And around her, the Maverick Heart hummed with every note.

The weapons were Ember's fists, and he wielded them with all the precision he could manage, by turns pummelling with hammer blows, then gesturing as precisely as a surgeon wielding a scalpel.

Missiles rained from open ports across the hull, creating a barrage of blows shattering stone and metal. The beams seemed to shoot from every pore, every part of his body. He was radiant, the seething, nuclear fire of a star emitting from his fingertips as the ship twisted and turned through space under Lexa-Blue's control.

Her decisions flooded his mind, allowing him to aim and fire at empty space, before targets were even in range, and then watch them seem to fall directly into his field of fire. Their thoughts were one.

Again and again, he struck. Masses of rock shattered beneath his weapons, while others shifted and moved under the vice-like grip of his deflectors.

But still the field defied them, held by the code induced by the rogue slicer, pulling back together as much as possible. Every time one gravitic stabilizer shattered under his guns, the power seemed to flow to those that survived. As he fought, he felt Vrick fighting too, wrestling with the twining, interconnected layers of code.

It was a game of attrition, but they were only one ship, and even he could see their armament reserves dropping faster than the field was breaking up. It was only a matter of time before he would have no more missiles, no more power to the beamers, possibly even no more power for the deflection system, as he could feel it overheating.

He fought on, data flowing through him and out through the weapons and deflectors.

We are fire. We are joy. We are the song.

And we will not be stopped.

In his mind, held so closely that none could hear, he screamed in rage and power. And the scream rose and broke free, becoming a defiant chorus. And the music flowed through him, to Lexa-Blue. To Vrick. And out into the universe.

Through their connection, Vrick felt the melody that was Lexa-Blue's transcendent joy at her unfettered flight. It truly was music, thrilling and rich, playing across es senses like the clearest, purest notes.

The realization came like a crescendo, ringing through all three of them, and out into the universe around them.

That, Vrick thought. Could that be it? Could that be the key?

Literally.

Ey cast es mind back, replaying the memory of es first experience of the code, hearing again the jarring rage of threnody that had itched at the edges of es mind.

For all es intellect, es taste in the human arts, ey recognized code as code. As algorithms and numbers. Ones and zeroes. Slicing was just the use of code, the wielding of these numbers.

Have I become so hullbound? ey thought. *Maybe I'm getting old.*

No, you've been thinking like a machine. And you've been fighting those machines as if that's all they are.

But this was Pi. One of the most prolific and proficient slicers known. Ey had admired the… magic of their code, for want of a better word. Ey had never seen any code like it before. It was virtuosic.

And that *was* the key.

Ey saw it in a flash, with the sudden, utterly human music coming from Ember and Lexa-Blue. It was their song. It was every piece of music they had ever heard in every context.

And ey listened. Listened to the thrill and glory of their resilience, their strength expressed through their nodes to em and to the universe beyond. Listened to it as music.

Ey heard it now, heard the structure, the notes, the tones. Heard it play up and down through octaves that their human voices could never have reached, never have sung in their physical bodies.

Ey grabbed at the code once more, feeling it twist and burn, rubbery and pliable, resisting es grasp at every turn, until ey finally held it. And looked again through that angry skirl of music, then through the undertones as well.

When ey had handed over the systems to Ember and Lexa-Blue, ey had hibernated so many other systems as non-essential in this crisis. But now, ey found the one ey needed, the translation and encrypt/decrypt modules.

With metaphorical fists, ey jammed the screaming, kicking code into the system, treating it like a new language, ripping it apart and analyzing it as ey might a deeply encrypted message.

But with the basic structure of Pi's music as the decryption key, the primer. The Rosetta Stone on which all meaning turned.

Es mind burned with knowledge as the code decrypted, all of its hidden meanings revealed. For the first time, ey saw it, understood it. Heard the song of hatred and apathetic violence that underpinned it all.

And that gave em control.

Ey saw it all, finally saw every rock and fragment in the mass of debris, saw what was left and the pattern of chaos that was intended. Ey saw where they would move, what force they would impart, what destruction they would cause if they hit Sound.

Ey reached for them all at once, the complex calculation of trajectory and velocity now just math, numbers, and interactions of forces, no longer hidden by Pi's interference.

And ey stopped them.

Waves of gravitic force poured through the stabilizers, exploding out from them at almost the speed of light. The violent, violet bruise of light from the network exploded outwards from the epicentre Vrick had programmed.

For a moment, it seemed as though a supernova had burst from the system's primary star, sending paroxysms down through the dark matter substrate and into the interspace threshold. The whole planetary system seemed to buck like some enraged beast, then quieted, leaving only a soft, pale point of light deep in the middle of the massive, now still debris field.

Where there had been diffuse, bruise-coloured glow, there was one light, its pulsating glow holding the field steady and quiescent.

One gently burning ghost light, on a now quiet stage.

CHAPTER THIRTEEN

The interspace ripple hit the *Gossamer* as Irad struggled to reroute the ship's drive initiators to get them moving again. As the ship's hull resonated with the shockwave, it travelled through his body, making him jolt upright, barely missing cracking his skull on the low ceiling of the maintenance way.

Oh, not again.

But it passed and the *Gossamer* held steady, though she remained adrift.

Relief surged through Irad's body. While they were out of the path of the debris field, they were adrift since the drive initiators had blown.

Without them, there was no way to get the drive field running again.

He'd accompanied Anyeis back to her mining crew, helping her triage the injured for turns in his small auto-doc, then getting the rest settled with food or drink.

But they were still dead in space, without long-range comm or drive systems, so he couldn't even call for help. He'd triggered his distress beacon, but even then, it would take time for someone to register it in the chaos of wrecked and damaged ships. He couldn't take the chance that whoever was out there doing triage would find them in time.

He was just about to crawl back into the access panel to have another go at the initiators when he heard the triple ping of the external scanners echo down from the bridge.

At least something still works. Maybe.

He worked his way back through the ship, heading fore, stopping only to check in once again with the mining crew. He'd turned them loose on his stores, so they had been fed, and he could see they were passing around a bottle of Onari brandy. He didn't blame them at all.

When he reached the bridge, he didn't even need to look at the scanners to see what had changed.

He could see what once had been a mass of shifting rock enveloped in the deep, twisted purple light of the gravitic stabilization system that had gone haywire.

But now, there was only a calm sea of stone fragments drifting lazily, constantly shifting away from each other rather than hammering together. Low and fore, he saw the throb of serene light that seemed to anchor the entire asteroid field.

He didn't know whether to laugh or cry from the onrush of relief. *One thing I don't have to worry about.*

As if on cue, the proximity alert went off.

Not funny, universe. Not funny at all.

But a check of the system showed a very familiar transponder code, and he was gripped by a relief so intense, he actually sagged into his chair.

His link signalled an incoming voice transmission routed through Know-It-All, bypassing his damaged commo grid.

Now, why didn't I think of that.

The ident for the signal flashed across his scleral displays. ***Gossamer, this is Maverick Heart. Need a lift?***

Very happy to see you. I'm at capacity over here, and they could all use some proper medical care.

Normally, this is the part where I'd tell you to power down your engines so we could take you in tow, but I fear that would be salt in the wound. Stand by for tow field on my mark.

For the first time in his life, Irad was happy not to have to drive.

It's kind of peaceful, she thought. *If you don't think about it too much.*

After she'd caught him, Keene had fashioned a makeshift tether between them, twining the suits' external strapping together to keep them from drifting apart. It felt far too tenuous for her liking, but it was the best they could do short of just holding on to each other as they had initially done.

As they had hung there, floating near the massive station, Keene had triggered their locator beacons, signalling for Irad and the *Gossamer* to return for them.

Below them, the stream of slag from the station tapered off to nothing. Behind it, the massive hatch closed, cutting off the glare of light from the interior until they were lit only by the stars.

Space seemed to shudder around them for a moment, though they had no idea that it was the attenuated leading edge of Vrick's code halting the asteroid field in its tracks. They grabbed for each other, feeling a sudden, uncomfortable stretch in the strapping holding them together. It was several minutes before they felt comfortable enough to let each other go and trust the webbing once more.

And still there was no response from the *Gossamer*.

Well, this is less than optimal, Keene said.

Just a bit, Malika answered. ***Plan B?***

Well, I've checked your system and your thrusters have just enough juice to aim us back at the station. Probably.

I'll take *probably* over *not bloody likely*, Malika said.

After that, I can probably get us back inside. Where we will be most likely arrested.

I'll take *arrested* over *dead*. But maybe not just yet.

Well, we've both got enough oxygen to wait it out a bit longer. I've set mine to ping once we get too close to empty for me to be able to do my work.

Officially the worst date I have ever been on.

Definitely not one of my better efforts, Keene said. ***Though you might want to compare notes with Ember on that whole alien invasion thing.***

He's right, they heard Ember say. ***That one was pretty bad.***

Malika let out a whoop of relieved laughter. ***You win. You win it all. Just come pick us up, and we can argue about it later.***

Look up, Vrick said. ***Look way up.***

They craned their necks, but the suits made it difficult. The Maverick Heart loomed over their heads, the shaped energies of her tow field holding the heavily damaged *Sparkling Gossamer* close on es tail.

I'm running on empty up here, but Irad has someone who wants to talk to you.

Tell me again how your friends are going to handle this quietly?

Malika's eyes welled with tears of relief at the sound of Anyeis's voice.

I never said quietly, Malika said, her voice cracking. ***I know them too well to ever have said quietly. But at least you're okay.***

And you will be too, once I get you on board, Vrick said, interrupting them. ***Sorry for interrupting. But we need to get you two sorted. I'm not overly manoeuvrable right now. I can slow down enough for you, but you'll need to get to me.***

My thrusters are shot, but I have an idea, Keene said, turning his attention back to Malika. ***Let me have your thruster control for a second.***

If it involves not floating to our deaths in space, I'm in, she said, and yielded control of her still functioning thrusters to him.

Vrick coasted to a graceful halt above them, altering orientation until es starboard side was facing them, and they saw es airlock open, releasing a warm flood of light from es interior.

Okay, hold on tight, Keene said, and Malika grasped him even tighter. He triggered the thruster field, giving them a gentle, but firm push toward the open airlock directly overhead.

For a moment, it seemed as if they were going to overshoot the ship altogether. Keene muttered a subdued curse and furiously adjusted the shape and direction of the thruster field, orienting them into position again.

Malika heaved a sigh of relief, then felt a sudden disorientation as their perception shifted and they seemed now to be flying sideways with the deck of the ship suddenly parallel to their direction of motion.

As soon as they passed the threshold of the airlock, they felt themselves gently held by the internal grav field, which took hold of them, and delicately turned them to match the orientation of the deck. Air rushed into the chamber and they settled softly to the deck.

Keene popped the release on his helmet, and it folded off his face and back into the suit. Malika did the same and soon their suits were bright colours on the deck, leaving them in only the underlayers.

Malika gulped in the sweet, fresh air, her chest heaving. "I'm going to hang that up later, if you don't mind."

Keene nodded, obviously enjoying the ship's atmosphere as much as she was. "I think it can wait."

He hauled himself to his feet and offered her his hand. "I need a drink."

"Only one?" she asked, following him out of the airlock and into the ship.

They found Lexa-Blue and Ember in the lounge, splayed across the couches.

Keene dropped down beside Lexa-Blue, lifting her legs and draping them across his knees. "So, what have you been up to?"

Lexa-Blue made some kind of indeterminate gesture with her hand but said nothing.

"Don't mind her," Ember said, his voice drawn with fatigue. "She's just getting used to the fact that she only has two arms."

Malika slouched beside him and rested her head on his shoulder, but when she registered what he had said, she came upright again, despite how tired she felt.

"I'll explain later," Ember said.

Too tired to press the issue, she settled back into the crook of his arm. "Okay, remember when this was supposed to be a simple 'get my friends their money back' sting? When exactly did it get away from us?"

"I think it was the potentially planet-killing meteor shower," Keene said.

"No, no, I think it might have been the screeching car chase through the streets," Ember said.

"I think it was pretty much when we said yes," Lexa-Blue said, not even lifting her head. "Not that I'm complaining. We did good."

"Yes, yes we did," Keene agreed.

One of the maintenance drones rolled up, a tray with a bottle of Fool's Gold and four glasses grasped delicately in its grip.

"I figured you could all use a drink," Vrick said, as the bot set the bottle of amber liquid and the glasses on the table. "And that you were all too lazy to get it yourselves."

"Anybody would think you were smart or something," Lexa-Blue said, the prospect of liquor rousing her from her torpor.

"I have my moments," Vrick said. "Now, pour yourselves a drink. We have one more thing we need to take care of."

Sombra, Pi decided as he ventured into the station's main business area, was his kind of place. He could taste the deals in the air, waiting to be made. He could feel the marks just crying out for his services, and just not knowing it yet.

He'd come here directly from Sound and Fury, taking a tiny capsule room in the transient section. He'd walked away from whatever was going to happen when he triggered the codebomb, not caring one way or the other what happened. Either he obliterated any remaining traces, or everyone would be so distracted by dealing with it that they would hopefully forget about him.

But if he was going to find another contract, it would be here. There was bound to be someone in need of the best slicer in the Galactum.

As soon as his transport had landed, he'd checked in, dropped his bag on the floor and sat on the bed, logging into Sombra's system. He'd uploaded a pretty general set of parameters, as he was willing to take on pretty much anything at this point, just for the sake of keeping his hand in.

His accounts were flush, but he'd lost a lot of equipment on Sound, and replacing it would be expensive, even though most of his tools were virtual and stored in his private innernet. Taking on some smaller jobs would not only add to his balance but would give him enough time to figure out if and where he wanted to put down some roots again.

He flagged the few possibilities that came up in his searches, sending out feelers to the posters, offering to meet, either virtually or in person, then set alerts to let him know if further possible jobs came up on the system.

Within the hour, he'd set up four meetings, two virtual and two in person with clients who were present and conducting meetings in person. Checking local time, he saw he had time to find food first, and his stomach protested as he realized just how long it had been since he had eaten.

He left the tiny capsule room and found the section of the main trading floor made up of rows of food stalls and eateries. He stopped at the first that caught his eye and ordered randomly. After a few moments of flashing utensils and jets of flame, the cook behind the counter handed him a cone full of rice, vegetables, and an unidentifiable meat.

He wolfed it down, standing off to the side of the kiosk, not bothering to enjoy it, or to notice the disdainful look from the chef behind the counter. Tossing the cone into the nearest recycler, he checked the coordinates of his first meeting in Sombra's innernet, accepting the directions provided.

He walked to the far edge of the food area, crossing into the hushed section filled with private meeting areas, turning right down the main aisle that smaller grottoes diverged from.

He'd barely taken ten steps when he heard the sudden change in the atmosphere around him, feeling the change in the way Sombra's system rubbed against his.

Then, he saw why.

There, in the aisle before him, was Tinsel. Well, a holo of Tinsel, standing astride his path, at least twice their normal height. And he knew enough to know that this was never good.

"Cyre Jostro," Tinsel said, the holo glittering around the edges, each sparkle of light as sharp as a dagger.

Pi bridled at the use of his long-abandoned name, the ripple of anger twisting around real fear as well.

"You have displeased me," Tinsel continued.

Pi heard the murmur of anticipation that went through the crowd, half fear, half hunger for a good show. He steeled himself, calling up his own anger to fortify his will.

"There are rules," Tinsel said, their voice frighteningly calm and reasonable. "Sombra does not do business with murderers, nor does it harbour them. Those with blood on their hands are not welcome within these walls. Have I been unclear?"

Pi said nothing, knew there was nothing to be said. His mind raced at the possibilities, expulsion most likely. He sent a quick query to the departure board, letting anyone with a berth know that he would pay top dollar for it.

"But this time," Tinsel continued, "you have not only angered me, but you have trespassed against those I call friends. Perhaps they should be a part of this as well."

Pi saw the air around Tinsel sparkle as the holo field expanded, filling the entire space of the aisle before him, then coalescing into five new figures. Lightning-quick, he recognized them. Cataloguing their appearances.

To Tinsel's right, a woman, beautiful even in her rage, her face framed in a fall of auburn hair. Next, a man, slightly taller, lean and wiry, his hair glinting like pewter. To Tinsel's left, another man, taller, broader and darker than the others. Next to him, a lean and athletic woman, her face marked by a scar and an artificial eye as deep black as her short-cropped hair. And finally, just a shape, a pulsing flow of energy.

"You've been a bad man," Lexa-Blue said, her name stabbing into Pi's consciousness, along with a digest of her role in foiling his plans.

He saw her in the limo, evading the drones he had sent after her, and then her unbelievable piloting skills through the asteroid swarm. Then, one by one, the information on the others hammered at his mind and memory, causing him to stagger as if physically struck. Sucking in a deep, ragged breath, he regained his footing, as the new memories balanced in his brain.

"People are dead because of you," the one named Ember said. "And a lot more could have joined them."

"And you messed with my girlfriend," Malika said, walking forward toward him.

Pi worked at not flinching back from her. She was just a holo after all, glittering around the edges. She stopped just in front of him, the hatred in her eyes black and burning. He was so lost in it that he didn't see the blow coming.

In a flash, she had pulled back and launched a brutal right hook at his jaw. The edge of the solid light field hit his jaw like a brick, sending him to his knees.

The holo leaned down, her mouth next to his ear. "No one messes with my girlfriend."

His vision fuzzy at the edges, he watched her walk back to join the others.

"You know, I'm really glad we paid for that transmission upgrade," Malika said. "Because that was so worth it.

Lexa-Blue stepped forward, fists clenched. "Can I hit him too?"

"Don't waste your energy," Keene said. "Vrick and I have something much better in mind."

The pulsing glow of energy rippled with what Pi could only interpret as malicious laughter. "Oh, no. I've arranged for one last, special parting gift for our friend here."

Pi wasn't going to wait around to find out. He reached for Sombra's innernet to check for some kind of escape route,

And there was nothing.

Shock almost drove him to his knees again. He ran a diagnostic, but his node was working fine. He reached for Know-It-All but received the same gut-wrenching emptiness. The sudden emptiness inside almost made him retch.

Without his connection, it was all gone. His credit, his code, everything.

"You've been cut out, like a malignancy," the energy pulse said. "And the wound cauterized. Your pathways to Know-It-All are gone. Your credits are gone. What you stole from the miners at Sound and Fury have been redistributed to those you embezzled them from. The rest will be divvied between an assortment of very worthy causes. For all intents and purposes, you are gone. And you won't hurt anyone that way again.

"You no longer exist."

Panic burned through Pi, searing along every nerve. Without access to Know-It-All, he had no way to get the reams of code he had written over the years. Beyond that, he'd barely be able to function in the real world, unable to access any of the information and systems that were controlled through the massive network that was the underpinning of all of Pan Galactum civilization.

"Oh, and one more thing," the disembodied voice said. "Tinsel has been so kind as to provide the use of one of Sombra's escape pods. When we are done here, you will be escorted to it. All of its internal control systems have been disabled. Under my control it will take you to a rendezvous with the Galactum Security Vessel *Night Star* where you will be remanded into their custody. All of the evidence against you has already been forwarded to the Public Prosecutions Division."

The amorphous energy shape roiled a moment, then went still.

"You may go."

The holos evaporated into glittery mist and were gone, taking Pi's future and freedom with them.

EPILOGUE

Ember stepped out onto the suite's balcony, and the door whispered closed behind him. At the railing, he lifted his glass and took a sip of the sparkling wine. For the first time in weeks, he felt relaxed. Even his pain was comparatively quiescent, nothing more than the murmur of a voice in another room, too quiet to be intrusive.

The corporate city below him was the same, though the lights shone brighter in the dimming twilight.

You'd never know that their world was almost destroyed.

But a sense of calm normalcy had fallen over the city once again, muting even the mourning for those recently lost. Mining ships were out again, at the fullest strength they could be after their losses. But a quick check of Know-It-All was all it took to show that there were new crews and new ships on their way. It was only a matter of time before they were at full strength once again.

Plus, all of Pi's malicious code had been cleared from the accounting and assay systems. All of the workers were ensured their fair share of the profits and bonuses from now on.

And they all lived happily ever after, he thought. *Except the ones who died.*

He heard the door behind him and knew from the weight of the step that it was Lexa-Blue. He turned and took her in. "You look nice."

"It happens occasionally," she said with a lopsided grin. "I keep a few things on hand in case Sindel wants me to look pretty."

"Or one of the others?" Ember asked.

"Or one of the others," Lexa-Blue said with a smile.

She was wearing a pair of form-fitting, high-waisted pants, in a deep purple that was almost black, and had set it off with a wide-sleeved blouse in a bold geometric pattern. Her drink, a short glass filled with a dark red liquor, glinted moodily in the fading light. "You look pretty spiffy there yourself, squib."

He was dressed all in black, the skirt of his formal suit long and dramatic, with a sharply cut coat over a cowl-necked sweater. "Well, it is a special occasion."

He lapsed into silence and stared out again.

"Stop it," she said, moving to stand beside him.

"Stop what?" he asked.

"You're beating yourself up about those people who died," she said, taking a swig from her own glass.

"Shut up," he said, but there was a definite undertone of humour and camaraderie underneath it.

"Both Vrick and Keene figure Pi would have triggered that codebomb no matter what. He could have set it off just for the hell of it, or because someone looked at him the wrong way. Those deaths are on him, not us. And it would have been a lot worse if we hadn't been here."

Ember was silent a while, digesting her words. "I know. In my head, I know. The rest of me just needs to catch up."

"It will," Lexa-Blue said. "And tonight will help. It's a good way to celebrate."

Ember smiled at this, and it was a genuine flush of happiness. "I'm excited for it."

"You know something?" she said. "I actually am too."

The door hissed again, and Keene stuck his head out. "Come and check out your handiwork."

They followed him back into the suite, and Ember took a moment to appreciate the view of Keene walking away. He was dressed in that suit that Ember loved so much, dark grey shot through with just a touch of bright blue, the skirt cut at a dramatic angle, and the crisp white shirt that looked so good against Keene's dark skin.

"Irad," Keene called. "Come on out."

The captain came from one of the rooms, his manner shy and uncertain, almost as if he were going to bolt back into the room.

"You look great," Ember said, and the genuine pleasure in his voice made Irad smile and stand a little straighter. The suit itself was pretty conservatively cut, but it fit perfectly, and the deep forest green set off his skin tone perfectly. The final touch was a simple copper-coloured band that pulled Irad's thick curls back from his face.

"The man of the hour," Lexa-Blue said, raising her glass.

"Oh, stop," Irad said, clearly flustered by the attention. "I didn't do anything special."

"There's a shipful of miners out there that would disagree with you," Keene said. "Not everyone would have flown into that mess of rocks like that."

"It was pretty fancy flying," Lexa-Blue said. "And I know fancy flying when I see it."

Irad blushed, but Ember could tell how much the praise meant to him. He decided to save the pilot from any further embarrassment.

"Come on, we're going to be late if we don't get moving,"

"It's too bad Anyeis couldn't join us," Irad said.

"The consortium has her and all the mining crews on extra rotations at double bonus," Keene said. "The execs desperately need to get production back on track but are so embarrassed by getting sliced that they're bending over backwards to make up for it."

"Good for her," Lexa-Blue said. "Stick it to the corpos whenever you can."

Their car was downstairs waiting for them, and it wound through the streets of Sound, toward the outskirts of the city. Irad had gotten over his embarrassment and seemed now to be almost bouncing out of his skin with excitement. Ember couldn't help but smile, feeling the rush as well.

"Try not to crash the car this time," Keene said to Lexa-Blue in the driver's seat.

"Hey, if someone comes after us, I can't make any promises," she said.

"It's just a good thing that the consortium decided to look the other way since we, you know, helped them expose the flaws in their system and saved the whole city."

"People get forgiving really fast once you save their lives. Or their money," she said. "Especially their money."

Ember shut out their banter and turned back to Irad. "Ready?"

"I'm so ready," Irad said. "Thank you for this."

Ember shook off the gratitude. "I'm glad we could share it before you left."

Lexa-Blue began to slow, and Ember looked out the window at their destination.

The theatre was resplendent, the holo facade awash with light. Designed to look like it was lined with individual bulbs, the marquee sparkled as the path of light chased around its borders. There, surrounded by the brilliance of the lights, the play's title in block letters: *The Moon Abides*.

Lexa-Blue pulled into the line of cars and rickshaws depositing people at the mouth of the extruded shield that joined the theatre to the city itself. When it was their turn, she activated the LI that would drive the car to the nearest parking area, joining them on the sidewalk as the car hummed away.

Inside, the theatre was even more gorgeous. Modelled after grand theatres from the long-distant centuries of Old Earth, every line was sweeping and grand, from the plain of the lobby to the sweeping, sensuous curves of the staircases. The luxurious design continued into the theatre itself, but from what Malika had told him, this was no holo. Balconies and boxes lined the gilt-adorned walls, and the seats were a swath of deep maroon velvet.

They found their seats, the best in the house, Malika had told them, and settled in. At his side, Ember saw that Irad held his program reverently, like a talisman. He saw Irad open it and then focus intently on every word, only looking up when he found Malika in the cast list.

"Look," Irad said, excitedly. "There she is."

Ember held back his smile, letting only the faintest trace reach his face. He remembered his own first time in a live theatre and wasn't about to say or do anything that might cast a shadow on Irad's night.

Irad must have pored over every word of the program as the rest of the audience filed in. Even Keene and Lexa-Blue were quiet on Ember's other side.

Finally, the seats around them full, the lights dimmed, and Ember heard Irad's breath catch in the dark, as he felt the other man's hand tighten around his.

"Thank you," the awestruck pilot whispered.

Amid a swell of luscious music, the house lights dimmed, and the curtain rose.

There, centre stage, lit by the warm rosy-gold aura of the footlights, Malika stepped forward, and the play began.

THE END

ACKNOWLEDGMENTS

I was going to dedicate this book to 'Nathan Burgoine before life, as it so often does, took a turn to a place I wasn't ready to go. But this book exists because of him. Because, number one, he has been a vocal cheerleader for the Maverick Heart crew from the very beginning. And two, because he said, straight out, that he loved Malika and wanted her back, which showed me how much I did too.

So much gratitude for my amazing Sistren, Linda King and Jennifer Saemann for their unwavering love and support as we navigated the loss of our fallen fourth, Sue Brooks.

Many thanks go to my Beta readers, whose support and eagerness kept me going in that limbo between completion, submission, acceptance, and publication: Michael White, Troy Anthony Young, Andrew Deobald, Ronda Johnson, and Tracy Montgomery,

Thanks to Cait Gordon for her unwavering support of the Maverick Heart team, and her sensitivity editing around disability and what it means in their future.

My thanks go to Glad Day Bookshop for keeping me caffeinated and fed during my post workday writing sessions and keeping me inspired with their support and their slate of always amazing events for writers.

And as always, thanks to the everyone at Renaissance Press: Publisher Nathan Frechette, for believing in the Maverick Heart crew and giving them a home, and his beautiful cover design. Managing Editor, Marjolaine Lafrenière, for keeping the process organized and on track. My editors, Joel Balkovec, Lorenzo Carrara, and Isabelle Shi, for seeing the things I missed and bringing a full polish to the finished product.

ABOUT THE AUTHOR

Stephen Graham King (He/They) is a writer of space opera novels, re-imagining the classic genre and its high-tech adventurers through an unabashedly queer lens. His stories have appeared in the anthologies *North of Infinity II, Desolate Places* and *Ruins Metropolis*. His books include his debut novel, *Chasing Cold*, and his *Maverick Heart* series: *Soul's Blood, Gatecrasher, A Congress of Ships*, and now, *Ghost Light Burn*. He is currently at work on the next book in the series, *Into Thieves' Rift*. He has also contributed several essays to the Spoonie Authors Network, has appeared at several speculative fiction conferences and as a guest on different writing, disability, and speculative fiction podcasts. He is also a long-term survivor of metastatic synovial sarcoma and an avid black and white street photographer. He can be found online, along with all his social media coordinates, at stephengrahamking.com.